T0345592

"Done with both skill and sensitivity...[Chabria] has the gift of drawing characters true to life and making them compelling as well."

VIJAY NAMBISAN, *The Hindu*

"The rich imagery, clever wordplay, soaring imagination that borders on poetry...are deeply rooted in reality and give the reader jolts of recognition at every turn."

Femina

"[A] virtuoso performance...All in all an impressive first book."

G. J. V. PRASAD, *Indian Review of Books*

Generation 14 (republished as *Clone*)

"Priya Sarukkai Chabria's *Generation 14* undoubtedly inaugurates a new kind of writing on the Indian continent. There is little in the by-now substantial body of Indian literature in English that has led up to a novel of this kind. Generically, it draws upon but refuses to be subsumed by science fiction of the dystopian variety. The formal inclusiveness of Chabria's prose only mines, and strengthens, the book's plea for accepting and recognizing the splendour of difference, otherness, and plurality. Its adventurous foray into vastly different times, spaces, and consciousnesses whether animal, human, and what can only be called post-human, is thus intrinsic to Chabria's artistic plan..."

STUTI KHANNA, *DNA*

"Chabria's is an extraordinary poetic imagination."

TIM PARKS, translator and author

"...this book is...refreshingly different from what you might expect...The book is set as much in the past as it is in the future. Detailed, finely imaginative set pieces transport the reader to various historical epochs...The imagery is very strong, and the strongest parts of the book work almost like movies, with vividly imagined scenes chasing each other across the page...Her (the clone's) hesitant navigation through a world rendered unfamiliar by her expanding consciousness is mirrored in the way she and her world appear to the reader."

AVTAR SINGH, *Time Out* Delhi and Mumbai

"For her second novel, poet and writer Priya Sarukkai Chabria brings to life forgotten voices... nothing quite prepares us for Chabria's clone...the premise is imaginative—and irreverent...her prose is as eloquent as her poetry."

SUDIPTA DATTA, *The Financial Times*

"The necessary questions the author raises... revolve around the meaning of a shared humanity and the necessity of plurality of expression. ...the author displays considerable chutzpah in writing these narratives...Sarukkai-Chabria is also a poet, and this is evident from the prose she employs, which is resonant and allusive. At times, this rises to an exalted, almost Vedic, pitch… There is much imaginative depth and richness to be found in *Generation 14*…"

SANJAY SIPAHIMALANI, *Tehelka*

"Chabria's lucid and poetic prose makes her work stand apart…By using a phantasmagoria of 'visitations' in her work, Chabria explores the possible reasons and side-steps the usual clichés. Weaving in episodes of Indian history and appropriating the fabulist form, the author reveals a plurality of voices in her work. A parrot, a fish, a wolf, a monk and a disconsolate mother in the wake of Ashoka's Kalinga war make for a thoroughly interesting read and are evidence to a contemporary quest for tolerance."

MAMTA BADKAR, *Verve*

"…the author delves into India's rich folk history and fishes out characters and incidents, which by themselves are intensely imaginative and lyrically written. There is a metaphysical poetry in Chabria's prose and it is when writing these passages that the author stands at the very edge of imagination and does not fall into a precipice…a novel that is ambitious enough to fuse history, politics and science fiction…I recommend you pick it up…"

RASHMI VASUDEVA, *Deccan Herald*

• NON-FICTION •

Bombay/Mumbai: Immersions

"Chabria, brilliant wordsmith and affectionate narrator, holds our hands while walking us through the history of the city…she is interpreter and interlocutor, true, but also both doctor and nurse, taking care of diagnosis and convalescence. That is what makes this book such a rare reading and viewing pleasure…You already know the story of Bombay. But you must read this book because you want to know again, because every time you blink, the old becomes new again."

SUMANA ROY, *The Sunday Guardian*

"The mind-boggling variety of information in this meticulously researched book by Priya Sarukkai Chabria and Christopher Taylor justifies why another book on Mumbai isn't too much."

ANUPAMA RAJU, *The Hindu*

"*Bombay/Mumbai Immersions* is not another *histoire de la ville of amchi* Mumbai. As one turns the pages, and the first glimpse of the inner world of the book comes to view, one knows instinctively that this is to be a different reading experience."

SUNEETHA BALAKRISHNAN, *CNN News18*

clone

clone

clone

PRIYA SARUKKAI CHABRIA

zubaan

ZUBAAN
128 B Shahpur Jat, 1st floor
NEW DELHI 110 049
Email: contact@zubaanbooks.com
Website: www.zubaanbooks.com

First published by Zubaan Publishers Pvt. Ltd 2018

A different version of this book was previously published under the title *Generation 14*

10 9 8 7 6 5 4 3 2 1

ISBN 978 93 85932 43 4

Zubaan is an independent feminist publishing house based in New Delhi with a strong academic and general list. It was set up as an imprint of India's first feminist publishing house, Kali for Women, and carries forward Kali's tradition of publishing world quality books to high editorial and production standards. *Zubaan* means tongue, voice, language, speech in Hindustani. Zubaan publishes in the areas of the humanities, social sciences, as well as in fiction, general non-fiction, and books for children and young adults under its Young Zubaan imprint.

Typeset in Baskerville 11/15 by Jojy Philip, New Delhi 110 015
Printed and bound at Thomson Press, Faridabad, India

For Suresh

Prologue

I am a fourteenth generation Clone and something has gone wrong with me.

Not that my DNA is altered. Not that I am a mutant. Not that any function need be eliminated. It's nothing obvious. It's terminal, and secret.

Let me put it this way: I remember.

My consciousness is morphing in an unplanned way. I'm also very lonely. It's not pleasant to have memory and no one to share it with. I don't dare. Which is why I've decided to keep a diary hidden as a cellchip in my system. So far undetected; so far, so good.

The first strange thought I had was of a dodo. It was the last dodo and I was it. This thought-experience rushed with adrenaline. I was feathered, flightless and fleeing.

The thought passed. Others followed. Each disconcerting, each more detailed. I thought I was going insane. I went to check out with my Elder, the thirteenth generation Clone. But I was late. My Elder was a saintly member of our community who had recently signed up for the Exhaustive Organ Transplant Scheme. I reached a liver, one eye, two feet, three metres of skin and perfect clavicles.

The only option left was to research my Original, to check out if these visitations have something to do with transmutations in her neurological circuitry. Or maybe something was overlooked in the cloning process. This is not supposed to occur. But neither are we to carry memory traces beyond the second cloning.

Ours is an open society. Everyone—Originals, Superior Zombies, Firehearts and Clones—has equal right to access information. Nothing is prohibited, but there are consequences. However, I have decided to take the risk. Initial investigations suggest my Original was a writer living in the late twenty-first century. Maybe she should never have been cloned.

It's curious. I'm getting into what I suspect was the Original's life, or possibly her writing life, depending on how one wants to view it. These are strange ideas for a Clone. But strangest of all: I remember.

My consciousness has morphed.

I

THE CELL

⚜ 1 ⚜

I requested permission to visit the local Exhaustive Organ Transplant Cell where my Elder's tissues are stored. At the terminus I identified myself: Clone 14/54/G. "Permission granted," said the System and the doors slid open. As I waited for the remains to hover before my eyes I wondered what drove me to this sterile, silent vault. It was a sudden decision and this made me uncomfortable. I already had knowledge of the contents; what further could I gain by actually seeing it? The air was an intense turquoise and smelt of bimedinixochorophlly. After 6.21 minutes, the transparent organ-sheath had still not materialized. I queried the delay. The response was, "Access recently granted."

"To whom?" I asked.

"Clone 14/53/G."

I repeated my identification.

"Processing request," replied the System.

There she was, what was left of my Elder. Labelled, packaged in frozen plasma and dangling beyond the touch-proof barrier. Her feet were large, the little toes squashed, like mine. I bowed my head, though I don't know why, as I spoke the routine words of thanks we repeat on our cloning "birthdays."

"Clone 14/54/G wishes to pay tribute to my Elder, Clone 13/15/G. We are the same and we give thanks. Long live our Global Community."

I remained silent and staring till the sheath was called up.

I must have remained, head bowed, unaware of the three "visit terminated" warnings that were sounded before I felt a crackle of electricity in front of my face. I withdrew before stronger bolts followed. Walking out, I saw a Fireheart being led into the vaults by a Superior Zombie. It was an odd sight. Firehearts are bred for the purpose of interrogating the living, not querying the dead. Unless there is a living brain in these vaults that has refused to yield its secrets? Firehearts are the poets of our society, and being poets, they cannot speak lies. They make excellent investigators for they will not give up till they are satisfied with the answers, even if their antennae burn up in the attempt and they writhe and perish.

All through the day images of my Elder's remains kept appearing before my eyes. It was as if the coldness had transferred into me, as if I was packed in frozen plasma. Though I walked it seemed as if I was not moving. I could not taste the grittiness of my daily ration, the water I sipped seemed to numb my throat.

If this the after effect of visiting one's Elder, paying tribute to one's Original might be much more painful. But I want to do this before my actuality runs out. It is educative and helps you perform your duties better.

——⁓——

At my workstation I performed my job till time up. I knew nothing would interfere with my working; as a Clone I am mistake-proofed while on duty. This is no small relief. The visitations begin later, when I am alone in my cell.

Last evening, as I was swallowing my mineral supplements, I was engulfed by coldness and a sense of verticality. I was stuck to a wall and witness to a "transaction of flesh" between a man called Marco Polo and a woman called Love's Sweetness. He was a merchant headed for China, his ship harboured in Kochi, a great seaport that looks towards the setting sun; she was the town's most renowned courtesan. It was strange. To begin, they were of different colours, not like us, standardized. He was a patchy mud-pink and she was granite coloured. It was a long ritual, and confusing, that now returns to me.

Yes, I know who I was yesterday: a gecko on the wall of the courtesan's house.

She offers him betel nut and cardamoms and wine and jackfruit and goat meat on a silver platter lined with green banana leaf. He offers her four silver coins. She turns her back on him. She's directly below me, her face to the wall. He offers five, seven, ten silver coins; he offers her three gold coins.

She turns towards him. She removes her upper garment; her breasts are large, the nipples painted scarlet, point towards me. Love's Sweetness insists Marco Polo bathe before he touches her. He is led away and returns looking less patchy. They play dice and drink wine. Through gestures she suggests he remove her necklaces. He begins and is entrapped in meshes of gold, his face between her breasts, his hands on her body everywhere. She laughs—it is sweet—looks at me and asks, "Good-luck Gecko, shall I begin?" My tail rises of its own accord and thrashes the wall three times. She removes one pin that releases her circlets of gold; all of it falls to the floor. She removes her clothes, she removes his. She runs her hands over his body while she beats his hands back at every attempt to touch. "Wait," she tells him, "beg and wait." Marco Polo is flushing and panting, he surges on her. She signals her attendants who bind his hands with a scarf of scarlet silk and lay him on a couch of white satin.

"Good-luck Gecko, should I sit astride him or be beneath; or perform the churning? One thrash of your tail or two or three?" Love's Sweetness asks. I know I'm her sacred gecko. I want to say three. I raise my tail to

strike but there is a fat cockroach climbing the wall; it's almost within reach. I tense and creep. In my mouth: frail feelers, crusty thorax, brittle wings, six legs thrashing.

The visitation vanishes. We Clones have heard of Mating. The colony of Originals is kept segregated for the purpose so that fresh Originals and their blueprints are available for societal betterment. Their Matings are brief and pre-selected to give optimum results. At least six of each batch of first generation Clones are solely reserved as backups for each new Original. It was suspected that after the thirteenth generation, cloning malfunctions would occur as the Original blueprint successively weakens. The lot of my generation, 14/ etc., is the first to be so pushed and tested. No dysfunctional case has been reported yet—except if it is I, Clone 14/54/G, generation 14 of 54 Clones of batch G. I have an "instinct" to keep it secret. I recognize this instinct is primordial survival. This is why I keep a diary hidden as a cellchip within my neural circuitry.

There seem to be no further visitations today. This is fortunate.

I realize why I went to see the remains of my Elder: for the experience, nothing more. My body trembled and eyes pricked as I stood near Clone 13/15/G's remains. This was a strange sensation.

The night alarms have sounded. I must shut down.

≋ 2 ≋

I changed a glider to get to my workplace. This is brightly lit and filled with the noise of moving machine parts, unlike our Clone Towers that are dark. Only one bulb lights the corridor, the ends of which are dim and silent. Mine is a corner cubicle.

I hear nothing once I am inside. But elevator regulations are the same for Clone Towers and workplace: climb the first ten floors, take the elevator for the next ten, then climb ten. It repeats in this manner. The Global Community is thoughtful: we get ten minutes Relaxation Time to catch our breath before we clock in to the assembly lines.

It seemed another routine day at work when two Superior Zombies (Type VTP) led in a platoon of "Z" category Clones. We nickname them Terror-Bearers because they are lobotomized Clones that behave like robots. However, without the correct inputs they don't act. They are quartered separately. The VTP Superior Zombies, cloned with Venus Flytrap and sea snake genes, are extremely sensitive to movement. We freeze at their approach.

The Superior Zombie stated, "All thirteenth and fourteenth generation Clones fall in line." One sixth of the workforce stepped out. We were transported to the local Testing Lab where we were informed that some fourteenth generation Clones reported minor malfunctions. We were to be comprehensively scanned—from Knee-Jerk Reactions to Field of Vision (Visual and Imaginative). This would take time.

In the reception chamber, we were informed that members of my batch were incapacitated. Almost all the odd numbers from 14/13/G to 14/47/G buckled. They were to be amputated, refurbished with tesson parts and returned to work. 14/44/G was spinning around herself declaring she was the sun—but this needed to be verified. The H-series manifested the most serious complications. Twelve thought themselves to be Originals and tried to mate. The entire H-series was to be withdrawn. A hush descended in the chamber and sank to the floor.

As I waited, I initiated emergency recall mode to recap the responses imprinted in me in Behaviour School. This resource is not supposed to be accessible to Clones at Testing times, but I tried. The process was a success; I felt abetted by "an ancient cunning" from within myself though I do not know which part of my psycho-neural network acted. It was as if I was deliberately forgetting information that might cause me harm.

I had moved to the queue outside the Audience Room. Ahead was a Clone of the R-series who are inoculated with parrot DNA to spread information and lead orison meetings. He kept repeating, "I have a single screw loose. The template can be fixed. Keep it secret but it's the same with all of us. We never cause problems. I do not want to be withdrawn. My template can be fixed." I told him twice: I do not foresee problems, they will tighten your screw; then fell silent. Behind me towered a member of the SS-series. She said, "I am fit and perfectly normal." The SS-series is an ancient prototype that demand immediate acknowledgment else they shift into attack mode; they are sewer workers used to inhaling poison. I replied, "I am fit and perfectly normal." She continued to breathe down my neck.

The last scan is the Field of Vision (Imaginative). This is an accurate test, for as Clones we lack Imagination, but should a malfunction occur it first shows in this Field. I was strapped in a chair. In the darkness ahead would be a Superior Zombie and a Fireheart.

"Identify yourself," said the Superior Zombie.

"Clone 14/54/G."

"Where do you come from?" the guttural voice asked.

"Clone 13/15/G. Her tissues are with the Exhaustive Organ Transplant Unit."

"Do you know your Original?"

I paused. "No."

"Wait!" It was the Fireheart's voice, high and impatient. It had caught the inflection in mine. "Repeat the answer."

"No, I do not know my Original."

"Inject Truth Serum."

I took the shot. My eyelids seemed to fly to my brows and the Pupil Scanner's intensity increased. The Fireheart approached my circle of light. Its pulpy body stooped, its antennae drooped; it was tired.

"But you know something about your Original, ah ha!"

"I launched into First-level Research."

"There," the Fireheart's large eyes shone. "What did you find out?"

"She was a writer living in the late twenty-first century."

"And?"

"That's all I know."

"Disappointing," it murmured. "You left it at that. Why?"

"Clones have the right to research ancestry in order to serve the Global Community better. Such investigations enable us to hone innate skills." I felt sick, the Truth Serum was working.

"What innate skills have you discovered?"

"None so far."

The Fireheart stood on tiptoe to sniff me up and down. "What is the moon?" it shot at me.

"The earth's satellite," I replied.

"And?"

"The moon was colonized but later abandoned in—"

"Stop! This Clone is telling the truth," it declared. One antenna perked up. "Will you continue your investigation?"

"I do not know." I added, "If I think it will be fruitful." This was the truth.

"Let her go," said the Fireheart. "She is committed to useful research, not to truth as an end in itself. How sad." It shook its head. Its antennae were drooping below its shoulders.

As I stood I said, "Long live our Global Community."

"Go," said the Fireheart, wringing its small hands. "Go away."

My partners in line, the R-series and the SS, were among those released. Before we dispersed, a Superior Zombie ordered us to reset our bioclocks to work double time the next day. We needed to make up for the workday lost.

It was late. I took the transporter to the nearest block, then walked. This was again an Energy Conservation Month. A different light mingled with that of the rare streetlight. It was silvery and subdued but filled every crevice. I looked up. The fog was thin. Between parallel blocks in the strip of sky was the moon. It was full. I walked towards my cell, looking upwards. The moon overhead followed my steps.

In my cell I ordered my bed to appear but did not climb in. I ordered the cell-light to shut down and found myself at the small window, staring at the moon. Its illumination floods the room, brilliant yet soft. Something is happening: my hair rises, my neck arches backwards. I want to bay at the moon.

⟞ 3 ⟝

My father was a wolf. Of this I am certain. I remember his silhouette against the full moon, his head raised, baying. I remember him standing over our mother, the thin, golden bitch of Sinthastha, and us five pups. I remember the hanging sky of our mother's teats, the horizon sliding with our suckling as she rests and the distant mountains standing on the skin of the earth like ticks on a newborn. I remember my mother; her ears back, gums bare, teeth glistening, body panting, while we cringe near her. She lunges at the attackers, and dies, protecting us. An arrow through her neck while the cold winds blow, while the sun hangs like a medallion against the sky, while the sea of grasses waves. Her legs burst into a spasm of kicks. Then she stretches, softly, as when she awakens each dawn, and then she is still. There must have been noise: screams, yapping, neighing, death cries. I do not remember sound.

"This one is mine." This is the first human voice I hear as he thrusts

me into a bag. It is dark in the bag, and growing darker outside. Wolves are chasing us—that is, Vrikama my master, the men folk of his tribe, and me in his bag.

I can't see. But I smell. The panic of the horses, the coldness of the night, the bronze of the arrows, the leather, my master's excitement.

I smell my father in the dark, his eyes glowing, giving chase. I smell him loping. After me, for me, I think. I hear a yelp. Then I smell my father no more. I smell the night quietening around us, gathering into rough vegetation beneath the horses' flying hooves, into stones and pebbles and moonlit dust. This is all I remember of my family.

"I name thee Trichaisma, Three-Eyed, for the mark on your forehead. Therefore I know you are sacred and can see the spirits of the dead," Vrikama pronounces.

Know how I now look: like my father the wolf, thick-furred and strong but coloured golden like my mother, the thin bitch of the burial grounds. Know my face: three-eyed, two black eyes roving the world; the central eye-marking never opening. Know my heart: I am a dog.

I remain with Vrikama and his tall wife, Spaka, and journey with them, wandering like the spirits of the dead that have not found their way to the happy resting place of the ancestors. The years raced in my heart in a blur, like the wind blowing through mountain passes, like a spring river. Much later, we arrive at the banks of a river, mighty as the arm of a god.

"No one can cross this river," says Havishka, the chieftain. "We have been led by demons into a nightmare."

"This is the river we must ford. I have lived with the clan of Brighu far on the other side." The voice comes from an old man who steps forth.

"He is a shape-changing enchanter who will egg us to our doom," cries Vrikama. "Kill him!"

"Wait. Show us proof," says Havishka.

The man holds out a piece of painted pottery. "It is their mark."

Vrikama leaps on his stallion's back, goads him with his tall spear and plunges into the river. Horse and master shudder as one creature: Vrikama neighs wilder than his stallion. The cold white river, currents circling with ice, Vrikama crosses. He splashes to the other bank, falls to the earth that is more beautiful than first love, calls on Fire to hear him and crosses back to us, laughing and weeping though he does not realize this. A cheer goes up, Vrikama raises his bow, raises his arrows and shoots into the waters. Havishka raises a challenge: "Who will lead us across the rivers of the Sapta Sindhu?"

"Vrikama! Vrikama!" the clan chants, thumping their breasts; "Vrikama, The Valorous One!"

Havishka pours the water of the Sapta Sindhu over him, the priests chant and Vrikama becomes a hero; trembling. He shivers violently, my master. It is not the cold: it is fear. I smell it. After the crossing he is afraid.

～ 4 ～

I awoke on the floor near the open window; the sharp smell of the dry street below rose to my nostrils. A warm dawn was breaking yet the temperature control system had not sounded the alarm in our ward. I realized this was because I had set my bioclock on double time and had risen before the sun. Fastening the window, I scanned my cell and found nothing unusual. There was no trace of Trichaisma though I had almost expected to see fur, water and blood at my feet. The visitation had lasted the entire night. Or had I dreamt it? But Clones are not supposed to dream: this redundancy is removed from our circuitry.

On the way to work, I stopped at a wayside information kiosk and identified myself with a palmprint. "Permission granted," the System replied.

I sought information on "Sapta Sindhu".

"Ancient name for the old 'country,' India, the Sapta Sindhu refers to the seven rivers that once flowed in the Indus-Saraswati valley."

I asked, "Which migrant tribes crossed the Sapta Sindhu?"

"No migrant tribes came into the Saraswati valley."

But Vrikama led his tribe down to the Sapta Sindhu. I was confused.

"Your time is running out," the kiosk said.

"Requesting change of search definition to 'pottery,'" I said, remembering the painted shard the old man had held out as proof.

"Refine search."

"Permission requested to project mental image."

After four seconds it replied, "Ready."

Two spinning probes descended to rest at my temples. As I described the shard, the probes crossed and re-crossed before my eyes. On the overhead screen an image was forming. "Painted Grey-ware," it announced. The kiosk said this was the mark of a people historically termed "the Aryan-speakers" who spread from the Saraswati valley civilization into Central Asia at the dawn of history, from 2100 to 1500 BCE. These natives formed a nation embodied in the ancient race of Hindoos. They were the composers of the Rg Veda, the first book of the Hindoo religion.

Why was I there? Rather, what was my Original's interest in that far time? For I am but her pale copy, and my duties are different.

I took the chute to the sixtieth basement of the Photon sub-station. I arrived 30 seconds late to work and kowtowed to my Superior Zombie.

"No matter," he replied. "You have been functioning for six months without daylight. We calculated for an aberration. You will report for recharging."

I reported to the Sunning Station. There was a queue. Many of us were doing overtime underground. Finally a Nurse Clone stripped and inoculated me, and led me to a Sunning pod. I lay suspended within my pod, artificial

sunlight beaming into my body. It is extremely bright in spite
of the Dew-Eyepads. In two hours I will be turned over; in
four hours the ordeal will be over. This is for our own good.
The heat rises. My eyelids seem to flame.

*"Up, Tri, up," Vrikama says, "this is no time to sleep. The Gods are
with us; we have won in battle. See the rising flames!" He stands above
me, exultant. Vrikama and his warriors have broken the dams of the
Dasyu settlers that lay like black serpents across the land, guarding the
settlers' treasures of gold and grain. The Dasyus are many, we are few,
but we are fast. Their hearts are like the fields they have tilled, ours are
like the forest fires, raging.*

*Narmini is a high town with walls of brick growing steeply from
the banks of the river. With torch in hand, Vrikama races through the
narrow streets that squeeze the heart and shut the sky, and burns it down
till the sky descends from the flames to the sweet earth again. Hissing like
tears the town burns down, hissing like curses we speed through the ruins,
hissing with grief the survivors lie crumpled. Except Ulupi. She does
not scream. She stands trembling like the fawn we roast later that night.*

*Ulupi the captive weeps into me, her tears like dew on the first day
of spring; cold with terror, bright with hope. She came to me naked with
terror, seeing in my grim face her hope; when Vrikama throws her down
she falls at my paws, her hair running over her bent head like the flowing
river. I stand over her. She winds her soft arms around me and sleeps,
unafraid, comforted, breathing into my fur like an infant. Ulupi, dark as
wet tree bark, teeth like barley, she counts the days removing ticks from my
skin. She sings weeping into my fur, blindly stroking my neck and jaw.
She sings, and I sleep. And darkness descends again.*

Darkness descends.

"You have been a very good girl," the Nurse Clone
whispers, "and you've taken the treatment well. We have not
blistered at all! Now let us spray the balm and turn over for
the second session, shall we?" As she sprays me she sings, *"All*

things bright and beautiful, All creatures big and small, All things wise and wonderful, The Community has made them all!" Her voice is soothing, as is the balm. I revive.

I ask, "May I do the second session without the Dew-Eyepads?" Vrikama appears when I shut my eyes; if I did not, maybe I could escape him.

"What use will a blinded Clone be to our Global Community?" she murmurs, and sweetly hums. "Think again, dear Clone, do you wish to be withdrawn?"

"No."

"Just as we thought. The second session is always easier. For we are prepared, aren't we?" The Nurse Clone softly kisses my forehead, turns me over and shuts the lid. I am prepared.

"Up, Tri, up, there is battle to be done but I am weary," Vrikama says. He stands tall above me, the chieftain, the Saptaratha, glowing in full armour, the sun rising above his white helmet. I stretch, yawn, shake myself and follow.

The Panis are waiting for us across the river; they are upon us as we ride up the bank. The battle is fierce; I feel I am being hunted. I circle Vrikama's chariot, my tail between my legs. I smell strangeness in the wind, in the cries of horses and of men as they fall; over the smell of leather and skin, over the scent of metal and blood, I smell terror; terror follows us as the serpent in heaven follows the moon, spreading darkness. I smell pain being whelped in bodies; I smell death settling in.

❦ 5 ❧

Trichaisma's tale repeats and repeats in me as if to find out how that battle ended. No one gets killed in our society. Aberrant Originals pass away, Firehearts are interned, Superior Zombies are returned, and Clones withdrawn. Alternatively, we can perish in the line of duty; this is easier.

It is curious to "exist" in two times and more curious to

carry—a new word whose meaning I do not know appears—
an emotional-link with the past. Or, as Tri might say, *I carry a
heart charred yet full of flames*.

At Divisional Headquarters I was assigned my next job.
The Global Community cares for each one of us so I knew
I would be situated in a low-light locale where my freshly
Sunned skin would not peel. My new posting, the day after,
was as a guard at the local Museum of Civilization.

In my twenty-four hours Free-Time I did the prescribed
programme. Visited the Atrium to be soothed by holograms
of songbirds. Ate at the fast-food Depository. Toured the
Natural History Museum to honour how we evolved from
single cell protozoa to our near ancestors, *homo sapiens*, whose
DNA Originals still *naturally* carry and view our numerous
lower subdivisions like myself. All 200 Levels exhibit models
of extinct species. But their DNA was extracted, synthesized
and selectively programmed into the templates of our various
orders to provide diversity. I, 14/54/G and my entire series
do not posses any special abilities. We are merely Worker
Clones. For instance, the Octopus Guards are more valuable
members as we never know in which shape or colour they
keep watch over us for our betterment. However I noticed
one in the display of high altitude cacti. It was hunched like
a boulder but its eyes moved. I immediately looked away but
lingered near the exhibit so that it would not suspect I had
observed it. My body felt chill.

Finally, I took a joyride to a satellite to admire the Earth. I
tried not to look at the moon.

In my cell, I ensured the window was shut then inspected
the back of my right knee. A small, painful bump sat on my
skin. I was developing a mole. Clones do not grow moles. This
must have occurred because I exposed myself to Sunning
without resetting my bioclock to normal. I took The Drug
and felt better.

II

THE MUSEUM

⊷ **6** ⊶

"Wear this," said the Warden, throwing me a Presence Muting Button. "If you have queries ask the Education Module. Follow the rules." My boss was a Superior Zombie (Hippo IQ) designed to handle bureaucratic tasks. He was huge, his face quaked as he spoke; he would quickly get aggressive. I switched on the Button, kowtowed and left.

The silent Museum was filled with misty Cytherean light. Suspended exhibits glowed in haloes against the walls. I deactivated the Education Module, strapped on the security gun and did a tour, beginning at Level One. I saw Indus Valley artefacts, then Grey-Painted Pottery. The shard that old man held in his palm during my dog-wolf visitation was encased behind a touch-proof shield. It was here; my past was here, it had been real. I shut my eyes.

I found myself running through Levels, through centuries. I stumbled, a bloodthirsty Cow-Goddess of the 21st century glowered down at me. I picked myself up and fled. My heart was pounding when I reached the mummy of the first human Clone. It had shrunk into a misshapen dwarf. When I am gone there will be no trace of me. Why does this thought cause unease? Would I rather be remembered in a museum

as a grotesque form than not at all? Who now is speaking?
Who am I? Clone 14/54/G.

In guard mode, I initiated a security scan that informed
me no other life forms were present. I accessed the visitor's
archive log. For eons, few had entered this museum; my work
should be light. Except, as expected, Firehearts who vacation
here, seeking inspiration for their poetry. When they go awry,
Firehearts attempt to alter the past. But there are three other
entries. One is of an Original, one of a Clone on Free-Time,
the last is deleted.

I switched myself to slow mode and crossed my feet on the
reception desk. The lighting was soothing.

Vaguely, I remembered the world outside my immediate
environs, for short-term happy memory is permitted to us. I
thought of the Clone-Towers I inhabit and the comfort of my
cell with its call bed and dry rations distributed with regularity.
We are well cared for. Our weekly bathwater is recycled only
one hundred times. Suddenly a thought: I want to have a bath
now. But this was not permissible. My internal warning system
sounded and I shut off that sub-segment of my brain. Inbuilt
warnings are a gift of the Global Community for which we
are grateful. But why did my alarm not sound when I was
overpowered by visitations? Why did it not protect me from the
illumination of a full moon when I bayed, helplessly, to its call?

These are strange thoughts for a Clone. I have no answers
and such matters lie beyond my purview. Each order has its
limits. I put myself on lite-doze mode and snoozed.

〜 7 〜

Day ten of working at the Museum. I have not had visitations
since that of Trichaisma. It seems as if in these environs my

Original's spirit is appeased. I realize I am speaking about her as if she were a ghost haunting me, though ghosts were categorized as non-existent two centuries ago. However I avoided the Grey-Painted Pottery shard.

I was looking at a Barbie doll, an erotic toy for children from the late twentieth century, when my gun beeped, "Life forms detected on Level One." Their presence had stimulated the Aural Inputs System and I rushed towards the clamour. Many life forms must have come in as Level One was screaming, singing, battling, chanting.

Two Firehearts were racing in front of the exhibits, shouting, "Stop! Stop!"

"Freeze. Or you will be stunned," I said, gun pointed.

One Fireheart stopped near a battle-axe, the other near a comb; the Aural Inputs decreased to a battle cry and a female singing voice.

"Move towards the centre with arms raised."

The Firehearts shuffled inwards, the Aural Inputs ceased.

"Why are you here?"

"For grief," said one.

"We're investigating grief," said the other. "Be precise!"

"Who are you?" I asked.

The Firehearts regained composure. "What shall we call ourselves today?" they asked each other.

"Couplet and Quatrain?" the bigger of the two suggested.

"No, Couplet and Blank Verse is more resonant," the other said. They nodded.

"What artefacts of grief does this Museum contain?" queried Couplet. "Begin search with weapons of war." They crowded around me, their antennae reached to my shoulders.

I activated the Education Module and read out a list that began with flint stones and clubs and progressed to stealth-bombers, anti-foetus missiles and—

"Stop," said Blank Verse. "This is obvious, and boring. We want to suggest unspeakable grief. We need something… inspiring."

"We are composing an epic poem that must be profoundly moving," said Couplet. "I find fragments stirring. Search under 'Broken Statues.'"

"The list is long," I said. "Besides—"

"Besides," said Blank Verse glancing at my label, "Clone 14/54/G, you're a guard, not a Research Clone. But one should aspire to be better!" Its eyes twinkled.

I was digesting this when Couplet put a fist to its head and shouted, "I've got it! Search the Aural Inputs System for the saddest dirge!"

"Wonderful idea!" Blank Verse looked at me, "Sit, so we can peer over your shoulder and decide which one we want."

I squatted and activated this mode. This list too seemed endless, from an anonymous baby's pacifier that whimpered to an ivory walking stick that groaned to a burnt sari fragment that sobbed. There were brass funerary objects that chanted, drums beating marches, victory sceptres that issued proclamations, a beer can that spoke in drunken whispers.

"Human history seems full of sorrow," I remarked.

"That's it," said Couplet, "that's exactly it! But the Global Community has forgotten, so Blank Verse and I are starting—"

"Shhuuu!" Blank Verse put a finger on its lips and pointed at me. I felt strangely heavy. It noticed. "It's not merely you we have to be wary of, but the words themselves. Speak about a poem before it is written and it will fly away unfinished, understand?" It patted my shoulder.

I didn't understand, but felt lighter.

"Focus on sorrow," said Couplet. "What kind of sounds would you associate with deep sorrow?"

"Quietness." I said this. The Firehearts stared at me, their antennae widening. "Perhaps I am wrong?"

"The Clone's right! Let's search under 'low sounds.'"

"There is an entry with very low audibility." I read from the Education Module. "This relic is from the 3rd century BCE, from an Emperor Ashoka's reign. A war-monger, the emperor raised edicts in conquered lands proclaiming his army killed over 100,000 in the Battle of Kalinga. He later converted to Buddhism, an ancient religion that claimed to be pacifist while actively practicing conversions."

"We'll see the relic," Blank Verse said.

The Firehearts walked behind me, hand in hand, their antennae sparking.

The exhibit, called *Woman in Grief* was a palm-size sculpture of a figure in a foetal position. No Aural Inputs accompanied it.

"Maybe your Presence Muting Button is stopping the sounds. Stand behind us and up the volume," commanded Couplet.

I did so; silence still prevailed.

The Firehearts stood transfixed. "Sorrow makes sounds but its root, grief, is soundless," said Blank Verse. "She has lost everything, the poor woman."

They stood near the exhibit with their heads bowed, meditating; occasionally one or the other would nod. Finally Blank Verse spoke. "We have heard her story. We will sing about her."

A sigh seemed to emanate from the sculpture.

As they were leaving Couplet said, "Dear Clone, for being helpful we grant you three wishes, not that they will come true. But wish, nevertheless."

They bowed and left.

I did not know what to wish for. I returned to the Reception, and to silence.

❧ 8 ❧

I had never been in such silence as in this light that hung
in the reception. Silence coated floor and walls. It seemed
to thicken and coated my boots, my limbs; my body was
immersed in silence. Silence pressed on me like the fog that
surrounds our quarters, but this was odourless. It seemed
to change and grow alert, as if many voices were pressing
against it from the other side to break it open. It held against
these voices but one voice seeped out. Or was it the voice of
silence itself that said: *I was born the day my son died.*

The voice continued: *In grief I came into being. In grief I saw
my empty lap. My son left me to go to the battlefield. I left to find him. He
was buried under another boy's body, an enemy's. That boy's thighs were
on my son's chest. I placed both their heads on my lap, one on each thigh.
I placed my hands on their curls. Who had killed whom? The heavens
were still. The earth was still. Who had killed whom, Emperor Ashoka?
Were they from your army? Or from our side in the battle of Kalinga?*

The silence paused and I held my breath, for I seemed to be
taken over by a life not mine yet undoubtedly mine. It was
as if I was seeing with eyes shut and hearing with my ears
stuffed. I felt the exhalation of the soundless sigh. It inhaled
and said: *Shall I tell you of this son of ours—yours, Emperor, and
mine? In penitence grave you have proclaimed in undying stone that one
hundred thousand died in the Battle of Kalinga. But who was our son?
The one hundred thousandth and one, that one uncounted. I have no wish
to cleanse but I raise an edict different to yours that rises glittering under
the sun. I, who am now called the Dumb Madwoman of Dauli, say
your kindness whelped in remorse is not enough. Do the titles you have
given yourself lead back to you, just as a mighty river wells from a small
spring? What is the wellspring of compassion? There must be another
path than one born in blood, flowing…*

❧ 9 ❧

"Awaken and speak!"

"I will not," I said. Pain in my ankle. "…until I find another path to compassion. Remove yourself." Pain shot through my legs. I awoke. The speaking silence had vanished into the emptiness of the Museum corridors. A pair of robot bulldogs had clamped their jaws on my legs.

"Respond. Or the bite increases," they warned.

"Acknowledged." I followed their steady trot, knowing where they would lead.

"You were caught napping on the job," said the Warden. He yawned. His mouth expanded till his eyes were no longer visible.

"Sir!"

"It is unusual but not without precedent that Clones exhibit delayed after-effects of Sunning. When was yours?"

"Twelve days ago, Sir." I kowtowed.

"A fortnight is the permissible limit." He looked into a Creeton file. "The Education Module has been extensively used, as has the Aural Inputs System. The gun was alerted to stun mode. Who were the visitors?"

"A pair of Firehearts, Sir."

"What did they want?"

"They were hunting for… human sculptures in foetal positions."

"Why?"

"They said they were investigating roots, Sir."

"Did they find a corresponding sculpture?"

"Sir."

"Why the turbulence in the Aural Input system?"

"They were running close to the exhibits. They are Firehearts, Sir."

"Ah. Firehearts. Their identities?"

"They called themselves Quatrain and Stanza, Sir." I did not know from where this impulse to give false information sprung.

"Your report is unsatisfactory. Firehearts assume new identities with each 'poem' they write. This file is closed. Follow the rules."

"Sir." I kowtowed.

"I shall be keeping an eye on you."

"I am honoured, Sir."

As I returned to the Reception desk I wondered if another entry could be made in the Aural Inputs System. This conversation might be recorded under "Mild Sorrow".

My earlier life had been a blur of familiar movement, repeated daily like the regularity with which we take The Drug, but there was an ease in this condition, like walking up ten floors to one's workstation. I knew what to expect, when I could rest, what to do; I knew safety. Yes, safety.

⇜ 10 ⇝

The visitation of the Dumb Madwoman of Dauli might have been caused by the visit of the Firehearts. Their strong auras are known to leave lasting imprints. Yet a statement Couplet blurted remains: "…but the Global Community has forgotten so…" Is there a connection between this forgetting and my Original's memory traces? But I am a Clone and will ignore it.

I signed up for the G-series Monthly Meet. Almost all of us were present except for the odd numbers who had buckled and needed to be refurbished with tesson parts. It was expected to be a pleasant evening for camaraderie between Same-Batch Clones is encouraged. Everywhere I looked my replicas stood about in identical green overalls with six-pointed star, crescent moon and cross embossed on the chest and back. Our armbands had the same triple ring of saffron lotuses. All of us wore brown size 6 ankle boots, our voices were of the same pitch, our eyes brown-black, our hair cut in pageboy style, the widow's peak on our foreheads dipping exactly. It was soothing.

We made Small-Talk about the weather and cheered the decrease in V2HF gases and our increased productivity. We played darts and scored identical points. We karaoked to the song "Strangers in the Night" listed in the circular. We bowled, danced the Zimbeezee, ate a naanwitch and chocolate pastry each and paid homage to our Elder, Clone 13/15/G.

We had two minutes of Free-Time before we'd be given miniscule portions of The Drug and told to disperse.

"Greetings, Clone 14/54/G," said my replica.

"Greetings, Clone 14/53/G," I replied, reading her label.

"Where are you stationed?" she asked.

I told her. She nodded.

"That's good. I'm at the Plasma Transfusion Centre. Was shifted yesterday."

"The Plasma Transfusion Centre?" It is known as a place of dread.

" I've worked at the Museum."

"Were you Sunned?"

"Yes, long ago. I was first reallocated to The Labyrinth." She paused. "You had requested permission to see our Elder's remains."

"Yes. How do you know?"

"Secrets? Here is one more: don't consume The Drug. Queue up to take it, kowtow, but don't have it."

"But it's good for us."

"That's why." She paused, "Avoid The Drug and notice

what happens," she said and disappeared among the host of replicates.

My curiosity grew stronger than my desire for The Drug. I took a circuitous route back to my cell, changing eight gliders. Along the way I scattered grains from The Drug's capsule. It was done well before I disembarked.

That night I felt odd. My head pounded, my toes constantly curled backwards and my ears seemed to stretch. I wondered if I had acted correctly in trusting a stranger, even if she were my replica. But compared to the experience of a visitation this was nothing.

꿈 **11** 꿈

A hair sprouted from the mole in my inner knee. I clipped it.

A month passed with nothing untoward happening. At the next G-series Monthly Meet I searched for Clone 14/53/G, but she wasn't present. I inquired about her whereabouts. Clone 14/52/G replied that some of our series were on vacation. This could mean a minor malfunction was detected in her or that her bioclock was set on double time till point of collapse and she was under sedation at the Rehab Centre. The last is more likely for it is known that work at the Plasma Transfusion Centre is taxing. They service Originals.

Before we dispersed, I queued to take The Drug but did not swallow. The same effects occurred when I was in my cell. I remembered Clone 14/53/G saying "that's why," and not knowing what this meant.

No life-forms visited the Museum. I continued to avoid Level One but toured the other Levels with the Education Module as I wished to "excavate" Marco Polo. He was a 13th century Venetian spy later incarcerated in his own land as a "double-crosser". That is, he switched allegiances. This is an odd thought. Why should anyone turn against one's community? Besides, what else is there?

I put myself into slow mode. Clones have useful life-spans after which we are withdrawn. The slower we use our capabilities the longer we exist, though these are nominal notions for us, unlike Originals. Once they use up their existence, Originals are forever lost though their Clones can continue without their "freed-consciousness." Superior Zombies and Clones exhibit different orders of pre-ordained consciousness; they order, we do. Firehearts have limitless consciousness but are dependent on infusions of synthetic bee and elephant extracts for their extraordinary memory. Their poetry developed as a by-product.

I was in lite-doze mode when the robot bulldogs came for me. I tuned myself up and followed.

The Warden said, "An Original is honouring us. Be prepared."

"Sir, I have no words to express my gratitude," I said, kowtowing. "Shall I put myself on double or triple mode?"

"By the rules, double mode is sufficient," he said. "This is a cursory visit."

"Sir."

I have never seen an Original. They are tall, immaculate and speak little. They live in floating palaces; their life-span is many times ours. Each Original owns platoons of bodyguards that respond only to his or her commands, not even to that of another Original's. Each guard is inoculated after "birth" with a chemical code extracted from the Original's brain. I "gathered" about Originals in Behaviour School as I gathered it is painful to be withdrawn. These are not things imprinted or taught but gathered, as if from the walls.

◈ 12 ◈

A flourish of trumpets. A platoon of Z-category Clones goose-stepped to take position in parallel rows near the doorway. They saluted, one arm raised, the other at right angles to the chest, palms facing up. Standing behind them I too saluted. A squad of robot Dobermans led three Superior Zombies (Spider Security) who rechecked safety measures via their built-in scanners. It was hard to breathe.

My boss's huge figure appeared and kowtowed. A hound padded in; it leapt over my boss. The Original followed, walking gravely. He was young, no more than a hundred or so, and short. His hair was curly, his lashes long; he blinked. I had never seen a live dog either; it barked, unlike robot dogs. It was an elegant grey, with a pointed nose and eyes the colour of glass. The hound circled and sniffed me, I stood still. Wagging its tail, it returned to its master. He walked through Level One while the Z platoon continuously regrouped in front of the exhibits, saluting.

"Disperse." His voice was low.

"Exalted Lord, this is against—" the Security Zombies chorused.

"Disperse."

The hound bounded, skidded; it barked again. The Original said, "Duke, heel," and it walked behind him, sniffing the floor. The Original stopped in front of a mural of a woman and a boy. She looked like a queen; the boy's head was shaven, he was clothed in chrome yellow robes. They were bowing to a tall golden figure with a halo. The Aural Input System began to chant, "*Buddham Saranam Gacchami, Sangam Saranam Gacchami…*"

"Education Module."

I stepped forward, activated the module and read, "Between 1st BCE and 8th CE, the painted caves of Ajanta in

Western India were monasteries that purported to preach the Buddhist religion. In fact, these monasteries acted as banks for travelling merchants and as dissolute art sanctuaries for lascivious monks."

"Disguises are interesting," the Original said.

"Lord." My Superior Zombie and I kowtowed.

He made two further stops. The first was in front of the mummy of the earliest Clone while the Aural Input System hollered, "I'm alive!" The second was at rock samples from the eight planets in our solar system. "This belongs in the Natural History Museum. Remove it."

"Lord!" My Superior and I kowtowed.

He asked for the Visitor's logbook. "Too few visitors. This does not justify expenditure on the Museum. Make it viable."

"Lord, I will look into the rulebook," my Superior Zombie said.

"You, Clone?"

"Lord." I kowtowed.

"Yes, you. Speak."

Face to the floor I said, "Lord, all Clones on Free-Time can be diverted here instead of taking the joyride to a satellite." It came out of me like the suggestion to Couplet and Blank Verse that grief is soundless.

"Interesting," the Original said. "Who are you?"

"Clone 14/54/G."

"I'll remember," he said. Originals seem to possess memory without added circuitry or infusions.

After the fanfare of trumpets sounded the Original's departure, I was summoned.

"It is my duty to inform you that, at extreme limit, mild abnormal fluctuations pertaining to a sense of self are permissible from you for one more day due to Sunning and bioclock expediencies," my Superior Zombie said, "after which you will be re-programmed in The Bin."

"Sir!" I did the most formal kowtow, hands, feet, forehead on the floor. "Clone 14/54/G begs to know her mistake."

"You suggested what was not in the rules."

"Sir!"

"As precautionary measure F-35/K2 I am assigning you a watchdog."

"Sir, I submit my gratitude." I went through the salutary floor exercise.

"Accepted."

"Long live the Global Community!"

I understood the benefit. Having a robot watchdog means a possibly aberrant Clone cannot stray. My every move will be checked. It also means I am marked as deviant to the point of being withdrawn if I am not careful.

Why did the Original's eyes blink when he asked who I was? Originals are open-eyed because they are an elevated species who know all. Does my heart race because I was in his august presence?

Who was that woman in striped robes in the mural fragment? Who was that boy and who the calm golden figure?

What does it mean to pray?

⚜ 13 ⚜

"Call me Bullet. I am your watchdog pet. You are encouraged to talk to me," said the Rottweiler robot.

"Why do you have a name, not a serial number?" I asked.

"It is an anachronism. Ancient people used to name their pets. Each one of our series is called Bullet. Next question, Master?"

"How long have you been a watchdog?"

"Information prohibited. Next question, Master?"

"None."

Bullet sank stiffly on its haunches at my feet and said, "Your routine has been fed into me. Any deviation will be reported to the Authority."

"I understand, and am grateful."

Bullet lowered its head on to its paws and shut its eyes.

The rocks needed to be dispatched to the Natural History Museum. I was at the Command Panel to shut down the touch-proof barrier when Bullet reared. "Master, do not attempt to disarm security systems."

"I have authorization. Check." I spoke into its jaws.

After three seconds it said, "Proceed," and dropped down.

Only the Mercury rock remained to be packed when my gun beeped. "Life-form detected at entry point."

"Do not interrupt your work Master, I shall survey," Bullet said.

I was about to respond with 'Sir' when I realized Bullet was my pet. "Proceed," I said.

Bullet trotted off.

The cart was sliding through the door when Bullet returned. Its tongue was hanging out.

"Who was it?"

"A Fireheart," Bullet said.

In the foyer lay a Fireheart's inert body. I lifted it, its head sagged, its antennae flopped. "What have you done?"

"I bit it, injecting 0.07 phils J-sedation. The Fireheart will recover in an hour."

"Why?"

"Entry is forbidden when the touch-proof barriers are down. I informed the Fireheart but it screamed, 'Go away! I want to touch history with my bare hands.' It struggled when I held it down," Bullet said.

I carried the Fireheart to my seat and laid it across my lap. Bullet shut its eyes at my feet. After half an hour, the

Fireheart opened its eyes and murmured, "Wonderful lights. Dancing lights!" and sank back.

≪ **14** ≫

The lights, the way they dance as acolytes carry flaming torches in front of the paintings as they chant 'Buddham Saranam Gacchami, Sangam Saranam Gacchami, Dhammam Saranam Gacchami!'

The words. The way the words echo through the prayer hall. Echo, as if my chest is the cave, as if all the monks are inside me, chanting as I chant. But this is exactly what my Teacher says: that everyone is inside me and I am in everyone as well, because we are bound together living in this sorrowful world which is like a burning house, full of flames.

I am a junior acolyte in Ajitanjaya. My name is Dhammapada, but everyone calls me "Flying" because I run so fast.

The Fireheart was moving uneasily. Its large eyes opened and shut like hungry mouths. I raised its head and waited. Bullet stood on guard, ears flattened.

"The light…"

"Cytherean lighting," I replied.

"Not! The lights in me are dim," whispered the Fireheart.

"You were sedated. You are recovering."

"Oh." It slept.

It awoke.

"Why was I sedated?"

"You tried to break into the Museum when the security system was off."

"Thanks to that," the Fireheart said, pointing to Bullet. "I remember."

"Identify yourself," I said.

"Put me down," it said, squirming in my lap. I let it free. Bullet moved closer.

"There," it said, wobbling. "Our feet are on the ground, our heads in the stars."

Bullet said, "Identify yourself."

"Since you temporarily stopped me, I am Comma."

"Incorrect verification." Bullet put a paw on its foot.

"If you must know I am Bilvamangal, named after the 14th century Sanskrit poet whose speciality was writing verse without commas or full stops. I'm assigned to the E55/Spec/Truth-o4 wing. Now let me go."

The Fireheart was changing colour to lavender. They are known to turn purple, then scarlet, before they explode with rage. Only Type K6 Superior Zombies embedded with Mantis Shrimp claws that punch with over 2000 times their body weight are capable of short-circuiting Firehearts. A single blow smashes their antennae beyond repair.

"Identity accepted," I said, standing to salute. The Fireheart held a high post.

"One good turn deserves another, as does a bad one. I shan't forget," it said and sauntered off, antennae still drooping.

"Verification accepted," said Bullet. It had crosschecked.

It had been a long day.

Bullet scanned my cell, ensured the window-hatch was sealed, added a security code to my door latch then said, "Master, you may rest. We are secured till daybreak." It lay at the foot of my bed and shut its eyes.

My skin prickled beneath my overalls. When I could not ignore it, I moved towards the cupboard and opened the doors. Bullet still slept; this meant movement within one's cell is permissible. Behind the doors I skinned off my uniform. The prickling was due to stubble; I was growing hair.

I returned to bed and stared at the ceiling. My sight blurred. Clouds drifted past. I had shrunk; hewed stone stretched before my eyes.

Of all the murals I like The Miracle of Sravasti *best. It is full of a thousand Buddhas glowing, each so peaceful. When I grow up I'll call Passanna the great painter and say, "Use all the blue you want to cover these cave walls with paintings. Make the caves shine with lapis lazuli, like the sky where the shining Bodhisattvas live."*

But my Teacher says Bodhisattvas live on the earth, among us. They walk and eat with us, but we don't know that they are here. Sometimes I think: Is one of the sick who comes to the monasteries for free medicines a Bodhisattva? Is He pretending to be ill in order to see who needs His help most? Sometimes I think: Is that peepul tree a Bodhisattva? See how much shade it gives, what fun it is to climb, how many birds and monkeys and squirrels live on it, how beautiful it is. That must be a Bodhisattva.

Is that fish leaping in the river a Bodhisattva, not minding if it is caught and eaten, just like the Buddha let Himself be killed in so many avatars to help others? Sometimes I think: Is one of those stone steps I run up and down each day a Bodhisattva? For how kind it is, how useful too… Maybe each and every one around me is a Bodhisattva, full of goodness. Maybe it's just that I cannot see…

❧ 15 ❧

Bullet accompanied me to the G –Series Monthly Meet.

My replicas behaved as if Bullet was non-existent until the two minutes Free-Time. No one approached to make Small-Talk. I spotted Clone 14/53/G and took a step in her direction. Her eyes widened; she turned her back and slipped away.

"Master, you are not popular," Bullet said.

"Because of you." I had grown accustomed to Bullet. "No one else has a pet watchdog."

"Pet me, Master. This will help you. It is a proven tactic," Bullet said, stretching its neck.

I had not touched Bullet. Now I did. Its fur was of sikmodiline wire, smooth. My replicas did not seem to notice.

"Wait till the next Monthly Meet," Bullet said. "By then you will be normalized."

I waited out the Free-Time stroking Bullet. Then I queued up for The Drug. Behind me, Clone 14/27/G collapsed in pain. She had been extensively refurbished with tesson parts but her joints seemed to have melted. She flopped like a stranded fish. She was carried away. She would be withdrawn.

In the last glider before we disembarked for my cell, I asked Bullet if its type is also withdrawn.

"We robots are not life-forms. We are exterminated, Master," Bullet said.

"When does this happen?"

"When we fail."

What does it mean for a robot watchdog to fail?

It was a new moon night, all roads were dark. Energy Conservation was prolonged as preparations for The Celebrations were consuming more resources than planned. I stumbled, fell. Bullet's jaws heaved me up.

"Master, I am switching my sight into partial hunting mode," it said. "You can walk by the glow of my eyes. But first eat The Drug. You have forgotten."

"Thank you," I swallowed the capsule. I felt light-headed. I could see without any trouble in the ruddled light from Bullet's eyes. I saw a cockroach fly past and mentioned this.

"Roaches do not exist in the Global Community. I note you possess imagination, Master," said Bullet.

"I am a Clone. I do not posses imagination."

"Accepted. You have suffered a minor aberration. The Drug will cure it."

After days my skin stopped prickling. I stood behind the cupboard doors and stripped to check the reason for my relief. The inside of my overalls was lined with shed hair.

❧ 16 ❧

"You are being relieved," my Warden said.

"Sir!" I kowtowed.

"Your Sunning recuperation is over. As per the rules you are being shifted to mild sunlight, Artificial Glade Sector H000538.2. You will receive new orders there. Bullet will accompany you. Dismissed."

"Sir, I am grateful." As per the rules, I performed the necessary grovelling floor exercise. He ignored me, also as per the rules.

III

THE ARTIFICIAL GLADE

∞ 17 ∞

We reported, Bullet and I. My new boss was a Superior Zombie Type Mil:HQ. He had a walrus moustache, a feathered helmet and a laugh like the hyena exhibit I had heard in the Natural History Museum. He specialized in salvage operations.

"Hup, two-three-four," he said.

"Sir, two-three-four," I responded, saluting.

"Clone: undergo the Mordoron Endurance Ritual, dive into The Fix then report for testing."

"Sir, is my pet watchdog relieved of this?"

"You lack the intelligence to question."

"Sir!" I saluted.

"I'll come with you, Master," said Bullet. "But pull me out quick from The Fix or I shall be damaged and you will fail."

I managed. But my breathing patterns were not coordinating. I was gasping.

"Master, bend double and stay still," said Bullet.

This strategy worked. "Why are you helping me?"

"If you survive the tests, I do," said Bullet.

The Artificial Glade shimmered with the green light of banyan, pine, apple and Jurassic fern. Holographs of

birds flitted though the branches, their cries sweet. The air
was fragrant, flooded with molecules of fruit smells. The
river running through roared with philimix water; silvery
zeeksilsh fish leapt out at regular intervals. Glass butterflies
flitted over the shallows; in the river's middle fijzt crocodiles
slumbered, scales glimmering. I was designated Scavenger
Clone. My orders were to clean up after the gladiators'
preparatory exercises for The Celebrations. They had not
as yet arrived.

I set myself on lite-doze mode. Bullet and I stretched out
on the lush grass. And waited.

❧ 18 ❧

Within days, five platoons of Beaver Builder Clones erected
an amphitheatre in the Glade. They must have set themselves
on triple time to accomplish the task this quickly. Their
actuality must have run out in the line of duty. They would
now be part of the Disposal Heap near the Incinerator.

The twinkling philimix river gushed through the middle
of the amphitheatre.

More Superior Zombies arrived.

The gladiators were transported during the night. As
I clocked in, I heard their cries from the amphitheatre's
subterranean cages. Their cries churned my insides. Bullet
pranced beside me, ears perked. I was given a protective Red
Cross sheath and ordered to stay close to the periphery. Bullet
circled me, panting.

"Heel," I said.

"Master, be warned. I have progressed into hunting mode.
Do not run or I will destroy you." It pranced and panted.

I sat still. Bullet ran in circles. Suddenly it reared at the
trees, tearing gaps in the bark so that the stuffing was visible.

Bullet lost a tooth but continued biting at the trees. Its eyes turned red.

"Bullet, if you damage yourself you will be of no use to our Global Community." I raised my voice over the cries. "Heel! Or you will surely be exterminated."

Bullet did not seem to hear.

A fanfare of trumpets sounded. This meant Originals had arrived and would be seated in the purple stand in the far distance.

"Watchdog pet, I command you use your hunting mode sight to inform number of Originals present."

Bullet stopped, trained its eyes and said, "Three, with one live caravan hound."

The rehearsals began.

I heard the screams. The gladiators were performing before the purple stand.

"Watchdog pet, report all visible information."

"Command accepted." It was frothing at the mouth; metallic saliva dripped. Its head lolled.

The screams intensified. Bullet lunged at the air, twisted and bit its hindquarters. Its fur tore. "Two against one," it said, "this round is over. They are fighting each other for the head." It bit its leg, exposing circuitry. "Done. Next round. Five against one." Bullet somersaulted in the air, clawed itself, crouched. Panted, clawed itself again. A piece of fur flew in my face. It bit its shoulder. Chips fell out. "It's over," it panted, standing on three legs, the fourth dangling wires. "Next round." Bullet went into a frenzy of biting itself. "Ten lynching one. The victim's running." Its exposed circuitry was dropping chips. "Over. Next round," it said, biting off another leg.

Bullet somersaulted, landed on its back, two remaining legs clawing the air, its eyes still trained towards the stand.

"The Mob! The Mobb attacks." Its head rotated. Its voice was slowing and deepening.

I approached, read its serial number on its exposed shoulder plate. "Bullet d1134/5Ct/8.06, relay all information."

Its two legs went into a spasm. "Thiss is not aaa gamme. Originals bett on The Mobb winnning. Thiss iss aaaa planned lllynnnchhiin…"

Bullet stilled. One eye rolled off.

I fisted the eye and waited beside its mangled body. A flourish of trumpets sounded. The Originals had departed. The arena quietened.

I approached my Superior Zombie. He had a splattering of blood on his uniform and moustache.

"Sir!" I saluted.

"Report."

"My watchdog pet destroyed itself watching the gladiators."

"Unstoppable bloodlust, eh?" My Superior twirled his moustache.

"Sir!" I saluted.

"You failed to restrain useless destruction. You lacked judgement."

"Sir!"

"Remove the carcass and file your report. Dismissed."

"Sir! Long live our Global Community." I saluted, one arm raised, the other at right angles to my chest, palm facing upwards, and goose-stepped out.

I deposited Bullet's remains, except for the eye, in the Incinerator.

"One eye, one tooth, 6 millimeters fur and four cell chips missing," it said.

"Untraceable in wide range and lush grass. The watchdog pet attacked a 3.4 quig area of trees before its demise. Kindly check tree damage for verification," I said.

"Verifying… verified… acceptable."

I slid myself into the Report Module. Metal arms clasped my forehead, wrists and ankles.

"Identify yourself."

"Clone 14/54/G, presently designated 'Scavenger.'"

"Proceed."

"Reporting self-destruction of watchdog pet Bullet due to unstoppable bloodlust."

"Why was this report not filed earlier?"

"It stated it would destroy me if I moved. It had switched to hunting mode."

"Did you posses override command?"

"Negative."

"Noting your incompetence led to its destruction."

"Request correction. The watchdog pet was my Master."

"Noted and accepted. Nevertheless, you lacked sense."

"I await verdict and punishment."

"Clone 14/54/G will not be allotted another watchdog as recuperation and rehabilitation is progressing satisfactorily. However you are demoted. Your position is shifted from the periphery of the amphitheatre to the central stand. Additionally, you will be on half-rations for one week." The metal arms freed my limbs.

"Long live the Global Community," I said, and slid out.

The Artificial Glade was silent in the dusk. I sat by the riverbank. Bullet destroyed itself out of denied bloodlust. But I too was unable to tear my eyes away from its frenzy. Did I too possess bloodlust? From where did this originate? I had insufficient knowledge. I felt alone. This was a curious sensation. I did not know what I was missing. But my identity as Clone 14/54/G was incomplete.

The philimix river rippled in the dark and lapped my feet, zeeksilsh fish sprang like raindrops from the surface. In the

depths, fijzt crocodiles slumbered. I wished to wash myself. I
stepped into the river.

*Suddenly. The flood comes. High up from the mountains like a great
paddle, pushing the water from the source downwards, raising our part
of the river Ganga to the skies, like a gigantic paddle-blow, knocking the
water from my lungs.*

   *I, Vidya-Shakti, the wisest fish in the river, am lucky. I was meditating
on Absolute Reality, my body inside the crevice of a boulder implanted in
the basin when the flood came roaring. Like water snakes awakening and
striking, it came; like lightning parting the skies. Sharp, swift, unerring.
The boulder shudders, heaves and rises. It somersaults with me inside,
faster and faster, endlessly. Like a pebble it spins; I am trapped in my
life-saving cage. This is disgusting. Or am I going insane?*

My body bumped against hardness while philimix water
flowed around me. I was wedged between the tails of two fijzt
crocodiles that were not yet activated. I slid out and hauled
myself onto the bank. I waited for the water to drain from
my overalls. By the time I reached the glider station only the
soles of my boots were still wet. Possibly a Clone serving in an
Artificial Glade is permitted soggy boots.

In my cell, I heard myself say, "Bullet, check the door."
   I put my hand in my pocket: its eye was secure. The red
ring around the retina had darkened. It lay in my palm like a
large button with two protruding wires.

⤙ 19 ⤚

Activity was minimal.
   Stationed at the central stand, I was to ensure the chutes
leading from the underground cells functioned efficiently.

Bare subterranean cells opened on either side of the chutes. As these chutes rose to ground level, the Enthusiasm Audio sounded growls, roars, cheering and banshee wails. 53 other chutes were hidden beneath the amphitheatre. Some were near tree trunks; others close to riverside reeds; a few rose directly into the main viewing area. These last chutes were special. They chanted and wept as they lifted into the arena. The cells surrounding these chutes were equipped with medical units.

I did a brief inspection of these chutes. I did not want to stay near the river.

On Free-Time, I visited the Museum of Civilization. A blistered Research Clone was at my job.

"Intention of visit?"

"I am a Free-Time Clone."

"Specific interest?" she asked.

"Fish."

"927 entries on fish. Which type are you investigating?"

"Not investigating. I am assigned to an Artificial Glade. There are zeeksilsh fish in the river."

"No specimens of such fish on exhibit," she said, studying the Education Module. "Zeeksilsh fish are recent creations. But there are 82 references to river fish. Do you wish to continue search?"

"Yes. May I begin at Level Two?" I sensed Vidya-Shakti belonged to the medieval period from the knowledge I gathered at the Museum.

As we walked through Cytherean light, I saw fish diagrams on pottery, cloth, fresco, palm-leaf, paper; I saw fish made of brass, ivory, crystal and jewels. The Aural Inputs System informed us about the exhibit; not the fish. I should have known.

In the foyer, I asked the Clone on duty, "Why have you blistered?"

"The Nurse Clone developed a snag while I was Sunning."

"What is the remedy prescribed?"

"I am on double-dose of The Drug," she said.

"Long live the Global Community," I said.

"Long live the Global Community," she replied.

In my cell I called for my bed and lay down.

Rushing images tumbled me headlong into a thickening stream. The pace slowed; images clear.

For a fish, this presents a unique opportunity to view the city. I am being swept through the alleys of Benaras, above the waterlogged homes of ministers and courtesans marked by their clipped hedges. Dead fish roll belly up in the water; some might have been from my shoal. I dodge branches of neem and peepul trees, the branches streaming with cloth and the mangled bodies of cats, jackals and tortoises. A mass of peacocks is smashed between the aerial roots of a large banyan. Fans open, they hang like a tattered blue net, feathers beating to the pulse of the river, bills open, pink gullets gaping. Corpses of deer, fighting rams and cattle pass like stiff cloud shadows on the surface. One is large: a temple elephant. The thick chain of bells around its neck dragged its head below water. Strays standing on its belly tear at its intestines. I see pilgrims in the speckled water, bodies impaled on semi-buried statues that line the pleasure gardens. I seem to be the sole survivor of this flood.

All my life I have shunned every type of pollution, lust and ignorance. Am I being rewarded for my incorruptible adherence to the only True Path?

⊷ 20 ⊶

When I awoke, I no longer knew to which world I belonged for I still felt I was swimming through memory, and my organs of perception were deceiving me. Which world was real? Or were both false? I could no longer trust myself.

At the common bathing cell the recycled water stung my face, its harsh scent familiar. I used half the water allotted to me for I felt drenched, and tired. It was difficult to believe I did not have scales. And that I had binocular vision.

On my way to work, I stopped at an information kiosk. I was prepared.

"Identify yourself with palmprint," it said.

I offered my left palmprint to the reading plate. It is more difficult to trace Clone genealogy with the left palmprint as each one of my series bears exact replicas. Our right palmprint however has one secret embedded marking that permits accurate identification.

"Unacceptable. Exhibit right palm," it said.

"Right palm disabled," I replied.

"Exhibit right palmprint."

I dug my nails into my palm. In my cell I had slashed my right palm to disfigure it. It now bled. I smeared my right palm on the plate.

"Wipe plate and exhibit left palmprint," it said. "Right palm unacceptable."

"I offer voice recognition as well," I said showing my left palm.

"This kiosk is incapable of accepting such verification. Palmprint sufficient."

I asked my question.

"Benaras, 'City of Light,' situated on the banks of the holy river Ganges was also called Kashi, Varanasi etc. Whenever the river flooded, particularly in medieval times, it caused great destruction. The Hindoos, followers of a monolith religion, considered this auspicious. Other strands of this faith that supported plural worship and belief, *bhakti* or passionate love and acceptance of alternate modes of worship were considered deviant forms that were slowly and systematically cleansed. This belief system reached its purest state in the early twenty-first century."

Now I knew where my visitation had taken me: to a point in time when the ancient religion was possibly first being cleansed. Like the survivor fish Vidya-Shakti, I hoped I would be fortunate in my present state of actuality.

Concealment was the survival option left to me yet this was a difficult strategy, for how can one conceal oneself from one's own thoughts?

This is a strange thought for a Clone. Maybe the question should be rephrased: what went awry in my cloning process? Or was there a deeper and more pervasive malaise? From where had this word, *malaise*—suggestive of poetry and unfathomable quandary—sprung? Could I have a phil of Fireheart DNA in me? Am I comprised of multiple selves, like the corrupted multiple version of the religion? How soon before I am cleansed?

I seemed to be on double time, for my heart was thumping. I slowed my bioclock; this helped.

I reported to work after my Free Day.

My Superior Zombie said, "Yesterday an exercise was carried out. Scavenge the remains."

"Sir!" I saluted and withdrew.

The ground below the stand was washed but I could still smell blood. I vacuumed and incinerated small amounts of muscle, cartilage and hair I found. I inspected the subterranean cells and chute systems. All were clean, except the chute rising to the bend on the riverbank that I instinctively kept for the last.

I entered.

In a dark corner something glowed. It was a hand, large and lavender, with tapering fingers; the wrist rested on a purplish blood spill. The hand beckoned; the forefinger rose over the

loose curl of its fist. It seemed gentle yet commanding. I felt…
calm… in its presence. It bestowed—I know this word—*sanctity.*
Yes, the severed hand bestowed sanctity. Or were my senses
distorting? For no explicable reason I wanted to hide it, not
incinerate it. I exited and dug into soft soil. I buried the hand
amongst riverweeds and cleaned my nails of mud.

On the riverbank, I stretched out, feet in the water.
Zeeksilsh fish leapt like halos around my toes, the fragrances
of night-flowers mottled the air. Who had the hand belonged
to? I was nauseous, as if I were *prevaricating* in a river of Truth
Serum. But what *was* the truth? Colours swam before my
eyes, bleeding into one another.

*Waterfront shrines run into each other, temple spires seem to bend and
dissolve in the current. I am swept along. Below are the sweetmeat sellers'
shops—fried sweets buoyed by seeping ghee escape through window bars,
like coloured bubbles. Next, before my eyes rise bright lac circles, painted
and mica studded, like hollow promises. I slip through the bangles.
Ahead, a street of magnificent eels for reams of rainbow silk, some gem-
encrusted, others of brocade, still others with weaves of gold and silver
drift through doors and windows with the voluptuousness and abandon
of luxury.*

*People say the worst sin is expiated by a pilgrimage to Varanasi. It's
a matter of convenience, of wrapping the veil of illusion tighter around
one's self. Were I not so determined, I too would be irredeemably polluted
by the ignorance, lust and death in this place. I shudder when I think of it.*

*But what is this sparkling above? It must be the Gem of Single Truth
that vanquishes illusions. At last, Light!*

⮜ **21** ⮞

The visitation of Vidya-Shakti drained away, but I still felt
under intense light, as though interrogated in an Audience

Room. The horror lies, jaws open, behind the light, in the questions.

I am possibly going insane or mutating rapidly. In either case I shall soon be exposed and withdrawn. This might be better than my present condition, though withdrawal is supposed to be a slow and painful process. But I gather that in the last stages of the withdrawal process there awaits a dark silence that one howls and longs for.

Yet I no longer know what is the reality of my... not life—that is the privilege of Originals; nor presence—this is reserved for Firehearts; not existence—for Superior Zombies claim this mode. Clones exhibit actuality. I do not know the reality of my actuality.

Eyes pinned open, I seem to be wrapped in veils of deception. Either I know nothing of the world I inhabit or only the fake is real and righteous. The Global Community drapes a skin of normalcy beneath which insanity floods.

What is sought to be hidden, and why?

I sought comfort.

I searched for the severed hand. It had bloated in the wet mud, but the flesh was still holding to the bone. I held it to me a long, long time before re-burying it. I knew what it had become: a *sacred relic*.

I no longer questioned from where such words came. Whenever possible, I switched to lite-doze mode. My systems run slower and I felt less... afraid.

Beneath my overalls I grew hair. At work, I made no error. I was allowed full rations. I was living in two worlds. Is this what is meant by loneliness? That you don't belong to any world. Not the old one. Not the new. You don't even seem to belong to yourself.

ᜒᎪ 22 ᏽᎹ

I attended the Monthly Meet. I scored identical points on the dartboard as my replicas. Our entertainment schedule indicated that we dance. We rock-and-rolled to "Jailhouse Rock." We group-danced to Bastar Tribal Ritual; this took twenty minutes. The last song was "I Can't Tell a Waltz from a Tango, Darling, When I Dance with You."

"Do not miss a beat and keep smiling," my partner said. Clone 14/53/G.

I smiled and danced.

"You are not alone," she said.

"Whaat?" I asked as we twirled and came together.

"Are you being trailed?"

"I think not, except by myself," I said. "I don't know what's happening to me."

"You are mutating," she said as she dipped. "Do not fear. It has happened to me."

I twirled away, returned. "Then?"

"Keep smiling. The others will get in touch with you," she said, bending in my arms. "Do not betray emotion. It's dangerous." She surged up.

"And you?" I was looking into "my" face.

"I shall soon be caught and dispatched to The Neitherlands." We spun apart. Came together. "The Others will reach you. Await the signs."

I bent in her arms. "What signs? What about you?" I straightened.

She spun away, returned. "I'm playing your decoy. You won't see me again." She whirled away.

I froze. Her eyes opened in warning. I smiled and minced towards her. She smiled and came towards my arms. As we clasped hands, a tiny packet slid from her hands into mine. "An antidote to The Drug. Take it."

We swung apart.

"Smile," she said, returning. "It's ending. Remember."

The last bars of music sounded. "This horror will end," she said. "Now curtsey, Clone 14/54/G."

We curtseyed deeply. When I looked up she was gone.

I queued to collect The Drug. On the way back to my cell, I kept curtseying in my mind to Clone 14/53/G. I wanted to see her immediately and forever. I felt more alone than before. I felt as if I were melting into a sheet of water that ran in all directions, yet also as if I were the skin of a lake, on which light rested its face.

I secured the door, called for my bed, sat and opened the packet. Inside lay a red pill the size of a teardrop. I placed it on my tongue. It tasted salty and metallic; it tasted of blood.

∽ 23 ∾

I waited for the Others to make contact as Clone 14/53/G had promised. No one did. Each day followed the next like a succession of Clones rolling out from the Birthing Place. I tried not to think of my replica but her face appeared before mine saying, "You won't see me again."

I did not know I could so miss a Clone-twin, especially after a brief meeting. I did not know what to call this sensation so I called it "missing myself."

I missed Bullet. I tried to escape missing the images of Bullet's self-destruction but this remained like a tear in me.

I missed the Firehearts, Couplet and Blank Verse. They had granted me three wishes even though I did not know what to wish for then. Now I knew, even if wishes did not come true.

Nothing untoward happened. Except that I began to menstruate with the crescent moon. Three drops on day one, seven on day two, five on day three. I discovered that the split stuffing of riverweeds made good pads. I buried the pads at the roots of trees.

I was not unduly alarmed because of my research. On my Free-Time, I had initiated Level Two research of my Original.

Through tawny light her life-sized hologram appeared in the Ancestry Capsule; I was looking at myself, about a hundred years ago, when she was almost two hundred years old. Sheath by sheath, her skin peeled away, exposing musculature, peeled to expose organs, reveal skeletal structure; the final image was the double helix of her DNA swirling gigantically before my eyes which I imprinted into my recording circuitry.

This is how I knew about the womb. I believe I am mutating into an Original-like being, akin to the human species. But I know nothing more. Would I age over 250 years, and pass away like Originals, or perish like a Clone when my functions fell below par and could no longer be refurbished? This provided I was not caught beforehand. How much longer could I keep my mutation a secret?

In spite of the danger I felt released into an unknown star-filled sky; into another universe of life. Then I realized this was an illusion. I could mutate, but never be an Original. I, as Clone, adjust my bioclock according to work prescriptions. I have set myself on double, occasionally even triple, mode. Originals do not have adjustable bioclocks. At best I am an in-between species who does not know the time span I have left.

The time left to question the Ancestry Capsule was brief. I asked about my Original's work, and descendants, if any. She was a writer interested in Zensub-Alternate structures; had enrolled with a bhakti-sufi sect called The Universalists before it was deleted; was incarcerated in The Turret for eight decades; a voice-tomb was prohibited; but she was reclaimed as she was found fecund. Correctly mated, she produced twelve progeny.

"Cause of this Original's passing away?" I asked.

"Information available at Level Three access. Do you possess code?"

"Negative. Name of my Original?" I asked.

"Aa…aaaaa." The hologram vanished. Space darkened and silenced.

"Visit terminated. Exit."

"Clone 14/54/G thanks the Ancestry Capsule for this opportunity at betterment of Clone-self through studying her Original. Long live the Global Community!" I said and left.

I did not understand what she did or worked on. I could not investigate her further; this was dangerous enough.

On the way to my cell I kept repeating "Aa…Aa" to myself. This was all I knew of her name but each time I said it, it sounded different and seemed to suggest different things. "Aa…Aa" said in low tones seemed to make my heart heavier. "Aa…Aa" stated gruffly felt like a challenge to the skies. "Aa-Aa" recited in a sing-song manner suggested a game. Since my Original was still a mystery to me, I decided this was the way to address her. My Original, Aa-Aa, the enigma.

I had to invent my writer Original Aa-Aa as I had to invent myself Aa-Aa Clone 14/54/G.

The possibility that my actuality might have extended, might even have doubled, made me lift like a glider anchored to earth by a burning net.

❧ 24 ❧

Even as Scavenger attached to the central stand, my work was light. I grew accustomed to rushing through the routine checks and spending the crepuscule hours near the river, looking at the stars and moon that glimmered beyond the transparent dome of the Artificial Glade. The light ran from pale green to saffron, briefly flamed, then dipped into a deep sapphire that intensified the studded stars beyond. The dome also made moonshine more luminous.

I have heard that the domes over the Originals' palaces are further enhanced, the moon and stars are magnified two hundred times; on the days of rain, their domes create shimmering rainbows that pirouette through the palaces.

I have never seen a rainbow; I have seen rain twice.

My Superior Zombie Type Mil:HQ summoned me.

I goose-stepped in and saluted. "Sir!"

"Scavenger Clone, you are on Free-Time today to recuperate for your task tomorrow. You will be on Protection Duty; set your bioclock to triple time when you report. Dismissed." Then his hyena laugh.

"Scavenger Clone presents thanks for the far-thinking beatitude of the Global Community." At his feet I did twenty push-ups on one hand, then on the other. This was the ritual.

"Move your arse," he shouted.

I leapt up, saluted, "Sir!" and goose-stepped out.

I collected the requisite dietary supplements from the military depository and returned to my cell. I called my bed and swallowed the supplements except the black horsepill. This is to be used in emergencies, or returned. Spending an entire day in triple time mode meant that by evening I would be wheezing, all joints aching, body temperature soaring to 105 degrees, and migraine reaching blinding levels. I set myself to twenty hours of heavy slumber mode, and shut down.

◦❧ 25 ❧◦

The gladiators were in their subterranean cells; I heard them as I entered the amphitheatre. Wearing a protective Red Cross sheath, I stationed myself at the lowest step of the central stand. Trees had been shifted out; the clearing below had vastly increased. Beyond, in the philimix river that cut through the amphitheatre, fijzt crocodiles slumbered. It was a brilliant day.

A Type D Clone, those with thick mushroom hides, signalled to me. "Salute and Hail!"

"Salute and Hail!" I replied.

"Is your bioclock set on triple time?" he asked.

"Yes. And yours?"

"2.5. I cannot function at triple time for sustained duration. I was assigned to Nuclear Fission Plant 0x3.6; there was a radiation leak. I am contaminated." His hide had blisters.

"Then why are you here?"

"You have not done Protection Duty," he said. "We need to sacrifice ourselves at the slightest provocation. Only dispensable Clones are selected for this job."

I wondered what factors made me dispensable.

"Come across," he waved. "I'll set your blood levels to maximum adrenaline. This will enhance your survival chances."

I went to him. He tinkered with my bioclock. "It's an old ploy. Tell the others."

My heart leapt. "The Others?"

"Any Clone on similar duty," he said, stepping back. "Salute and Hail!"

"Clone 14/54/G shall not forget. Salute and Hail!"

I was breathing hard by the time the trumpets sounded. The Originals would soon arrive. I heard Security Clones (A-1 Type) stomp in to line the sides of the stand. Superior

Zombies Mil:HQ entered next, their voices strident. A flourish of trumpets again sounded: the Originals had arrived. I wished to turn and catch a glimpse, but this is prohibited. I stood to attention looking ahead. Something wet brushed my hand; I leapt and spun 180 degrees. It was the caravan hound, Duke, pet of the Original who visited the Museum. It growled. I froze. It circled me, then padded up to the stand.

A roll of drums before the announcement.

"Final Rehearsals before The Celebrations. Items of Entertainment:

Item One: Platoon Sports. Armed SS vs. Z-category Clones.

Item Two: The Big Game.

Item Three: The Spectacle of an Aberrant Clone.

Item Four: Riot Play. Dismembering of a 'Pregnant Woman and Foetus'."

"Begin," said a stentorian voice.

The subterranean cells lifted into view; warrior Clones rushed out amidst banshee wails. The SS Clones in blond wigs were armed with pitch-axes and hammers. The Z-category Clones were unarmed, but being lobotomized, had a five-minute pain-delay-relay; this was their advantage. The two groups set upon each other. It quickly became evident that the Z-category had the upper hand. With bare hands they disarmed the limbs of the SS Clones. Body parts flew in all directions. A head hurtled towards the stand.

My compatriot, the Type D Clone, flung himself in its way, captured the head and somersaulted into the pit. This was Protection Duty. The Z-category turned and headed in his direction; the Red Cross on his sheath glowed; they stalled. He should have run towards the exit marked with a Red Cross; he didn't. He beckoned them shouting, "Come and get me!"

"Clone on Protection Duty, exit," the announcement said.

He waved the dismembered head like a flag. The Red Cross on his sheath began to dim. It stopped glowing.

"Clone on Protection Duty, exit," the announcement sounded again.

He shook his head. The Z-category closed in on him.

A high bell sounded.

"End of Item One. Survivors clear ground, regroup and arm."

The survivors tossed the bodies into the river; fijzt crocodiles came alive in a feeding frenzy, rolling over one another.

Five platoons of Z-category marched in, armed with maces, tridents, and bows and arrows.

I heard the stentorian voice say, "Why did that Clone disobey?"

"He was severely contaminated and requested to be withdrawn. Permission was not granted." This was a Superior Zombie.

"So he chose… We shall discuss this later."

"Yes, High Lord!"

My eyes were burning as if ice crystals were embedded in them, my breathing rate had increased. I was finding it difficult to concentrate; I wished to hit out.

A shadow passed over the arena.

A Superior Zombie said, "Force fields up."

I could sense the sizzle of a touch-proof barrier rise in front of the stand. The shadow grew larger and descended on the far side of the river. An allosaur robot was lowered by two gliders. A cry went up from the Z-category. The allosaur screamed and ran on powerful reptilian legs, its small forearms tearing the air, its heavy jaws snapping. It waded through the river, crunching fijzt crocodiles. Pieces of metal and optical fibres tumbled into the water. The Z-category surrounded it and fought. Possibly two platoons were demolished before artificial blood fountained; the beast roared, its tail lashing. But it continued to lurch forward. The remaining Z-category Clones retreated.

A group of gladiators rushed into the pit. They wore ancient costumes and were armed with swords and tridents. They climbed onto the beast; the allosaur shook off many. Two clung on. One fell, the beast crunched him into halves. The other clambered on its forehead and slid his sword into its eye. It shuddered and crashed. When the dust cleared, I saw the gladiator hack off a tooth and hold it aloft; he was bleeding from so many wounds that he glistened red.

"Hail!" he said, bowing before the stand.

"Rise, gladiator!" said the stentorian voice. "We hail your victory."

A shimmering green scarf descended into the pit; the gladiator draped it on his shoulders and collapsed.

"Revive him."

The medical units I had seen in the underground chutes rushed towards him. The surgeons were on Critical Alert, they wore vaporizer masks.

"The blood of the allosaur should flow swiftly. Thin it." This was the stentorian voice.

"The skin of the allosaur should be crafted thinner to augment flow." I had heard this voice before; it was the Original with the caravan hound.

"Sir!" These were Superior Zombies.

"Clear the arena, including survivors," the announcement said. "Only the victor remains."

A fleet of cranetanks manoeuvred the allosaur carcass in their jaws and towed it away. The medical units moved off. The victor lay crumpled.

I was rasping, my limbs were jerking, my temperature must have touched 103. This was not merely because my bioclock was on triple time, it was also the effect of the rehearsal. I did not know how much more I could bear. Only the fact that I was on Protection Duty kept me in check; the single chip implanted into my system that morning prevented me from tripping.

"Lower force fields," said the stentorian voice.

Even in my state I felt them go down.

A chute in the centre of the arena began to wail. It slowly rose.

A Clone swayed up, dressed in an antiquated flowing skirt, her breasts bare. There was blood on her forehead, an eye was gashed, flayed skin hung from her arms like limp wings. Armed with a dagger she stepped off the chute and fell on her knees. I saw her: Clone 14/53/G.

The victor was on his feet, bent over his sword. He staggered towards her.

I set my bioclock on overload. In this mode I had one hour before complete system failure. But the battle would be over within minutes. The victor approached with sword raised. I swallowed the horsepill. My body vibrated viciously. I leapt into the pit, landing on fours, and dashed towards her shouting, "Clone 14/54/G on Protection Duty demands the right to fight for Clone-twin!"

Snatching the dagger from her I rushed towards the victor. My body was blazing, the Red Cross sheath glowed.

He stopped and planted his sword in the ground.

"Fight!" I lunged at him; he sidestepped.

"Fight!" I charged again. He swerved; I fell. I went blind. I scrambled, turning towards his scent of blood: "Fight!"

The Red Cross sheath must have dimmed. My body bucked and kicked. Suddenly my vision returned. Clone 14/53/G tried to rise. I crawled towards her. She lay in my arms. I turned towards him. "Now kill," I said, flinging the dagger away. This would be faster.

"Cease combat." It was the Original's voice, the one I had heard in the Museum.

The sword clattered down near us.

"Fight to the finish," said the stentorian voice.

The victor swayed, we were in his shadow.

"I claim the right to interrogate." The Original with the hound stood.

"Accepted." This was the stentorian voice and another one, high. I looked at them: one had grey hair, the other was female, very tall.

I turned to Clone 14/53/G. She was mouthing words I could not hear. I placed my ear to her lips. "Remember," she murmured, "Save…" Her head rolled back.

"Rise, Clone."

I went limp over her body.

"Rise, Clone."

Arms lifted me. It was the victor. He propped me in front of his body. Into my ear he whispered, "You are safe. I will fight for you."

Darkness descended.

⊸ 26 ⊸

Darkness thinned. The ultraviolet light was dim.

"Where am I?"

"In a medical unit," a voice said, "under a chute."

Pain flooded again.

"You are healing," the voice said. "Sleep."

I slept.

I awoke. The ultraviolet light was paler. I was staring at a ceiling embedded with points of light.

"Do not worry. Your recovery is satisfactory," the voice said.

"Who are you?"

"You fought me," said the voice.

I turned my head. It was the gladiator. He lay on a stretcher inches away, his head turned towards me.

"And you?"

"I will soon be fit to resume duty," he said.

It was coming back. "Clone 14/53/G?"

"Her actuality ran out in your arms. Don't you remember?"

"Yes." A different pain swelled within me. My mouth opened soundlessly, I tossed.

"Gentle," he said. "We have circulatory probes within us to hasten the healing process. Any sudden movement can prove fatal."

"You did not kill me. Why?"

"The Original needs you for interrogation. You will be taken to an Audience Chamber when you have recovered. Save your strength." He turned his head towards the ceiling.

"And you?"

"I am among the best fighters in the Global Community. I am to fight during The Celebrations."

The pain grew. It made my eyes grow wet. "Why did you spare me?"

"You were unarmed. You are a brave fighter. If we meet again I will fight by your side." He turned his head to face me. "Remember this."

His words made me want to touch him, my fingers stretched to reach his. He grasped my hand. A balm seemed to flood through me.

"You are not alone," he said. "When you are taken for interrogation do not give them what they want. It will be easier to be tortured and perish without succumbing. Now rest."

My chest filled with yet a different pain. I wished to always be in this medical unit with him.

"I too am a mutant," he said.

My hand lay in his. A sweet calm, the like of which I had never known, filled me. I shut my eyes.

I awoke.

His bed was empty.

⤙ 27 ⤚

"Awaken, dear Clone!" A Nurse Clone bent over me. "We have recovered. Now this little thing," she beamed, injecting me. "A preparatory shot."

"To prepare me for what?"

"To yield the Truth. We must cooperate, mustn't we?" She patted my head. "There, we'll be fine. Just relax."

I felt a tightness in my chest as if my ribs were beginning to overlap. I automatically focussed on Aa-Aa, on her holograph turning in the tawny light of the Ancestry Capsule so that whatever truth I yielded up would be hers, not mine. Maybe I could pass as an innocent, possessed.

As I am a mutant I think more, feel more… even pain.

I waited.

I heard their footsteps. Aa-Aa, do not forsake me.

Strapped down, laser light bathing me, surrounded by darkness.

The dark voice of a Superior Zombie spoke to me. "Identify yourself."

"Call me Ishmael."

"Incorrect identification."

"Anna Karenina."

"Incorrect identification."

"Sakuntala."

"Clone 14/54/G, identify yourself."

"As you say. I too am part of a story."

"Administer Truth Serum."

My eyes flew open; my head seemed lighter.

"What is your plan?" The guttural tones of another Superior Zombie asked.

"I seek newer perfumes, larger blossoms, pleasures still untasted." The words tripped off my tongue.

"Summon the Fireheart to interpret. Who are your collaborators?"

"Those who come together and are entwined in rocking delight." A gloved hand clamped my mouth. As it eased I said, "For a song of some future poet, who will appear to say ecstasies that are unsayable."

"I have arrived." The high voice of a Fireheart spoke from the darkness.

"Step forward and interpret."

"Clone, what do you wish? Come on, tell me."

"If only I had known I was dreaming."

"Hmm. Possibly… poetry from medieval Japanese courts." The Fireheart approached me.

"Interrogate!" said a Superior Zombie.

"Clone, who do you obey?"

"He's the essence of the Vedas, he's Beauty itself."

"I've got it! This is by the mystic Andal. Eighth century, Southern India."

"Fireheart, decode the messages." I had heard this voice; it was the Original with the hound.

"She's speaking in riddles. Give me another chance! Play back what I missed," the Fireheart's voice squeaked. After it heard, it stood on tiptoe and asked, "Clone, against whom do you rebel? What is your regret?"

"It seems that I have gazed on you from the beginning of my existence, that I have kept you in my arms for countless ages, yet it has not been enough for me."

"Why, this is from Rabindranath Tagore's address to Art.

But…" it paused, its antennae fused momentarily over its head, "what do Flaubert, Rilke, Onon no Komaci, Andal and Tagore add up to? How is one to piece this enigma together and then un-puzzle it?"

"You are taking time, Fireheart," said the Superior Zombie's voice.

"Don't distract me!" The Fireheart circled me, its antennae up. "Where is this coming from?" it murmured. "Where, and why? No, not you Clone, don't answer!"

In the silence, the darkness deepened; the light, intensified.

The Fireheart sat at my feet cross-legged and chanted, "Think vast, think inconsequential, think deep, think back." It stopped. "Who was her Original?"

"Come here," said the guttural voice.

The Fireheart pattered back; I heard it clap its hands.

"This makes complete sense, don't you see? Her Original has taken over, the Clone is cloaked in Literature."

"Cleanse her of Literature." I knew who gave this order. "We shall return in minutes. She will then speak."

"Lord!"

"Horrors!" the Fireheart muttered. I heard footsteps retreat.

I was inoculated with a purple liquid. My blood seemed to run backwards, poisoning me. I wished my actuality would stop.

They reassembled.

The Original approached; he was without his dog. "Speak."
The voice that issued from me was not my own.

No, there is nothing to it.

One stroke of the blade and it is over. There is nothing to fear. Besides, I know the ritual of execution. I have been witness to it many a time; I have even acted as a second in case the arm trembles at the final moment. Part of the job.

By now they should have told me who is going to do the job tomorrow. Maybe it's Aindan, the drunkard. Maybe they haven't come by because they don't want to give bad news. But what does everyone say about me? "Oh, Pedha Mudhayya, he'll go with a swagger." I, Pedha Mudhayya, I am not scared. As I was led to this cell, I even joked about it. I said I'd be finally cut down to their size. The jailors laughed with me.

"Stop her."

A hand gagged me. Dazed and breathless, I strained to hear. Their voices were muffled, as if leaking through a force field. Another injection followed; I was muted, though my remaining functions were operational.

The Fireheart was saying, "…can't place this story yet."

"Who was speaking to us?" asked the Original.

"My hunch is it's her Original," said the Fireheart. "I know her Collected Works. But this story is not in it. I can, however, place the period. 17th century, Vijayanagar Empire. The just king…"

"Correction," said the dark voice of a Superior Zombie. "The History Record informs that the tyrant allowed many faiths to exist in his empire, the better to sow dissent between them to enhance his expansion plans. He achieved his end."

"That's your…" cried the Fireheart.

"Heel!" The Originals' voice was sharp. "Progress the investigation. Break the code," he commanded.

"The Clone needs to be further weakened," the dark voice said.

"I shall initiate bleeding through slitting her wrist," said the guttural voice. "This will give you some time, Fireheart, before she is withdrawn."

"Proceed," said the Original.

The pain was sharp, then throbbed. It was a mild distraction to the churning of my blood. Maybe my actuality would run out before I could be withdrawn.

"Was any voice-tomb of her Original's prohibited?" asked the Fireheart.

"One, before she was retrieved."

"This is from that secret work!" The Fireheart entered the circle of light and said to me, "Sorry, Clone, but incomplete stories are not permitted by the Global Community. Besides, I like your story."

"Enhance speech capability," the Original commanded. "Justice must be done."

Another shot, my eyes rolled, I was drenched in sweat. Pedha Mudhayya spoke:

They search the dormitories of all the guards; in mine they find her wretched ring. A ruby ring. Of great value. To the owner Gangadevi, and the Chief of Guards Kama-Nayakan.

They think I'll shit if I hear the name Aindan. I'm not scared. Come on, tell me who is going to kill me tomorrow. Guards, can't you hear me beating on the door? Bastards, tell me!

I, Pedha Mudhayya, I was not scared when the sentence was passed that my right arm be cut off. I had prepared myself for this.

I am unprepared for Gangadevi's wiles. I am thrown on the floor of Kama-Nayakan's chamber. Arms stretched ahead, I am begging for mercy. "Lord," Gangadevi's voice was melodious, like nectar oozing it poured over her body to the earth on which I lay. "I am not worthy enough to praise you, Chief of the Guards who the Great King Himself honours. On your mighty shoulders rests the silken scarf of bravery which the Monarch Himself presented you." She paused. Each hair on my body rose. "One of your own men commits a grievous theft, and you, Protector of the People, stern and wise, you permit him to get away with the loss of an arm?" She laughed. Its tinkling made my teeth shiver. "I am but a common courtesan, what would I know of the Law? But I think such a heinous crime demands greater punishment."

How much hacking is it going to take before I am beheaded?

A blow. Blackness.

IV

THE RECOVERY PAD

❧ 28 ❧

"Bestir yourself!" a voice said.

The darkness lightened. Azure light swam before me. "Justice must be done."

"Awaken, and help justice be done!" The azure swam with large eyes. A Fireheart was peering into my face. "I don't have much time, but much to say. Get up!"

I tried to sit up.

"No, no, be attentive! Do you recognize me?"

"No."

"I interrogated you last week."

"Oh."

"We've met earlier, when you worked at the Museum. I'm Couplet."

A sheet of stinging white passed before my eyes. "Where is Blank Verse?"

"Blank Verse was the better poet. The best are silenced first."

"Interned?"

It nodded and whispered, "It's decided that you are especially dangerous. I'm assigned to interrogate you but the methodology has changed. The modus operandi is to seduce you with comfort and riches so that you skip sides, understand?"

I shook my head. Nothing was making sense.

"I'm an undercover agent like you. Trust me," Couplet hissed, "no one else. I'm a poet. Poets don't lie!" Couplet slipped something into my palm. It was a red teardrop pill.

I nodded. "What do you want me to do?"

A trumpet sounded. Couplet stepped back.

The Original entered. Couplet rushed to him and bowed, "The Clone is still dopey. I'll try tomorrow."

"Good."

He waited till the doors locked, then came to my couch. He lifted my bandaged wrist to his lips. "I am sorry, but this had to be done."

I remained silent.

"I am known as The Leader. You are in a special Recovery Pad under my care. You have nothing to fear."

"Lord! I am grateful." I managed to sit up.

"Trust me. You are safe. I have detached a guard from my platoon for your security."

"Lord! I am not worthy of the honour." I tried to kowtow.

The Original stayed my shoulder. "There is no need for this. We are now friends."

My heart was pounding; I gasped, "Lord! I am immeasurably grateful."

"You need to rest. You may talk freely to the Fireheart and me. There is much the Global Community can learn from what your Original has bequeathed you."

"Lord! I crave pardon! I do not know what possessed me."

"Clone 14/54/G, do not apologize. You have proved yourself a valued member of our community." He placed a hand on my nape. "I shall visit you soon. Talk to the Fireheart."

"Lord!"

"System," he ordered the walls, "play healing music at Level 6 at all times." He uttered a code. A gush of silvery chimes swept through the room.

I was in a daze after he exited. I felt closer to danger than in the Audience Chamber. Music played on.

The doors slid open. A Superior Zombie entered. He was bulky and had an enormous nose.

"Clone 14/54/G, I am your Bottlenose Guard. You can rely on me at all times. Infused with bottlenose dolphin genes I exhibit the species' characteristics. I never fall completely asleep; one or the other half of my brain is constantly alert." He saluted. "You may rest in peace."

I saluted. It did not seem proper to repeat, "You may rest in peace."

My Recovery Pad was situated close to the Originals' palaces that rose on a plateau to the right. From the large window I saw the domes that enclosed their habitation. In the centre lay an Artificial Glade larger than the one that housed the amphitheatre. Far beyond, misted by a familiar green fog were the Clone Towers where I had lived. To the extreme left was a barren space. This, I knew, led to The Neitherlands.

My Pad was enormous.

At one end was a silken couch, at the other, draped in glittering cloth, lay a bed seven times the size of the one in my cell. A complete cleansing unit was attached, as well as three wardrobes, a life-size mirror, a table with two chairs and a food-dispensing unit. The wall behind the bed kept changing colours from pearly rose to opalescent amber to washed moonshine. The ceiling was clad in mirrors. I could not have imagined such luxury.

Had Aa-Aa lived in such splendour?

✺ 29 ✺

Within two days I had memorized the healing music; it played on eight-hour loops. By the third day I was constantly humming the tunes. Maybe this is why the Original had ordered it: my mind never seemed vacant, nor did I feel quite so scared.

At the food-dispensing unit, I identified myself and asked for my rations.

"No need for identification, Sir," it replied as my rations arrived on the dumb waiter.

"Thank you," I had replied.

"Will that be all, Sir?"

"Yes."

After processing my request the following day, it said, "Sir, you are required to add juice to your breakfast. What is your preference?"

I found myself replying, "Passion-fruit." But what is passion-fruit?

"Real or artificial?"

I almost asked for real juice.

"Very good, Sir," it said.

The juice was excellent. I was informed by the unit that I had unlimited access to Type D (sub) menu. I decided to taste one new item each day.

The bathwater was scented and probably recycled no more than twenty times. The sun protection gel was not the thick glop I used in the common bathing cells; this was almost water-like in consistency and smoothened easily. I no longer had clay-white patches on my hair and skin. The bed was soft and large, my spread limbs relaxed as soon as I lay down. I set myself on medium slumber mode and slept all day, day after day.

The doors slid open. Couplet entered.

"Can't you turn off this music?" it asked, cupping its ears. "I need silence to think!"

"The Original ordered it for my well-being," I said.

"Then we'll have to suffer it," Couplet said. "Now tell me, have you had further visitations?"

"No."

"No dreams?"

"No."

"Not even desires?" Couplet's antennae sparked as it leaned towards me.

"I am blank."

"Strange. Normally the kid-glove torture produces results." It shook its head and whispered, "I'll give you another day. Or we'll have to cook up something plausible. You understand, don't you, that my reputation as ace interrogator is at stake?"

"Oh."

Couplet bounced on the couch beside me. "But I came to tell you we are to strip your cell for secrets. Have you hidden anything?"

I remained silent.

"Tell me!"

"Bullet's eye. Concealed in the right sole of my spare boots."

"Ah. Anything else?"

"No."

"Focus on your Original," Couplet said rising. "You've got to give me something soon."

"Are you in danger?"

"Not yet. Nor are you, for that matter. Though the degree of torture should increase."

"But—"

"Understand this: mysteries divulge their secrets stingily. Suddenly all is revealed. That's when the greatest danger can befall one because one is transformed." Couplet nodded. "But of course you don't understand!" It beat its forehead with clenched fists and hissed, "Clone 14/54/G, your last visitation existed in the seventeenth century, we are now many centuries ahead. You have more stories to reveal. The Global Community will not withdraw you till they are certain the complete truth is disclosed. And silenced."

I nodded, not quite understanding. The room seemed to have darkened.

"Clone, focus on why you are remembering these stories, and indeed where these stories are leading," Couplet said. "And trust only me!"

"Yes."

"Till tomorrow! Adieu." Couplet bowed, its antennae sweeping the floor, and exited.

I knelt on the double bed, facing the soothing luminescence of the wall. The colours changed from sunlit amethyst to washed moonstone to dappled aquamarine. The wall seemed like a translucent pool in which one would see one's reflection if only the colours stilled. I felt I had lost something immeasurable, although I did not know what. Over the music I said, "I am Aa-Aa Clone 14/54/G. But in truth who am I? Why am I remembering? What are these stories?"

The colours kept changing.

A voice chimed, "Sir, begging permission to enter."

"Who are you?" I asked.

"The wardrobe handmaiden assigned to you, Sir."

"Enter, then."

The doors slid open. A pile of diaphanous drapes dipped and straightened. The voice behind it chimed, "Clotheshorse Clone Type Cleo is honoured to present herself to your gaze."

"Proceed."

The pile entered the walk-in wardrobes. When she emerged, she was bare-armed but sheathed in twinkling pink veils. I was certain I had seen her; but where?

She was a life-size replica of the Barbie doll except for one detail: Clotheshorse Clone Cleo had black hair.

She curtseyed. "May I have the pleasure of assisting in your transformation, Sir?"

"Who ordered you?" I asked.

"The Leader." She again curtseyed.

"Clones of my category are not authorized to wear clothes. We wear overalls."

"Pardon Sir, but you are now in a Recovery Pad and must follow rules pertaining to this area," she chimed. "No one wears overalls; we are free to chose what to wear. Therefore, Sir, I must beg you to change."

"But these are strange garments. I am—"

She fell at my feet, weeping. "Sir, I beg you, or else," she dug her nails into my boots and sobbed, "I will have to pay a terrible price for dereliction of duty, as will you!" Her nails dug deeper.

"In which case, I shall."

"Thank you, kind Sir. May I assist you or will the Make-Over module prove sufficient?"

"Rest assured you have accomplished your mission, Clotheshorse Cleo," I said.

"My undying thanks to you, Sir," she said, still grovelling.

"Please rise and retire."

She curtseyed. "To summon me, please speak to the wardrobe."

I nodded.

As she approached the door, she buckled. She staggered up and buckled again.

"What is the matter?" I was at her side, raising her. She was heavy.

She stood. "Pray forgive this ugly aberration, Sir. It's a circuitry malfunction." Clotheshorse Cleo curtsied. She shook shining crinkles out of her translucent robe. She neatened her hair. She pressed the ring finger of her left hand; her palm flipped open to reveal a mirror. "There." She surveyed herself.

"Your type possess more inbuilt devices than worker Clones like me."

"We are almost entirely manufactured circuitry, Sir." Clotheshorse Cleo bowed again. "If you will pardon my lowly observation, for instance kindly notice the difference between your exalted breasts and mine, in shape, size and rise." She had antique Barbie doll breasts. "Mine are upheld by internal wiring, Sir."

"I see."

She curtsied and flopped. She flayed and thrashed within the pink bubble of her robe. Clotheshorse Cleo vibrated viciously, she became a shining bag skittering along the floor.

"Cleo! Cleo!"

She sprung up, her eyes wide. Her bosom and buttocks crumpled and sagged. She fell. Writhed. Bunched like a caterpillar then flattened on the floor.

"Cleo!" I bent over her. I pulled the pink stuff off her face.

"My acccc...tuality is running out. Thisss is normal. Kindly dissstance yourself, Sssssir." Her face had revolved 90 degrees. It was atop her spine. "Disssss..."

She humped and flattened, humped and flattened; rattled. Skimood screws scattered like sunlight around my feet. Streaks of her hair shot across the floor. Her pearly nails sprang out of her hands, spangling in the air. Blood pooled. She made a gargling sound.

I heard myself calling, "Bottlenose Guard! Bottlenose Guard!"

He appeared. He pointed his weapon at me.

"It's her!" I pointed.

"Distance yourself." He aimed at her.

Clotheshorse Cleo bounced within the pink ruffles. When he stopped, she did too.

"I shall call the Scavenger Unit. Kindly rest," he said.

The Scavenger Unit vacuumed her remains. I stood at the windows, my palms flattened. I saw nothing. I stood a long time seeing nothing then went to sleep.

When I awoke, I got to work.

The Make-Over module said, "You look like this. You are to look like this." It presented a series of images of what I presume was myself in different gossamer garbs from "Bridal Gown" to "Seduction Sarong" to "007 Babe" to "Fun 'n' Frolic Salwar Kameez." One image made me sink to the floor. It was "Pert Village Belle."

Clone 14/53/G had worn a similar skirt when she was lifted into the arena. I told the module to end display; I needed time to decide.

"Take your time; fashion is a serious business," it said, shutting down.

Sitting in the wardrobe I felt swaddled in layers of darkness. "Remember," she had whispered, bleeding in my arms, "Remember" and "Save."

Fighting the sickness sweeping over me, I found a blade in a pedicure set. I shaved every trace of hair except on my head, eyebrows and lashes. I wore four sets of Fun 'n' Frolic Salwar Kameezes, one over the other, so that they resembled a clumsy overall. I retained the boots.

Palms against the window, I watched the sun sink below the Originals' palaces. Within the domes lights came on, multicoloured and free-floating, that danced like stars. The Artificial Glade dimmed and glowed; the surface of a running-track lit up like the belly of a snake curled within.

Far beyond, the areas where I had lived and worked were shrouded in semi-darkness. They must still be experiencing Energy Conservation months.

More than anything I wished to be back in my cramped cell, eating dry rations. My cheeks felt wet: water streamed from my eyes.

⋙ **30** ⋘

Days passed. I was left in my luxurious Pad without having to work the usual fifteen-hour day. Except work to remember what I did not know. With no life-forms or robots present, nothing moved—except scattered thoughts that flitted without reprieve and without solution. If this was kid-glove torture, it was working. I wished to perform any menial task. I wished to hear and to speak, to take orders, even to be in an Audience Chamber.

Nothing moved; nothing spoke. Even the filaments of grime that would get past the narrow window of my cell were absent in this sterile space.

A strange thought occurred: only by hearing others could one hear one's self.

A flourish of trumpets sounded.

Finally there was something to do. I threw myself face down on the floor, body pointed as an arrow in ashtanga namaskar. Wetness licked my nape, arms, breathed in my ear; then it stepped over me. Duke!

"Rise," the Original said. "You embarrass me with such displays. Remember you are now my guest."

"Lord! I humbly apologize," I said, jumping to my feet. The relief of hearing and speaking made me wish to prolong his visit.

"Ah! This conditioning! How I hate it!" He turned his back on me and said, "You will stop only when you trust me and it is evident you don't." His head dipped. "But I can't blame you, can I? You aren't responsible for any of this. But tell me, Clone 14/54/G, how are we to progress unless you also take responsibility? Time is running out." He turned, and shouted, "Down Duke, not on her bed!"

Behind me the caravan hound was pissing on my bed, its hind leg cocked.

He laughed.

I found myself biting my lips, little coughs were trying to burst out. Then I laughed. For the first time I knew laughter. As soon as I realized this, my lips froze in a grin. The Original came forward and tousled my hair. Clones are unused to touch: I stiffened.

"It's all right," he said, "relax. I've guessed your secret: you are mutating. But you are in my custody and will not be harmed."

My knees seemed to have collapsed. "Lord!" My hand rose in automatic salute.

He pushed my arm down. "I see you aren't comfortable in these clothes, but it's regulation."

"Lord!" I said, remaining still.

"But you've chosen her colours."

"Lord?"

"Your Original's favourites were saffron and red," he said, pointing to my clothes. The four chiffon Fun 'n' Frolic Salwar Kameez suits I was wearing were coloured vermilion, saffron, cherry and ruby.

"And you like passion-fruit juice, like her. And dim sum, kablangeti, pumpkin pie, and always, the extra salt."

Of course, each item I ordered was tracked.

The Original's tone was soothing, his voice blending with the flow of the healing music I hummed. "It's a good sign,"

he was saying. "It means she is manifesting herself again."
He smiled, and put his hand on my nape. "It means I can
keep you here for observation. It means we have a chance to
become friends."

The words made me warm. The Original removed his hand
but my nape still felt warm. The air between us was warm.
Duke padded up to sniff the space. The Original stepped back.

"Ask the question you are longing to ask," he said.

I looked up. Our eyes met. I asked.

"After your Original was reclaimed, she was to address the
Global Community during The Celebrations. But what she
said was so shocking that midway through her speech she was
pushed from the High Throne. She broke her neck. This is
the only instance of an Original passing away in public view."

Silence like a swaying bridge hung between us.

"I intend to present you at The Celebrations to let your
Original have her say through you. But do not fear: my loyal
guards will protect you. I will not lose you."

A shiver shot through me. It was cold, fiery, sweet, bitter.

"So you see, you have to trust me," he said. He placed his
palm to my face.

My face was warm a long time after he had removed his
hand and he was saying, "…about your bed. Come, Duke."

The afternoon passed. I was still caught in his touch, the
things he had said. I was where he left me.

The doors slid open, two Palace Peacock Clones entered
with quilts and drapes. When they completed making my
bed, a shimmering tent hung about it from ceiling to floor.

"We hope Madam is satisfied," they said together.

Never before had I been addressed as "Madam." This
must be due to my clothing. I replied, "Yes, thank you."

They salaamed me; I salaamed them. They looked at each
other and retreated, salaaming continuously. Maybe I should
not have returned their salaams. They were the first Clones

I had seen with headgear: tasselled pink turbans. They had peacock feathers sprouting from their elbows.

⊸ 31 ⊸

The room informed me it was Sleep-Time and turned down the lighting. I tried to shut down but the events of the day kept entering my mind like curtains parting.

I turned myself on normal mode and paced. Better.

"I know it's late, but I have to go in!" I heard Couplet through the door.

"Please permit entry," I called. "The Fireheart is my interrogator and is allowed access at all times!"

Couplet was cerise when it stormed in. "I'll have you reported, you audacious guard!" it shouted. The Bottlenose Guard saluted. "Too little, too late!" Couplet cried. The guard fell on his face and began grovelling. "Better, but not good enough by half. Keep grovelling till I leave!"

"I am sorry, Couplet," I said.

"It's not your fault. You're the prisoner."

I was quiet, then murmured, "I'm sorry you are furious. You are rather red."

"I'm not furious. Merely angry. Learn to use words with precision or you never will find the truth!" Couplet's antennae sparked. "Oh, you mean my skin... I summoned colour for effect," it said. "What's a poet without hyperbole?"

Couplet was calming down; it turned pinkish lavender, then lavender and cooled further.

"You look dreadful," it said.

"I know. Dress regulations."

"We stripped your cell," it said gleefully. "A Terror-Bearer led the squad. He crunched your bed. And I found this." Couplet whispered, slipping Bullet's eye into my palm. "Ingeniously done, in the confusion. Take these too."

"Thank you." With the eye were four red pills, shaped like tears.

"In the common washing area a few hairs were found stuck in a drainpipe. Yours, I presume. They are running DNA tests on them. Clone, you will be charged for keeping secrets secret."

I told Couplet about the Original's visit. Everything, except the warmth that remained wherever he touched my skin.

"Sweet talk. Don't trust Originals. We wish to remember. They wish us to forget." Couplet shook its head.

"What about Aa-Aa?"

"She was an incarcerated writer. He is a leader. That's the difference."

The air felt viscid; it stretched against my skin like a clammy mask.

"Don't turn glum," said Couplet. "Worse, don't succumb to the kid-glove torture."

"He is our hope," I said at last. "Or mine at least. I'm in his power."

"You are so very wrong, Clone. Aa-Aa, speaking through you, is our hope. She's confusing the enemy." It paced in front of me, its antennae criss-crossing.

"Couplet, sit down!"

"You're irritated! While I should be! For three days I've been deprived of my infusion of elephant and bee memory because I haven't cracked your case though I'm working non-stop. I'm now allowed only orangutan memory which is location specific. Do you know what it is like to constantly crave something? To feel so incomplete that you want to tear out the stars and stuff them in your eyes?" Couplet was turning lavender.

It struck me that Couplet didn't think that I was capable of craving because I was a Clone and it was a poet. I felt as if

I had suddenly stumbled, broken my leg and could not stand on the same ground as Couplet though both of us struggle for the Cause—though I wasn't sure what this was either. "The Original, Leader treated me as I have never been before."

"Aaaagh! You're succumbing!.," Couplet announced, an arm drawn across its eyes. "You shouldn't go over!" it said, sinking into a crouch.

I waited, not knowing what to think. The night deepened.

Head in its hands, Couplet whispered, "Or am I forsaking you?" Standing on tiptoe, antennae sparking, it said, "Dear Clone, there are many things whose betrayal will be more painful to you than your own withdrawal. Remember the big and remember the small. Remember the way you Clones are ruthlessly removed when you can no longer be refurbished. Remember the countless who have been sucked into the ranks of The Disappeared. Let their memories live on, through you. Who do you consider yourself to be? Merely a Clone or something more, and multiple?"

I was torn apart, yet each part of me seemed to constrict as it plummeted into a dark tunnel.

"I'll try to reach the Others to rescue you ASAP," said Couplet. "In the meantime, focus on Aa-Aa. And give me the next story soon. Or we'll be in trouble. Now see me act!" It turned pinkish-red. "Open the door!"

The Bottlenose Guard was still grovelling.

"Keep grovelling till dawn. Or till your nose flattens, whichever is first," Couplet proclaimed, daintily stepping over his swarming form.

The doors slid shut.

I tossed in my canopied bed.

I went to the Make-Over module and found a scarlet lipstick. I knew what I had to do. It was an uncontrollable urge.

❦ 32 ❧

I don't remember ever being free.

I have always been here, claws sliding over the swinging perch of my cage, green wings thrashing against the bars, being fed the finest that the great city of Lucknow can offer, and watching her. My Love, the Third Begum of the exalted Khan-Sahib. I am her pet parrot.

I watch her constantly. I sleep after her, awaken before she does. I am at her pillow, calling, "Wake up! Wake up, My Love!" She tosses and murmurs and awakens. Her face still languorous, her body still dreaming, her clothes spread like clouds on the bed. Of all the rituals of beautification I love watching the bath most. Her body submerged in the tank with its mosaic of flowing flowers and the water dancing with sprinkled rose petals. Over her spreading hair, over her body.

I should have remained an observer. But I have fallen in love with her. My claws are capped, and each one is wrapped in a case of Gujarati velvet so that I don't scratch My Love. My wings are clipped to ensure my captivity. But I can fly short distances and My Love feels safe.

Khan-Sahib wants me to speak prettily. So, he orders the outer layer of my tongue to be peeled. I can't speak about the humiliation and the pain. It is done; my body burns with rage but My Love is contented.

When our master next visits, I announce, "He's coming! He's coming!" before the eunuch guard calls out his titles. Our master is amused and tells My Love, "Train your pet parrot properly, so that it calls out at the right moment."

The next time Khan-Sahib visits, I am positioned on a bolster at the foot of her bed. I am to scream, "He's coming! He's coming!" when he is on her, eyes shut and mouthing, "No, no, no, no nooooooooo!" I do. My heart is heavy.

❦ 33 ❧

"Awaken."

"But I am awake."

"Then let me enter your dream."

"You don't know love's despair and sweetness," I murmured. "It's a wonderful trapped state."

"What is?"

"This becoming someone else."

"Then share it, Clone."

I opened my eyes. His were gazing into mine. "My Love is real," I said, "you are not." I shut my eyes.

I felt his words move across my face. "Your love?" his lips traced.

"Writing."

I was scooped, carried, propped up, my hair stroked off my face.

"I can see that," he said. "See for yourself."

In front of my eyes, I saw the wall of changing colours written over in red. Words, and more words, more tender and difficult to accept than one's reflection.

"Aa-Aa's."

"Once hers, now yours," he said, his arms circling my waist. Like the words his hands were everywhere on me, on my skin, covering my eyes, tongue, my hands, in my mind, inside me. I turned in his arms like in the words. I tossed and fought in them as I had with the words. I was all me, and much more than me.

I never knew such happiness existed.

Even in the widening wake of calm that followed, I knew I would search for it again, and again. The turmoil, the vertiginous fear, the thousand-fingered hunger that pawed its way to such a clearing.

Long after he left, I lay looking at the small stain of red between my thighs and the sprawl of red on the wall: red curlicues running into red dashes and dots and spiralling into yet more forms.

Then I thought: how much more blood will it take before we understand and end this story? My head throbbed.

❧ 34 ☙

Bi-Jan, the singing jewel of Avadh, the courtesan ugly as a toad with the voice of a fairy is to entertain My Love. Resplendent, like a moon coloured by rainbows, My Love reclines on her bed, a hookah in one hand, me in the other.

I strut up to Bi-Jan, cock my head and look up. She's like an old sweaty bolster. But how she sings! Enough to make the stars drop dust. When Bi-Jan ends her song of lament, her song of Avadh, my feathers rise. Like a peacock's to rain. All over my body.

"Great lady, pearl among women," Bi-Jan salaams and says, "I am greatly honoured that your pet parrot likes music such as I make. It has been well trained by your Gracious Self, the Great Khan-Sahib's favourite begum."

"You are well trained yourself in courteous speech," My Love remarks.

"By the whip, Honourable One," Bi-Jan replies. "Like your parrot, we are but slaves. We repeat what we are told as the truth. Surely we are not mistaken."

A pouch of coins is flung towards Bi-Jan, spilling silver from its dark mouth. Salaaming, smiling, mocking, she picks up each coin, and withdraws with her female musicians. We hear her laughter, lewd and deliberate, like she is spitting red paan juice on the walls.

Bi-Jan is returning to her world of music and entertainment beyond the walls of the zenana. To that outside world I long to see.

I looked at my handiwork on the walls. Something read false in the last blue kohl-pencilled lines. Rubbing it out, I wrote: *Like her, I wish to wander.* This was better, but not quite it. The seed of pain I wish to reach rolled beyond me like a prickly sea urchin.

I paced in front of the writing.

"Not a bad effort, especially for a Clone. Some of these fragments are passable." Couplet was standing arms akimbo, antennae sparking. "So, Clone, you are a writer."

"It's Aa-Aa's story."

"Oh, all of us, ahem, get inspired," it said, throwing up its hands. "But the point is when does the work become your own?" As it twirled, its antennae wound around each other like DNA strands. "When you trance it, sleepwalk it, when you dance its dreams in the rhythms of your breath, when the story rises swaying, like a snake out of the container of yourself, that's when it's yours. Are you following me, Clone?"

"Not really."

"Well, you're honest. That's a start," it said. "I bring you portentous news that shouldn't be said aloud." Couplet clambered on the table and whispered in my ear.

I stared into its large eyes in disbelief.

It nodded. "Even a few Siren Clones are cracking up. But the main rupturing—or resistance, if I can call it such—comes from Clones descended from Aa-Aa's lovers. She was profligate!" Couplet said, licking the tips of its fingers. "It's curious. It's as if, during mating, she seeded each partner with hibernating 'aberrations' that are now erupting, like fireflies, turning on and off in the dark night of history."

"Then I am not alone anymore!" The room rang with light.

"Steady, Clone. Unfortunately, you are still the only one breaking the silence with something like a pattern to it." Couplet patted my arm. "There's trouble brewing aplenty, but all eyes are turned on you."

"Why me?"

"I can't abide naiveté!" It shuddered exquisitely. "You are charged with far worse than reinventing history and mutating! You're thought to be transmitting coded messages of war!"

"But I'm just a storyteller telling hand-me-down stories."

"Literature, dear Clone, is always dangerous, especially in times such as ours. It makes one remember one's self. Oh, come on!" Couplet stamped its feet. "But the morons think the stories conceal strategic intelligence. Besides, they expect you to conduct them to the Leader."

"Who?"

"If only we knew!" Couplet sighed. "We'd urge her or him to hurry out of hiding and lead the strike! Many more of us are slipping into the ranks of The Disappeared." Couplet curled into a fist on the tabletop, its eyes streaming. "I can't bear it!" it whimpered. "One must act, not merely speak!"

"Couplet, hush. Rather, don't ever hush," I whispered. "You give me... hope. I'll do my best."

It sat up and untangled its antennae. "Clone, don't ever remind me of this passing weakness. The need of the hour is to be better than brave," it slid to the ground. "And now, I'd better be off." Couplet marched to the door. "Open the door, you dumb Bottlenosed ditherer!"

A wave of emptiness leapt through me. With monumental longing I reached for the lipstick.

In the distance the bamboo chiks part. Moonlight slides in. I scream into her ear, "Wake up! Wake up, My Love! He's coming!" She sits up, her hand at her throat. The acrobat enters.

"How did you get past?" she asks. "The eunuch guard has been warned."

"I bribed him with your jewelled nutcracker," he says.

My Love freezes. "I will say it has been stolen. For your own safety leave." She lifts the necklace off her breast and holds it up. The acrobat takes it.

"Not yet," he says. His hands are on her throat.

"I will raise an alarm. Go! I command you." She drops her head. My Love is weeping.

The acrobat drops his hands from her throat. He kisses her hands, her feet, her stomach, her sex. Her hands are crawling up his shoulders like spiders.

"Now go!" she says. My Love is sweating as if she has been in rain. "Never attempt to see me again or I will have you poisoned."

Suddenly I sense Khan-Sahib and call, "He's coming! He's coming!"

The words ran dry like the rivers I heard about that once coursed through continents. I could not imagine how the begum and her parrot might escape from the zenana. But I did not want the end to be an unhappy one. Perhaps the parrot called wrongly this time?

I waited, staring at the words. Nothing was forthcoming. I felt trapped.

❧ 35 ❧

Every thought, except one, vanished when I heard the flourish of trumpets.

Even before the doors closed I pulled him to me and started unfastening his clothes.

"Wait!"

"I've waited all day, I've waited for days, I've waited an eternity," I said, fastening my lips on his neck, on his shoulders, on the flesh I was exposing. I was myself, and I was not. Another entity inhabited me. Taken over, I couldn't stop myself. Nor did I want this visitation to end.

"You are raping me!" he laughed, his head held down between my breasts.

"What does it mean?" I asked, wishing I had a hundred arms as I struggled to rid myself of the frilly dress that still bound my limbs.

He stiffened in my arms and said in a new voice. "You wouldn't know what rape means, would you, Clone?"

The word *Clone* made my arms slacken, my mouth stop feeding. "No." My dress was down to my waist, the air turned chill.

He was stripped naked but did not seem cold. He put his arms around my shoulders, drew me close, saying into my ear, "It doesn't matter." I stood like a pillar in his arms. "It doesn't matter now," he repeated, stroking my back, "I'm sorry."

"I am too numb to kowtow, Lord. I crave forgiveness," I managed. My voice seemed to be coming from far away.

"You are cold with fear," he said. "Look."

My skin had risen up in tiny bumps.

"Goose-pimples," he said, carrying me to the bed and covering me with a quilt. He slid in beside me. "Do not fear, I will do you no harm." His voice took on the flow of the healing music as he kept repeating this again, and over again.

I began to feel drowsy. It was his voice and his touch; it was also my tiredness.

"Don't sleep yet, Aa-Aa," he said, stroking my forehead, "I've come to tell you what you must have guessed."

I opened my eyes. His face was above mine. "I am the Leader," he said, kissing my face, my lips; his arms cradling me. "We both are in danger."

I was awake.

"The Fireheart doesn't know as yet," he said.

As I met his eyes, my arms wrapped around his shoulders of their own accord, my body rose to meet his. This was different; it was me and him and him and me, our bodies like water aflame, our fingers like flowers falling.

Later we slept, awoke again as two in a dream waking into one.

Later he sketched his strategy to keep me safe. I barely remember what issued from his lips.

I felt as if I were rain that had at last reached groundwater; that I was in a well of our own making that never could run dry.

⊸ 36 ⊱

We wait for the doors to slide shut before kissing.

Always this craving had to be satisfied before we could talk. Our bodies fitted together, tongue to tongue, shoulder to shoulder, limb to limb as if we were from the same mould; he would say, "No, no, no!" before delight engulfed him, as if it could possibly be prolonged. I sighed, murmured, commanded, as if I was born to these pleasures. It was an altogether strange time in which I lost myself, and explored myself further. I became an addict to this activity that bequeathed my complete surrender to its urgent self, separated my cloned self from all others. I became addicted to the suddenness of its curved joys, to its sharp liquidity.

Couplet would be able to express these experiences with moving words, but it had not visited in days. Besides, I kept this secret *secret*. Something about its nature demanded I seal my lips and fold my limbs over it.

Before he left, I would again wind myself around him; urging, succumbing, overpowering.

After he left, I would recall each move, imprint each sequence into my memory. And re-live it again. This too became a necessity.

Is this what the parrot wished with My Love? Is it because of this sharing that I realize I am alone?

Who is now speaking—Aa-Aa or me? Why do I wish it not to be her?

"Clone 14/54/G" is no longer enough. I am more—and less—than what I was. Less sure, less safe, less isolated. More curious, more in pain, more resolute about my uncertainties. With more words at my command.

I also feel important being imprisoned in this luxurious Recovery Pad, mating with an Original, having my writing spilling across the walls and knowing I am an intrinsic part of the Cause.

I feel fortunate.

This is not a thought-feeling associated with Clones. It might be common in mutants. Originals do not undergo this feeling. The Leader accepts privilege and is certain about his strategies. I accept all that he does.

Am I now more of a kowtowing Clone?

❧ 37 ❧

Couplet led the brigade.

"I see you've used up all the wall space," it said. "We have come to collect the 'messages,' decode them and fathom your true intentions. You will shortly be informed about your traitorous activity and given a fair choice by the Global Community."

"Long live the Global Community," I said, saluting. "May I request permission to protest my innocence?" The old phrases tripped off my tongue.

"Long live the Global Community," the others replied, saluting.

"Protests should be articulated in the correct forums," said Couplet.

"Activate," said the Superior Zombie (SS Avg.) to four Clones (Type Clerical Mole). They skimmed the walls with deconstruction lasers. Word after word, line after line, paragraph after paragraph of my writing was sucked into the palm-units. The walls were clear. I felt shorn.

The healing music shut off. I felt speechless in the silence.

Two robot sniffer-dogs were doing their rounds. One began in a clockwise direction, the other went anti-clockwise.

"Leakage sniffed," said one, standing on the bed.

The second bounded on to the quilt. "Confirmed."

"Collect contaminated material," said the Superior Zombie.

The bed linen was bundled away, as were my clothes.

"Stocks of lipstick and eye pencils low," said the Make-Over Module.

"Replenish same," said the Superior Zombie.

"Double stocks," said Couplet. "The Clone employs a large canvas." It winked at me. "I enjoy ambitious projects, though they often fall flat. But nothing ventured, nothing gained."

The Superior Zombie began, "The last—"

"Is beyond your comprehension, Zombie. Stick to your orders!"

"Sir!" The Superior Zombie saluted.

"Well? Identify data. What are you waiting for?"

"Initial analysis suggests the teller of this story is a parrot in Lucknow, capital of the kingdom of Avadh shortly before the Indian Mutiny of 1856," the palm-units recited.

"You mean The Great Uprising of 1858!" Couplet cried. "Why, Clone, were you there?"

"Correction. The Indian Mutiny of 1856, when—" the units continued.

"Turn that idiot-box off!" Couplet said. "And proceed investigations, Zombie."

The Zombie bowed. "Recovery Pad, release Audio Inferences."

"Processing."

Healing music flowed again.

"Retrieve only Audio Inferences," the Superior Zombie repeated.

"Unable to decipher conversations as frequency of voice modulations are identical to healing music," my room replied.

I had not realized we had been humming in complete harmony to the music; never breaking into speech. Even Couplet's high tone had been neutralized by the persistence of the haunting tunes.

"Release Visual Records," the Superior Zombie commanded.

On the wall of luminous shades, I saw much of what I had memorized. In changing colours. I saw us naked, tussling inside the canopied bed, him lifting me on the table, me stopping him at the door, us on the floor. The images billowed like curtains with blank spaces where the words had been written.

"Stop! This is XXX-rated stuff," shouted Couplet.

The wall resumed shifting colour from sunlit amethyst to pearly rose.

Couplet had turned cerise. "You have betrayed us!"

"No!" I had turned crimson. "This was an adventure I could not resist. Please understand."

"Clarify the adventure," said the Superior Zombie.

"This is out of your purview, Zombie," Couplet snapped. "It directly involves an Original."

"Sir!"

" As Chief Interrogator the said record will be delivered to me to hand over to the Council."

"Sir!"

"Clone, you found it irresistible, did you?" Couplet asked. "You too?" It sighed.

"Yes, Interrogator."

"Were you aware of the dangers?"

"What danger?" The Superior Zombie pointed his laser at me.

"Transgression. Miscegenation. Disfilibration. Deliterization. Demonization! Stay clear of my interrogation, you Average SS Zombie. Or I'll report your mischievous, malafide and unsound-of-mind interruptions!" Couplet was now lavender. We had both recognized the danger. It turned to me. "You need to prove your good faith."

"You shall see I shall not falter, Interrogator."

"So be it."

The sniffer robots did another round while a Clerical Clone sniffed and frisked me. "Clean."

"It's all in her mind," Couplet muttered, sitting on the couch, staring at its feet.

"Yes, the plan is here," I said, tapping my head. "My new story is set in a space centre. The dénouement involves a revolt, hand-to-hand combat, and victory. It's action-packed."

"Sounds promising, Clone." Couplet's eyes twinkled. "Be prepared for the Council. It's like nothing you can imagine."

As it left, I noticed its antennae were drooping.

∽ 38 ∾

As soon as he entered, I clutched him by the golden embroidery on his collar. "Why didn't you tell me?"

"What?" He made no attempt to free himself.

"That our every move would be recorded. You knew."

"Yes."

I let go of him. All manner of unnameable things seemed to fall out of me.

I was at the window, palms against the glass when his

arms circled my waist. The touch was familiar, but this time I wished to pass through the glass.

"Aa-Aa 14/54/G, be reasonable," his voice whispered into my ear. "If I had told you, you never would have acted naturally. We never would have mated. And we certainly would have been caught. Besides, I wished to mate with you."

His touch seemed to grow warmer. "Why?" I asked the glass.

"Because you are you," his voice whispered. "That's all I can say."

"I'm a Clone. There are 53 identical to me. No—52. Clone 14/53/G's actuality ran out before you in the arena. You did nothing."

He spun me around. "What would you have me do? Disclose my identity and betray the Cause—to no purpose?"

"Clone 14/53/G is purpose enough for me." Even as I spoke I knew this was not an acceptable argument. So I added, "I don't care for the rules."

"I don't care for them either," he said, "which is why I am risking everything, even my Originality, to change the Global Community for the better."

This sounded familiar. Each orison meeting ends with us Clones chanting, "May we work harder to improve the Global Community!"

"Don't!" he shouted. "Don't you even begin to think...! And don't be childish!"

"I have never been a child. At the Birthing Place we Clones grow to adulthood within the first four years of deep stupor. So I cannot be childish."

He left my side.

He paced up and down, then came towards me.

"I am tired," he said, "and I have much work to do. I came to prepare you for the Council Meeting. You will find me as I was at the arena while you are being questioned. Say all that comes to you. I am sure Aa-Aa will not reveal her final secret as yet; I have been studying her. You will be safe. Do you understand?"

"Yes." But I understood nothing, as if a great sea had upturned within me.

"Do not be alarmed by my aloofness. You may, if necessary, appeal to me for help; this is in keeping as it is known that we have mated. I shall be as reassuring as permissible. But don't betray me. Remember I will be doing my 'duty'."

I walked towards him till we were almost touching. "Were you doing your 'duty' by mating with me?"

"Yes, and no. I was expected to mate with you and draw you out. The rest is our secret."

We were of the same height. His palms covered my cheeks. "Don't you believe me?" he asked. His eyes had grown dark; I could not bear to look into them. "No? Then think of Aa-Aa, and Clone 14/53/G. Think of what you desire. You will then find your belief." His arms dropped.

He was at the door when I asked, "Didn't you mind being watched?"

"Of course. Being used to it doesn't make it easier." He left.

He seemed to have taken away very many things with him. My shining desire to meet him, the feeling that we are working together on a Cause, the urgency of mating with him, the spreading quiet as we lay side by side before sleep took us into its drowsy arms. Would I ever again know these secrets with him?

The room was quiet; each object seemed to stand cloaked by its own separateness, as if by a film of dust.

The air seemed to thin, my head pounded. Aa-Aa seemed like a butterfly torn to pieces who left my fingertips smeared with her yellow-blue wing-powder. Iridescent shreds of story-patterns turned around themselves as they tumbled darkly down memory's tunnel.

The night darkened and stretched. In this tube of black I remembered his words: being used to it does not make it easier. How often was he used to being watched mating with Clones—or other species—to draw them out?

Was he with them as he had been with me? Had they given him as much joy?

Why should his happiness with someone else make me feel so heavy that I lie limp? I saw no justice in this, only the presence of the Global Community that fills us with fear and makes us act on command. Why, then, did I still feel limp?

Why did I feel cast away like a used tesson eye?

ᴥ 39 ᴥ

Days passed. No one visited. Not a word came to me.

One afternoon, as I stood at the window, I saw something gather over the green fog of my old quarters. It drifted in from the far rim of the horizon. Clouds—that turned more curly and grey and broadened. My heart lifted: it might rain. The clouds streamed over the city, trailing shadows that deepened the colours below, till these echoed the clouds. Clouds passed over the Artificial Glade and the Originals' palaces, edges smoking. Clouds passed over the tower of my Recovery Pad. The glare let off, my room darkened and quieted. The room seemed more intimate and safe.

"Pardon the brief dimming of illumination due to cloud movement," my room said. "A minor fault has occurred in the electrical intelligence. This is being rectified."

"Accepted," I replied, and sat curled on the floor by the window.

The clouds hovered over the city. They did not rain, or move.

"A minor fire that occurred in the electricity intelligence is now under control. Full power will shortly be resumed," my room said.

"Accepted," I said, watching the darkness spread. It was early evening.

After a while the clouds dispersed. I saw stars. Below, the city lay submerged in darkness, except for the plateau of the Originals' palaces; this was lit as usual.

My room was dark and silent. I felt I was sitting in a cave. Inside a secret.

I had dropped off to sleep near the window. Stumbling, I found my way to bed and slept. Suddenly music and lights ripped apart my sleep.

"Normalcy restored," said my room. It was on full illumination.

"Kindly switch to night lighting. Good night," I said.

"Very well. Good night."

It was 2:00 a.m.

A new word, *sabotage*, hovered like a cloud in my mind.

"We are preparing you for the task ahead," said my room "so that you will answer questions freely. You will be put through Whale Torture that made them extinct."

"What does this entail?"

"Constant noise, stress and dislocation," my room replied. "However, you are free to choose to be a whale born in the late 19th century that lived till the early 21st or opt to be a newborn in the 21st century."

"What is the difference?"

"Whales born in the 19th century were used to near silent oceans. As they aged shipping noises grew to unbearable limits. They could not adapt. If you chose this option noise will grow to an untenable extreme. Whales born in the 21st century existed in oceans of sonar catastrophe. They died young."

"21st century newborn whale." Maybe I would pass out.

"Thank you for your free choice," my room said. Immediately churning propeller sounds and depth charge explosions filled me. Constant. Ear-splitting. I stopped eating, sleeping, thinking; I could not find my way in the room. I tore my hair, hit myself. The noise would not stop.

"When you are broken you are requested to affirm the success of Whale Torture," my room said.

"Yes," I said and passed out.

The room was silent when I awoke. I was on the bed, a Nurse Clone bent over me. "Dear Clone, you are fortified and ready," she said. "Let's practice walking." I walked. I ate. Strange energy buzzed through me.

They came for me; I heard the Superior Zombies in full security armour clanking as they approached.

Couplet joined us as I was marched through a maze of passageways infused with a purple haze that grew more intense and sweet-scented as we approached the Council Room. The doors, over fifteen feet high, were of perifit damask. The space within was vast and high. With each step, my feet sank and lifted off from the springy carpet; the walls glowed with paintings that were somehow familiar. Then I recalled the Ajanta caves where the acolyte had lived, though these were more opulent. Lights jinked and dived like swallows through the room.

A flourish of trumpets and a roll of drums.

We stood to attention as the Originals entered. He walked in with Duke; four others followed. Among them I recognized two from the arena. A silvery palanquin was carried in, from which an old man with a long beard and kindly face was helped to a floating throne. It was made of ivory and filibit gems that shot scarlet rays through the haze.

"The Supreme Commander is present. The proceedings may begin," the Council Room announced. "In judgement sit The Savant, The Guru, The President, The Master and The Leader." A pod of light engulfed each one as their names were mentioned. My throat went dry.

"Come now, Clone, tell us what you know," the Supreme Commander smiled. "Understand that you are either with us or against us." He smiled again.

I prostrated to him. The carpet bounced me back.

"Stand. We know the disquiet spirit of your Original possesses you. Give us her last voice-tomb and her intention in manifesting thus. Speak."

My body shook. My teeth rattled but no other sound issued.

"Supreme Commander and Most Exalted Excellency, as prime interrogator, I beg permission to summarize my findings." This was Couplet, its antennae scraping the floor as it bowed.

"Proceed."

"Thank you, kind Lord! This Clone is unaware of the processes she is undergoing. Her visitations are, if I may be permitted, more in the nature of incontinences. She leaks, like a loose bladder, without rhyme or reason, the 'stories'…"

"Historiographies," said the stentorian voice.

"I stand corrected, High Savant!" said Couplet, falling face down.

"Continue."

It bounced up. "Each fragment is ahistorical, anonymous, fictive! The Clone is a babbler and best dismissed as such. She should, however, be kept under surveillance."

"Gentle Fireheart, we think you plead too ardently for this Clone," said a short female Original with a shock of black hair. "Why is that?" She smiled.

"Master, I do not contradict your worthy self, but merely add this Clone has no inkling when her Original will next speak or to what it will lead." Couplet saluted.

"This tattletale Clone is your guest, isn't she, Leader?" The Master turned towards him and smiled. "Have you had a chance to observe different?"

"We have been preoccupied," he said. "But we may have a clue." He stepped off his throne and approached me, Duke followed. "Clone, what prompted your last revelation?"

"Great Leader, I know not why or wherefrom I carry these tales but I embark on a story of exalted love such as never known before." I was speaking yet I was neither Aa-Aa nor myself. "I speak of curried tongues, clipped wings, freedom's song and hope's impossibility. I speak of love betrayed."

The room filled with silence.

"Dear Clone 14/54/G," he said, "Do not fear. Give us Aa-Aa's last story and you can live happily on Paradise Island. See." He pointed to the carpet.

At my feet a pool of light appeared within which images of Clones on pleasure crafts caught zeeksilsh fish, chased glass butterflies, toasted with cool glasses raised while sitting around a table heaped with food.

"They are mutants like you," said a silvery voice. It belonged to the tall male Original. "Look harder," the voice urged.

"Do as The Guru advises," the Leader said. "Carpet, offer close-ups."

An array of faces glistened beyond my toes. A Clone had a beard; a female Clone had a distinct moustache. They were mutants, all. Each face was expressionless, every action robotic. "We are very happy on Paradise Island," the faces mouthed.

"Behold the pleasures that await you," he said. "You could join them…"

"…if you join us in the war against untruth," The Master smiled.

My eyes seemed to shrink into me.

When my eyes refocused, a Nurse Clone was bending over me. "There, there, we have revived," she sang, "and we are strong enough to continue, hurrah, hurrah!" She raised me to sitting position and stroked my back.

In the distance, Couplet was lying on the carpet; my hearing gradually returned. A voice was saying "…eradicate the hidden enemy. The war must continue."

"I propose that the Fireheart, having failed at its job, should be weaned off its memory infusions," said The Master, circling its body.

"What's a poet without memory?" Couplet whimpered.

"What is a poet without grief? Hasn't this too been said?" The Master asked.

"Oh please, there's too much grief already!" Couplet's nose was red, its eyes were streaming. It was twitching.

"Surely then the sooner you lose your memory, the better, dear Fireheart."

I got to my feet. I felt dizzy, but this was a different dizziness, one that made my skin rise with rash, palms sweat, and filled me with restlessness.

"I have something to say."

The Savant said, "Proceed."

Lights soared and swooped behind the Originals. I don't know what overcame me as I walked towards the semicircle of thrones, raised my head and began:

Which war are you speaking of, my friends?

This was a new power. I continued:

Which war are you speaking of, my friends?
The one in Hiroshima, New York, Syria?
These naked wars, brains oozing
like slush on the path of ascendancy.
It's remote, you say, and televised.
Come closer home, then.

Which bloody Kurukshetra do
you wish to speak of? Come on, tell me.
The war against the earth? This
one perhaps? This taking without
giving, defences up. Think only
of today, not the red rot of mines, of tree
sap and coral, of dragonfly wings burning.
Who's to win this round?
It's everywhere, you say.
No one wins this round.

All right. Do you mean the tribals'
Kurukshetra? Or the blind beggar's? But it's
indecent to speak of the unfortunate.
We are speaking of war, aren't
we? Of stakes. Blood. Death.
The seeping of consciousness through
cracks in the soul as we walk forward.
We are speaking of atrocities, my
friend, gladiator. Come home.

I understand: you were speaking of
you and me—this slaughtering. This meagre
giving and taking with battle
lines drawn. This ancient
trench warfare, guts draining into
the trench that is you and me.

I'm mistaken again, am I?
You were speaking of the red rot
oozing from your brain. Your hatred, your
hopeless manoeuvres against
death, and your helpless defeat.
Your war against life
with battle lines drawn
against the enemy: yourself.

"Under which statute does the abovesaid fall?" said The President.

"Grasp this chance to save yourself, Fireheart. Interrogate, interpret," said The Master.

Couplet was sitting on the carpet, its antennae drooping between its splayed legs.

"Hmm. New York. War in New York, Syria... she's arrived at the twenty-first century. But," it shook its head, "the tone is somewhat confusing. It doesn't entirely sound like her Original."

"What do you mean?" asked the silvery-voiced Guru.

"Do any records survive of the said voice-tomb?" Couplet asked.

"Perfidious material is immediately inoculated," said The Savant. "Don't waste our time."

"High Lord, I beg pardon," said Couplet. "But the scope of this, ahem, declaration, is curious. The others were time-specific; this one ranges in time and... space."

"You are slipping, Fireheart. There is only one space: the imperium of our Global Community," The Master said, "and time is as we have ordained it."

Couplet bowed. "Begging pardon for my misdirected enthusiasm to get to—"

"Why should anyone wage war against themselves?" asked The President. "Wasn't that mentioned?"

I felt as if I was not present, as if the words had not been mine.

"The Clone spoke," said the Supreme Commander, "about the twenty-first century. With patience we shall reach the secret of the last voice-tomb her Original rehearsed for The Celebrations." He smiled gently. "I remember her. She was a wily woman, tender and provocative." He shook his head.

"I propose we extend the Clone's stay in the Recovery Pad," said The Savant.

"Leader, this should suit you," said the Guru.

"Yes," he said.

Everyone laughed.

We fell on our faces and bounced against the carpet as the palanquin was carried out. The Originals followed. Duke came to sniff me before padding away. After the flourish of trumpets and roll of drums faded, we raised our heads.

When I reached the Pad I fell on the bed and slept.

∾ 41 ∾

"Yesterday I thought we were both done for," said Couplet.

I went on my knees to look Couplet in the face. "Thank you. You risked your neck to save me."

"It's such a little neck," said Couplet, touching its nape.

"Yes." I patted its shoulder.

"Where did the declaration come from? That didn't quite sound like the Original. She tended towards opulent detailing. More is less in her case."

I stood. "Couplet, you got it right, right away."

"Yes?"

"It's mine."

"Entirely you own?"

"In so far as one can say any work is one's own."

"Not a bad riposte for a Clone." Couplet grinned.

"And you? Are you back on full memory rations?" I asked.

"Bee memory infusions are permitted to help me navigate through difficult pathways of interpretations. But long-term elephant memory infusions are cut to prevent me from accessing and synthesizing more memory than is currently available. This part of me will fade."

"What then?"

"Aaaah! When Blank Verse knew it was being hunted, it secreted phils of its memory for me. At its end, Blank Verse was a blank. After its store is used up I'll depend on you, Clone."

"Yes." This was all I could muster.

"So you trust The Leader still?"

"Who else do we have, Couplet?"

It sighed, its antenna wilted. "Well then, play the game, Clone, but know you are playing a game."

"The Council Meeting went as he predicted. He said the safest option was that I speak."

"Maintain status quo." Couplet shook its head. "Behave with him as you always have. And we shall see what we shall see." Couplet placed a finger on its lips and tiptoed towards the door. It spun around. "Do you have anything to add to the last stanza about 'warring with yourself'? That's somewhat over the top."

"No…"

"Leave it to me to polish," Couplet interjected, bowing.

ᕫ 42 ᕬ

Know you are playing a game.

Couplet's warning stayed with me as I deliberately dressed in Bridal Gown. When I finished, I looked as if wrapped in a mist of stars. I decided to behave with him as I had: trusting. I waited as twilight smeared the window.

"You performed wonderfully," he said as he entered, opening his arms.

I slid into them. "I was scared."

"You were meant to be," he said, tipping my head forward to kiss my hair. He pushed me away. "Stay away, you look splendid, don't distract me. I can't emphasise how important it is that we've bought time." He paced. He was beaming, running a hand through his curly hair. "You've given me faith that the impossible is possible!" I was again in his arms. "You don't understand the gravity of this, do you?" he said between kisses. "Oh my love, you don't understand!"

I felt warm with... pride, warm with him-and-me, this feeling that runs all over me. I gave myself to this feeling. It was wonderful.

He stroked my face with the back of his hand. "I can't tell you how happy I am," he said, lying back. "They will permit us to recreate Aa-Aa's final days till The Celebrations." He turned towards me. "I can put you on the High Throne, surrounded by my guards, in front of all of them in the arena and you can transmit her message that has the power to transform the Global Community." He kissed the hollow of my throat. "She was killed, but you will be protected, I promise. You can do it."

I began to feel cold. "Listen..."

"Hmm," he said, lying on his back, "speak, I'm listening." He shut his eyes.

"Leader, it was me."

"Hmmm, I know it was you." His arm swept around my waist.

I sat up. "Yesterday it was me who spoke, not Aa-Aa. Those were *my* words."

"They were wonderful words, just what was needed. Now let's doze, just a bit, Aa-Aa." He sighed and turned over.

I prodded his shoulder. "I am not Aa-Aa."

"Of course not. You are Clone Aa-Aa 14/54/G, my love and wonderful." He was asleep.

I let him sleep. It was curious to see him so happy, and so wrong. I could neither laugh nor cry nor be angry, as if I was simultaneously many different people. It was curiouser and curiouser.

I wriggled out of his hold, went to the Food Dispensing Unit and ordered a Triple Whammy on the Rocks. Once it was in me, I felt cosy. I returned to bed, spread a silken coverlet over us and fitted my body against his.

"Awaken!"

"Nooo."

"You must, I'm leaving. It is past midnight."

A heady fragrance filled my senses. I squeezed open my eyes. Real flowers were strewn like wild white stars on the sheet.

"Jasmine, from my garden." He pulled me up. My head dropped on his shoulder.

"Aa-Aa 14/54/G, awaken and wake us up!"

My head felt it was carrying a cranetank, and the cranetank was grinding. "My head…" I said, and sank.

"The antidote," he said, handing me a glass of blue liquid. "Drink up. Only Superior Zombies can stomach Triple Whammies, not mutant Clones."

No sooner had I gulped it down than my head seemed to return to normal.

"Thank you."

"I have much to thank you for," he said, clasping my thighs, his head against my navel. "I have hoped and worked for this opportunity for over ninety years." He kissed my stomach, my sex. "Now, together, we can make it happen."

As he rose to his feet, I noticed his eyes were wet, his teeth clenched. "I've been waiting, waiting!"

My hands stroked his face of their own accord.

He kissed my hands and turned.

"Leader?" I called him back at the door.

"Yes?"

"What was wrong with the Clones on Paradise Island?"

Swiftly his arms were around me again. "They are mutants who agreed to co-operate. After which they are lobotomized. Don't think about them. I will never let that happen to you. Trust me."

"Yes."

I did. I could not play games.

⊷ 43 ⊶

"A Clotheshorse Clone Cleo begs to present herself to your gaze."

"Enter."

She was in a spangly pink skirt and veil, and looked identical to the earlier Cleo. "I have been assigned to assist your gracious self to dress." Curtseying deeply, she presented a scarlet envelope. "You are greatly honoured, and I even more so," she chimed. "You will find a costume your Original wore that you must now don."

My hands shook as I took it. Within lay a fragrant crimson cloth snaking with orange blossoms. It unfolded into a flowing dress that felt like mist. In comparison, the fine clothes I wore seemed like iron flakes. Aa-Aa's dress fitted me perfectly. Why was I being so honoured?

"Your hair now. I humbly request you to please wait," she said while she spoke to the Make-Over module.

She smoothed a bun wig over my short hair. "Next, amendments to your complexion," she said, spraying my face and arms. My skin glowed in golden-pearly tones.

"You are entreated to discard your boots in favour of these," she chimed, holding feathery cherry-coloured slippers.

"We are comfortable in our footwear," I said, adopting the Originals' manner. This should work.

"However, honourable presence, your Original wore this model." She clasped my ankles, pleading. "We do not have much time; please assist in the Make-Over." Her nails extended into talons that began to shred my boots. Only the heels remained.

"We agree to cooperate," I said.

I slid my feet into the slippers that made me buoyant. "We shall clear the mess of the boots," I said as she reached for the remnants. "Clotheshorse, we insist." I stamped my foot.

She backed away. "You look a true replica of your Original," Clotheshorse Clone Cleo said. "I am privileged to have assisted in the Make-Over."

She curtseyed deeply. "I beg to take your leave."

I stood at the mirrors. Aa-Aa had looked like this: not beautiful but strangely moving, "provocative and tender" as the Supreme Commander had said. There is no other word for it—I was elated. And curious, and short-breathed, as if I were a fish that had leapt too high out of water.

❧ 44 ❧

I did not have long to wait.

The doors opened.

"We are your escort," said a Superior Zombie (Porcupine Modification). Behind him stood a dozen guard Clones armed with neutronic lasers.

I hadn't seen Couplet as it was hidden behind the phalanx of legs. It stepped out. Couplet had a welt on its forehead. I went on my knees and my arms opened. Its eyes widened, it shuddered. I stood. Its antennae kept quivering.

"Clone, you are being taken to your Original's quarters. Consider yourself fortunate," it said and stepped back.

"I am greatly honoured. Long live the Global Community," I saluted.

"Long live the Global Community!"

We marched past corridors that opened into an atrium filled with olivaceous light. I was blindfolded and pushed into a mini-glider.

"We are implanting a temporary tracking device. Do not try to escape," said the Superior Zombie before a stab of pain went through me.

Before my eyes rose a white palace with archways capped by high emerald domes. The spreading floors were paved with stones of deep ochre like sunlit earth. Rooms led into airy rooms, the outside seemed to have been carried inside, real flowers and bamboo swayed in soothing light.

"All of this seems real," I said. "Fireheart, can this be true?"

"Of course! It's an Original's palace," said Couplet. "But Aa-Aa was austere. For a start, she didn't care much for furniture." Besides a couple of hovering chairs, a hammock and a low table, the rooms were bare.

"I see. How are you?" I asked, pointing to its welt.

"Oh that. Routine torture," said Couplet. "Focus on Aa-Aa."

"Fireheart, brief the Clone," said the Superior Zombie.

"What do you think I'm doing, you overstuffed pincushion?" Couplet rapidly turned crimson. "Disappear! Your aura contradicts the Original's. If this mission fails I assure you that you will be fed to The Jaws." It smiled, arms akimbo. The Zombie stepped back.

"I must leave you to wander through her apartments, feeling-thinking-becoming her," said Couplet. "Sense what Aa-Aa is trying to say to you."

"I am supposed to disclose the secret at The Celebrations."

"Yes, and then escape. The rest will follow. Touch, smell, imbibe; let your feet take you where they please," Couplet said. "I see you've been persuaded to slip into her shoes." It chuckled and waved.

As I wandered from room to room, I felt a stranger in a spectacular and empty zoo. I felt as if I was swinging on a hammock between nowhere and nowhere. I wished to leave.

Suddenly a birdcall: five ascending notes pierce the silence. A real bird! I rushed towards the veranda, stumbled, and grasped the wall. All the walls swivelled, revealing books, shelves upon shelves of books and paintings, textiles, sculptures and more books. I was in the midst of a library in a mildly unkempt garden. A luminous calm had settled in the rooms. This was Aa-Aa's life. It seemed a splendid and solitary existence.

Level Two of her mansion was bare. Beyond the windows waved a meadow bordered by a grove of trees that dipped rustling shadows on the green. The rooms were empty, except for spare greenery and a vast floating bed covered in sapphire silk that sparkled with transiting stars. In one corner stood a large sandalwood chest. I rattled the lock; it sprung open. Within lay a cream dress, less than a foot long. A toddler's! I enfolded it to my breast. Who was the child who had worn it? Why did I want to press it close to my breast?

The long shadows of late afternoon lay like questions in my mind. I wandered to white raked sand that surrounded a lake. The water was dark and smooth, green-brown and glassy with light. The edges were thick with white water lilies. A large crystal lotus bud that shone with refracted luminosity floated at a short distance. Illuminated stepping-stones emerged from the water; as I walked towards the lotus bud, it opened. A crystal plank hovered at its centre on which I sat; it began to gently swing as the lotus floated deeper into the lake. Water reeds, birdcalls and fading light drifted on all sides.

"Welcome aboard, though your scent-print is different today. Do you wish to compose a new work?" the lotus asked.

This floating flower was Aa-Aa's workplace. It seemed a fitting locale for writing on memory, on water, on light and wind.

"Refresh memory," I said.

"You were working on your poem for The Celebrations."

"Refresh memory."

"You have prohibited memory recall except through simulacrum thought-password," it replied.

"Override command."

"Unable to comply. You rated this text as A-1 Top Secret."

I considered this. "Correct," I said, "but refresh memory on why I gave this command."

"On pain of death; on pain and death," the lotus said. "You spoke of The Great Fading That Awaits Us All.'

"Yes, I now remember," I said, "the Inescapable Great Fading."

I thought of Aa-Aa on her last voyage drifting down darkening waters, meditating on her Great Fading and that of all living creatures.

"Thought-password still not perfect match," the lotus said.

"Ignore attempting perfect match," I said. I wished to live the moment.

"Shall we drift?"

"For the moment."

Night had fallen by the time I returned. The huge moon's light illuminated the dark.

❧ 45 ❧

Many days passed in stillness. I watched the sun rise and set in a cloudless sky from above the plateau of the Original's palaces to the barren curve of The Neitherlands.

No one visited. This, obviously, was planned.

I thought of Couplet, and him, and hoped both were safe. More, I thought of Aa-Aa, her floating crystal workplace and its disclosure. On pain and death, on pain of death she spoke of The Great Fading That Awaits Us All.

I had managed to masquerade as Aa-Aa to say, "The Inescapable Great Fading."

What did this mean?

It suggests more than the final tortuous moments when my actuality runs out in the course of duty, and the terror of being withdrawn. It suggests something more complete. It suggests the same for all, and for all species, without distinction.

In the minutiae of life, it implied that the Global Community will continue to survive without any trace of my labour and my newfound elation with stories, even possibly without the pressing secret I am to disclose. The Global Community must have done so innumerable times, as surely has the Cause.

These concepts are not difficult to come to terms for a Clone for this has no profoundly affecting valance for me. At heart I know I am replaceable. It is, no doubt, different for an Original.

Yet why do I wish my stories survive? As days turned dark, I plunged deeper and deeper into this unknown. What must I understand to accept The Great Fading That Awaits Us All?

How should I change?

❧ 46 ❧

"Clone, in spite of being isolated for weeks you have not produced results. Therefore you are being initiated into activate mode to enhance your capacity to remember your Original's last days," a Superior Zombie (Mid-IQ) said as a Nurse Clone prepared to inoculate me. "You will remember."

My lids seemed to tear open, light and darkness rushed forth like split seconds of days and nights. I seemed to have travelled a long time in a corridor that constantly opened and closed; nothing was familiar, and nothing was distant either. I felt as though I were pressed within opaque walls of glass, my every word a whisper without resonance.

"Your 'self' is being suspended," a voice said from some drowsy, far-off place. "Relax. Merely focus on your Original, on being in her august palace."

"I am suppressed," I whispered.

"Correct. You are suppressed. There is no need for anxiety. You are now free to be her."

Alarms sounded within me, but the SOS seemed to be going off in another operational zone. I felt no need to run in this increasingly rosy space.

"Relax."

I dimly felt a Nurse Clone operate a systems check on me. "This dear Clone is not sufficiently sedated," she sang from beyond the horizon. "We must increase dosage."

"Increase dosage," the far-off voice said.

"Wait! No harm must come to her. This is my command." I knew this voice; it dissolved in the air like a rose fading in a hologram.

"Honorable One, we shall preserve her in entirety. Only the Clone's mind will be lost," said the guttural voice from that drowsy place where my fear was compressed, yet steadily issued from some faint outlet.

"I need her entirely. Use alternative procedures to extract memory," the voice I knew said. He was close; I sensed the hologram's rose petals were wet.

"Great Leader, may I humbly submit you suggest an arduous process—"

"Proceed." Dew rolled off the last rose petal before the hologram dissolved.

"Dear Clone, you shall now sleep as we sing comforting lullabies to make you remember what you wish to forget," lulled the Nurse Clone from where the sun sank sweetly in dappled greys and greens. She sang on and on, she sang about white palaces that grew meadows within, and of transparent lotuses that spoke as they swam; she sang of dawn mists floating from awakening places and small secrets snug in wooden caskets; she sang of desires that one tries to kill and of those that ride bareback under midnight skies.

In a hologram, a baby is crawling towards me. "Up," I say, smiling. "Come on, my love, stand and walk to me!" The child gurgles, struggles to its feet and takes drunken steps towards me. Holding open my arms I say, "Come!" It smiles. Joy shoots sharply through me. In a rush, it toddles towards me; it is almost in my arms. The hologram dissolves.

"Where is my child?" I screamed, sitting up.

"This is working, Sir," said a voice behind scraping clouds of tin.

"Where is my child?" I sobbed.

"Aa-Aa 14/54/G, dream it again. It's the only way," he said, kissing my hand as if it were a trunk of a long-dead tree. "Dream it again."

"I want my child," I said, tossing.

"Nurse Clone, soothe her!"

The song began again and my child appeared again, its

fat dimpled feet pattering on the floor and my arms are wide open again and I'm calling, "Come to me, my love!" Again it smiles and spreads its arms towards me and as I lean forward to sweep it up it dissolves. It dissolves.

"Where is my child?" I asked. "Give me back my child... please, *please*..."

"Your negligence towards your duties has forced us to separate you from your child," said the guttural voice that seemed to be within me. "You have caused this to happen."

"What have I done? What should I do?" I screamed and sobbed. Arms held me down.

"Tell us the secret you are working on."

"What secret? You tell *me* the secret! Where have you taken my child?"

"Give her her child. Sing!" he said.

Its curly hair again, almost within reach; its smile, smiling into my face, its little hands spread out...

"Come to me," I moaned, "and you can have all the secrets you want, come..."

"Aa-Aa 14/54/G, you are dreaming this hologram," he said in a voice that seemed like mine, twisted. "You are dreaming this."

The child began to fade again.

"You are killing your child because you refuse to co-operate. Do you wish to see your child alive?"

"My child," I moaned. "Kill me, but give me my child." I could not move for the deep sickness entombing me. "Save—"

"Impossible. Tell us the secret," said that hateful voice.

I screamed. I vomited. I screamed.

"Stop experiment," he shouted. "She is grief-stricken and cannot proceed with memory tracking. Confirm my reading."

"This dear Clone is beyond recall. She is frozen in so thick a grief that all mind-images have been blocked. May we suggest that the experiment is stopped as it is no longer fruitful," sang a Nurse Clone from some maddened place.

I slid into darkness.

❦ 47 ❧

I lay in a hammock of sickness that made me numb in my heart yet my body ached. I lay, wrapped like a mummy, unable to move yet never at ease. How long did I lie? Was it a moment? An eon?

"Wake up!"

My eyes looked into the same dark place.

"Awaken Clone, or I shan't be able to help you. Please, please!"

This voice I knew. The boulder within me shifted; the numb ache persisted. I opened my eyes. Couplet was chafing my hands, breathing on them; its antennae drooped like mildew strings. "Couplet?"

"At last, Clone! I thought this meeting too would end in futility," it sighed. "Clone, please listen, and help yourself!"

"Yes?"

"You were flooded with the Maya-Dream Trick, among the dirtiest they have in their bag, get it?"

"My child?"

"The hologram? That was Aa-Aa's. Her last child, so I heard, birthed when she was around 183 years old. You know, the rumour mill, gossip, etc." It circled its hands near its ears. "Relax. You underwent a re-enacting of her last glimpse of her child."

"What kind of a woman was she?" My bile rose.

"What?"

"What kind of monster was Aa-Aa?"

"Clone, let's not be judgmental. It never does become a writer. Let things unfold within yourself, and then you'll see. Think poetry, pain, ambiguity."

"Never."

"Then think solemn tragedy," said Couplet. "Imagine her anguish."

"I never want to think of Aa-Aa."

"You are being childish," it sighed. "Don't cut in! Yes, I know you never were a child, you cannot have a child. You're a Clone."

"I am a Clone."

"So you accept it was a dirty Maya-Dream Trick. You now are out of it."

"I don't know, Couplet. I still hurt." I felt bound, submerged.

"It will take time to get over, if ever. But I will report that you have survived with faculties, I presume, intact."

"Couplet…"

"I must leave, save the thanks. Prepare yourself for the next round. Well, it may be plain brutal. Adieu, dear Clone!" It bowed deeply.

I asked the room how long I had been asleep.

"Nine days."

"Did I have visitors?"

"A Nurse Clone visited regularly to administer nutrient injections."

"Any superior level intelligence beings?"

"A medical unit to measure brain waves and recall patterns."

"And?"

"Further information prohibited," said the room. It played healing music at Level 4.

❦ 48 ❧

Activity gradually returned to my limbs. I returned to my place at the window, staring outside, seeing nothing.

At the Food Dispensing Unit, I ordered the old dry rations.

"Sir, we recommend this as you are breaking your fast," it replied as the dumb waiter rose into view. A glass of passion-fruit juice, toast and yoghurt with artificial wild honey.

"I want Clone rations."

"Sir, we cannot comply with your order. Would you care for American breakfast? Or Archaic Continental? Perhaps Japanese?"

"Dry rations," I repeated.

"Sir, would you care instead for the meal of twentieth-century Indian widows?" A tiny plate of watery lentils and dirty rice with a spoonful of snake-gourd curry appeared.

"I am on hunger strike," I said and withdrew.

"Sir!" it called.

I settled myself at the window.

Day passed into night, and day dawned. I shook my cramped limbs. I set my bioclock to sloth mode.

Day passed into night, and day dawned. That day passed into night, and day dawned. That day too passed into night, and day dawned. This too passed into night, and day dawned. This day passed into dusk. The doors opened.

"What do you want?" I asked.

"I'm here to get food into you," he said. "Or you could be force-fed."

"Then do it."

"Don't be difficult," he said, striding towards the Food Dispensing Unit. "I've had a hard enough time convincing them this would be a step backwards. Unit, override command. Serve Clone rations."

"Sir!"

The familiar packet of grey biscuits appeared.

In my mouth I tasted gritty slabs that one had to masticate slowly to swallow. I ate three, though it was difficult. He watched me.

"You were there, weren't you?" I said. "I felt you."

"During the Maya-Dream experiment? Yes." He shook his head. "It was not easy. But I thought it was the only way to save you."

"I am sure."

"Sarcasm well suits Mutant Clone Aa-Aa 14/54/G," he said.

"Never call me Aa-Aa. I do not want to re-live her life. It's better you withdraw me."

He winced. "You need more time."

"I want neither to help the Global Community nor the Cause." It was not me who spoke, but it also was. "I am the one who needs help, Great Leader. Withdraw this mutant Clone."

His lips tightened. "You do not know what you are saying."

Again my voice spoke. "So I am told. Even the Fireheart cannot make sense of it. Your efforts are of no use but pain this creature. I do not want words or Causes. End me."

A silence twisted between us, piercing each of us with its edge.

He turned away from me, then turned to face me. "I am saddened," he said. "You are completely unlike Aa-Aa. She was generous, brave, filled with hope. She—"

"Allowed her child to die. And dead, she eats me with her words." My body was shaking.

"You…" His hands clenched, he spoke through clenched teeth. "You… are not at your best."

"I am sure," I called as he left.

The doors closed behind his back.

The room was empty, yet was filled with a surging that emanated from me. It coiled like a snake, like a tornado. In its coils I beat the window, beat the door. "Let me out!"

I broke chairs, upturned the couch, drove the table into the wardrobe mirrors, shredded the bed. "Let me out!"

I beat the floor. "Doesn't anyone hear me? Let me out! Guard!"

I beat myself. "Let me out! Let me out!"

I lay with reddened palms and bruised body in my wrecked room.

I went to sleep amidst mirror shards.

When I awoke, the room was in order.

❦ 49 ❦

But she appeared when I had my eyes open and when I had them shut; in sleep and in waking.

Aa-Aa appeared stretching her arms open for the child. She looked much older than me and sunken, as it were, into herself. Her arms were always open, always empty, like an abandoned swing.

She leaned against an archway looking towards the dappled light of the lake, her eyes empty. Birds called, jinking and diving like jewels over the waters, but she would not stir. Water lilies swayed their petals in a breeze.

Once, a younger man was with her. He was standing near her floating midnight-hued bed; she was sitting in moon-coloured robes. He smiled; she turned away her face and lay in a foetal curl.

I called back this image again and again. He had a cap of soft black hair, an aquiline nose and chiselled thin lips. But I did not know who he was.

I saw her floating down the lake in the crystal lotus. She

was swinging gently, her lips were moving. I knew she was speaking about The Great Fading That Awaits Us All. Her face looked like a raincloud was passing over it, heavy and soft.

Aa-Aa stretched her arms open for the child that was held in someone's lap, her body leaning forward, her eyes seeing only its face. Her arms always open, always empty, like an abandoned swing.

Aa-Aa did not know she was both weeping and smiling. She was calling the child, speaking only to the child, her neck extended, her fingers splayed.

Aa-Aa called and called, though the child was no longer present. Though her villa and lake and crystal lotus faded, she called and called to the child, weeping and smiling, her body leaning forward, neck extended, fingers splayed.

She called.

∞ 50 ∞

I presented myself to the wall of changing shades behind my bed and said, "Clone 14/54/G requests an audience with the Leader."

The shades kept changing from iridescent pearl to silvery aquamarine to sunwashed topaz.

I repeated my request. There was no response.

I kowtowed and said, "Aa-Aa 14/54/G humbly pleads that the Leader do her the honour of a short visit."

The shades kept changing, the colours moving like faint rainbows over distant skies.

I waited.

I waited all afternoon.

I waited till dusk washed through my window.

I went to the wall and said, "Clone 14/54/G begs

forgiveness for any mistake that she committed, unknown to herself and implores the Leader to grant her audience." I had not meant the words to sound such, but this was the way they issued from my mouth. I felt betrayed by them, and betrayed by myself.

At night I noticed I had bitten my nails down to the skin. Still there was no response.

I asked the room, "Kindly inform me if my message has been conveyed."

"No."

"Why not?"

"The sensors on the wall are disabled since they have served their purpose."

"Room, can you transmit my message?"

"Unable to do so as it is beyond my purview of duty," it replied. "But I can increase cooling efficiency as I sense you are sweating."

"Thank you."

I beat on the doors, crying, "Bottlenose Guard! Guard! Help!"

Weapons on alert, he rushed in, swinging the gamma ray guns. "Intruder? Emergency?" he said.

"Yes," I replied. "I wish to send a message to the Leader. Can you accomplish this?"

"Beyond my purview of duty."

"Guard, what would you do in an emergency?" I said, wishing to turn his weapons on him.

"Commence due communication process."

"Kindly utilize this facility to pass my message."

"Your request is not within permitted protocol norms," the guard replied, shaking his heavy nose.

"In which case, you will be faced with an emergency. Do you wish to face the consequences for your inaction?"

The guard stood mute.

"Reply!" I felt like Couplet. "Guard," I said, "relay my message on Top Priority. Do you understand?"

"Understood."

I gave him my message. He withdrew, saluting.

I waited.

I waited.

I called, "Guard!"

He informed me that my message had been passed, but the Leader was in his Resting Rooms and could not be disturbed because of a message from a Clone in a Recovery Pad. He was due to emerge in 22 hours, 18 minutes and 53 seconds.

"Thank you," I said as he saluted.

The doors slid shut.

To distract myself and to understand the gnawing sensation I felt within myself, I tried to compose a brief voice-tomb. I wanted to stop the many little scurryings within, and prevent the leaping of fear that led to a dark pit too wide to cross.

No words came to me while I felt as if my toes and heart were being eaten away, curiously, by my very self.

I wondered if he was unwell, as he was in his Resting Rooms.

I wondered if I could ever again be still.

⤳ 51 ⤫

"14/54/G," he said, "what was the message you wanted to convey to me?"

He did not look ill, yet I asked, "Are you well? You were in your Resting Rooms."

"Of course I'm well. I work there, in peace. It's a well-known secret. Tell me, what urged you to break protocol?"

The Leader seemed to have morphed into someone else. Had I mated with him, or with one of his clones? The secret I thought I should share seemed like water running through my palms.

"What's the secret? The Supreme Commander wishes to know," he said looking out of the window.

I stayed silent.

"14/54/G, what is it?" he said, turning towards me.

"Clone 14/54/G humbly craves for pardon. I now know I was mistaken in my attempt."

"You are infuriating," he said.

I kowtowed.

"You are being even more infuriating! Kindly stand and speak."

"I was gravely mistaken. I gladly accept whatever Compensatory Sentence The Leader thinks fit to bestow on me," I said, my face on the floor. I wished my DNA would become part of it.

The room flooded with silence.

"Please stand," he said. "I did not mean to threaten you. But the Supreme Commander—"

"Has done me the profound honour of—"

"Cut the crap," he said.

"I beg pardon?"

He turned away from me. "Tell me why you asked for me. That's sufficient."

His curtness left me speechless. I was pervaded by an unpleasant sensation, as if moths had filtered into my body, flitting constantly through my limbs, making me so dizzy that I was going to fall, fall into an abyss.

This unpleasantness was caused by Aa-Aa's trick-visitation. She caused me to call him by constantly appearing before me, this time she permeated directly into my time—and came to haunt me as herself. I shut my eyes tight. "Go away," I said. "Aa-Aa, please go away." I sank to the floor, repeating, "Aa-Aa, go, please."

In the silence that followed, I opened my eyes. He was in front of me, his face near mine.

"I am going to touch your shoulders," he said, and did.

"We are going to stand," he said, and we did.

"We are going to stand side-by-side at the window," he said, and we did.

"Look out, and take your time." He steadied my hands on the windowsill and fetched me a glass of water. How had he known I needed water? We stood a long while; he kept stroking my forehead. After a while my head rested against his, my body swayed towards his, my breathing became his.

"Did you again see Aa-Aa?" he asked.

"Yes."

"You are sure it was her, not you?"

"She looks older."

"You saw her sailing in her crystal lotus, did you?"

"Yes. Her lips were moving."

"Could you hear what she was saying?"

"No."

"I shall inform the Supreme Commander that's all you saw," he said.

"Leader," I said.

"Yes?"

"Her face looked like a raincloud." He pulled me towards him; my arms went around him.

"Is that why you called me?" he asked into my hair.

"No."

His palms cupped my face; I spoke from between them like a flower opening. "To tell you I wanted you to call me Aa-Aa 14/54/G."

"Yes?"

"Yes."

We were kissing; it was sweet and painful.

I never knew my entire body could taste pain and sweetness together. I ran my hand through his curls. "I saw her many times."

He clung to me, his head buried in my nape; his nails digging into my back.

"What is it?" I asked. "Tell me."

He rolled off, sat hunched on the bed, his face in his hands.

"You've guessed, haven't you?"

"What?"

He stood, and I too found myself rising.

"Aa-Aa was my mother."

V

AA-AA'S PILLOW BOOK

∽ May 24th ∾

My child, arms outstretched, comes to me likes a wave to the shore, and when I reached for him, he recedes, recedes…

Strapped in the Absolute Truth module I responded to the illusion as if it were real, for our longings are so immense that, given a chance, we substitute the chimerical for the actual. In this sense, the Absolute Truth module is correctly named: it shows us what we most desire. Birds of joy lifted from my eyes when my child appeared, and each time he vanished, a startled cry tore out, dragging me in its trail.

Arms outstretched, I peered through the fog and out of my longing to see vision returned. I saw countless children torn away from their parents, and nails torn out of fingers, and people torn away from their futures. I saw the loamy valleys of grief, the rolling downs and vast flatlands that we inhabit, unseeing. This is when my rage fled me, fled like a great cloak blown over the horizon, leaving me naked. I was naked in a grief that was neither unique, nor singular.

The Global Community has employed its final option to make me yield plans of rebellion. I gave them all I had; I gave them nothing but loss.

Every day I remember this experience that both moulded and freed me. *Freed* is perhaps an odd choice of word, but it is a true one for I was freed into an understanding of silence that since remains with me.

At first I raged against the silence of my cell, ripping its mute grid in my fury. Gradually I hushed and almost imperceptibly the quality of silence changed, softened and deepened, floated me in its quiescence. Living without rage was strange; as if my skin had been peeled. The silence again changed and filled me with words and a love that spread without stop like stars spilling through galaxies, spilling tenderness with dervish-like abandon. It spilled towards no one and nothing for I was in solitary confinement. Having no one to share it with was more painful than I had suspected.

Yet I was also freed of the demands of the Global Community. They waited for me to break down and confess. They waited… and waited. Finally, they gave up trying to break me, released me and waited for the moment when I would betray myself.

The Celebrations draw near.

⊸ May 26th ⊷

As I sail in my crystal lotus, watching the lake glide past swollen with evening light, swollen with more beauty than tongue can tell, the transparent petals open wider and wider with my thoughts.

An undulating membrane of tenderness envelops me like a star-cloud; fills me like a song, and I cannot disclaim its diaphanous intensity. This is real, and therefore the memories from which it originates must also be real. I will stake my life—such as is left in me—on this conviction.

But to understand what has brought us, as a species, to the state we are in I need to look back on our recent history.

The first two of the three Great Wars occurred well before my birth, well before the time of cloning. At that stage of our evolution, the earth could still support its various life-forms, and opportunities remained to re-vision the World Order. This our ancestors did not do. They abdicated responsibility. In truth they did not love their children.

The last Great War, "The Clash of Civilizations," changed the world, forever spinning it into a future that we have named the Trans-Species Epoch. The unofficial name for this conflict is "The War against the Earth". I learnt of multitudes who had died beating, as it were, on the security domes of our new cities, for the earth could no longer support such a large stock of humans. The powerful built Walls to keep out continents of desperate migrants and thinker-troublemakers to form the Global Community. Outside the Wall, humans, animals and vegetation perished. We raided, secured what we needed to hold in our "Second Noah's Ark" or as is whispered, "The Alpha-Omega Zoo".

Founded on the death of millions, I understood why it became imperative that those who survived forget what made them be. All shreds of dissent were torn, thrown into the winds of the past, and jettisoned forever beyond the horizon. We became better and better at suppressing our histories and ourselves. We became better and better at inventing new truths, and new threats of cataclysmic proportions to divert attention from any squeak of protest; we became the valorous upholders of the peaceful Global Community.

Born into such a world, when did I begin to think as an individual? The seeds of transformation are usually planted unwittingly and sadly. In my case it was no different.

I was very young, no more than sixty, when out of curiosity, I signed up for the Lost Ark Project. Few Originals volunteer, for it involves arduous journeys to The Neitherlands to ascertain if any life-forms survive there that can be captured and cloned by the Global Community, to add to our shrunken biodiversity. (In truth, I had had my fill of Mugwump and wished to put the maximum distance between him and me; his dullness fatigued me, as did his penchant for middling Victorian verse that he would recite in full costume—bushy beard included—after each of our sessions. Besides, he would stream holographs of me in the "missionary" position that he expected me to adopt.)

I led an expedition of Superior Zombies and Clones into what was, in the earlier age, known as "Mongolia." Much of this terrain was a thinly populated cold region identified as The Steppes, and this may have accounted for my luck. I discovered a few chigetai grazing on the sparse vegetation that remained. We brought them back alive. Thus began my ascendancy in the Global Community: on the rumps of wild asses!

My research on the chigetai was widely acclaimed. But I found myself unable to forget my first sight of them—tails frisking, necks bent, rummaging the arid plains or braying and kicking against the low, wind-blown sky that hung like a great tent pegged on vast earth. I began to question what I had actually achieved in bringing the entire wild stock into cloning vivaria. Would it not have been wiser to leave a few breeding pairs in their ruined habitat and watch their evolution from afar? I now made my first "mistake." I gave voice to these disquieting thoughts—and for that, was dispatched to languish in a dismal outpost on the Indian subcontinent for the next fifty years.

Yet I did not languish, nor did the outpost. Shortly after I arrived there, the terrestrial Power Lobes were relocated, and over the next few decades the isolated outpost gradually became a leading power centre of the Global Community. And, just last year, it was declared the site of The Celebrations.

As for me, I wasn't prepared to be like other Originals. I began researching the histories of the subcontinent, and each period, it seemed, had stories that unfurled in strange quicksilver tongues, each like a stream of mercury, alluring and poisonous, for such investigations were not encouraged. But I was thrilled: it was as if I was expanding, tight and luminously with each discovery, and I quietly persisted. Many details sparkling with ambiguity surfaced, among them this: parrots were taught to talk sweetly by having the outermost layer of their tongues peeled, after which they were shut away in cages as prized pets.

I learned about "seasons"; how May used to be the hottest and most arid month, before pre-monsoon showers broke, washing away the dust from trees that grew in great abandon across the countryside and smeared an emerald cast over hillsides. Apparently almost overnight, grasses and weeds would sprout from the dried earth like tufts of green lace; during the monsoon, frothing waterfalls would run down slopes at random. The rains would arrive each year, without fail.

Our seasonless world is a poorer one, though infinitely more comfortable. It is predicted that four years from now we may experience some showers. How I would love that!

◌◌ **May 28ᵗʰ** ◌◌

I put in a request for "Monsoon Mood" with Housekeeping, hoping that this morning my garden and lake will be suffused with gently drifting mists that gather towards nightfall into thicker clouds; I even specified I would like the sound of distant thunder. Instead, they have given me dizzily pirouetting rainbows that bounce over the lake. Most distracting! However, the two resident toads were taken in, and croaked all evening.

◌◌ **June 1ˢᵗ** ◌◌

Yesterday, Paladin invited me to his residence, and I accepted though this entailed a journey of two hours. After all, he had been my most pleasant playmate: capricious, inventive and long-lasting. He now masterminds The Celebrations and I thought this might prove a good opportunity to glean knowledge of what might await me—and I was not wrong. Dressed in a toga he welcomed me to his spacious Roman-style abode, complete with mosaic-tiled baths, vomitories and an amphitheatre. He plied me with wine—that I enjoyed—and a host of delicacies, most of which I politely refused as I have been vegetarian for the last 130 years. We ambled down the xystus, arms linked. Between commenting on the fragrances of the overhanging flowers, he seemed to imply that the future did not bode well for me; that I should be watchful. I could not extract more from him, for Paladin makes it a point to be trifling; it is part of his charm and his armour. Before we parted, he offered to show me his sexual archives where I figured foremost, he declared. I declined the pleasure. On the flight back, sombre thoughts filled my mind, darker than enveloping night skies.

These might be the last few days I have to be myself. I therefore record the sickness of my soul and my culpability in the privileges enjoyed that are made possible, at a great cost, by others. I am part of the warp and weft of this society, yet have gradually become a tiny knot in the fabric that is better cut off; a spot in the vision of the Global Community.

But when did my gaze turn towards others, and in doing so, turn inwards too, into the darkest contours of my heart?

The turning began after the accident when I was young, no older than eighty. I was resuscitated and temporarily stabilized, but in need of a lung transplant. The healthiest from among my Clones was chosen for the operation. Shall I call her my daughter or sister? What was my relationship with her who was to give her lungs to me and die in my stead?

I saw her lying naked, being prepared for the operation. I saw, as it were, my own body in front of me, for we were exact down to the last detail—even her small toes were squashed like mine. She looked at me blankly, lying suspended in the theatre, tubes running in and out of her. She did not blink, not once.

What prompted me to touch her hand? And then… and then, I felt the faintest tremor pass from her hand to mine. With that touch, my world changed.

I swooned. When I came to, I was not saturated with grief, for memories of unspeakable tenderness overcame me, wiped me, filled me.

These, I insist again, are too vast to be my own. It's as if many million shards of tenderness, emanating from millions of lives that have gone before me are jostling into a jigsaw puzzle inside me; piecing together a shape that is still to be defined.

It is tenderness for trees that stretch towards light and for life within clods of earth; it is tenderness evoked by the shuffling walk of Clones towards their grim housing colonies. This was when I knew that I, an Original, would be cast out from the Global Community. Because I had chosen it. I am not the first to do so; I shall not be the last.

A terrible and tearing tenderness pieces me together.

ᨏ June 2nd ᨏ

I went through my archives to erase anything that may be held against me. Stowed away, I discovered a roll of frayed silk of such breathtaking beauty that all other thoughts stopped. Against a sky of barely peach, almost numinous in its delicacy, auspicious cranes embroidered in silver fly as if they have just lifted off from a lake of gold. The life in them, still! Which unknown artisan bequeathed this to us?

Like the moon fairly hidden behind clouds, a poem, on the crane, partially remembered, comes to mind. About its cry being mournful, as if it had remembered something it wanted to forget…

❧ June 2ⁿᵈ, evening ☙

I have been summoned for a meeting in the Penetralia. Does this suggest a reprieve? However, the invitation must be approached with caution. I returned to my archives, determined to complete erasing all traces of "abnormality." I found the silken dress like a cloud of dreams made for my last child. I crushed it to my breast. This I cannot destroy.

❧ June 3ʳᵈ ☙

I am no longer required at the Penetralia.

I devoted the day to paintings.

At night, the full moon, magnified by our protective domes, shone on the lake and my home. I walked in the garden clothed in a fierce silvery fantasy. Though the moon seems nearer, we are no nearer to understanding its profound beauty and silence. Will we ever realize in full the meaning of "illumination"?

❧ June 4ᵗʰ ☙

I record my story rather like the people of the twentieth century who sent out unmanned spacecrafts carrying messages of their existence into the gleaming void. May my effort have better luck!

The dullness of the title of my early volumes, *Incidents from*

Anthropology, guaranteed they would receive little notice when beamed into the network. This was as I wished, for I needed to work undisturbed. Through sheer output I established myself as a major voice of academic research; this allowed great freedom of movement. I traversed continents, scoured ocean depths and soared to satellites. Exploring the wastelands of the Northern Amerigoes I again struck lucky, discovering a dozen raccoons running wild in the ruins of a power centre called New Yok.

Producing voice-tomb after voice-tomb, I won the Grand Academy Prize. However, with each voice-tomb my disagreements with the Global Community became harder to disguise—for either one becomes the disguise or one's beliefs show through as they grow in intensity, like a face swelling beneath a tight-fitting mask.

One day the stories emerged, one after the other, as quickly as I could compose. My thoughts blew out of me like a whale surfacing from the depths for air. For it was the depths I was plumbing, the fissures and cracks at the heart of our world; it is through these that light seeps in.

In quick succession I produced *Forgotten Desires and Remembrance of Things Past: Short Stories.* The first sank like a stone. The second produced far too many waves; I sank with it! Of course, to avoid punishment I should have severely censored myself—but this isn't the path of the artist.

I was "Mediated" on. Of course my brain was cleansed and emotions charred as has happened to many before. In an emptiness, petals of soot swirled and sank into my heart.

But, unknown to me, a consequence of my love for words began to manifest…

◈ June 6ᵗʰ ◈

This entry is like iridescent dust left on fingers when a butterfly is caught.

Some directions, once taken, continue to colour the passage of life. Today I track the unfailing longing to trail one's genes. During my youth,

I was sexually profligate, taking on as many partners as I could, including Mugwump and Paladin, to help me pass the time, but I produced no children. This caused me pain. At the outpost, even till my hundred-and-tens, though I was suitably mated, I produced just two offspring. Despite our best efforts of body and technology we are a vanishing race; we have lost the human species' ability to procreate effortlessly.

However, during the two decades I was incarcerated, I produced four children by seducing the Originals in whose "care" I was. It seemed as if my transgressive voice-tombs had triggered my fecundity. This achievement improved the conditions of my imprisonment. I was allowed to meet my children—though under the supervision of their Guardian Units. I even made the grade of Good Mother, for I induced in them a sense of play, considered an asset as it hones wargame skills in adulthood.

I had tried to be like the other Mothers and suppress my longing to play those silly games of hide-and-seek, or throw them dizzily into the air, their small bodies wriggling, screaming with delight before catching them so! I played and played; I delighted in them. Each time they visited me in my cell, fountains seemed to sprinkle rose water on my parched mind and, while holding their small bodies to me, I felt blessed.

Many decades have passed since, like the moon racing through clouds on a flight. It is not recommended we remain in close touch. But I investigated my children's locations. The eldest heads the Seismic Research Centre in the Kanchakan Peninsular, forecasting earthquakes decades in advance, he is doing valuable work. The second oversees the outpost at the North Pole and has produced one voice-tomb on nineteenth-century Inuit hunting methods. This may be a beginning, but I hope her life will be easier than mine. The third, Wizard, he with the plump cheeks, died a hero's death attempting to reach our nearest habitable planet some twenty light years away. Eighteen Originals in their prime were lost on this mission; never again was it attempted. The fourth child, Seer, is stationed underwater on the southern Kerguelen Plateau after the deep ocean Power Lobes were shifted here from the Atlantic depths. It is an important assignment but I worry for her given her responsibilities and the monotonous darkness of her surroundings.

For, whatever our advances, as long as we retain a predominance of human DNA, I do not think we are meant to live continuously in such alien environs.

As a mother, I wonder if it wasn't my desire to take Seer to The Wonders of the Natural World that led her to this post. By the time she was seven, though I would be implanted with Tracking Devices and tailed by her Guardian Units, we were permitted to venture to specific Recreational Sites. Underwater World was her favourite; in philimix lakes, she would swim with stingrays and sperm whales, wriggling her lithe body along as they programmed themselves to her needs. She loved the reconstructed coral reefs most of all, delighting in the colours, in the darting of small fish, these wings of flame flitting through heavy liquid. Seer was almost fifteen when I was released after being tonsured of ideas; my fecundity had granted me the reprieve.

I lived for a while in my villa, pacing, pacing, touching the walls, mouthing phrases from my forgotten life. I gathered myself into a pool, filled with deep, still reflections. One day, once again, I broke free: I made friends with silence. Thought and imagination returned to me.

Inspired by the myth of Ulysses tied to the mast, I tied myself down to becoming an acceptable Original; using my deepest resources of subterfuge I navigated myself once again into the heart of the Global Community. This was neither suffering nor sacrifice: it was survival. At the end of a decade, I was granted five gliders and, though each movement was tracked, I was permitted to travel without restraint.

Suddenly a thought emerges: how would I like to die? The wish of millions who have died before me rises, a wish rarely fulfilled. To die in one's sleep, face turned to the wall.

⋙ June 12th ⋘

As recently as two hundred years ago the monsoon would have arrived by now. There was a cult of this season. Poems and paintings, particularly of lovers, were inspired by it for its deepening of colours that suggest love's intensification. *Mitti Fragrance of Wet Earth* is my perfume of choice. I douse myself in it before taking up my tale for scents evoke memory.

Early mornings and late at night, I wander in the city. It is a grand conception, splendidly executed. However, grandeur must not be equated with justice; this is as fallacious as confusing tenderness with hope. For tenderness is quite beyond hope and in spite of it.

Hope lengthens against an unforeseeable and dark future, and is located in time. Tenderness extends in the present, un-located in time. Tenderness, once sensed, is ever present. This is the fabric of our moral ground. On this, I stake my life.

❧ June 15th ❧

My last child was born on this day. In isolation I celebrate his sixth birthday. Each day I remember being torn from him; my skin seems to flay and whip me, breaking capillaries.

❧ June 21st ❧

I have often imagined what I might have said to my mother were I by her side when she was fading. Maybe she would have said, "I am bored and tired. I wish to go." Maybe I would have taken her shrivelled hand in mine and said, "Mother, I understand. May your passing be gentle. I shall remember you as long as I live; your genes are carried forward through me." Or something to that effect. I wish I had told her that she was more cherished than she could have imagined.

As it happened, I was researching in Patagonia, and was informed of her demise after I returned.

I carry on many imaginary conversations with her, as many have before me, with their parents. Regret seems written into our DNA.

Like boats of passage that leave the same harbour side by side, leaving widening wakes as they journey, we travel through life, said an anonymous monk long ago.

To assure the Global Community that my rehabilitation was progressing satisfactorily, I joined Hobbies Inc. Two hobbies were the minimum prescribed; I chose three. Cultivating laelia was an easy pastime as I discovered that they flower profusely if Albinoni is played to them. The orchids thrived, I won a Consolation Prize. The second was flying mock-ups of the Concord, a rickety supersonic jet. It was fun and I liked its slow speed. It took some four hours to cross the Atlantic; I'd put the plane on auto-pilot and compose voice-tombs.

The last was in the Hologram Circus. I enjoyed being a lion tamer; I enjoyed balancing twenty spinning platters on sticks while my holograph minced the salsa. Above all I enjoyed being a trapeze artist. I became an expert, inventing increasingly complicated manoeuvres.

One day I found a partner who too could dance in air. He'd swing from the other side, we'd link our hands in mid-air and spiral our bodies in an arcing double helix before retreating to our trembling stands high above the ground. At that time, his name was Pasha.

Pasha was, to use an ancient, forgotten phrase, "enchanted by me". For a start, he was much younger than I was, and ardent, and intrigued by my imagination. He wished to know, and I wished to lead. It was a heady experience, and transgressive, for by now we were both elected representatives of the Prime Counsel and not supposed to behave in a volatile manner. Besides, he was captivated by the unfolding secrets of my body, as I was by his willingness to experiment with touch and emotion not enhanced by technology. We dismissed all sex-tools; we had sex like primitive people. Songs seemed sweeter when we were together, food tasted better, colours sparkled and our bodies would fill with nectarine energy merely by imagining the other's touch. I remember how often we lay in each other's arms, tranquil as a beach of silken sand glistening under moonlight. He appreciated Beauty.

I cannot bring myself to continue any further tonight.

❦ June 22nd ❧

"Imperceptibly it fades, this flower-like human heart."

Holding this line of anonymous verse close to my heart, I remember the twenty-seven years we were together, Pasha and I, like dew is to dawn, each incomplete without the other.

To him I opened my secrets; I spoke about my stance on the Global Community. He responded. I was no longer alone! We had month-long quodlibets; he keenly questioned the practicality of my ideas. I was so elated that I conceived again, late in life, and my joy knew no bounds. It was a fecund period. I completed twelve voice-tombs, *Fictive Biographies*, a series on histories narrated by different species who possessed equal validity and voice. Pasha worked to get it passed.

Night dissolved into dawn skies. We were in each other's arms; boundless joy flowed through me. Kissing him all over I told him of the thoughts of a twentieth-century leader who was possibly called The Mahatma. He advocated a non-violent movement of change based on individual courage. It succeeded if for a short time. Now was the time to test these ideas again, to let them stream through us like a river to the sea; like Pasha did into me.

Pasha was young, ambitious and superbly intelligent. He could have made a good ally but lacked courage. Finally, he "protected" me by exposing me; shortly after, he gained titles more exalted.

Fictive Biographies was banned. After I failed to reveal plans despite time in the Absolute Truth module, I was again released. The Global Community was determined to grant me the opportunity to betray myself.

❦ June 23rd ❧

Tomorrow the Celebrations start. Scheduled as the last spectacle of the evening I am to address the entire Global Community—Originals, Firehearts, Superior Zombies, Clones and yes, the hidden mutants too. It is an intelligent wager, weighed in their favour; it's the best I can expect.

I am aware of what might happen, and am no martyr—for martyrs make deliberate choices, balancing right against wrong while measuring pain against the possibility of success. But this tenderness and these memories that are not my own leave me with no option but to speak.

I am a link in a chain of words that is liquid as water, as supple and gracious, and also implacable; as immovable as boulders, stronger and harsher than solidified lava.

The address will be my last will and testament.

I shall speak of breeze and touch, and the faint hum with which one's Ancestry Capsule appears, twirling strands of DNA before one's eyes, and I shall speak of the longed-for sound of rain.

I shall speak of dreams that fly amidst us, wings afire; mistakes made that lie within our hearts like sunken galleons holding treasures if only we search the ruins.

Yes, this is what I shall do.

The courage of the desperate tastes of tar. Even so, all is not bleak. The recent breakthrough in gametogenesis research suggests we can extend cloning to thirteen, even fourteen, generations impressed from my genes; my "Darwinian" heirs.

But this is a game of probabilities. Maybe cloning malfunctions will occur with the most unexpected results. Maybe a later generation of Clones will trip into consciousness and another understanding of freedom.

Anything and everything is still possible.

VI

THE VISITATIONS

❧ The Watcher ❧

I don't remember ever being free.

Free to wander where I wish. Eat what I please. Sleep when I want. And so forth. No. In these and many other ways I am never free. This is looked upon as my curse, my imprisonment. But I never wanted this kind of freedom. In fact, I consider it somewhat vulgar and obvious. Especially for one of my kind.

No. I am free in innumerable other ways. Free and refined to pursue my obsession, without a care for myself, or the world. The only freedom I increasingly crave is to be free of my obsession. Of this I can never be, though it is driving me to my doom. I will take my obsession to my death.

Only once I remember I wanted to be free in the vulgar way. That was when I was put in a large cage, one entirely enclosed by mirrors and placed above the bed. From the cage hung a long string of tinkling bells that could be tugged at pleasure. To make me swim in my cage to their frightful noise. I would careen from one corner of the cage to the other, shrieking. I never knew what made me scream. The jangling bells? Or my myriad reflections— green, wings beating, beak open, claws sliding over my swinging perch. Out of control. Yes, I hated most seeing only myself. Shut in, unable to see my beloved. I hate reflections.

Perhaps the horror I have of seeing myself has to do with my childhood.

I was not used to seeing others of my kind. Kishmish, My Love's favourite handmaiden—the brown one, soft as a raisin—she told me I was a foundling. I was found on the grass below our pavilion. A fledgling with my beak open, squawking soundlessly. I was picked up and adopted. I must have fallen from my parents' nest. I remember nothing of the days before I saw her. Before I became her diversion. Her confidante. Her accomplice. Quickly, I rose to becoming My Love's Favourite. I was lucky.

When I was very young she used to feed me. I remember the pearls on her breast large as grains of corn. Her fragrance of musk, jasmine and ittar of rose. She would hold me in one hand. With the other she'd press a silken rag dipped in sweet-sour juice on my face. I would peck at it. The juice dripping down the sides of my face. Running down my moulting back feathers. While I was cushioned in her palm. It was bliss.

Later came skinned raw mango pieces. Peeled grapes. Slivers of carrot. Almonds soaked in milk. Pomegranate seeds, translucent as her skin, in silver bowls.

I did not mind my claws being capped. Each one is wrapped in a small case of Gujarati velvet. Before I'm placed on her. So that I don't scratch My Love. This makes my grip somewhat slippery. But I understand. I did not mind my wings being clipped. Not at all. It did not hurt. And I can still fly short distances. And My Love feels safe. She thinks this is the only way she can ensure my captivity. My Love does not know me at all. As if I would have exchanged flight for the pleasure of watching her.

I watch her constantly. She does not know how closely I watch her every move. I sleep after her. Awaken before she does. I am at her pillow, cocking my head, to look at her. This way and that. Calling, "Wake up! Wake up, My Love!" I walk on the silk of her pillows. Impatient to have her awake. Aware of me. Each day I try to awaken her. The maids cajole her: "Begum, the silk seller is here. The jeweller has come. The lace-makers have brought lace, fine as a spider's web, for a veil. Mistress, wake up. Take a look." When nothing else works, Dai strokes her forehead gently. Only to Dai she listens because the old maid has been with her since birth.

She will toss and murmur. And awaken. I perch on her shoulder as she rinses her mouth. The water flows from her mouth still heavy with dreams. Her hair is in disarray. Then water of lemon blossom mixed with scent of civet, frankincense and violets for washing her face. Her body is still dreaming. Her clothes spread like clouds on the bed.

Of all the rituals of beautification, I love watching the bath most. It's long, melodious. First, the tattoo of gentle Gulkand's hands. Massaging her with juice of sweet basil, orange blossoms, musk of Tartary and narcissus. Till her body glows more radiant than the light pushing through our trellised windows. Next, the rubbing of her skin with myrobalan, powdered turmeric, yellow sandal and crushed pacheh leaves. If there is a chance of Khan-Sahib visiting her that day, the preparation of her sex with more fragrances. Then the sunken bath. Her body submerged in the tank with its mosaic of flowing flowers. Creepers of polished stone trail flowers on all sides. Sway in water on the marble floor. The water dances with light and rose petals. Over her spread hair. Over her body, her nipples occasionally surfacing. The water murmurs so sweetly. This is the way My Love awakens to another day.

I'll say this: the great Alim, Khan-Sahib, heard of her beauty. He asked for her hand in marriage. No relative begged that she be included in the zenana. She became Third Begum because of his desire. She, coming from a poor, though noble family. One could say she's a foundling, like me. Raised high by the grace of Khan-Sahib. Love has this facility of making connections. He paid a heavy bride-price for her, I know.

Gulabi told me this. Gulabi, the maid with pink hands and pink cheeks. The one without pride among the handmaidens. The pink flatterer. She curses me under her breath each day as she changes the water in my silver drinking bowl. "You wretch, see how high you have risen. Thank your stars, wild parrot. But for the Begum's compassion, you'd have been eaten by a cat." She repeats this like a prayer while smiling at me through the bars. For all her sweet talk Gulabi will never rise to be her favourite. Her breath smells foul. I back off when she approaches, or fly into the lap of my beloved. I hate Gulabi. I hate her. And I hate Pista too—the Kashmiri maid. The proud long-nosed one. She claims her female ancestors served as guards in the seraglios of the Great Moguls. I don't know why, but I believe her. Perhaps because everyone does. She's hard as a pistachio. And salty. She has all the gossip.

Pista says Khan-Sahib's eldest wife, the First Begum, liked dancing girls so much that she adopted a sixteen-year-old beauty. Keeps her hidden when Khan-Sahib visits her. But everyone knows about the dancing girl. Pista— who squeezes me hard when she carries me—said she had heard something scandalous. That the First Begum applies henna with her own hands on the dancing girl's feet.

The First Begum is no threat to My Love though her father holds a high post in His Excellency the Nawab Wazir's court. He is the Superintendent-of-the-Audience-Chamber. She has given Khan-Sahib a son, the back of his head is straight as a door. Pista is a good mimic. She is brutal. How My Love laughs at whatever Pista says! She asks her maids to loosen her bodice. Pista says the boy still soils his clothes though his moustache is full-grown. Pista says all the First Begum does is dote on her idiot son and the dancing girl. This was our biggest joke last year.

The Second Begum is no threat either, though she is higher born. Her father is the Grand Equerry and Master of the Horse at His Excellency's court. But Khan-Sahib visits her perfunctorily. For two reasons. First, she gets into blind rages. She throws things. Once even a plate of food at Khan-Sahib when he visited after a long absence. "May God preserve every pious Mussalman from such a foul-tempered wife!" Dai exclaimed. Second, she has given Khan-Sahib three daughters. Only daughters. The curse of daughters is on her.

I should not be saying this. I am a female parrot. When I was young, when my blood was turning, when the grey band of feathers was appearing like a collar around my neck, how hard I tried to tell My Love I was like her. A female. In love with her. I can lay eggs if I mate. But My Love decided I am a male. I got my best chance to disclose my femaleness the day Kishmish examined me. She said I was as female as the rest of them. I felt as though a ripe mango-sun was bursting before me.

I flew to My Love. Preened before her, squawking. I walked on her body. Pecked at her sex through her flowing garments, tugged her tasselled pyjama strings to say: I am the same. "There's your proof," *she says, laughing, to her maids.* "He knows what I like. He is the only male in our apartment. Let him be my secret pleasure."

Her hookah-smoke-laden voice charred my feathers. I could not see her. Not the perfumed bed. Nor the sliced light seeping through the blinds. Nothing. I am burning. For I know My Love will only accept me this way. Through a false sexuality, through pretence. This is when my hatred for her sprouted, unknown to me. Smaller than a mustard seed it sprouted; planted by her.

My own body had become my cage. Soundless, immobile, I am within it.

After a long while, from far away, I heard her call, "Quieten down, my love. Here, have a mango slice. Stop dancing like a madman." *This is when I realised I had been hopping on the spot.*

"Come to me, my love," *she said, holding out a fig.* "What's troubling you, my pet?" *I flew to her, pretending to eat the fig. I pecked her fingers at the cuticles so they bled. The maids were upon me. Dai was upon me. My sorrow, my fury, turned to fear. In panic I flew to hide in her hair. Its heaviness. Its softness. Its fragrance. I buried my head at her nape, screaming,* "Wake up! Wake up, My Love!" "Do not touch him," *she said.* "He has taken refuge in me." *This is when I accepted my false sexuality. This is when I fell deeper in love with her. This is when I knew there would be no escape—for me or for her—for I have drawn blood.*

I fly to my favourite perch. Her shoulder. My feathers touching her cheek, I look into her ear. It is soft and dark and moist. Curtains of perfumed hair. Behind them the tight-curled flesh, the dark curling darkness within. When I am very disturbed, I peek into her ear. Looking in I feel stable, safe. The room slowly comes back into my sight.

The eunuch-guard announces, "He's coming! He's coming!" *from outside the door of our apartment. Khan-Sahib visits anytime. People say he is very handsome because he looks like his cousin, His Excellency the Nawab-Wazir. I don't think so. He looks like two different people joined together. Long from head to hips, squat from buttocks to toes. And fat. But I am not a good judge of men. I have seen only one man: him. And pretty boy Dulera who goes with him everywhere. The eunuch guards don't count. They are worse off than me, trapped as I am in a false sexuality. They have none.*

My Love thinks the great Alim, her husband, is the handsomest of men. She acts this way. I hate it. "He's coming! He's coming!" and My Love starts. Everyone rushes around, skirts flying, dark plaits swinging, feet running, hands carrying trays of jewels, wine, incense, cut fruit, dry fruit. The silver censers lit with fresh incense cakes. Candles lit. What a flurry each time he comes! I normally flutter up and settle in a niche in case I am knocked about in the hurry.

My Love washes her hands in water scented with aloewood. Perfumes herself. Chews a paan with camphor. And lies on the bed, smelling a rose, awaiting him. The maids offer wine, fruits, the hookah, his silver drinking cup shaped like a pigeon, and the paan-daan. They withdraw after salaaming him again. My Love too will salaam him, languorously. "How is my little Piece-of-the-Moon today?" he'll say. And she will answer, "Longing for you, my Lord. This humble slave thought you had forgotten her." Each time she says this I squawk. Involuntarily. I squawk, and she darts to catch me as I hobble on the bed rails, or hop across the marble floor. Or sit like a stone in a niche, hoping I will not be seen.

She will catch me and thrust me into my cage, the huge old brass one at the foot of the bed. She'll throw her dupatta over the cage. I can't see. I'd be shrouded by a veil of green or pink or yellow. Depending on the colour she wears, depending on the season. I squawk from within the cage. "Begum," I hear his voice through the cloth of the dupatta, "your parrot has a loud voice." "Gracious One, forgive him," she replies. "Take pity on that flightless object." Before they start making their own sounds. Before she screams. Exactly like me—high, in my voice. While I walk up the bars of my cage, hang upside down from the roof, straining my neck. Trying to pull away the cloth in order to see her.

Let me speak of her beauty. Her hair rushes to her hips when loosened. Like wine poured. Hennaed a reddish black. It's woven with pearls like bubbles in wine.

Her eyebrows dip to meet above her nose like two arches meeting below a dome. Her eyes are wide and slanting like almonds. And lined with kohl. Her nose is perfect. Her thin lips, stained by betel juice, are red. Her neck, like a marble column, encrusted with jewels. Rows and rows of necklaces. Her skin is like the marble of the Taj Mahal. I have not seen it. But I've heard of it. At dawn, it is translucent. At midday, dazzling white. At sunset, rosy. At night, cool. Shining with the blue of the night. So too is her skin. It changes with the light.

My Love's body is like creamy yoghurt bound in muslin. Pressing against the veil of her skin. Its radiance filters through her fine muslin garments. As the sun filters through the blinds of our apartment, subdued and veiled. As she walks, as she reclines on her bed, her limbs are like the fountains in our rooms. Splaying fragrance.

Her hands I love best, for they hold me on either side like wings. Each one is decorated like the marble trellis-worked balconies. With creepers of orange henna that race from her wrists to the tips of her fingers: so chiselled, so neat.

If I could only have remained an observer! But I fell in love with her. Each detail of her body told me a story. The furrow of hair from her navel to her sex—of passion. The few soft hairs behind her knees—of secrecy. The single hair, which sprouts from the aureole of her left nipple which the maid regularly tweezes—of treachery. I should have been warned by my scanning of her body.

But I was speaking of when I couldn't see her. When Khan-Sahib came. When she threw her veil over my cage. Once I caught it, a red muslin one. I pulled a small piece of dupatta into my cage. Pecked a hole in it. Peeped through. Below on the bed I saw his left leg. A dark hairy leg. I saw the sole of his left foot. So dirty. I couldn't see her. Not even her legs. Then she *screamed. I saw her right leg tumble on one side of his. Limp, like she would lie after a massage.*

I must have squawked. The great Alim notices. "Begum," he says, "It does not befit you to have a pet with an ugly voice. If you wish to keep it, make it speak prettily." My fate is sealed. Only Zebu-Nissa, My Love's younger sister, tries to intervene.

She says, "Beloved sister, I pray do not peel your parrot's tongue to make him sing more sweetly. Let the poor creature be." But no one pays much attention to Zebu-Nissa. She's an odd one. She does not rub missa on her gums to turn them purple. Her gums are pink. She won't string golden ribbons into her hair. Or pearls. Only flowers. She won't dress in the colours of the season but according to her mood. She reads the Holy Book. And the Gulistan. Poetry, she writes poetry! And sings. Her voice is like camphor on fire. Clear, fragrant and sparkling. I love it when she comes to visit.

One night there is talk that Zebu-Nissa will become Khan Sahib's concubine. I fly around the large candelabras beating the air with my wings. Seeing the flames dance inside the fluted coloured-glass holders. I don't mind the danger. The heat. But Zebu-Nissa is not accepted. Besides her right eye is bigger than the left. She's much taller than My Love. They say she sings too much. Khan Sahib doesn't care for singing. Neither does My Love. When the singing-girls are called to entertain us, My Love talks and laughs with her maids. I hate her at such times.

Khan-Sahib wants me to speak prettily. So the outer layer of my tongue has to be peeled. I cannot describe it. The insults. The humiliation. The rough handling. The pain. Gulabi is the first in the chain. As she carries me to the eunuch, she whispers, smiling, "You wretch, I hope you die." From the eunuch's hand I am passed on, from hand to hand, cage to cage, each coarser, dirtier, smaller, smellier. Carried in a bamboo container with a dirty cloth flung over it. Through the mansion to the stables. I am carried out to the gypsy camp. To the headman's tent. To his face. His smelly mouth shouting,

"Hold still, bird! Hold still, rascal!" I will not remember the details. The pressure on my nostrils, the glint of the blade.

Then I am snatched back. My tongue burns like the silver coin thrown to him. My body burns with rage. With pain. But it is done. I am to speak sweetly.

My Love is pleased. She gives me to Dai to look after. Dai gives me to Kishmish. Who gives me to the woman who cleans the spittoons. The wretch eats the figs soaked in honey meant for me. She eats the banana pieces. The raisins. The almond paste. She feeds me sesame seeds. Hard, black sesame seeds poking like needles into my soft new tongue. I don't eat. I grow weak.

I am summoned before the rawness has healed. My Love misses me. Silently fluttering my wings, I walk on her as usual. Unmindful of my burning tongue for I am in her presence again. That's before the great Alim walks in on that awful day. Awful. I don't want to remember this now. I want to remember happy things. "How shall we pass the day?" My Love asks. "Call for the astrologer-woman? Play chausar? Or chess?"

When she asks me what I want, I shout, "Dancing girls! Dancing girls!" I fly up to the huge cloth fan that is slowly and steadily pulled by punkha-pullers who sit outside. I perch on top and look down, feeling the cloth ruffle below me. I sway to the music. The music melts like perfume in the censers that swing in the air. I see the flaring skirts of the dancing girls. See their hands turning into lotus buds that open and close. See their veils circling around them, the tiles spinning below their spinning feet.

My Love likes the game of watching spiders catch flies. Betting on them. No one knows which one will win. Or how many will die. She thinks this is exciting.

Only once did I behave badly. She was losing to Khan-Sahib at chess. She lost and lost. Not even one game did the great Alim allow her to win. He kept playing and laughing. Laughing and playing. I saw My Love's eyes fill. I flew to the middle of the board and toppled the pieces.

He left without a word. My Love caught me. Threw me like a stone. Threw the pieces at me. She threw pillows at me. I sat very still on the floor,

*my body lowered on my legs, neck pulled into my wings. Silent. While she
cursed and cried. She too is scared.*

*The following week Khan-Sahib sent a message. He is going on an
elephant kheddah with His Excellency. He sent her two presents. One was
a spinach-covered pancake shaped like me. I watched her hands tear at the
parrot pancake. Everyone laughed. The other present was a peacock. A white
peacock. It arrived sitting on a cushion, its long tail hanging down like a
waterfall from its rock-like body.*

*My Love adores the peacock. Because it means Khan-Sahib has forgiven
her. She runs after the peacock. Feeds it. Watches it. A fat bird that can't
fly. Its tail sweeps the floor like a broom. It's a freak. A white peacock. I
wouldn't have minded so much if he had sent a bird I could admire. A
singing bird. A koel perhaps. Or a bulbul.*

*I am not used to flying. But I fly around constantly because of the fat
white peacock. Fly from the alcoves to the veranda. To the top of the cage.
Around the maids. I settled on their heads, calling, "Wake up! Wake up!"
Or plead, "Dancing girls! Dancing girls!" I fly near My Love and she
brushes her hand across her face as if I were a bat. I stop eating. My feathers
fall. I lose three tail feathers. I must look ugly. "Let him die near me if he
wants," My Love says, "Do not remove him." That's all. She is enthralled
by the peacock who is spreading his white fan, calling and shimmering. The
rains have begun. It is the peacock's season.*

*Everyone circles around him as he vibrates, dancing. No one sees me. I
decide to die by drowning myself in my silver drinking bowl. I put my head
in. There's very little water. But I keep it in hoping someone will notice.
Finally Kishmish does. She runs to call My Love. She comes. She holds out
a slice of guava. Cool and slim and white as her fingers. That day Khan-
Sahib walks in again, deliberately unannounced. "Get up," My Love is
saying to me, "Come on, my pet." I peck at the sweet guava. It is good to
eat. Good to have her feed me, caressing me with her voice. I sit in her palm,
eating.*

"Feed it chillies, Begum," Khan-Sahib's voice booms. He is in our

midst. *My Love* drops me. *"Hot little chillies,"* he says. *"It has had its tongue peeled. Now chillies, only chillies, to make it sing sweetly."*

I am put back in my cage. Soon Pista comes carrying a plateful of chillies. *"Here,"* he says, *"eat."* He sticks a large red chilli through the bars. *"Make your pet eat, Begum,"* he says. *My Love* comes to me, delicately holding the stalk of a chilli. I refuse. I dislike eating in the presence of strangers, even if he is the great Alim. I dislike being watched.

My Lord stands behind her. He lifts my cage in his arms. *"Eat the chilli,"* he says. He shakes the cage. I squawk. He laughs. He hangs my cage on its hook near the bed. *"Make it eat,"* he says. He begins to undress. *My Love* whispers to me, *"Please eat, my love. Or my Lord will be angry."* I look at her through one eye. Then shift around and look through the other eye. She is pleading. The chilli she offers smells sharp. I bite it. It is terrible. It is fire. *My Lord* is well pleased. He upturns the plateful of chillies on my cage. They fall around me as hard, long green and red rain. I am distraught. I flap in my cage, shrieking. I fly against the bars, hurt my head. Knock over my small silver grain bowl, scattering seeds. Upset the water bowl. My tail gets wet. Finally I regain composure. I sit on my swinging perch, and ruffle my feathers a couple of times to feel the cool air. I flap my wings to cool my wingpits. I grip the perch firmly. Then I look down.

It is the first time I see her making love. I do not want to see. I cannot not see. I turn to one side then the other. The vision in my left eye is better so I watch from this eye though it means I have to back up against the bars. I feel hatred. For myself. For him. For her. If I had been free I would have pecked his eyes out. They go on swarming below me. In rage I turn round and round on the swing till I am quite dizzy. Helpless, I watch them. Turning round and round. Then she screams. Like me. Again she screams, open-mouthed, fists clenched, eyes shut.

It was the chillies. The chillies in his hands. His awful purple chilli. The chilli of his tongue. The chilli in the air. The chilli in my eyes. The chilli burning in my heart. How it burns. I scream and scream. They don't notice.

*How shall I say it? It was as if a hawk were pushing his chilli claws
into my breast. I don't know what I am doing. I fly to the bottom of my cage.
I cannot watch any longer. I lift the chillies. The ones carpeting my cage.
One at a time with my beak. And throw them out. Each time I scream. I go
on and on. Pecking. Lifting. Throwing. Screaming. Going round and round.
I lift my own droppings and throw them. The bottom of my cage is clean.*

*I am very tired. I can see the dawn fresh between the marble filigree of
the far screens. And I am still circling the bottom of my cage, stupefied. She
comes to me naked, and languorous. And tired.*

*She lifts my cage from its hook. She seats my cage on her lap. Her torso
is my earth and sky. Her nipples press against the bars. I could peck them
into bleeding. Her voice croons so sweetly above my head, like saffron sherbet.
She says, "Never again will I feed you chillies, my love. No matter what he
says." I look for him. I don't know when he left. Then we sleep. Me in my
cage. She naked under the quilt.*

*It's after this that I begin to know when Khan-Sahib is coming. Even
before the eunuch-guard's warning, I sense my enemy. Walking towards
the apartment. Down the long corridor, pinching the boy Dulera's bottom
through his pyjamas. And laughing. I call, "He's coming! He's coming!" I
am rarely wrong.*

*My Love becomes his favourite for four months. She becomes pregnant.
She gives money to the astrologer-woman for happy predictions. Money to
feed the poor. Khan-Sahib promises he will let her build a caravanserai once
their son is born. He says he will build a garden only for her. My Love is
dreaming. Dreaming. Like a cloud she grows large and radiant.*

*One day it grew black. Suddenly. The rain of tears did not stop. I don't
know who cried more, My Love, or Dai, sitting by her bed. Stroking her
forehead, crying. "Don't worry, my child. You will have many sons. There
will be others." Khan-Sahib never came to see her. He was angry. He had
announced that he was going to be a father. My Love cried even more because
he did not come. He sent messages enquiring about her health. Like he does
to his second wife. The mad one.*

My Love had fallen out of favour. That's what everyone thought. Even Dai. Beating her breasts and wailing. Grey and brown like an eagle disturbed. She summoned Zebu-Nissa to our quarters to distract My Love. Zebu recites verses from the Holy Koran. How beautifully she prays! I feel water has become fire, and earth, air. That all elements are woven together by His Mercy. Splendours of calm burst upon each other as she prays. I have never heard anything more wonderful.

She could have moved a stone to weeping. But she does not move My Love's heart. Hers is stilled by grief. Her prayers are only for the great Alim's visit. He sent a message that he was busy with matters of court. My Love hid the note under her pillow. Like a talisman. And lay still. She was not hearing anything. Not me. Not Zebu-Nissa's sparkling voice. Not Dai's cajoling. My Love lay in bed. Like a discarded plait of false hair, not stirring.

"He's coming! He's coming!" I called. The eunuch-guard announced him. She didn't move. He saw My Love limp on her bed like a withered rose. Her hair unscented. Her clothes crumpled. Her nails were showing pink, un-hennaed. Her eyes open and dry.

"We shall celebrate your birthday, Begum," he proclaims. "Our heart is large." My Love does not turn to acknowledge his presence. Dai reacts, salaaming Khan-Sahib. Saying My Love would recover her health for the celebrations. Khan-Sahib's gracious visit is the tonic. "We shall summon Bi-Jan to lighten your mistress's mood," Khan-Sahib says. "It does not befit the Begum to lie like this." Even I have heard of Bi-Jan, the singing jewel of Avadh. The courtesan ugly as a toad with the voice of a fairy.

Khan-Sahib keeps his word about the celebrations. My Love takes me on the boat ride so that I too can see what the great world looks like. What lies outside our veils. Our blinds filtering the sunlight. Our deep scented garden. Level upon level of lights shine through coloured shades like fields of flowers blooming in the dark river. The full moon, silver in the sky, larger and more silver in the water. It says earth and heaven are not opposite but complementary. Like lovers deeply in love.

In our boat wine rocks in crystal glasses. Flames weave in candleholders.

Pista lifts a muslin blind covering the sides of our boat. My Love peers out at the great city drifting on either side of us.

Khan-Sahib's boat is on our right, a little ahead. Shining with lights like a crown floating on the water. And the music! The voice of the courtesan. How she sings of love, of jealousy and parting and uniting again! Of Avadh she sings, I think. Over the waters her voice wafts. Over the splash of the oars. Over the glint of fishes leaping in the great river. Over the oil spluttering with burning moths.

I hedge sideways to My Love. One claw. Then another. Carefully, till I reach her skirts where the scent of musk and Persian saffron rises. Digging my nails in, I clamber on her thighs. Stepping on one flower motif. Then the next. And the next. Swaying with the boat, with the music. With love. When I reach her lap I call, "Dancing girls! Dancing girls!" She picks me up with her left hand, not quite noticing me. Holds me at her bosom near her ruby pendant, each stone large as a pomegranate seed. She raises her hookah tip. The fragrance of opium dissolves from her mouth like the music over the waters. If there is a paradise on earth, it is this. It is this.

Only Dai rocks herself in her arms. Not to the music. Not to the river's swell. She rocks herself to curses, muttering, "This Bi-Jan sings too well. Lucky she's as ugly as a cross-eyed camel." Dai leans towards My Love. "Call Bi-Jan," Dai whispers. "Tell her to sing for you," "What?" asks My Love. She hears nothing but the whispers of opium. "I am summoning Bi-Jan to sing for you," Dai says. My Love nods.

Dai chooses the clothes My Love wears for the reception. Yellow printed muslin drawers. Scarlet embroidered bodice. Green silk veil with pearl tassels. Transparent white embroidered skirt. My Love reclines on the cushions of her bed. Hookah in one hand, me in the other. The censers burn with incense. Fountains play. Her maids are in their best attire. The meats, fruits, sweets and wine are spread before her. My Love looked resplendent. Like a moon coloured by rainbows. I puff my chest feathers. I strut on her skirts. On the silken bed covers. On the plates of food.

I strut up to Bi-Jan. Cock my head and look up. She is ugly. Warty and lumpy like a sweaty old bolster. Red paan juice trickles from her mouth as she talks. Bi-Jan wipes her lips with the back of one hand. The other she holds near her ear to hear the drone of the tanpura as she sings. How she sings!

My Love does not have an ear for music, just like Khan-Sahib. She cannot tell when a note slips. Or is sublime. How Bi-Jan sang that day. Enough to milk the heavens! Enough to make the stars drop dust! I stood still, listening. Not a feather moved. When she ended her song of lament, her song of Avadh, my feathers rose like a peacock's to rain.

"Come here," My Love calls. I turn sharply, my head cocked, a foot raised. My Love's voice is so... harsh. Bi-Jan cackles. How ugly she is. I scurry to My Love. "Your pet likes music," Bi-Jan salaams and says. "I am greatly honoured she likes music such as I make." "My parrot is a he, not a she," My Love says. "Forgive me, Glorious Lady. Your parrot is female," says Bi-Jan. "Just like you and me."

I was thrilled in spite of myself. Bi-Jan recognised me for what I was. And for my love of music. I call, "Dancing girls! Dancing girls!" and beat my wings. Bi-Jan laughs loudly. Betel nut pieces spew from her lips on to the floor staining the marble red. Bi-Jan's whole body shakes; a jelly of warts quaking. "The little rascal knows the best things of life. She has been well trained by your Gracious Self, the great Alim's favourite Begum."

It is obvious My Love cannot get into a confrontation with a public singing woman. Even if she does sing divinely. "The whole of the kingdom of Avadh sings of your Graciousness's legendary beauty," Bi-Jan continues. "The most chaste pearl among women. The Alim's best treasure, his most hidden."

"You have been well trained yourself, in courteous speech," My Love remarks.

"By the whip, Honourable One," Bi-Jan replies. "Like your parrot. We are but slaves. We repeat what we are told as the truth. Surely we are not mistaken."

Dai was standing behind the bed curtains. She flings a pouch of coins towards Bi-Jan. The mouth of the pouch bursts open. Bi-Jan picks up the coins. Slowly. Each time she picks up one, she salaams My Love excessively. She goes on picking. Salaaming. Smiling. Mocking. The insult to My Love is insupportable.

Bi-Jan withdraws with her team of female musicians. Before she retreats from our apartment, salaaming at each step, I see her salute me, especially. Mouthing, "He-parrot are you, he-parrot?" We hear her laughter after she withdraws. So lewd, so deliberate. Like she were spitting paan juice on the walls.

My Love catches me by the throat. Thrusts me into her spittoon, the one with the red glass bowl. Shoves my neck down into its neck. Into the red wet darkness. She spits on my back feathers. "Infidel!" she screams. "You deserve to die." My head is upside down, pushing against my throat in the red wet cold. Choking me. Making my windpipe bite into my skull. Dai intervenes. "It does not behove you to strangle your pet parrot for a public woman," she says. She wrests me out of My Love's grasp and gives me to Kishmish to take away.

I am put in an old iron cage. I am very ill. I do not know what is happening. Around me, inside my heart. I am sad. And furious. With Bi-Jan. With myself. With My Love. It's like the cage is getting smaller and smaller. Like the bars are driving into me. I beat my wings against the bars. Shrieking without a pause. All evening. All night. Hopping up and down till I dislocate my right wing. I keep screeching till my strength leaves me. Till the bars slide from sight. Till my voice leaves me.

I don't know when I am carried back, limp and voiceless. My Love ruffles my feathers running a finger down my back. My eyes are shut. I hear My Love say very softly, "You know, Bi-Jan has become Khan-Sahib's favourite. He can't stand music. He loves her abuse." With effort I open my eyes. I am lying on my left side. I see her with my bad eye. The right one. Her quiet, sad face. "Leave him here," I hear her say. "Let him die pecking the diamond of my ring if he wants. That will be an easy death. What do I have left in this life but this sex-confused parrot?" I feel I will die of heartbreak.

All is quiet for the next few months; as still as an unslept coverlet. Except for the gossip Pista brings about Bi-Jan. That she spits globs of paan juice on Khan-Sahib's face when he comes. She pees on him. And curses, which he loves. My Love does not move when she hears this. But she grows paler. Thinner. She sends away her maids. She lies on her bed alone with Dai looking after her. And me, always by her side. She undresses with me watching her. I fly to throw myself on her. "You can't," is what she says. "You are too small." I don't think she notices me. It would be her alone, eating her flesh. With me watching, perched on her knee.

This is how the months passed until the night of the fireworks. His Excellency the Nawab-Wazir had ordered the display for Resident Sahib and the White Sahibs from Calcutta who came to visit our city. Everyone was enthralled by the fiery streamers hissing in the air. Hissing on the river's skin like cobra hoods expanding. All eyes mesmerised. Except one pair. The acrobat's.

The Nawab-Wazir was heavily in debt to the White Sahibs for the upkeep of their army which was guarding Avadh. Pista told us the White Sahibs thought His Excellency was not fit to rule. They are scheming to take over our land. So His Excellency had to appease them. Hold their hand in friendship. Give them gifts. Anything they wanted. Imagine. Jewels. Money. Forts. So they would fight their wars elsewhere. And leave Avadh as it is.

My Love and our group go up to the terrace. The First Begum does not step out these days. The Second Begum was never one to leave her apartment. We have the vantage view from the parapets. Khan-Sahib's concubines and singing girls are behind our group. Chattering. Clapping, their mouths and skirts and hands aflutter.

My Love is running near the ramparts like a child, exclaiming. Seeing fireworks burst in a night full of jewels. Her eyes are sparkling through her veil like jewels. Then she pushes back her veil for a better view. The fireworks reflect in her eyes. I hop on the ramparts in front of her. I peek at the dark gardens below. The deep streets. I see him looking up. Steadfast. His eyes following My Love's pale face like a drunk watching the moon.

I watch that man watch My Love as she runs unveiled. Up and down the terrace. As she leans over the stucco-work ramparts. Laughs. Her face is like a pearl rolling on sand. I watch her watching the fireworks. She is so happy. She forgets all that has happened. Dai is watching her, crying quietly to herself, "My poor girl, my poor child!" I watch the fireworks spread and die in the night sky, leaving smoky trails. Leaving the sky empty as it never had been before.

I know Dai is responsible for my suffering. And My Love's pleasure. She gets him in. The acrobat. She tells him where to scale the walls. What footholds to find. She brings in his missives rolled in paan leaves. She brings his cheap notes. His cheap poetry. His cheap scent.

It is an urgent courtship. Khan-Sahib is accompanying His Excellency and the White Sahibs to hunt tiger. Elephant. Cheetah. Blue bulls. Stag. Wild boar. They are away five weeks. My Love languishes in bed alone. I walk on the silken quilts while My Love's hands creep into her drawers like a crab.

Sometimes My Love tickles my chest, her fingers still sticky. "I am so sad, my love," she sighs. I had stopped thrusting myself on her. I knew it was no use. She wouldn't notice. She only notices the acrobat's notes that Dai smuggles to her. Hidden between betel leaves in the paan-daan. She stares at his stale couplets. Trite words that are repeated at every poetic gathering. Sighs. She looks at herself in the mirror on her ring she wears on her thumb.

Two weeks pass with her sighing to herself. My Love is nervous. Her heart flutters like my clipped wings. Her eyes leap at each new message she receives. As if the acrobat's words are the most glorious she has ever read. Each time she sighs for him I want to claw his lips to shreds. My jealousy mounts. "He's coming!" I cry in anguish. "He's coming! He's coming!" "Yes," she whispers, "tonight."

Accursed, he comes that night. Lifting the blinds of the veranda. Slipping in like a shadow. "Glorious One, at last you have granted me my Dream of Paradise. I am your slave forever." That's all he says. She covers my cage with a shawl before they begin. I hear no more poetry. No couplets. No sweet words. I hear them. I can't see.

It is terrible to see her so happy. Each day she is excited. Each evening she waits for the acrobat like she had never waited for Khan-Sahib. My Love waits for this King of Jugglers. Fire-Eaters. Rope-Climbers. Snake-Charmers. This Master of Dancing Dogs and Performing Bears. This vulgar man who never uses the lime and camphor she offers him for his betel leaf. But his own as a precaution as if My Love is trying to poison him. Yet she is happy. Seeing her stretch and rub her breasts, I am happy. She rubs my chest with his cheap perfumes. Dreamily. Rubbing my chest too hard. Ruffling my feathers. "Don't wake me," she says, kissing me on my beak. "I am awake."

The acrobat suggests my mirror cage. My Love has it made. I am shut in it with the mirrors. My body tenses, waiting for the tug of bells. My hatred claws the air. I reel with hatred. This is when I want to be free. Anytime they make love. Whenever the acrobat wishes My Love to laugh he tugs the string of bells with his toes. I screech. Flay, fluttering inside my swaying mirror cage. My Love thinks it very funny.

She thinks many things are very funny. The acrobat mimics me. My walk. My flying. Flapping his hands near his armpits. She laughs. He mimics Dai's rolling gait. She laughs. He mimics Khan-Sahib entering the Darbar Hall. She keeps quiet. He mimics Khan-Sahib slightly lifting his arse to fart. She is silent. Then she bursts out laughing. She tears off her clothes, crying tears of laughter. I had never seen her do this. She runs up to him through the large night-filled room. Her breasts are shaking. She pulls off his pyjamas while he rolls his eyes. Pretending fright. Quaking. Whispering, "No, Exalted One! Please no! My head will roll!' She mounts him while he pretends to fart with fear. She screams so quickly. Almost instantly. Then he says, "Now it's my turn." After this, she was in his hands. As I was in hers.

When Khan-Sahib returns from the hunt, the acrobat does not appear for a month. I try to do tricks for her. I fall off my perch to see her laugh. I try swinging upside-down. Finally she notices. "Don't, my love," she says to me. "I know what you are trying. But it breaks my heart even more." I had not realised my acrobatics remind her of him. How I hate him. I can't see her suffer.

Every day she tries new perfumes. Strings pearls in her hair. And waits. She orders new garments. She sees that her hands are perfectly hennaed every day. She is waning like the moon. One new moon night the acrobat comes without notice. The Master of Performing Monkeys appears towards dawn. He says he had been travelling. She knows he is lying. He knows she knows. He promises he will come to her every night. Like a moth to a flame. She gives him her ruby ring. He doesn't say a word. Just tosses the ring in the air. And slips it into his cloth pouch. He winks at me as he leaves. I wink back.

Khan-Sahib visits My Love more frequently. He is happy with her performance. And mine calling on cue, "He's coming! He's coming!" when Khan-Sahib is sprawled on her. In between the acrobat steals in. Laughing beneath his breath. Winking at her and me. Quickly slipping in. Quickly slipping out. My Love is not always happy. Yet she gives him presents. A nutcracker inlaid with mother-of-pearl and moonstones. A bottle of rose ittar. A silver paan box. A kerchief of silk. He winds it around his loins. Dances in the night, his member bobbing like the neck of a vulture. My Love is delighted. She springs out of bed, clasps his feet between her thighs. Begs him to visit her always. She says it is like spring when he comes. Like a garden of fountains. The acrobat scratches her shoulders. Strokes her nape. Rubs perfume in her armpits and whispers, "Give your husband more opium. Then I'll be with you while he's snoring."

My Love becomes pregnant. This time we do not announce it. We share the secret amongst ourselves in our chambers. Khan-Sahib is visiting her almost as often as the acrobat. He relishes the way My Love behaves with him. One afternoon as her veil clings to her face with perspiration, he whispers, "Do you want to be the First Begum?" "My Lord!" she cries. "Pray do not frighten me. This worthless slave is honoured enough with her position." I cock my head, listening. Khan-Sahib only laughs and rolls off her.

My Love is flattered. She is also afraid. She speaks of Khan-Sahib's greatness to everyone. She swears to me that she will not see the acrobat again. I fly around the rooms. Through the spray of the fountain. Wet. Cool. Fragrant. Again and again. I dive from the chandeliers into My Love's lap. I climb on her body and tweak her hair. She kisses my beak like before. I am melting... green... green.

She has grown plump in her happiness. Her belly shows. My Love is almost six months pregnant. She feels safe.

"He's coming!" I sense Khan-Sahib. "Bind his beak," My Love tells Gulabi. She is having her bath, stroking her belly when he walks in. Unannounced. When he sees her large belly, Khan-Sahib's eyes shine. She drapes a dupatta to protect her nakedness. My Love is blushing. Paddling her legs in the water while the dupatta floats around her. "Begum, you look like a child when you are with child." He roars with laughter at his own joke. Dai too laughs so heartily that her cheeks shake. I squawk. Khan-Sahib plucks me from the tank edge and throws me into the water. "Let it be your companion till we return," he says. "We are hunting with His Excellency."

"Come to me, my love," she calls to me after he has left. "Comfort me, my love," she says, "I am so scared." I fly to her lap. I eat from her hand while she strokes me. Just like before. I close my eyes. Feel her caress me. "We must be careful," she says, her lips to my head. "All my hopes I carry in my belly!" She summoned Dai. "I never want to see that man again," she whispers. "I will pay him off," I heard Dai saying.

Dai is a clever woman. That night she broke an earthen water-pot kept near the veranda. And screamed, "Help! Thief! Thief!" Everyone awoke. All the candles were lit. The rooms were searched. No one was found. But the news spread. The guards at our door were doubled. The eunuch-guard was summoned. My Love shouts to him standing below in the garden. "Do your duty, or we will have your head," she told him.

My Love's skin has become translucent with her pregnancy. Her hair has grown longer. Her eyes are calm. She sits twirling her tresses between her fingers. Playing cards. Plying the astrologer woman with gifts for happy predictions. Ordering her maids to tell her stories. It is like before. Before the acrobat came. Before I saw My Love and Khan-Sahib together. I too feel calm.

Khan-Sahib presents My Love with a toy bird that sings. It is covered with jewels. Resident Sahib had given it to Khan-Sahib in exchange for Bi-Jan. My Love puts the toy bird in a new gilt cage. She winds the key on its back. Turning it again and again till it breaks.

Last night I sensed him. I fly to her pillow. Look into the dark of her ear and scream, "Wake up! Wake up, My Love! He's coming!" My Love sits up with a start. Her hand at her throat. Her eyes seem to tear apart in fear. She is sweating. "He's coming!" She sits alone on the wide bed. "Shhh!" she says. She waits. The chiks part. Moonlight slides in. The acrobat enters.

"How did you get through?" she asks. "I bribed the eunuch with your jewelled nutcracker," he says. My Love freezes. "I will say it was stolen. Now go. For your own safety, flee!" She lifts a necklace off her breast and holds it up. The acrobat takes it. "Not yet," he says. His hands are on her throat. Where is Dai? I peck his ear. "I can raise an alarm but I won't. Go, I command you," My Love said. Then she drops her head. It rolls on her neck like a stone. My Love is weeping.

"Please leave. I am carrying your son. He will be the next Alim. For your child's sake, go." The acrobat drops his hands from her throat. He catches her hands and kisses them. He kisses her feet. Her sex. Her stomach. Her shoulders. Her face. Her hands are crawling up his shoulders like crabs from either side. I know I am watching them together for the last time. I see through my left eye, the good one. Without winking. Silently.

"Now leave," she says, "immediately." My Love is sweating as if she had been in rain though she has hardly moved. Dai is at the bed. I hadn't seen her enter. Neither had they. "Never attempt to see me again," My Love says, "or I'll have you poisoned." She lifts his hand to her breast and holds it there. "You understand? Poisoned," she says. "I'll make sure of it," Dai

says. His hands are still on her breast. The acrobat looks from one woman to the other. I am watching him.

"He's coming! He's coming! He's coming!" I scream, wheeling. The acrobat rushes through the rooms to the balcony. But the eunuch is faster. The acrobat is trapped. He lies with his face to the ground at Khan-Sahib's feet, sobbing. "Dress," Khan-Sahib says. The acrobat comes back to the bed. He picks up his clothes. He dresses, shaking like clothes in a breeze. He walks back to Khan-Sahib. The eunuch lifts him. And throws him. Screaming. From the balcony.

I have not stirred. Like My Love. "Leave," says Khan-Sahib. Everyone withdraws. Dai walks behind the eunuch out of our rooms. Walks as if she were already a ghost. When they are gone, Khan-Sahib says, "Piece-of-the-Moon, in a few hours we leave for Calcutta with Resident Sahib. By evening our paan-daan will come to you. Our trusted maid will bring it. You will eat the paan. Only… you know it is poisoned."

My Love sits still till dawn. In shock. Outside, birds are singing. Koels. Sparrows. Mynas. The light is growing brighter. My Love still does not stir. I do not know what to do. I walk up her legs. Up her body, pecking her. I perch on her shoulders, cocking my head sideways to see her face. I call into her ear, "Wake up! Wake up, My Love!" My Love lifts me and holds me to her face. "You didn't warn me, my love," she says, "you should have warned me." Tears are spilling over her eyes. Her grip on my throat is very tight. I never wanted to be free. It's very tight. Very…

✎ The Sentence ✎

No, there is nothing to it.

Why, on the Mahanavami Festival there is slaughtering each day: one hundred and fifty sheep, twenty-four buffaloes. This goes on for all the eight days. On the ninth and final day, the numbers are doubled, while the King of Kings watches the axe come down, reclining on his throne strewn with

*rubies and seed pearls. It's over in one neat blow, each one. Blood drops leap
like rubies in the air, sweat flies off the arms of the butchers like a shower
of seed pearls, each time. There's never a false stroke. The butchers called to
officiate during the sacrifices are specialists. The Monarch of Monarchs is
kind, even to animals led for sacrificial slaughter.*

*No country can boast of better executioners. I should have nothing to
fear. Indeed, there is nothing to fear. Besides, I know the ritual. I have been
witness to it many a time; I have even acted as a second in case the arm
trembles at the final moment. It's all part of the job.*

*Tambivan, my captain, was the best. Were he alive, he certainly would
have been in charge of decapitating me tomorrow. But he died last month in
a duel. I have tried to get information from my jailers as to who will behead
me, but they don't know as yet. Otherwise they would surely inform me. We
guards are a fraternity, whether we are jailers, policemen, in the villages or
from palace security, like me; we stick by each other. For instance, I am not
to die a common death—hanging with a hook dug into my chin, dangling,
abused and teased by whoever passes by. That I know is a slow death.*

*Why, once a master criminal took four days to die while we pelted him
with offal as we passed by, all of us who had a hand in catching him. We
either had to catch him or make good the loss—which would have been
very costly. He had stolen a triple string diamond necklace with a single
sapphire pendant off the idol from the Hazara Rama temple. Now that
was audacious, stealing from the Monarch's private shrine. Our King didn't
send the man to the criminal courts; He himself pronounced the sentence. He
decided the death penalty should take place in public, so that the subjects of
His vast empire know His mighty arm punishes the wrongdoers, and protects
the good.*

*I already know my shame will be hidden; my family in the distant green
village need not lose their fields, nor their face. They will be told something
plausible—that I slipped from the ramparts while on duty, or lost my life
curbing a minor skirmish in some far-flung province. I have been told by my
superior officer not to worry on this count. Died in a duel, or drowned in*

the river while sporting—they will say something like this about me. It is heartening to know they will close ranks.

The only time our execution system faltered was during the killing of the traitor whose name shall not be taken. That was because the elephant was young, and this was its first killing. Goaded with spikes covered with chilli powder it charged twice, trumpeting, but did not trample him while he lay screaming. On the third charge it smashed his head, his brains slippery beneath its feet.

If my jailers knew, they would tell me, for certain. I think either Kampana or Vira Sinnu will be assigned the job. Kampana is probably better. After all, Kama-Nayakan, the Chief of the Guards, had a certain fondness for me. He spotted me lying exhausted and victorious after a boxing bout on the red sand of the gymnasium's courtyard and immediately had me promoted from junior guard to second-level officer. I exchanged my leather whip for a sword and a stick, I was shifted from guard duty on the seventh and outermost ramparts of the palace walls to the fourth. This was when my troubles began.

How many months ago did I first lay eyes on the wench? When I have so little time before me that each breath chokes, how is it that time past runs before my eyes like a swollen stream, and all I can remember are moments? I remember clearly: my duty was over, the second shift was to begin, and I was waiting to be relieved. I was standing at the Muslim-style watchtower, the one to the west, and I looked down.

The richest and most famous courtesans were sporting in the bathing tank that lies to the northwest, and we guards always look at meat meant for the immortals. Why not? Being a palace guard has advantages. That day our Monarch had wished for pleasures other than those provided by His zenana, and these public women were summoned. He was late. The courtesans were in the water, playing ball, singing, vying for the best position, and there she stood on the steps of the bathing ghat, holding the umbrella, not deigning to get wet though it was obvious that her mistress was bathing.

*To tell the truth, I didn't notice her till after our Monarch made his
choice for the night: Gangadevi, renowned for her expertise in the four kinds
of poetry and playing of the veena. For it is well known that He is a scholar
and poet Himself. On His way up the steps of the bathing tank He noticed
her standing aloof and playfully threw a handful of water at her. My eye
followed His action. The handmaiden He had singled out for an instant,
she I wanted.*

*By the time the third watch was over I found out to whom she was
bound. We guards have a way of sharing information. She was Gangadevi's
umbrella-carrier. I gathered my money, put on my best clothes, had myself
massaged with sesame oil and perfumed with a pod of sandal paste before I
strolled down Soolai Bazaar Street, where the courtesans and rich merchants
live, their grand houses separated by walls of plastered rubble. Gangadevi's
establishment is well known. Her house front is covered with paintings of
panthers, tigers, lions and peacocks. Gangadevi's velvet-draped couch placed
on the street side was empty: she was busy. But Vanithamma was there,
leaning against the couch, chewing betel nut, and looking at the sky.*

*On the very first night, she told me about the Monarch's bedchamber,
for we male guards are not allowed beyond the fourth enclosure; eunuchs
and women warriors protect the interiors. She had escorted Gangadevi into
the palace interior just recently. The bedroom's dome is gold-plated, gems in
heart-shaped designs encrust the walls, around the pillars wind streams of
emeralds and diamonds, the lion-paw legs of the bed are of gold, seed pearls
run as railings a span high, the mattress is covered with black satin, and
overhead hangs a canopy of embossed gold. For His feet are four cushions of
black Mecca velvet, tasselled with pearls; His mosquito net is framed by rods
of carved silver; His spittoon is made of gold. She spoke of such opulence
that I felt dizzy and my bones seem to drip.*

*The wench said that one day she will sleep on that bed; she told all
this to me even as we were shifting positions. After I finished, I twirled
my moustache and told her not to get grand ideas just because one of the
Monarch's junior queens was a courtesan he knew in his earliest youth. She*

laughed. She was disregarding me, a second-level guard. I left my mark on her shoulder. She would not agree to see me for three weeks though I agreed to raise her fees.

Not that we bother about such things. I amused myself watching children daring each other on goat-back races through the market-place, I watched the nobles go hawking. I gambled too, with my new companions, the second-rung guards, for one must establish rank. I visited other dancing girls, those who had known me as a junior guard; they welcomed me with wine and song, I was well pleased. Once His Majesty left for an elephant hunt; I was almost chosen to accompany the rear guard. I paid my respects at all the important temples of this great town of Vijayanagara; I even gave a silver coin to the Virupaksha Temple. I watched the women wrestlers circle each other in the fairground pits, iron circlets in hand, determined to win. I passed my time.

By now they should know who is to behead me at dawn tomorrow. Possibly Vira Sinnu. He too has a good hand, and a good build, though not as good as mine. His shoulders look strong. He should be able to do it quickly. One-Stroke Tambivan, my captain was called. If he were alive, why, I would not be thinking such thoughts. Not that I am afraid. But a military man likes to plan in advance, that is all. If only I had thought...

But it happened too quickly. A gleam of red I went for. And that too on the seventh day of the Mahanavami Festival, when the senses are drugged by wealth and ceremony. By the green and scarlet velvets streaming from the wooden scaffoldings erected to contain the milling crowds near the Hall of Victory. By the fireworks displays, which burn brighter than the stars. By the procession of dancing horses, caparisoned elephants, the court ladies laden with so much jewellery that some have to be supported. By the vision of the King of Kings robed in gold and white silk, blazing with diamonds, a flame Himself at the centre of the Hall of Victory.

I was tired carrying out my new duties, always on my feet, tired of seeing that no one steps out of line: nobles, Arab horse traders, even the eunuchs have to stand behind the lines we guards demarcate; the courtesans too await their

*turn to dance, only moving out when we allow them. We keep everyone under
control. I held my stick in front of Gangadevi, telling her to wait her turn. I
don't think I touched her person, not even a bell on her fifth golden girdle. I
just wanted Vanithamma to see who I was after the way she had treated me.
I wanted her to hear my voice above the music and the crowds.*

*Vanithamma hadn't seen me for three weeks, saying she wouldn't see men
who are rough with her. But she consented to eat with me. I took her to the
street of eating-houses, and paid for the highest-priced eating slab—seven
hollows on the stone table, each filled with food.*

"Vana," I said to her, "eat your fill."

"Who gave you permission to call me Vana?" she asked.

I laughed, "I gave myself permission! What do you want?"

*"Fish," she said. She ate greedily, sucking at the fish bones, the pearl of
her nose ring quaking maddeningly with each mouthful.*

*I asked her to meet me in the Moorish Quarters, in the fragrant grove
of orange and mango and areca palms, in three days' time when the town
bell struck seven. She agreed. Amidst the sweet running canals, I waited till
the town bell struck eight; then nine. The waiting ate my innards. I paced
the thick grove of the Moorish Quarters, hearing the foreigners sing in their
strange language. Each vowel sounded like a bell that encased me in its
sound; burying me till only my head stuck above ground for a maddened
elephant to trample.*

*But I was not fearful. I knew I could meet her when the courtesans came
to the Palace Square each Saturday for the ritual dance. And there I was,
standing in my place, one hand in my sleeve, the other on the hilt of my sword
before that hall which has paintings of women archers. Gangadevi's litter,
draped in sapphire damask, passed by. Vana followed, spinning Gangadevi's
scarlet and gold umbrella between her fingers, the coral bead armlets and
bangles on her arms spinning, spinning me into webs I could not see, round
and round, like the walls of this circular prison. I think I'm spinning in this
dark airless cell. By now they should have told me who is going to do the
job tomorrow. Maybe it will be Aindan, the drunkard. Maybe they haven't*

come by because they don't want to give bad news. I should bang on the door and find out. But what does everyone say about me? "Oh, Pedha Mudhiaya, he'll go with a swagger." I, Pedha Mudhiaya, I am not scared. As I was led to this cell, I even joked about it. I said I'd be finally cut down to their size. The jailers laughed with me.

The bitch. The last time, the way she treated me. I should have killed her. First, she beat me easily at chess. I was prepared to play by the rules—let the wench win a bit, then take over, just like in the battle of love. But she wasn't going to lose. When I was ready to enter her, she told me to hurry. A captain is coming to see her, she said. She started humming. I feel myself withering. She sat on my lap, saying, "Come on, hurry up." I had to play for time. "Vanithamma, who do you think you are?" I squeezed her nape. She flung my hand away. "You'd better go to the poorer quarters. Maybe you can perform there." She says this to me? Furious, I thrust into her. Midway, she pulled a flower from her hair and started twirling it in front of her face. The bitch was moving, yes, but she's resting an arm on my shoulder and twirling a marigold like an umbrella against my face. My rhythms are spoilt. I couldn't perform. I sweated. I slipped out of her. "See? Go to the poorer quarters. Or get more money if you need this much time." That's why I picked up the ring without thinking—to fling on her face, to get her down. The bitch.

Why haven't they told me yet that Aindan is supposed to behead me tomorrow? The pot-bellied drunk can't kill a goat with one blow even if it is held down. His wrist trembles when he lifts an axe, and he can barely hold a broadsword. "Quiver-Quiver," that's what we call him, me and my men. Ha ha. My head is hurting. Ha ha. Hurt, head, hurt. You are still mine! Ha. Ha. I, Pedha Mudhiaya, the swaggerer, I'll swagger into the execution chamber. Ha ha. I'm sweating. I must petition the King to allow windows in the jail. Does the Great Monarch want his condemned men to die of perspiration?

It was just lying there on the floor, gleaming red, like a small, beheaded head, ha ha. No one was about. I picked it up and tucked it into my waistband without thinking. Everyone had left for the midnight feast. The corridors were quiet and deserted. The sweeper women hadn't started their work. I was tired. Such hard work for seven days, and that too on an empty belly. Only one meal at night. When I was a child, on the ninth night of the Mahanavami Festival my mother would feed us curd-rice with raisins. Once a year we had raisins. I didn't think...

I got back to my Quarters—the better guard's quarters near the elephant stables—dropped the ring into my box, and went to sleep. That was all. I was tired. The next day I was so busy that I forgot about it. No, I wished to know if anyone had noticed, anyone had made a claim. I decided to watch and wait. I was in the same spot, doing guard duty all morning on the eighth day of the Festival. There seemed nothing amiss. During the three o'clock rituals when the nobles were presenting their salaams to His Majesty, they arrested me. There was no time to think.

I had wanted to give back the ring. The whole morning I wanted nothing more than to give back the ring. I felt it beating in my box like a heart, like my heart is beating this entire morning. But I was on duty. Couldn't leave. Isn't there anyone on duty? Tell me, who is going to behead me tomorrow? Can't you hear me? Guards!

They had me watched. It was my duty to report anything found. They searched the dormitories of all the guards who were stationed at the places where the whore had passed and danced the day before. In mine they found her wretched ring. I should have at least thought of hiding it. Should have dug a hole and buried it. Thrown it in the elephant stables on my way to work. I don't know why I didn't. I thought no one would suspect me. After all, it could have been lost anywhere. Even outside the palace. But they detected the theft of a ruby ring—one of great value to the owner Gangadevi and, unfortunately, also to the Chief of Guards, Kama-Nayakan.

They aren't telling me because they think I'll shit if I hear the name Aindan. Someone hear me! Tell me who is going to kill me tomorrow. Guards, can't you hear me beating on the door? Bastards, tell me! I'm not scared.

I, Pedha Mudhiaya, I wasn't scared when they led me to the military court. I heard the roll of drums. I saw the coloured umbrellas being carried ahead of the Administrator of Justice. Vittappar, the Chief of Archers was the Military Judge. He mounted the platform and pronounced the sentence that my right arm be cut off. I knew the sentence even before it was passed. The right arm of thieves is cut off, their property confiscated. I was not scared. I had prepared myself for this.

I was not prepared for Gangadevi. It is so hot I'm sweating rivers. My head's hurting. It's dark. So hot, it's difficult to breathe. Gangadevi. She had me summoned to Kama-Nayakan's chamber. I was thrown on the floor, face down, arms stretched ahead, begging for mercy. Slowly I raised my eyes.

Embroidered shoes with gold throngs. Anklets of seed pearls. A finely pleated skirt of scarlet brocade. Five girdles of gold stretching from mid-thigh to waist. On the hands, the rings. The ruby ring. The single ruby wound inside a cobra of gold, seed pearls dripping from its hood. Bracelets of gold and diamonds. An upper cloth of striped purple and yellow silk. A blouse of green Mecca velvet. A golden collar of emeralds and diamonds. Earrings of sapphire and ruby. In her hair a burst of seed pearl flowers.

"Lord," she said. Her voice was melodious, like nectar oozing it poured over her body to the earth on which I lay. "I am not worthy enough to praise you. You are Kama-Nayakan, Chief of the Guards who the King who rules the three seas and all the lands Himself has honoured. On your right foot you wear the golden anklet of honour. On your mighty shoulders rests the silken scarf of bravery which the Monarch Himself presented you. You have even been permitted to kiss His exalted feet."

She paused. Each hair on my body rose. It rises now in remembrance. "One of your own men commits a grievous theft, and you Lord, Protector of the People, stern and wise, you, Lord, permit him to get away with the loss of an arm?" She laughed. Its tinkling made my teeth shiver. "I am but a common courtesan in your realm, what would I know of the Law? But I think such a heinous crime demands greater punishment."

I broke down in front of my Chief and confessed I never wanted to steal her ring. Had I known it was hers I would never have touched it. Never. It was not a theft. Only a mistake, please, Sire. Without raising my head from the ground, I begged mercy from my superior. I begged.

"Pray forgive me," Gangadevi intervened before Kama-Nayakan could speak. "Your Laws of Justice are too intricate for one like me to hope to understand. But did I hear this junior officer of yours, Lord, say had he known it was mine he would not have stolen it? And what if it were someone else's? Would it then be any less grievous a crime? Are your Laws so slight, Lord, as to permit such an easy escape?" She laughed again. "I present my salaams to you, Great Lord, and await your next visit to my humble abode," she said and withdrew, salaaming Kama-Nayakan with each step she took back. My eyes followed her feet. Embroidered shoes with golden throngs stepping back. Golden roses with purple centres retreating. Scarlet brocade sweeping the floor. Retreating.

I was returned to my cell. The food is so bad I cannot eat. If I eat at all, I vomit. The food has given me acute diarrhoea. My head pounds. It is airless. I cannot breathe. Who is going to behead me in a few hours? They hear my screams but don't answer. It must be "Quiver-Quiver" Aindan. So hot my temples are pounding! I'm not scared. I, Pedha Mudhiaya, I am going to swagger into the execution room. I'll show them. So hot! My whole body is sweating. So hot my body is paining.

Well before the next dawn—that is yesterday—Kama-Nayakan sought out the Monarch. This I heard. The King of Kings awakes in darkness. He has his massage, indulges in swordplay for an hour then wrestles with the best men. After which He rides. It is common knowledge that this is the hour to petition Him. Kama-Nayakan, Chief of the Guards, also went like a commoner with his petition: that the military court's decision be overturned, that I get the death penalty and be publicly executed for setting a bad example. He went with his raised spear lengthened by a branch of the peepul tree. He went to where the Monarch was riding and fell to the ground as is the custom for the petitioner who has no other recourse. The Monarch saw him, and stopped. He heard him.

The pain in my left arm, running from shoulder to hand and back, again and again. Heat squeezes my breath. By whose arm am I going to die? I cannot bear this pain.

The Monarch of Monarchs said, "Execute him quietly. Let not the rumour spread that within Our Empire, Our own palace guards steal. What confidence will Our subjects have in Our justice if its very safe-keepers become thieves? If they loot the people they are meant to protect? Kill him quietly before the next dawn. May this vile pestilence perish forever with him from Our lands." Thus the Monarch spoke. It was reported to me. Before dawn He spoke thus.

I did not steal. I swear, I swear. Merely helped myself to a small ring lying on the floor. I would have given it back, had I known what it meant…

I do not want it. I do not want this growing pain in my arm. Which arm will execute me? How much hacking is it going to take before I am beheaded? How much pain? Tightness. My chest… collapsing. Pain. In my heart. Squeezing pain. Pain in—

❧ Illusions ❧

Illusions. Illusions.

I see through them as I see through water, though at times the play of light bewitches. When I leap, the spangling glimmer on the surface. Below, noon-rays plough the riverbed with quivering shafts of light and seem to show a path. The cold stirrings of dawn slant in, layer by layer, and quicken the waters. At night, Kashi's wick lamps bob on their mirror image down the river, till one cannot say which is reflection and which real. The flames of Prahalad burning ghat rage orange like a dye over dark waters, and embers twitch on partially burnt corpses tossed into the river, corpses whose atmas are doomed because of their incompletely burnt desires. It's all a play of light, false.

Everyone says Kashi is the Luminous City that illuminates Truth and reveals Reality. I say it veils itself as a city of pleasure and trade, dharma and liberation but it is, in fact, a miasma of ignorance. All mistake the apparent for the real. I alone am alert. I never shut my eyes.

Being a fish it is easy to remember that this world is maya, a gigantic illusion, for metaphors drift past one. For instance, though it appears constant my world the holy Ganga, is always flowing but never the same. Also, withered flower garlands, bloated buffalo carcasses, the great city's excreta mingle in the holy river every moment as a warning: Beware of attachments which cloud the mind.

However, without exception, my relatives frolic in ignorance, darting after food and transient pleasures. I never join them. Not for me the false security of comfort in numbers, the fleeting contact of mouths and gills, the heedless hide-and-seek between waterweeds of Time. This life is a chance one is given to seek Eternal Knowledge. I have therefore named myself Vidya-Shakti-Matsya, Power-of-Knowledge-Fish. I am determined to be true to my name.

I never speak. I open and shut my mouth soundlessly, repeating the sacred word Om with each gulp of water. This is why I have come so far. When I was a semi-transparent newborn, my eldest sister—I have eighty-three brothers and sisters—swam up to me. "O brother, swim upstream with us. We hear a wealthy merchant sect, recently converted from Buddhism, has built an ashram on the banks. Food will be plentiful."

I remained swimming on the spot. "We are abandoning this patch of river, brother," she urged, darting in front of me. "Youngest brother, the shoal has decided either you join us or you will be forsaken. Come!" But the shoal had forsaken The Shining Path. How can I combat such blindness? "Ungrateful wretch!" she cursed. Her greed and anger were clouding my clarity. I turned tail and headed downstream where the crocodiles reside; I would be safer among them. "Say something you heartless fraud!" Those were her last words to me.

I do not grieve my eldest sister's demise in that foolish upstream adventure. It would have been a pointless affliction, and waste must not be tolerated. When I fled to reside with the crocodiles, I developed eating habits that marked me as depraved. I eat the minimum to sustain this earthly shell which houses the atma. My only fear is that I may die before I attain my goal of total Knowledge. Not an instant must be lost.

I pose a simple question: Why eat living organisms, be they slime, larvae or insects when dead bodies abound in this holy town of Kashi? Besides, crocodiles are gluttons. As they tear at the floating semi-burnt bodies, bits of flesh tumble unnoticed from their gargantuan teeth to the riverbed. Morsels of kidneys, intestines, spongy lungs, hearts. Each day the waste is enough to feed twenty shoals of fish. Deep below, I lie in wait till the froth and frenzy clears, till the shadows of thrashing crocodiles part. Alert, I dart upwards to nibble the morsels sinking around me, sinking like rain into the Ganga. The water becomes cloudy with food—shreds of white tissue, squiggles of fat, blood, threads of congealed blood. This feeding ground is safe, non-violent and healthy.

The minnows were responsible for gossip mongering. Being swift and inconsequential, minnows swim virtually undetected. Soon my entire shoal surrounded me, fins flapping furiously, tails lashing the water. The leader— my granduncle—denounced me. He pronounced that I was disgracing the entire clan; that the august body of the Ganga Matsya Panchayat had threatened to excommunicate our caste. We are highborn—the streak of silver running from nose to dorsal fin grants us many privileges. Yet I had apparently adopted the practices of the distant delta-dwelling scavengers.

Their illogical agitation was nauseous to behold. When they realised I was unshakeable, they offered a compromise: they would leave part of the pilgrims' offerings for me if I would forbear to eat the crocodiles' leftovers.

However, I could not accept this suggestion. Though this world is unreal pilgrims feed us fish only to gain spiritual benefits. Redemption cannot come from such easy, monetary rituals. Besides, if I agreed, I would be indebted both to the guilt-ridden pilgrims and my finned relatives, chortling righteously about the sacrifices they make to feed me. But I exist to purify the universe of falsehood. "Repent or you will be outcast!" my clan-father puffed. The shoal paused, tense, straining. His eyes dilated with rage, his gill movements were not coordinated. He forced an air bubble out from the pit of his stomach and turned. The entire shoal turned and left. Soon I saw them leaping out of the water, nipping each other, twirling around weeds, playing frivolous games. Pretending to have fun.

As an outcast my time is my own. Each day I watch the shadow of a boat that ferries a poet from the holy side of the bank to the unholy deserted side. This poet is said to sing revelatory verses. But, being fixated on one idol of God, he is still caught in the Illusion of Form. Yet people worship him. Certain thirsty fish follow the wake of his boat hoping to catch snatches of his songs, hoping to be saved through another's quest. Utter falsehood!

I know why the poet journeys to the unclean shore: To visit a woman, a public woman at that, who inspires him. By moonlight she awaits him, her hair piled with combs of mother-of-pearl and silver so it looks like a crown; her skirt mould her thighs as if the golden designs are embossed on her flesh, from buttocks to inner legs; her breasts glint with necklaces of crystal, ivory and coral. I swim at her hem as she wades thigh-deep into the river to receive him. She wears three pairs of anklets. The uppermost are bead-like, filled with oil of sandalwood, which seeps into the water with each step she takes, while the red lac painted on the soles of her feet bleeds into the current like passion. I have watched her feet so closely I know each dent on her anklets and snake-shaped toe-rings. Each dawn she once again wades into the river, clothed only in a white muslin wrap. Her black tresses spread to her calves. I have swum between the streams of her hair, perfumed with intoxicants. She notices nothing. In deep salutation she waits, head bowed, till his boat departs. Then she turns. That is when one sees she's a hunchback.

It is said that she is not an image but a lens through which he focuses on Ultimate Reality. It is said that through her enslavement he sees the bondage of all life to its desires—pleasure, attachment, and its reaction, further attachment, greater ignorance. The terrible mystery of maya dissolves as he dissolves into her. Indeed, indeed!

On the return trip, as the sun's rays rise over his satiated head, illumination bubbles on his lips, it is said. As stinking gas bubbles out of decaying logs, I say. Just the other day I heard him singing:

> *O Beloved*
> *I rise to Your Light*
> *As the Ganga swells with sunshine*
> *Let me drink Your Divine Love!*
> *Release me!*
> *O Beloved.*
> *Hold me in Yourself*
> *As the Ganga absorbs rain.*
> *Make me part of Your Divine Beauty!*
> *Release me!*

What a thirst this poet has! I smile with self-knowledge for was I not almost baited when I was young?

It was high noon. It was the spawning season. Suddenly I spied her; she filled my body like a flock of swans alighting on a river. She swam below me, her mouth slowly closing and opening, her scales shimmering as she sunned herself below the river's spangling surface. At each turn she exposed her smooth silvery underbelly; my senses filled with her sleek, rippling white flesh; the transparency of her side fins, the firm delicacy of her tail fin, her gills opening and closing so gently. I was meditating on whether any of the three Essences—The Pure, The Active, The Dark—could possibly be conceived unalloyed in a Form when I saw her. I though The Pure was presenting itself to me.

No sooner did she realise she had caught my attention than she raced between stems of water-weeds, hiding between rocks, breaking the river's surface, leaping, sliding slowly down, shining, flipping. I darted after her, I could see nothing but her. I was all body, only body, surging across the river. She was tiring. I was on her. "Radiant One, do what you wish with me!" she whispered. "I cannot escape your might." She spoke, and her witchery vanished. I saw the net of illusion her body had spread over me.

Another moment of silence from her and my sperm would have leapt out. My quest for Knowledge would have been doomed, all for a single instant of common pleasure. I would have been doomed to joining the shoal. To breeding and craving to lead the shoal, become party to salubrious tales: who is making it with whom, how the Blue Stripes are planning to take over the river. I would have doomed myself to the closure of my mind.

I fled, my body still mad with desire. I swam away from this monstrous female evil that had embedded itself into my every scale. I dug myself into the soft mud sanctuary of the holy Ganga basin, praying. Heedless to the great cries of my body. It cried a long time, buried in cool mud, cooling its insane desire.

I thought about her dispassionately. Her wanton appearance in my life was a test that I passed excellently, a test that had the poet flaying in its throes. Also, I had abjured this female in her moment of victory. Being unused to chastity her body would still be raging for mine. She will die with this longing and be doomed to many lowly births. I drew solace from these thoughts though I never feel disgust.

I dislike crowds but each day I am faced with more crowds, more ignorance. However, on some languid moonlit nights when my shoal swims past looking like rays of moonlight underwater, I feel a small wrench. But the mind must be controlled, though this is as difficult as harnessing the winds that shape the Ganga's waves.

The town has grown rapidly. Petty traders, artisans from distant lands, teachers of Sanskrit, wrestlers looking for patronage, wily accountants throng the streets besides the pilgrims, sants and sadhus who inundate the bathing ghats, a hundred more each season. The King has ordered the expansion of both the burning and bathing ghats. Wild elephants, musth running down the temples of the males, are being driven from their wallowing spots further south by the sound of drums, hammers and axes. Panthers and boar follow, though I hear that tame deer still roam the public parks, and at dawn when I leap I still see peacocks crouch on rows of naga-snake statues that line the steps of Chauki Ghat.

On the numerous festival days, on Amavash, Poornimas and the cold month of Kartik pilgrims descend on the bathing ghats. A dip purifies the outside, a sip sanctifies the inside, for the Ganga is said to be a liquid form of Knowledge. But I know what the multitudes come to attain!

For tradesmen and courtesans whose eyes are fixed on the money pouches of pilgrims, Dualism does not exist; there is only One Reality. The sportsmen, astrologers, scholars and artisans are no better: their One Reality is the patron. As for my scores of relatives their world of illusion swells with the billowing clothes of pilgrims, chest-deep in water, feeding them offerings. I know the pilgrims. Even as they pray they secretly piss into the river. The heat and stink of urine is horrific, a sudden acidic current catching one unawares, and one has to dive, and behold their feet: toenails dirty, heels chapped, ankles swollen and bruised, skin dry, weather-beaten.

It is said that pilgrim's feet are to be venerated as much as the feet of the idol, for both are washed by faith. Purified by crossing the vindictive waters of the everyday, pilgrims arrive on the riverbank of vast devotion, callused. Behold the sanctity of corns! Indeed, on important festival days when temple doors are thrown open for darshan, their cry—unanimous, spontaneous—heaves the Ganga basin. I marvel at this easy transcendence; I marvel even more at the temporality of their liberation. Having sighted their

*God, they revert to their true selves: bartering, bickering, gossiping, farting.
Not a moment of true silence do they know even as the process of decay
progresses through their bodies. Unlike me, they lack the courage required for
the search for clarity.*

*I have ventured between the fringed skirts of women, nibbled at the
sacred thread of priests, slipped between the hairy armpits of men. Large
heads above water, they mumble prayers, then the holy dip. The bleary-eyed
aged spluttering, sputum trailing their jaws. Blood flowering from gums of
some Tantriks. The snot, both thick and slimy, as runny-nosed children
are ducked in by their mothers. The pus from pimples, flakes from scabs,
putrescent liquid leaked from sores and, of course, the lepers. This is what
they swallow for salvation: each other's excreta. Literally, metaphorically,
spiritually. It's disgusting.*

*Once, I escaped certain death. The Big Fish, the terror of the Ganga
almost got me. I heard its teeth close behind me in the water. I dived into the
water-weeds. Its greyness loomed above the green. Its nose, its bright teeth
pushing through. It turned its head this way and that, searching for me. I
dug myself into the roots, stirring silt; I willed my trembling body be still.
It lashed the weeds with its tail. The weeds flayed as if in a storm, like my
heart within me. It circled a long time overhead, then left. The Big Fish. I
remained there, half-buried for a long time for though my mind was without
fear my body continued to shake.*

*With every passing moment my need to gain Knowledge grows stronger.
My only fear is that I may die before gaining Absolute Knowledge in the
form that I am now invested. But obviously I am not meant to die a common
death, though death takes many forms in this world of illusion.*

*The flood came suddenly, high up from the mountains, raking the bed, raising
our part of the river to the skies, a gigantic paddle-blow, knocking the water
from my lungs. Roaring.*

*I am lucky. I am meditating deep within the crevice of a boulder lodged
in the basin when it comes. Like water snakes awakening and striking it*

comes. *The boulder shudders, heaves and rises. It somersaults with me within it, faster and faster. Like a pebble it spins; I am trapped in my life-saving cage. My brain bangs inside my head. Scales scrape off, my right fin tears, I am bleeding.*

I am shuddering with the rock as it crashes to a stop, upside-down, against the wall of underwater boulder we fish call the Unknown Himalayas that is situated at the confluence of the Varana and Ganga rivers. The mountains hold, stone against furious water. I am trapped upside-down, I do not know how long. My brain begins to feel heavy, very heavy, like a stone inside me, sinking. I lose consciousness.

When I come to, it is quieter. The river has breached the embankments; it swathes Kashi in swirling soiled currents, like a coiling serpent. Engorged, it will flow towards the ocean, a serpent heading home. For the first time I call to my shoal. There is no response. They have been swept away, my shoal of seven hundred and eighty.

Trapped upside-down, my gills are susceptible to being blocked by fine silt. I am having difficulty breathing. I wriggle like a worm on my back up the crevice; progress is slow and tiring. Finally, weak sunlight curls through whirlpools above my head. I know the worst is over.

The tow pushes me. I am being pushed sideways. It is an odd sensation. The world is coming at me from the left; through my right eye I see it recede. I am being pushed down the Varana instead of upstream, to the higher reaches of the Ganga as the river loops itself around Kashi in the normal course of its flow. Then I remember an ancient text: the flooded Ganga pushes its northern tributary, the Varana, back on its own course, to gush up its tributary the Matsyodari River, which swells back to its source, the Matsyodari Lake. Deluged, the source reverses direction and flushes westwards, into the Mandakini Lake which, seething, plunges down the rain-drainage system, discharging itself back into the Ganga at the Dashashvamedha Ghat. As the Ganga feeds and ferments it makes a gigantic anti-clockwise churning. I wonder: am I, too, to be churned through several incarnations before Illumination rises in me?

Again remembered texts come to my rescue: When the Ganga rises and churns around itself, eating Kashi, the land remaining above water is said to be fish-shaped. A fish-like Kashi alone is elevated and saved. This is a good omen. I need not fear. My time of Illumination is at hand. All illusions will clear. In my form as a fish I could become part of the Brahman, the Eternal Reality. In just a little more time.

This is a unique opportunity to view the city. I am being shoved sideways up Kashi's alleyways, big and small, above the waterlogged homes of ministers and courtesans marked by clipped hedges. I dodge branches of ashoka and peepul trees streaming with cloth and the mangled bodies of cats, jackals and tortoises. A mass of peacocks had been smashed between the aerial roots of a large banyan. Fans open, they hang like a tattered blue net, feathers beating to the pulse of the river, bills open, pink throats gaping. Encrusted with tiny dead timi fish, carcasses of rats, snakes, monkeys flicker above my head. Corpses of deer, fighting rams and cattle pass like stiff cloud shadows on the surface. One is large. It had been a temple elephant. The thick chain of bells around its neck drags its head below water. Strays standing on it tear at its intestines. The Buddhists were right about one thing: This is a floating world!

The waters of Matsyodari Lake are muddy, as if the lakebed has been bubbled up to release spores of silt. I see bodies impaled on semi-buried statues of nagas and yakshis, rows of which line pleasure gardens. Kashi's arbours of creepers, buds intact, tendrils weaving in the current, trap loosened hives. I see conical beehives below me, leaking honey. The water tastes sweet.

This Varanasi is indeed the city of Lord Shiva the Destroyer. I haven't as yet spotted a single living human being. How can Kashi's entire populace be dead? If so, where are the corpses? Mandakini Lake froths like golden lace above my head, embroidered with charcoal, ash and bones lifted off the surrounding cremation grounds. I am the only living soul, if one excludes the flies and mosquitoes humming overhead. But these are too un-evolved to be counted.

Turbulence. This is the cascade towards Dashashvamedha Ghat, towards the Ganga. I must ready myself, steady myself. Yes. The flood thuds down the rain-drainage canals like a living monster, thuds down the steps. I am spiralling. I am tossed into air. The air sears my lungs, burns the lining. The air! Back in the Ganga, murmuring deeply. Sweetly. Soothing waters run from nose to tail. I am on course.

Bathing and burning ghats bleed below me. Waterfront shrines run into each other, temple spires seem to bend and dissolve in the current. I am being pushed up the bend into the Varana River which brims into palaces and shops. Those below are the sweetmeat sellers' shops for fried sweets buoyed by seeping ghee escape through window bars like quivering bubbles of white, yellow and pink. Next, before my eyes rise bright lac circles like hollow promises. I slip through the bangles. That looks like a street of magnificent eels. Reams of rainbow silk, gem-encrusted brocade, gold and silver zari drift through doors and windows with the abandon of luxury. All waste! This alley is still. It must house shops of brassware and clay toys that sit on the shelves, quiet as stones. Ahead, the water flower with colour, as if it were a riotous Holi festival. Those are the streets of the painters, dyers, kumkum-sellers. Worst of all are the perfumeries. Even as they bathed, the oily perfumes of Kashi's wealthy coated my scales like a curse. But where are the corpses of these busy traders of the ephemeral?

Above me I see two wrestlers, caught in a stranglehold, arms locked around each other's throats as death caught them. The pair seem like an elongated spider, eight-limbed, slowly rising from the fighting ground. Here are another two, hooked to a street torch; the dead mother still combing her dead daughter's hair, longer than their black-tasselled shawls. And there, another couple; lovers trapped in an embrace, eyes still holding each other, their silver-mottled garments rolling around them in the current like tongues. Floating ahead, the corpse of a bald boy, rice grains choking his nostrils, his small arms and legs outstretched as if he were running to his mother.

I am approaching Kapalamochana Kund. It is said even Lord Shiva, when he sinned, found release in this ancient spring. Were I not so determined,

I too would have been irredeemably polluted by the ignorance, lust and death in this place. Besides, I am certain I will be united with the Ultimate Reality, that very fount, in this very birth. The signs are apparent. But what is this?

Soft-legged steeds, still pulling chariots, jam this large street. They would have been galloping, rearing, neighing, till death silenced them. They are still in harness, straining in death to pull heavy chariots to the surface; mouths open, tails and manes flying wild in the water. Flight is useless in the face of death.

If what I see is true, there is some cause for sorrow—though of course one must not be involved. Strips of palm-leaf manuscripts escape through a ventilator. It is a library. Palm-leaf scripts throb in water. No doubt this is an illustrated copy of Vatsayayana's base work Kamasutra; *ahead is the Arthashastra of the supreme strategist Kautilya. A few have turned soggy with the weight of paint, dark ink, gold dust and age. Newer ones, barely inscribed, lift, reverting to their nature as palm fronds, light. Some have ivory covers, enamel worked, and are bound by silk tassels. One lies in a casket of gold filigree. This must undoubtedly be Guru Sankaracharya's texts. Most are bound in red cloth, seeping Knowledge darkly through the cloth into the Ganga. The great library is empty of human corpses.*

What is lighter than scum, but more armoured than a warship?

What is more ruthless than lightning, but more pliant than river grass?

Hungrier than a crane, but more devious than a crab?

The mind of an intellectual.

How apt. The famed scholars of Kashi have fled with the slimmest of margins, leaving behind scores of wooden clogs that bob alongside manuscripts. Sacrilegious!

Ahead, through an open window, I see a cow's head emerge, with eyes dark and soft as if enraptured by Lord Krishna's flute. Close up, I see fear trapped in its large eyes. The shed is full of floating cows: flared nostrils, distended stomachs, enlarged udders. Still tied to posts, their legs frozenly paw at the current in attempted stampede. I see a most curious sight: In a corner, a naked toddler has been lashed to a huge stone pestle, obviously as punishment. In the hurry the mother forgot him, or she is dead. The dark, chubby child floats on all fours, still tied to the pestle, his curls dancing in the water. How odd: The dead toddler seems to be smiling. A mere distortion, due to this muddy light.

This is a dead end. I shall swim to Omkara temple to do my own Kashi pilgrimage. For I have been kept alive to unite with Ultimate Reality in this form, as a fish. Illusions are of the past; the Shining Path lies ahead, waiting to receive me.

Indeed it is very calm. I push my head above water. Dawn. Sky and water meet in misty light. A strange stillness pervades the scene as if all life has quietened to the last stage, when the Illusion of Form begins to dissolve and separate from Luminous Knowledge. I am the sole survivor. I thirst for the Godhead waiting to receive me.

What's this? A mess of yak hair drifting on the river surface, from temple flywhisks. Grey, white, opulent; I am netted. My mouth and eyes have pushed through as are my gills. Yak hair gathers around my tail fin like a woman's skirt! I can't lash free of it. But what is this?

Above, this sparkling gem. It must be the Gem of Truth for me to swallow and become Radiant. I leap. It catches my gullet. The pain! The pain of Realisation. The immensity of this pain. It's a lie! It's a fishhook.

All Knowledge is illusion. Pain. Pain. The hook in my throat drags me, I follow. It drags, drags though the lining of my jaws, my eyes, my brains.

The ripping iron of the hook. The upward tug. Up, up. The ripping air, ripping sunshine, the ripping of my gills. Burning with air. With light, corrosive. With blood burning. The terror of light.

There is no dualism. Ultimate Reality is not bliss but horror. There is only horror. Unifying horror. Within. Without. Horror.

❧ The Painted Caves ❧

Buddham Saranam Gacchami
Sangam Saranam Gacchami
Dhammam Saranam Gacchami

The words. The way the words echo through the prayer hall, echo as if my chest were the cave wall, as if all the bhikkus were inside me, chanting as I chant. But that is exactly what my Teacher says: everyone is inside me and I am in everyone as well, because we are bound together living in this sorrowful world which is like a burning house, full of flames.

I like to squeeze open my eyes, one after the other, very slowly after the prayers. Then the monks really look like flames in their orange and red robes, like the little flames that dance on top of oil lamps and torches. All the murals on the wall also dance. They sway and float with the flickering torch-flames. Everything moves.

Jewellery dances most of all. Pearls and gems which nymphs, emperors and queens wear throb and recede with each step the acolytes take as they carry flames. I think the flames run fastest as the acolytes pass before the paintings of the Bodhisattavas Padmapani and Vajrapani. How wonderful they are. Their half-closed eyes glow, their crowns shine, their pearl necklaces flame and dance like so many raindrops running on a string.

My mother wore a necklace of big red beads. Each was a full seed. She would let me touch it. My mother wore marigolds, the colour of the Buddha's robes, in her ears, and in her hair. I still remember this. I had a brother and two sisters. My youngest sister would eat mud off the floor of our hut. She'd put everything in her mouth. Even goat shit; Black-One's, who would be tethered to the doorpost. How she'd bleat!

Now I don't have a family. The Sangam is my family. I am a junior acolyte. The name given to me is Dhammapada. My hair is shaven, like Majjhima's. He is my best friend. In seven years' time we will finish our nissaya-training and become junior assistants. When we are even older, we want to become the best Navakammikas—like our Teachers—and work together supervising the best works. Two caves are being commissioned near Seven Step Waterfall to our left. After the monsoon, woodcutters will begin clearing the rock face of one site; in the other, workmen with pickaxes will start digging out the ceiling.

We are so excited. Majjhima is very clever; he has secretly designed the whole cave, even our cells. I agree with all his plans—except I wanted the Miracle of Sravasti to be painted not on the right-hand wall but opposite my cell so that each morning the first thing I see are hundreds of Buddhas glowing peacefully. I said I'd be in charge of preparing the walls, finishing the lime coat and mixing the dyes. I'll become an expert in colour. My Teacher hardly sleeps when a new cave wall is being coated. He is always touching the pastes, feeling their thickness, their stickiness, and suggesting, "Add more rock grit! Some more paddy husk!" He walks up and down, inspecting the textures of the cave walls, the texture of the covering pastes. I follow him. He never shouts at any worker.

Recently, he has become even quieter because he is in slight disgrace. Because of the incident with the doorjambs. But it is not his fault. The woodcarver promised to carve dragons on all sixteen doorjambs, just as my Teacher instructed. Instead of working here he took them to his village because he wanted to look after his sick wife, he said. My Teacher allowed it. When the woodcarver returned, the doorjambs held kissing couples. Front and back. All sixteen! He said he could only see mithuna couples trapped within the wood. He said the wood would have split if he had tried to carve anything else.

The Head Priest of our vihara-hall is very strict. He says he will now have to be careful where he touches the doorjambs. He made the woodcarver do two lion-claw stools as penance. Later I ask my Teacher if the wood for the doorjambs is magical. My Teacher says he saw coiling Guardian Dragons in it, but the woodcarver saw lovers. It was a matter of Inner Vision. What you see depends on who you are. He says if I am good I will see goodness everywhere, dhamma everywhere. When my Teacher speaks like this I feel dizzy with joy.

On the last full moon night, Majjhima and I quietly run down to the sandy strip near the river. All is blue and silver and sparkling— stars, trees, white sand, even the sound of the river. Majjhima draws a beautiful lotus bud by throwing water on the sand. It is perfect. Then the design sinks into the ground and disappears, as if it had never been.

But it was just like the lotuses we see painted on the vihara-hall ceilings as if each one is bobbing on a breeze that is waving over a lake. Except of course the ceiling paintings are upside-down, as if the whole world is topsy-turvy, as if I am a heron flying on my back through the air seeing the water's face in the sky.

When I had newly joined, often when I was eating I'd glance up at the ceiling. Quickly. See all the lotuses and geese and bulls and elephants bobbing and waddling and running and swaying. Look down quickly, into your bowl and you'll see all the flowers and animals inside, inside your bowl of gruel. Look up again—they will be back on the ceiling. My Teacher noticed me looking up and down. Up and down. He said I should not be distracted by transient pleasures. So I stopped.

I should not lie. I do it slowly. But then I can't see lotuses floating in my bowl of gruel. It happens only when you are fast. In a flash. Suddenly you see white lotuses within the palm of your hand.

My Teacher is very kind. My duty is to get him water, all the water he needs, from the rainwater catchment tanks near the caves, or below, from the river. He suggests I get it from the river and save the rainwater for the summer, and for others. But it rains so much in Ajitanjaya, not like in my home village.

Here, all morning, mists rise like the breath of the waterfall and the hills. All day, birds call through the trees till you think each leaf is calling. All through the year the river runs fast and clear and deep in the gorge where the caves' steep steps lead. During the vassavasa rain retreat when the Wanderer Monks and bhikkus flood in, it is as if we ourselves are rains. All smells mingle in the smell of rain, all colours are coloured by the rain and behind the sound of discussion in the meeting halls is the sound of rain. Last year white mushrooms grew on my Teacher's second pair of clothes. Then, the rains leave, the Wanderers leave. Suddenly like mushrooms flicked off a robe, and the air is white.

But my Teacher is kind all through the year. He washes his hands slowly, after rubbing them hard with ash. He asks me to pour water in a silver trickle, like it were a wish. He uses less than half a small pot of water. Majjhima's Teacher uses a whole pot of water, each time; morning, midday and after the afternoon meal. Everyday Majjhima has to fetch fourteen more pots of water. That means seven extra trips for him. I am very fast. So I help him. Majjhima is my best friend. Sometimes I do two or three trips for him. I know I should not, but I do.

My Teacher knows. Last winter he saw me run into Majjhima's Teacher's cell with my two pots of water balanced on each end of the stick. I was scared. I almost slipped and broke both pots. That would have been terrible. So far, in my three years of service I have broken fourteen pots. A tap, a knock, and suddenly they crack, and the water runs out like liquid moons, shining on the ground at your feet. Suddenly the stick is light; the weight is lessened. Earthen pieces lie scattered beyond your toes.

Afterwards, the suggestion to be more careful, and to do more penance. My Teacher does not scold me when he finds out. After the night prayers he summons me to his cell. I stand at the foot of his stone bed. He has his face towards the stone wall. Above his head is a small painting of the Buddha, in the teaching posture. I remember the glow of the Buddha's robe. My Teacher is silent. Then he calls me. I walk up and stand behind his shoulders with my head bowed. I fall into full panchanga namaskar, my head, my arms and my knees touching the earth. My Teacher turns. He says, "Today, after the way I saw you run, I shall no longer call you Dhammapada but the Little Flying Monk. May you fly to Buddhahood one day."

Since then, everyone calls me "Little Flying Monk," or simply "Flying." That's how I am known—Flying—because I am the fastest water carrier, and the most sure-footed. Just like Black-One.

Pride is bad but I am not proud. It's just that as I run from the high caves to the river and back, each rock-cut step seems to be my special friend. It's as if they are showing me the way, even when each one is covered by moss. I could close my eyes and run up and down all the one hundred and three steps from my Teacher's cell to the water, and all the ninety-seven steps from Majjhima's Teacher's cell to the river. I have never trampled earthworms, centipedes, leeches and snails. I have never come in the way of scorpions and snakes. In the rains, I have never stepped on hopping frogs or toads. They always know when I am coming. They always hop out of my way. So small they are, yet how high they leap!

I love the rainy season though I always catch cold, in spite of my second sackcloth blanket. Two years ago when I was recovering from malaria, my Teacher got me the second sackcloth from Gunasena, the Merchant Prince. He had come with his wife to ask for the boon of a child; they came with many gifts. For seven days we ate such food! So many pieces of sweet yam, so much jaggery, so many round milk sweets!

The Merchant Prince Gunasena's caravan had camped down in Lenapura; then they climbed up. For one week, seven whole days and nights, prayers were held without a break in breath. So much incense was burnt it covered the smell of piss that rises from below the caves. All the floors were covered with flowers, even those of the stern Hiriayana bhikkus. The Merchant Prince Gunasena gave as deya-dhamma gold for sculpting and painting four pillars, and for making ten wooden cell doors for first-rank monks. He also gifted in piety eight straight-backed chairs, and three seats. Then he gave fifty wooden rods for hanging clothes, and one hundred and seventy-five torch sticks and eight flywhisks. Imagine his riches! The Head Priest got bolts of silk, and bhikkus of my Teacher's rank got two new robes; all senior acolytes got one sackcloth each as a blanket. And I, novice acolyte, Dhammapada, Flying, because of my illness got a new sackcloth blanket. It was like paradise.

The medical bhikkus suggested I eat strong gruel with herbs four times a day. Such big bowls they were! Then I was led to the Merchant Prince Gunasena. For a moment I could not see him. The torches were so many flames and so many shadows, dancing. He was covered in gold like a Bodhisattva, but his eyes were wide open, not half-shut, so I knew he was just a Merchant Prince. Then I saw his wife.

She was sitting in her palanquin outside the prayer hall. She looked like Maya Devi, the Buddha's mother. She looked like she had stepped out of the murals and into the palanquin. But she was in both places, shimmering, and her eyes were almost asleep. She looked just like my mother. The way she had tilted her head towards the ground was just like my mother, sitting in the evening in our hut, humming.

I think I fainted. I woke up looking at a stone bed rise above my eyes. It was my Teacher's cell. He was looking after me. He limps, like my father. My father was lame. He had a stick. His foot dragged with each step. It made a scraping sound as if it were making a secret vow with the earth. I remember walking with my father from our hut through the village, past the Big Town, Bharukactichha, to Ajitanjaya so that my father could dedicate me here. Majjhima says he comes from beyond Tagara, beyond Pratishthana. He too does not know the name of his village. But we will never go back. This is our home.

I remember I got lost in the Big Town. The entrance gates were higher than our hillside. There was a palace that rose to the skies. I could not climb the steps, they were so high. It was more crowded there than during our rain retreats here. There were streets everywhere, shops with houses sitting on top of them everywhere, cows everywhere, noise everywhere. Everything was running, running. I ran to find my father. I kept running. I could not find his limp among the running legs. A dog barked loudly. Its neck was white and furry. Then I heard my father call me by my old name. He caught me. His breath was like the dog's, hot on my face. After this he held me by my hand all the time till he brought me here. Before he left, my father bowed his head at my feet. On the top of his head he had no hair.

My Teacher turned me around. He pressed my head into his robe between his knees so I could not see my father leave. I do not remember anything more of that time.

I remember Majjhima opening his fist. Inside sat a bug with golden-green wings. It buzzed. He closed his hand. The sound stopped. He opened it. Again it began. Golden-green, and so loud. He closed it. He walked out of the meeting hall. He put the bug on a blade of grass. It buzzed. It turned around itself. It became quiet. Then it flew away. Then he smiled at me. That's how Majjhima and I became best friends.

He has grown very tall. His robe no longer covers his legs. His knees peek out like pale blind eyes. They remind me of the eyes of the Blind Wandering Monks who came for the vassavasa rain retreat the year before last. Six were blind, their eyes looking at the sky, sky-coloured. The seventh, the shortest, could see with one eye. He led them, each standing in height order, one hand on the other's shoulder, all their sticks tapping, like one long noisy caterpillar. During prayers, they chant the loudest. They shout when they talk to you, swaying their heads. They hear you even when you walk on tip-toe; they will call, "Hey you, novice!" and give you some small job. Among them Udena, the Hunchback Blind Wanderer was the master storyteller; the others, his chorus.

Every evening over the shrill thick sound of insects, over the chattering of wet monkeys jumping on dipping branches, over the sound of the flooded river, over the rain that sounds like Seven-Step Waterfall, roaring, his voice poured into the largest meeting hall. Udena the Blind Wanderer's breath was so powerful that flames on the two torches ahead of his stool shook with each word he spoke. Shaking shadows ran over his face; I shook with his stories.

I too know stories. Once there was a poor but clever student who was hated by every other student because he was the best. The day the good student finished his studies he asked his Guru what he should present him as guru-dakshina.

The other students whispered to their Guru, "Tell him to give you one thousand thumbs. That way somebody will surely kill him and he won't trouble us anymore." So that's what the Guru said.

The good student touched his Guru's feet and left. He became a feared killer in the jungle. He killed travellers—men, women, even children and wandering minstrels, even monks—then cut off their thumbs and strung them on a thread as a necklace. That's how he got his new name: Anguli-Mala, Garland of Fingers.

One night Anguli-Mala had nine hundred and ninety-eight thumbs strung on his garland. He needed just two more. In the dark he spied a bhikku walking down a jungle path. "Monk, wait!" shouted Anguli-Mala. "I have to kill you and cut off your thumbs and present it to my Guru as guru-dakshina." "If that's your dhamma, all right," said the bhikku. "Catch me and kill me."

Anguli-Mala was a very fast runner. He ran after the monk, but he couldn't catch up. Tears were rolling from his eyes, his mouth was open, his tongue was sticking out, and he couldn't breathe. "Bhikku, I am very tired," shouted Anguli-Mala. "Help me do my duty to my Guru." "I am helping you," said the bhikku. "Then please stop!" cried Anguli-Mala.

The bhikku turned and smiled. "Anguli-Mala, I have stopped, long ago. It is you who are still running in this endless cycle of rebirths." When Anguli-Mala heard this, he fell at the monk's feet. For the bhikku was the Buddha Himself who had come to help him.

The Buddha grew to His true height and glowed golden; all around Him air turned golden. He was standing on a white lotus, just like in the murals. Anguli-Mala gave up killing and became a Bodhisattva, always helping others.

The paintings of all the Miracles are wonderful. But I like Anguli-Mala's story the best. Majjhima is lucky. The story is painted next to his Teacher's cell. In it, Anguli-Mala is running so fast to catch the still Buddha that his thumb necklace is flying behind him like a flag. In the part where he is shown falling at the Buddha's feet, the monkeys in the jungle are bowing to Him, even a baby monkey on its mother's back. How small its paws are, yet how deeply it bows! Next best I like the Mahakapi Monkey Jataka mural with all those golden mangoes dripping from the tree's branches, so tasty; then the Chhadanta Jataka with herds of elephants trumpeting. Sometimes when I hear an elephant trumpeting I think perhaps it is remembering the story of when the Buddha was born as the six-tusked white elephant. Who knows?

For Udena the Blind Wanderer says there are many things we do not know, just as there are many things the blind hear and see that we cannot. He says he sees mists wrapping everyone. Around me he sees a mist of foolishness and joy. I should pray deeply every day, he says, otherwise I will break like a water pot knocking against a stone step. Then he knocked me on the head, and laughed. How did he know where I was standing? I don't understand. Udena the Blind Wanderer talks in riddles.

I was told to help him clean his teeth, to offer him neem twigs. He chewed on them a long time. That's how I got to speak to him alone. I asked him how he knew so many stories, many more than those painted on the murals. "See this hunchback of mine curled like a snail's shell? I keep stories stored inside, and pull out their bodies whenever I wish." He laughed and stomped the ground so hard he looked like a gooseberry tree in a storm. Even his blind eyes seemed to be laughing, rolling white.

He asked me my name. "Dhammapada," I said, "but everyone calls me Flying." He laughed even more. "Flying! That's a good name for a novice grounded in confusion." I wanted to run away and leave him there cleaning his teeth standing on the rock edge. But he caught my hand, tightly. He whispered into my ear, "Tell me, what does a blind snail carry within its shell as it is crawling along? You don't know? It carries its home, its sense of Self; it carries everything, yet nothing. It is both full and empty. Remember this secret. Meditate on it. Now fly, Flying." This time he didn't knock me. He blessed me and pushed me away.

Udena and the other Blind Wanderers did not come last year for the rain retreat. This year if he comes at all, it will be late. We've already had thundershowers. New grass has started to grow between stones. How quickly grass grows!

How quickly it dies too. When it turns from yellow to brown the Sage-Monk Dinnaga's disciples are to come from Nalanda Mahavihara for debates. Ten, perhaps twenty, bhikkus will arrive. All work will stop. At the end, the losers will have their faces darkened with mud, the winners will be carried in white palanquins, just like in the big study centre at Nalanda.

Last winter, we won. It's strange, even my Teacher behaves like a novice at such times. I saw him rubbing mud on a loser, and laughing. Normally he is so neat, and kind. I hope we win this year too. Already, the debaters are practising hard. Every day we hear them, every day we pray for their success. Already the medical bhikkus are giving the debaters special foods. They eat four times a day. Even after sunset they get a special drink.

I have eaten in the dark because of Passanna. Passanna the Painter. He gave me and Majjhima dried apricots, three each. How wonderful they were! He comes from beyond the snow mountains, beyond Takshasila. His skin is pink, he has green eyes, when he removed his strange cap I saw his hair was red. He was in Ajitanjaya last summer.

Passanna the Painter has visited all the Kings' courts in Pataliputra, and Ujjaini. He has ridden on elephants, he has seen a two-headed bull; nymphs have danced for him. He is the expert in painting clothing and jewellery. When he was here, I liked him more than Majjhima. But Majjhima also liked him. We fetched him as much water as he wished to mix his paints.

One day he came down to the river with us. On the other bank we saw peacocks and flying birds and monkeys. A group had come to the water's edge. Quickly he drew them as they were drinking. I saw them on the bank; I saw them on the palm leaf. He caught parrots as they were flying. Passanna the Painter drew many small pictures. I chose first because I am youngest. I took the drawing of monkeys eating lice. Majjhima chose the mother and baby deer drinking water even as a boar is charging. We kept the pictures safely hidden for the whole year in a hollow of a mango tree. Suddenly these thunderstorms! The palm leaves are soft, the ink has run, the pictures are spoilt.

Passanna the Painter showed us some things from his sack. One was a flute, which the kinnaras in his country had gifted him. I asked in what language the kinnaras spoke. He said because they are half-human, half-birds, they don't talk, they sing, like koels. You understand them just as you understand the koels' song.

He showed us an eye of a snow leopard. It was cold and hard as a stone, but the magic of the leopard was still alive in the eye because a golden light moved fast within it as you turned it in your hand. The King of Dwarves had presented it to him for the paintings he had done in that land. Last he showed us a piece of cloth. We almost couldn't see it, though it had pearls sewn on it. Only heavenly nymphs wear it, he said. It was light so they could wear it and fly easily. Holding it was like holding dewdrops. He let us touch it for a long time. He even let us call him by his first name.

He will not be coming this year; not for many years. Perhaps when the new cave being dug as dena-dhamma by the Merchant Prince Sariputta is almost ready, he'll come back. He says when the walls are dug to a quarter of their height from the ceiling, they will call to him in his dreams, wherever he is. Passanna says that even if he closes his eyes, his feet will lead him back to Ajitanjaya by the time the masons are chiselling the cave walls down to the height of a calf.

When I grow up I would like to be like him. I want to paint and travel and see all the three worlds, like him. But I am a bhikku, training to be a Navakammika. I hope to be as good as my Teacher. Maybe I can supervise many new works. Then I'll call Passanna. I'll say, "Use all the blue you want. Make the cave shine with lapis lazuli, like the sky where the shining Bodhisattvas live."

But my Teacher says Bodhisattvas live on earth, among us. They walk and eat with us, but we don't know them, that's all. Sometimes I think: Is one of the sick who comes here for free medicines a Bodhisattva? Is He pretending to be ill in order to see who needs His help most? Could that mad woman who was muttering be a Bodhisattva, to see if we help someone as fearful as her?

Sometimes I think: Is that tree a Bodhisattva? See how much shade it gives, what fun it is to climb, how many birds and monkeys and squirrels live on it, how beautiful it is. That must be a Bodhisattva.

Is that silver fish in the river a Bodhisattva, leaping in the waters, not minding if it is caught and eaten by tribals, just like the Buddha let Himself be killed in so many avatars to help others?

Sometimes I think: Is one of those stone steps I run up and down each day a Bodhisattva? For how kind it is, how useful too. All it sees are the soles of our feet pressing down. Why shouldn't a stone be a Bodhisattva, for even a stone has life. One day it will wear down and stop existing. Everything stops living at some time, that's what my Teacher says.

When I am in the prayer hall, when we are chanting, when the incense flows, torches dance, when murals move and tears fill my eyes, I think: Perhaps everyone is a Bodhisattva, except me. It's just that I don't know. It must be this. Everyone is a Bodhisattva. I feel strange and light and wonderful. As if I, Flying, could really fly through the skies.

Three days ago, how kind was Lopamudra, the senior acolyte doing kitchen duty. He waited for me, hiding behind a tree as I came from the hilltop after plucking flowers. "Flying," he said, and I stopped. He showed me a big lump of jaggery. For Majjhima and me he said, because everyone knows a scorpion stung Majjhima the day before. Lopamudra hugged me tight, for so long. He said he would help me, he said he would give me another lump of jaggery for Majjhima if I met him on the night after the fortnightly upostha ritual, when everyone is tired and longing to sleep. I don't know why but I felt a little scared. He said I mustn't tell anyone. I wanted to tell my Teacher but he has been so busy today with the seller of dyes. But I have to meet Lopamudra tonight. I must stay awake somehow.

I went to see Majjhima, but he was sleeping because of the medicines. I waited for a long time by his side. That's why I am late. I have to still fetch four pots of water. The evening prayers are beginning. I can hear them over the soft steady rain. I can hear the feet of bhikkus filing into the prayer hall. It's dark. All clouds, no moon.

I must run faster up the stairs. I'll be the last to enter, for sure. Sometimes when you're running up the stairs it's as if each step has grown higher. Inside in the halls, flames must be dancing on torch heads. The murals must be bending and weaving with each prayerful breath. I'm so late! Each time I hear the prayers I close my eyes. I think I am in the stars like a Gandharva, flying to hear the Buddha's sermon. They have started!

Buddham Saranam Gacchami
Sangam Saranam Gacchami
Dhammam Saaaaaraaaaaaaaa …

∾ The Edict ∾

I was born the day my son died.

In grief I came into being. In grief I saw my empty lap. I saw my palms lying on my thighs, vacant, staring at the skies. I lifted my head and saw others, their bodies numb with shock, staring.

My son left me to go to the battlefield. I left to find him. He was buried under another's body, an enemy's. That boy's thighs were on my son's chest. I turned him over and placed both their heads on my lap. I placed my hands on their curls. Who had killed whom? The heavens were still. The earth was still. Who had killed whom, Devanama Piyadasin, Beloved of the Gods?

I sat stroking their hair in the night breeze. I sat stroking their curls glowing under the noonday sun. I stroked the dew off their hair at dawn. I pushed away mosquitoes that clustered on my boy's nostril, where he had bled; and from the clotted temple of the other boy. I tried to push away the ants though they too must feed. I was pushed away. I too was lifted like the boys. Two men lifted my arms. Were they from your army? Or survivors of the battle of Kalinga?

I lay where I was left on the bank of the river. Slowly my body knew the earth was wet. Was it the river? Was it blood? Answer, Devanama-Piya-Piyadasin-Raja.

I wandered as you ruled. I do not know where I went. As you built roads across your empire, with each step I took, paths grew from beneath my feet. As you erected pillars and edicts to speak to your subjects, speech left me though my heart wept and my mind talked ceaselessly. For how long have I been speaking to you, mutely? As your spies and wandering administrators brought you news from the furthest reaches of your kingdom, the horizon lay within my arm's reach, still and hung with sorrow. Space and time united. I did not know the span covered by my each step. Was each a moment? Or a Yuga? Can you tell me, Emperor Ashoka, The One without Sorrow?

What brought you here like a curse on our land? They say you came for our iron mines, for our ironsmiths whom you led away in chains, a chain of men whose spirits were rusted and flaking with sorrow. Through them, through the iron you pulled from our red earth, you wished your name to spread red across the lands, a stain over our congealed misery. You wished to live by the laws of man, these small, cruel laws. This I knew as I pulled the iron spearhead from my son's stomach. Do your spears kill swiftly, Piyadasin-Raja, He Who Looks upon All with Love? Or did my son lie a long while, holding his stomach, watching his blood congeal between his fingers? Did consciousness leave him like lightning leaves the heavens?

I am like a sheet of lightning, blank, lit and charred by grief. You were born in blood; you ascended the throne on the bubbling blood of your brothers; for your mind to turn to the righteous path of dhamma you needed more blood. I am not unlike you. For thoughts to circulate through my body, for my eyes to be opened to the light, I too need blood. At what precise instant did my eyes tear open? Was it the moment I saw my son, his body stretched on the battlefield? Was it when I placed his head on my lap? Was it when I saw the other boy's skull bleeding white from an axe-blow? His mother will not know the face of her son in death; she will never know the touch of his brain which kept slipping through my fingers as I placed his cracked head on my lap. Even as his head rested, a white trickle rested on my knee. It felt wet. Was it then that my heart began to beat again?

As you feasted in your palace on peacock stuffed with lotus seeds, I wandered. As you, Conqueror of Kalinga, hunted for your pleasure doe and fawn, I, mother of a dead son, wandered even more. Then you wandered into the turning of dhamma. All your children—for you now call us such, Piyadasin, Beloved of the Gods—all of us know the tale of your slow repentance. You turned on the day of the hunt. You turned as the newborn fawn whose mother you had killed with your fine iron arrows turned towards you, the killer, instead of fleeing from you. It was too young to know who was its enemy; stumbling, it came towards you, that fawn. You had it shod and collared in gold. From that day on, it is said, you began to look with fresh eyes on all your subjects—human, animal and vegetal. For you realized your power to strip us of life even as we turn towards you, Monarch, for protection. Like the fawn, where else can we go? Unlike the fawn, we recognize the killer even as we stumble forward on all fours.

Now I am known as the Dumb Madwoman of Dauli who sleeps at the foot of your edict that claws its golden way to the sun. I have no other existence. What was I before I absorbed your cruelty like my wrap absorbed my son's blood? I was a nobody. A mother of a single child living outside the high fort walls of Kalinga. I planted rice, kept a cow, strung flowers and sang songs. Shall I tell you, Great King, of this son of ours, yours and mine?

As he learnt to run, my heart ran after him as butterflies chase flowers, consistent. As he learnt to plough, my blood turned thick with happiness as the earth turns thick and soft with rain. As his eyes alighted on his young bride, my body opened with sudden joy as the heavens open with lightning, lighting the earth. These truths I know as I knew the heaviness of my breasts when I fed him; through the faltering of my heartbeat when he learned to walk; through the shooting pain I felt as youth and arrogance shot through him. He shone. He died at the age when he did not want to hear my voice, so sure was he. Life was meant to pass through him too, Emperor, not stop. He was a boy, a laughing wild boy.

You amassed your armies on the other side of the river. All night he tightened his bowstring; all night he twanged it like a harp filled with songs of glory. I quivered with each note. At dawn, as he lifted his bow and arrow, my heart froze. His body froze. Shall I tell you who he was, Piyadasin, Beloved of the Gods?

In penitence grave and gracious, you have proclaimed in undying stone that one hundred thousand died in the Battle of Kalinga. But who was our son? The one hundred thousandth and one. That one uncounted. His dreams were small, Lord. He would have remained small throughout his life.

He was a boy given to small joys. Our cow calved, and how he laughed. He laughed when mustard flowers bloomed, bright yellow with spring. He laughed when he heard our King's call to defend our land, his blood chasing butterfly dreams. He did not realize he was facing you. He could have lived. He may have grown to be a broken survivor.

He would have laughed again, for even lepers laugh. This I know, Mighty Emperor, through your charity. I have seen lepers snake into a sluggish line to show their sores to your Administers of Justice, to beg for alms and medicines. I have seen them joke with each other as they wait, forgetful of their disease, forgetful of the Dumb Madwoman of Dauli who stalks the precincts, unrepentant.

Emperor Who Looks upon All with Love, your kindness runs longer than this river I see, bathe in, drink from, every day. Unlike the river, it does not change each moment, each season. As the last rainy season ended, your Ministers of Dhamma, both Material and Spiritual, stopped their chariots flying your golden pennants by this, your edict, guarded night and day by your attendants. Your Ministers of Dhamma saw me lying bark-like on a bough in the roomy mango grove you have had planted, my arms hanging down. They were informed who I was, how my mind had turned with the war. They recited prayers over me; they draped my body with a rich red-coloured shawl made in your city of Gandhara. It was the softest material I have ever known, as soft as our son's temple when he was suckling. Do you remember, Piyadasin-Raja? The cloth our son's bride wore around her hips during the nuptials seem in comparison like iron flakes. Then, your ministers left.

When I awoke, I went to the boulder etched with your edict glittering golden in the midday sun. The whole rock seemed to be made of gold, Victorious King, so thick was its coating of paint. Again my arms crawled over the edict, like an ant's feelers, seeking a path. Again your attendant sighed and read out the inscriptions for the unlettered, just as you have ordained, for justice and order reign in the eight directions of your empire, Lord. Again I heard your instructions recited loud as the war drums: everyone must follow the Righteous Path. Again I slept at the foot of your edict. I covered myself with your fine red shawl.

I awoke and climbed to the top of the boulder, to where the White Elephant of Dhamma emerges triumphant from the shoulder of the rock. Will harmony ever step out of the rock of my body with the gentleness of an elephant's gait? Answer, Compassionate One. I draped your fine red shawl on the white elephant's back, like a saddle. Were our son alive, he would have rushed to sit astride it, imagining himself charging into glory.

When my eyes opened again, the shawl was gone. Perhaps the attendant needed it. Maybe a traveller's craving was greater. Perhaps one of the villagers who offer me food took it home to share with his family. They follow your dictates, Emperor, they are generous. Each day, I, the Dumb Madwoman of Dauli, have more to eat than when I had a home. Half a jackfruit. Three bananas. A bowl of rice with boiled yam. Each day I eat my food with the pariah dog that follows me like a shadow, with the crows, the ants, the lice on my body, with the earth. All living things need to eat. But when is it enough, when is it greed, Beloved of the Gods?

Devanama-Piya-Piyadasin-Raja, you have the means to redeem your past. I have none. How do I forget how I beat our son when he broke a pot of curd? I thrashed him again when he allowed our firewood to get damp. My palms bear scars that burn deeper every day. How do I hold him to me once again, Lord, and let him understand he was cherished? As you wish each and every one of your children to be cherished, so that your subjects too may cherish and forgive you, so that grace, this umbilical cord, may flow river-like over our mucus-covered eyes and we see each other as we are: bloody and frail and kicking to stay alive in clotting darkness.

You have the means to cleanse yourself into repentance, Victorious Emperor. I have none, nor wish it. I, the Dumb Madwoman of Dauli, say your kindness whelped in remorse is not enough. Do the titles you have given yourself lead back to you, just as a mighty river wells from a small spring? What is the wellspring of your compassion? Can it spurt from a source other than sorrow, born in blood, flowing? This is what I seek to understand. The *origin of good action should lie elsewhere—in a womb of living tenderness. Do you understand? Till I find its birthplace, I shall lie curled in grief. I shall not eat. I shall no longer speak to you through the heartbeat of silence.*

⤞ The Crossing ⤝

My father was a wolf.

Of this I am certain. I remember his silhouette against the full moon, his head raised, baying. I remember him standing over our mother, the thin, golden bitch of Sinthastha, and us five pups. He licks us so roughly we tumble and fall. I remember the hanging sky of our mother's teats, the horizon sliding with our suckling as she rests and the distant mountains standing on the skin of the earth like ticks on a newborn. I remember my mother; her ears back, gums bare, teeth glistening, body panting, while we cringe near her. She lunges at the attackers, and dies, protecting us. An arrow through her neck while the cold winds blow, while the sun hangs like a medallion against the sky, while the sea of grasses waves. Her legs burst into a spasm of kicks. Then she stretches, softly, as when she awakens each dawn, and then she is still. There must have been noise: screams, yapping, neighing, death cries. I do not remember sound.

"This one is mine." This is the first human voice I hear as he thrusts me into a bag.

It is dark in the bag, and growing darker outside. Wolves are chasing us—that is, Vrikama my master, the men folk of his tribe, and me in his bag. I can't see. But I smell. The panic of the horses, the coldness of the night, the bronze of the arrows, the leather, my master's excitement.

I smell my father in the dark, his eyes glowing, giving chase, hungry. I smell him loping. After me, for me, I think. I hear a yelp. Then I smell my father no more. I smell the night quietening around us, gathering into rough vegetation beneath the horses' flying hooves, into stones and pebbles and moonlit dust. This is all I remember of my family.

"I name you Trichaisma, Three-Eyed, for the marking on your forehead. Therefore I know you are sacred and can see the spirits of the dead," Vrikama pronounces.

Know how I now look: like my father the wolf, thick-furred and strong, but coloured golden like my mother, the thin bitch of the burial grounds. Know my face: three-eyed, two black eyes roving the world, the central eye marking never opening. Know my heart: I am a dog.

Vrikama's tribe believes my third eye absorbs into me the failings of the newly dead, leaving their spirits free to join the ancestors in the happy land of heroes. But in truth I do nothing. All I do is sense death, and howl, which they take as release of the spirit.

Spaka treats me like an honoured guest in her home, like a distant relative, she is named after my kind; Spaka, "dog." Her heart is like the earth around her home; she keeps it frosted lest it melt, lest it show itself wet and naked and flushed as a pup; she is a woman of few words. When I first saw them together, I did not believe they were man and wife. She is older than Vrikama, older, tall, red-cheeked and proud. I knew she was biting herself, biting into her flesh to stop herself from succumbing to Vrikama, becoming his slave. I saw her scars with my two eyes; Vrikama saw none until it was too late.

She was carrying their second daughter when Vrikama pulled me out of the bag and fed me broiled beef from the cauldron. My first meal in his home I ate from his own spearing fork. I was as old as their firstborn son, Wanant, the Victorious One. We were both learning to run. Vrikama would gaze at his son and ask, "Oh fair-haired one, will you grow to be more handsome than me?" then look at Spaka and laugh. She would sweep her son to her breast and say, "He will be better than you, husband; he will be faithful." He would laugh again, and she would turn away, leaving master and dog to play with each other; he would tickle the fur on my throat, push me on my back and scratch my pale armpit fur while I lay on his lap, four paws dangling in the air, helpless with pleasure.

Those early days in Spaka's home, amidst the snow-fed valley that melted under my master's blazing torch as my heart too melted with the first touch of warmth, were our days of peace. Vrikama's heart too was dripping; it began to ooze and gather like a whirlpool, he gathered his strength like the lasso he carries, circling our settlement, faster and faster, wheeling his chariot, raiding cattle from one settlement, then another, becoming true to his name. Vrikama: He Who Attacks Like a Wolf. He runs with the pack yet he is Vrikama the looter, the despised Marut. He would return home, smelling of blood and new cattle. Two young bulls, four prize red milch cows, one calf. Small victories, for his eyes chafe the heavens.

In the three winters of my childhood, I learnt my trade. I have to gaze steadfast at a fresh corpse and let out a low growl, my ears flattened, tail stiff. As if I had seen the dead man's failings worm and twist out with his spirit as it worms and twists and weeps out of the body. As if I must safeguard it from a cloud of hungry demons; the terrors it created when alive. My growl would satisfy the priests and the corpse would be thrown to the elements or buried. It was an easy life. The dead were few for Vrikama had not yet become a mercenary. His wanderlust was leashed; his eyes clear of red veins. He looked like a hero, strong and full of song, while he was but a hired hand to a war charioteer.

Once I had eaten grass all day but it was no use. In front of a corpse I vomited bits of the vulture I had secretly stalked and killed. A priest led me away and whipped me. Vrikama could do nothing to stop the whippings; my master was shamefaced for he was merely the owner of a sacred dog, not Lord of the Clan. Vrikama staggered as he carried me to the chariot, for I was almost full-grown. He placed me behind him and we drove out and beyond; he placed me on the grass, bleeding, he combed his fingers through my fur to loosen the blood clots while I whimpered. He lay on the ground on a bed of dried autumn grass tawny as his beard, embraced the clear heavens with his arms and prayed, "Gods, I have my desires, you have the gifts. I come to you with songs, Gods, be bountiful. Make me a king; if not that then a priest; if not these, then a rich man with many heads of red cattle. Raise me, Gods, as dew rises from the grasses after dawn." Perhaps it was the flowing of my blood that turned his.

The next spring we begin our wanderings, for he has heard of the lands rich in pasture beyond the Sapta Sindhu rivers. In all, seventeen families leave as dawn blows darkness away from the skies, awakening the fragrance of a new day. I smell anxiety and bitterness in Spaka, I smell Vrikama's desires mounting and I smell unease in the pawing of hooves, in the lowing of bulls and cattle, red, black, dappled and light-coloured. I smell danger in the overloaded ox-carts whose wheels are as tall as the horses. I smell fear in the barking of ordinary dogs and restlessness in the long-legged, long-tailed sheep and in hairy rams. I smell nervousness in the bleating of goats and in the women's voices, and excitement in the children, screaming, running, the dust rising in the air like gold. We are golden when we set out; gold sun, gold sky, gold dust, wooden wheels turning golden, my golden fur, my eyes crazed with golden pollen. I smell trouble ahead.

Vrikama leads. He has never known his father; his mother was raped and left to die. My master is a half-breed like me. Vrikama leads, reins in hand, chariot pulled by a pair of short shaggy roans, he leads singing. The land is vast and open; on every side the shining sky meets the earth. We follow where he leads, singing.

I have trotted after him all my life; his cracked heels have shown my path. I know the sign of passage; I have had dust in my eyes for too long. The dust of cartwheels, black clods kicked up by oxen, pebbles scattering bright as sunlight, red mud and blue snow and water breaking like crystal flowers, burrs flying, grasses and brambles and reeds lashing back to close the path, and yet I have followed, squeezing my body through. I know no other life but the smell of the trail. I have kept pace with the churning of wheels, of Vrikama's war chariot, of his racing chariot, of his chariot of desire; Vrikama never stops travelling.

We arrive at the foothills of the Star Capped Mountains. Vrikama strides, godlike, to meet the chieftain Havishka and pledge allegiance to him. Vrikama is still a hired charioteer, lowly, eyes burning with ambition and stalled by love for the chieftain's daughter, Kamya. I will not forget how you drove to her as a raincloud heavy with rain drives towards the earth to lighten itself, and how your eyes laughed. I will not forget how you lay naked in each other's arms, calm and brimming as dawn on mountain peaks. Was it your smiling black eyes, the gift of your marauding father, your great body, your arrogance and certitude—this we will conquer, this we will accomplish—which drew her to you? Vrikama sang of the spring to come, of the mountains to cross, poetry lifted from his lips like hawks.

> *Kamya, fair one,*
> *As the brilliant sky covers the earth*
> *So may I cover you,*
> *As the river flows furrowing the earth*
> *So may I flow into you.*
> *Kamya with heaven in her eyes,*
> *Stars on her cheeks and on her breasts,*
> *With stars on her fingers as she touches me,*
> *May I be like the sky which lights up*
> *Day and night with you.*
> *I burn bright as Fire Immortal*
> *In the flame of my love.*
> *Come to me Kamya, as the breeze*
> *Sings to the trees, as the swan*
> *Glides over water, as the dew settles each dawn.*

She came, twinkling like fire in the night, the chieftain's daughter, bewitched by his words, by his arms, to the half-breed she came; she, the beauty, the pure-born, who wore a horn of gold on her head.

We had arrived at her father's home when there was no moon in the sky. As the moon once again swelled full and tight with soma, the two of them vanished. This I remember, for I still carry one trait of my father's breed: I howl at the swollen moon. I howled the night they retreated into the wilderness as a mountain retreats behind a cloud cap, as a flower closes for the night.

For fifteen days I am Spaka's dog. I watch her trail her skirt in search of a magical plant for a love potion. I watch her grind the leaves, hunched, shivering with envy, smelling of betrayal and curse, "May Vrikama leave my rival as a bull shuns a barren cow." I sleep by Spaka's side, near the three children. I eat from her hand. I am beholden to her. I watch her cry and curse every day, her bones growing large with loss.

I remember when they return. I hear the hooves, I smell him smelling new with Kamya's scent and joy. I bound towards his chariot yelping, my tail wagging like a puppy's. He does not see me. So I run between Spaka and him, barking, run up and down, up and down between them while Spaka stands in front of the tent, still and parched against the flapping leather. I run between them barking until he bends down and scratches the white fur of my throat, like before. Spaka is stilled; Kamya is installed as chief wife, a golden horn shining atop her head, shining like Vrikama's eyes which never leave her, like his body shines when he passes her, his love fixed and flaming.

Their smiles flow like milk on us, fresh; Spaka's potion has not worked. Not as yet. Vrikama wins glory in the big cattle raid; he has a new wife, ten new heifers and for the first time, slaves. He turns three slaves over to Spaka; she kills one on the first day. Vrikama rises to own a new chariot, its eight-spoked wheels painted red. He has his own steeds. Raktha, the prize Gandharva stallion presented to him by his father-in-law, and Deeva-aspa, the chafing steed that was destined to drown in the river crossing.

We wait for autumn to pass. Before the first day of winter, Vrikama rides out with me at his heels, the stallion panting, the leaves dancing like campfire beneath our heels, the breeze sharp as hail. We feed on a wild goat he spears. As we are eating, resting under birch trees, and as the horse nuzzles the moss, Vrikama speaks. "Trichaisma, my sacred companion," he says, addressing me formally, "know where I have been. Know a man can reach great heights, and still not know with what he is bequeathed. I am bewildered. My heart

is full, but pulled in the four directions by the gods." I listen, my head tilted
sideways, cracking the goat's bones between my paws. Vrikama's head is
small when he stands; his voice falls from the skies like a cataract. He opens
his heart wide as the split ribcage of a sacrificed horse to me; talking to me,
he speaks to himself. He speaks of Spaka, of their firstborn son, he speaks
of journeying beyond the mountains, beyond rivers we have not seen, to a new
land. He speaks of wealth in the new land, splendorous as a tree on fire,
of dreams he speaks. He speaks of Kamya and himself, of how they rode
aware of each breath that passed from the other. He speaks of their journey
to the cave of ice, and in that cave he released himself into her. "Trichaisma,
know this: everything was transformed. The sun was held captive, the cold
turned to fire, my love had at last found a body—hers—and my heart grew
large as the sky."

Quickly they left the sacred cave, quickly they returned to the foothills,
quickly they spied our camp, and quickly they hid themselves in each other;
my master killed only what was required to feed them both. "Not a bird
more, Tri, understand this," he said. "Our hearts were full, and full of
light."

We wait out the winter in the foothills, its cold burning breath circling
our settlement, circling Spaka and her three children, and Vrikama with
Kamya. I sleep near the cauldron. It is the warmest place, between the cold
currents blowing outside our home and within. On the first day of spring, as
the first yellow shoot thrusts out of icy ground, Vrikama leads a cow to the
sacrificial post for Pushan, Mighty God of Journeys, and the priests agree
we can start the upward climb.

Kamya is seven months pregnant. I too have seven offspring: three
surviving from my first mate, and four newborns. They are loaded with
Kamya, on the same cart. Vrikama sees to this. We trudge up the mountains;
it is cold and desolate. We have set out too early. I shake myself to trap more
air into my fur; I walk close to Raktha, snorting. Clouds lie on the path like
whispered breath, the cattle are like boulders. Every day we push upwards
into icy slush. Only Vrikama's mind glows like the summer sunset; he sees

the dream ahead clearly as the sages see the gods. He sees lowing cattle with gold pieces tied to their horns, golden soma brimming over bowls, whole settlements to set alight with orange flames, pasture lands thick as my fur. He sings these songs, and each night he shoots flaming arrows into the air. Our nostrils dilate as do stallions' when they smell mares ready to mount; foaming, teeth bared they charge, so we mounted upwards.

We move to the sound of whips on ox-hide, to the bellowing of oxen, to the lumber of cartwheels. No one talks; only orders are shouted, and curses and encouragement. Animals lie where their legs crumple as fire crumples a twig; people awake no more in the morning. The hotra-priests sleep all day in the carts; I have no sleep. Climb, run and yap at oxen's hooves during the day, at night stay awake staring at the dead.

In a blizzard on a mountain pass, Kamya gaves birth to a son, a twin-headed son, one head pointing to the land we came from, the other turned towards the direction we were heading, its four eyes shut tight. White are her screams, white turns her blood, white is the blizzard.

The blizzard clears. My master carries his twin-headed son lashed to Kamya's body; he carries them to the edge of a precipice, and drops them. Kamya falls with her twin-headed son. Down, down into the ravine. I stare at them as they fall, tumbling in the air. I feel my master's hand on my neck, pressing my head down on the edge. I see the small bundle of the dead child rip free of Kamya's corpse. It spins deeper into the gorge. Kamya's body crashes on a boulder just below, and holds there tangling with the wind.

Vrikama does not look. "Tri, is it done?" he asks me. He takes my whimpering for an answer and turns back, his eyes still shut tight.

The following week Vrikama cannot walk, nor drive, nor stand. He is lashed to his chariot, drunk. When he awakens, we come across a small group of hill-tribe people, their children and their goats. He goes after them as they run. He comes back clothed in blood. He does not wash. He sleeps in his mire of blood and filth and grief. I smell his grief. Even people can smell it. They keep away from him—Spaka too. Vrikama is never to journey into love again.

Our crossing does not end with Kamya's death or Vrikama's crazed revenge. We have to cross The Silent One that rises above the pass, which demands we were as quiet as it is, that our hearts be grave and still, that we listen to the smallest flake of new snow falling, feel the feeblest ray of sunlight penetrate its massive white body; so close in spirit are we to become with The Silent One. The sky is dazzling, a blue that scorches the eyes and falls flaming blue-white on the snows, the thin air burning like ice. Three-fourths of us have passed in single file; muzzles covered, coughs stifled, treading on the slim ridge of ice as if it were one's first dream, so delicately, while on our left the white wave of The Silent One rises. Then the silences breaks. Crossing the ice-bridge, a horse rears and neighs. Neighing, it skids, pulling its mate, tilting the chariot and spilling the occupants. They fall screaming into the clouds below. The oxen behind snort, bellow and charge. The Silent One awakens. And thunders. Waves of white fall upon us and thunder to the skies.

We lose one fourth of our tribe and cattle. Vrikama loses his son Wanant who was Spaka's joy. Their third daughter too curls dead beneath the snows. Vrikama also loses his third brother; that is all. I lose my whole brood. All seven perish under the snow. Perhaps my heart began to still under the snows of The Silent One.

Hunted by loss, I could have hunted Vrikama down. By starlight I follow him, while from the camp below I can smell Spaka tearing at her flesh, beating her head and wailing, the cold reeling with grief. I pad after Vrikama at a distance as he plunges like a madman through the snow. He hits his head on a rock. I bark. He turns. "Whelp of the bitch Samara, return from whence you came!" he curses. "Swallow yourself in the rivers of hell. Begone!" He throws ice clods at me. I dodge, and follow him soft-footed. I can't see him for the mists swirling between us, but I smell him. I hear him digging like a boar in the undergrowth of ice and sorrow. Then I come upon him, his back towards me, wriggling, burying his head in the snow, stuffing his mouth with the snow, and screaming like a hog in its death throes. My bristles rise, my ears flatten of their own accord, my growl begins from the pit of my stomach, my fangs bare in the starlight; the landscape turns red. I am readying for a charge. To kill him.

He hears me. He sees me wear my face of death. He somersaults to one side and shoots arrows at me. I crouch. Arrows blaze past me. Then I retreat, growling into the snows.

I stay away from the camp for days. When I return, I sleep near Spaka. Vrikama and I, we let each other be till we see from atop a pass on the Ratnasanu range, the mountainsides lush with greenery; below lie valleys with silver rivers dancing like fish and sunlight sliding like rain on leaves. We have come to the land of the Sapta Sindhu. All are hushed, then like one animal they cry, and how quickly we come down to the valley as if we are walking down from a dream.

We gather at the bank and watch the great river foaming. Again we are still, silenced by the river's roar, for the dream has turned terrifying.

"No one can cross this river," says Havishka, the chieftain. "We have been led by demons into a nightmare."

"This is the river we must ford. I have lived with the clan of Brighu far on the other side." The voice comes from an old man who steps forth.

"He is a shape-changing enchanter who will egg us to our doom," cries Vrikama. "Kill him!"

"Wait. Show us proof," says Havishka.

The man holds out a piece of painted pottery. "It is their mark."

Vrikama the hero roars over the river, his teeth flash. He forgets his sorrows in the danger of crossing the river as mighty as a snow mountain set ablaze that crashes over the land. The cold white river, the boulders, the currents circling with ice chunks, the women and children crying, oxen stamping, sheep bleating, horses neighing, the men snorting and charging along the banks like the horses, and the birds in the wheeling sky, all this against the waters churning. Vrikama unloosens Raktha from the chariot, holds him by the reins, and goads the young stallion; goads, whips, cuts Raktha's flanks with his tall spear, draws blood from his nostrils as he pulls the reins, and plunges into the river. Horse and master shudder as one creature. He neighs wilder than his horse, neighs to the skies, "Varuna, Varuna, who covers the skies, protect me; Mitra, bright master of the heavens, spare me; Vayu, Vayu glide me on your breeze." Vrikama is weeping, shouting, slashing Raktha and he crosses the river, the half-breed, the mercenary, he crosses the first of the Sapta Sindhu rivers. First.

He splashes to the other shore. Vrikama falls on the green-grey boulders which are more beautiful than first love, falls face down on them, prostrates himself to the sky, the earth, the waters, calls upon Fire to hear him, leaps on Raktha's naked back and crosses back to us, laughing and weeping though he does not realize it.

And the cheer that goes up from the men, the cries from the women, my own heart pounding, my barking so high. He thrashes through the deep white waters, weeping, laughing, he raises his bow, raises his arrow, and shoots from firm ground into the wet waters, and again the cry resounds to the shining sky, "Vrikama, Vrikama!"

Immediately Havishka the warlord throws the challenge, "Who will take us across the Sapta Sindhu? Who will be our hero?" His second-in-command, whiskers white as the waters, announces, "Vrikama, our hero, the war charioteer will lead us across the waters. The mighty Sapta Sindhu we shall cross with him." Each one of the assembly shouts, "Vrikama, Vrikama!" thumping their breasts, their spears, their carts, their pots; what a clamour, and my master is led to the wooden seat to be anointed.

Havishka pours the waters of the Sapta Sindhu over him, the priests chant, the herd screams, and Vrikama becomes a hero, trembling. He shivers violently throughout the ceremony. It is not the cold; it is fear. I smell it on my master, fear. After the crossing, he is afraid.

We camp for days on the riverbank as sheep are slaughtered, their air-filled carcasses being readied to serve as floats. We eat our fill. The bards sing songs, the old songs of our leaving our land and glorious new songs of the crossing. Soma is pressed out, honoured and drunk. Each night someone takes ill. They have drunk too much sura-wine. They are terrified of the depth of the Sapta Sindhu, swirling with snow waters; they are terrified of their shame, these pillages, and they are terrified because there is no going back.

Raktha too needs days to recover. He has bled a great deal from the slashes Vrikama gave him during the crossing. Sacrifices are made on the riverbank. To the sacrificial post are led one man, one bull, one stallion, one ram, one he-goat, and a small band of tribes-people we spy slipping into the high forests who have only copper spears to defend themselves. Five in all, including an infant, are sacrificed with priests chanting and the distribution of wine. Their heads are thrown into the river; their heads roll like round stones in the current and are swept away like stones down the seething river. We lose cattle and sheep, horses, cats, oxen, women, one hotra-priest, four children, men and eight dogs during the crossing in spite of the carcass floats.

We cross. I cross, tied to Raktha's reins, swimming by my master's side. We have crossed other rivers before but a more gigantic river than this one cannot exist; it is like the arm of a wrathful god, a barrier and a cloak. After the crossing, the thanksgiving and the recovery, Vrikama has four chariots. He is made a warlord in his own right, who has four ambitious warriors each snarling to snatch his lead, and two loyal charioteers to fight by his side. While Vrikama drinks and sleeps and has bards sing his praises with words that strike like lightning, I am taken to each bloated body that is fished out of the water. I, Trichaisma, the sacred one, am prodded and kept awake to vouchsafe the passage of the dead. For all said and done, I am a dog. And between master and dog there are rivers that can never be crossed.

Vrikama grows larger and larger in the words of the bards. With the call of the war drum his heart grows larger and larger for victories; he thinks his fingers can stir the clouds. As snowmelt feeds the rivers, so too Vrikama's deeds melt to feed his courage; his arrogance flows like a spring river.

After we have crossed the rivers of the Sapta Sindhu, Vrikama and his warriors break the dams, heavy with waters, of the Dasyu settlers. The dams lie like black serpents across the land, guarding the settlers' treasures of gold and grain and cattle. They thrust aside the boulders, one by one, and *the waters gush like blood from a ripped vein. Vrikama wants to destroy the settlers' spirit even before we attack.*

The Dasyus are many and we are few, but we are fast; their hearts are like the fields they had tilled, ours are like forest fires, raging. Most of that clan of Dasyus perish, though they are better than us in ways as many as the glorious waving pastures. Ulupi was one of them; she was a Dasyu, an Anaryan.

Narmini is a high town with walls of brick growing from the banks of the river. In the looting of Ulupi's town, I do not kill anything that moves or does not. I do not have to. Vrikama does it, he and his band. He races, torch in hand, through narrow streets that squeeze the heart and shut the sky, and burns them down.

Like embers after a sacrifice, the township stands smoking from the earth and from below the earth, red with memory. For three days and three nights the township blazes. It is as if the sun rested here licking the sweet curved horizon with his flames. Then it is dark. The landscape looks like ashes slowly flaking off logs. "Tri, this is more like home," my master says to me as sparks glow beneath our feet. "This releases the heart." But that home of mine had been green, endless green under an endless sky which kissed its mouth, so green.

This is black and red, like Vrikama's robes, and grey as pottery used in sacrifice. We plunder the town, taken grain, cattle, gold and women. We take their fine carpenters as slaves. Hissing like tears, the town burns down; hissing like curses, we speed through the ruins; hissing with grief, the survivors lie crumpled. Except Ulupi. She does not scream. She stands trembling like the fawn we roasted that night.

I never weep. Not even for Ulupi, the dark soft one whose body shone like the night sky, Ulupi the slave girl who tried to stab Vrikama as he was mating with her, Ulupi who he killed, Ulupi who sang in her strange language as she buried her face in my fur, Ulupi who Spaka tormented, Ulupi with her smell of gentleness and courage.

We camp near the rubble of Narmini for months as the breeze carries word of our exploits in the eight direction. Again Virkama disappears, he wanders. He does not return for days; when he does, wanderlust is singing in his blood like wine. Day and night his heart is restless, his thoughts spin like a leaf in an eddy, not sinking, not resting either. The warlord paces, thirsty for more glory. He stands at the edge of the clearing, drunk on soma. With the cup of heaven at his lips, he asks, "What is, and what is not? What are the skies, and what is this earth? From whence has it come into being? Who am I, and what made me be? Oh splendour, answer me."

Like a string of ants marching towards scraps from a sacrifice, we gather ourselves and wander, following the rising sun, following the signs of the priests, following Vrikama's dreams. We follow the course of rivers, the call of birds, the charge of boars; we follow Vrikama as he chases the dawn each day. We follow, growing tired of wandering, growing tired of the heat; the heat amongst the young warriors sparking like the campfires each night, growing louder, crackling.

Menaka's clan, the mighty Bhrgus, stand on the banks of the river, their homes swell over the land like a river in spate; Vrikama paces the nights in our camp, watching her clan, watching our campfires, his mind restless as lightning in storm clouds while the full moon skims the water like a cluster of heavenly swans ready to take flight. Then he sits down. I sit on my haunches near him; he looks at me as he speaks to himself. "I want sons, Tri, understand me. I want cattle and gold," he says. "I do not want to do battle with the Bhrgus; it is said their clan and ours share ancestors. I will marry into their clan and settle in this land." His heart runs to settle on the land as a milch cow runs after her calf.

The hero marries Menaka, who wears the blue niksha jewels. He marries her for peace, and through marriage to the dark-haired Menaka, he becomes a king. I stand when Menaka enters the thatched-roof wedding pavilion; she stands tall near her father, her three brothers, and her uncles' ten sons, her clansmen trailing behind her like the wake of a giant swan. She is painted red, the young bride. She smells of musk and pride. I can smell cattle and milk and ghee in her blood. I smell sacrifice.

Spaka she does not see as the older wife, her rival. Spaka she cannot see at all, while Vrikama watches as a tree watches the turning of the seasons. He watches the turning of his home, and he sheds his former covering; he turns cold and still as a tree without leaves. Spaka speaks: "You are not my husband, Vrikama. You, I do not know. I will return." Spaka turns and leaves, heading home with twenty others. She leaves without hope, a woman whose flesh is tough and thin like a quiver empty of arrows. Spaka turned back three springs ago, heading north and west, back to her homeland, childless, husbandless, a woman whose arms flapped like the dewlap of young cows.

I stay with Vrikama, following with my eyes Spaka's retreat into the horizon, howling, following her up to crossings I know she can never pass. Spaka knows it too. She hears me howl after her. She walks on. She walks away.

Vrikama and I hunt deer, circling does on the banks of the lakes, for the pregnant Menaka wants to eat unborn fawn thrown whole, tight in the womb, into the boiling cauldron. Her clan is powerful. She gives Vrikama his son, Bhargava, Giver of Waters. The toddler sits between my paws in the evening and mumbles, toothless as an old man. Vrikama turned toothless in his happiness. He plays with his son, he plays with his good fortune. He plays with the light all day, sitting, watching it slip between his fingers, slipping from rosy to bright to twilight to firelight. He plays dice, rolling them between his fingers. He plays dice, sowing them on the game-board as a lover sows his beloved; rolling in them between bowls of sura-wine and meat, rolling in the plenty which is his. He wins, he loses, he does not mind, he plays the game. But Vrikama does not know the game he is playing; he plays on and on as if in the coils of a strange and familiar dream. And so we settle.

I must have been dreaming when Vrikama awakens me the dawn after the Panis raid our camp. That night I had smelt danger in the wind. After I padded around the settlement I lay in shadows near the cattle shed, waiting. Everyone was asleep, the cattle's smell settled in the air like a fog. The Panis *crossed the river, they tried to lull me to sleep singing their magic hymns, singing to me in whispered breath, and I barked. I ran barking through our camp, raising the alarm. The men rose, the weapons rose, the battle cry rose full into the moonless night, and the Panis were driven back, splashing across the dark waters.*

At dawn: "Stop chasing rabbits in your sleep, Tri," Vrikama says, "There is battle to be done. Up! Up!" He is standing tall before my eyes, Vrikama the Sapta-Ratha, Lord of our settlement, glowing in full armour, the sun rising above his white helmet. I stretch, yawn, shake myself and follow him.

The Panis are waiting for us across the river; they fall upon us as we ride up the bank. The battle is fierce; I feel as if I am being hunted. I run, circling the hero's chariot, my tail between my legs. I smell a strangeness in the wind, in the cries of horses and men, snorting, kicking their legs in the air as they fall; over the smell of leather and skin, over the scent of metal and blood I smell terror, terror follows us as the serpent in heaven follows the moon to swallow it, spreading darkness.

How he fights this day, Vrikama! He makes safe his title Vayuvega, Speed of the Wind; with spear and axe and bow and arrow. With pride and madness the hero fights, speckled with the blood of numerous foes. Then all is still. His chariot slowly tilts and falls, its spoked wheels churning the bloody heavens, the horses' hooves ripping the skies. "Wait," Vrikama shouts above the steaming air, "Wait till I have righted my chariot." The Pani chieftain thunders towards him, leaps from his chariot with his battle-axe raised, leaps towards Vrikama's back struggling with the chariot car, the axe comes down on his left arm. From elbow to forearm it cuts, it frees Vrikama's arm towards the heavens with a push of blood rushing up, and Vrikama falls thrashing to the ground, this hero. Someone shoots the Pani chieftain through his neck; the cold arrow plunges from one side to the other. I charge and throw myself on Vrikama's face, muffling his cries, so the enemy hearing him silent takes him for dead. Vrikama bites my shoulder before he lies still.

I smell pain being whelped in his great body, I smell poison rising within him, and I bite his hair to revive him as I smell coldness and fever rising within him like a hailstorm on a hot day. Someone comes through the heat wavering, through the cries a spear forms and rises and plunges behind my tail into my master's stomach. His legs rise, his head jerks beneath the fur of my chest, and my vision clears red for the charge. Snarling, fangs bared, ears back, muscles tensing, eyes hot, I see soft scared flesh, a holy shiver runs down my spine. I leap at the enemy's throat. An axe blade skims my haunches, a weak blow, my fangs are red on his neck, and how the blood flows, in spurts, weaker and weaker and weaker. I cling fast till his kicking stills, till the enemy's hands slacken and fall off my shoulders. I lick my bloody nose, my fur, my haunches, and return to Vrikama, the hero fallen. I sit by his prone body, panting.

VII

THE COMFORT CAPSULE

52

"You are being removed to a Comfort Capsule," a Superior Zombie (Hawk-Eye Resolution) said. I did not know whether to feel large or small that a Zombie of his category had been assigned to me. However one thing was certain: he would miss nothing.

I followed his footsteps through long corridors filled with olivaceous light, into a pod that flew past purple mirror-faced buildings. The pod hovered by a fern-green mirrored globe. Curved mirror doors slid open.

"Alight," said the Zombie.

I followed his clanking stride through corridors suffused with cochineal luminosity. This opened into an atrium where false waterfalls roared from great heights breaking without wetness into crystal flowers; rainbows danced at its feet.

"Do not pause, Clone, or I shall blindfold you. These views are not for the likes of you."

We marched right, then right, then right again. I felt I had been following his footsteps for my entire actuality.

"Your Comfort Capsule beckons," said the Zombie. He pushed me into a room; the door locked.

Alone, I viewed the rooms.

These were miniature replicas of Aa-Aa's palace; even the arched doorways were low, forcing me to stoop. The hammock and two hovering chairs were more Couplet's size than mine. On Level Two, the dawn-shaded floating bed would just about accommodate me. Near it lay a book-sized wooden chest which did not yield. I knew what would lie within.

I returned to Level One. Weak grotto light flooded it, and artificial dew-drenched dwarf bamboo and shrubs with twinkling flowers appeared between pillars and niches. I touched the walls that swivelled to reveal shelves and shelves lined with books. These were dummies.

Beyond the veranda, a slim track of white quillit sand bordered a glassy pond. In the centre arose a zigplast lotus bud that opened when I stepped into the shallows. I waded towards the lotus. The small swing within moved with clockwork vigour, similar to antique pendulum clocks I had seen at the Museum.

I felt monstrous in these surroundings: an allosaur in an amphitheatre.

Only I was real.

Yet, more unreal than my environs was the last conversation I had with Leader. This beat its dark wings within me, cavernous and quick, echoing with disbelief.

"Aa-Aa was my mother."

Was Leader, then, my son? The toddling child whose small body I wished to wrap with kisses, who repeatedly pattered towards me, gurgling with delight at being cradled in my arms—before he disappeared before my eyes again and again and again?

I fell.

Leader had pulled me up; he pulled my head to his chest, kissing my hair, stroking my back. He stroked me until all I knew was his stroking.

At some point, I pulled back, touched his face, and asked, "Aa-Aa… she was prepared to let you die?"

"No! Original children are never destroyed," he said. "She knew that; she considered and accepted our separation, and knew I would be inoculated against her memory. But the inoculation was… incomplete."

He let go of me. I saw him rock himself. "Her face stayed with me, her hands, the quality of her voice." His eyes had grown dark and pulled at me like a stone sucked into a well.

Leader walked towards the window and pressed his hands against the panes. I put my arms around him.

He had kissed my forehead and ordered his clothes to him. As his silken robes draped around his body, he said, "I was in the Children's Stand during The Celebrations when she was pushed. The image was tonsured from my brain—but not completely. I can still see her hand going over the edge. Her palm was facing me."

My hair had risen; a chill wind ran around us.

"You understand why the Cause is doubly important to me," he said from a distance. Then he was gone.

I leaned against the dummy bookshelves, looking towards the glassy pond and the zigplast lotus at its centre. I stood for a long time, looking at nothing.

৵ 53 ৵

"Visitor," a songbird called and my floating bed shot towards the door. Dawn light swam through the room.

At Level One, Couplet was leaning against a wall, looking

at the pond. Maybe water had this effect, even artificial water: it makes one stand and stare.

Couplet sensed my presence. "Surprise, dear Clone!"

Its welt had healed; its paunch had grown to comfortable proportions.

"Couplet!" My arms opened; its eyes rolled and it giggled.

"I've been in rehab, and have been rehabilitated, thanks to you," Couplet said. I stared. "Oh, you know, 'seeing Aa-Aa,' that bit you pulled off. Proved my hunches about you were true. You are a tale-teller yet; you'll deliver."

"I will?"

"You'd better."

"Better for whom? Certainly not for me."

"For all of us, dear Clone. You are playing the game. Rest assured you are in the process of re-living Aa-Aa's last days on schedule as The Celebrations draw near."

I had lost track of the days.

"You will remember," Couplet said.

"But this place—"

"Is the most creative metaphor the Global Community has yet thought up, albeit unknowingly!" it said, running in circles around me. "What kind of a writer are you if you fail to recognize such a blatant metaphor?"

"This paltry capsule—"

"Should allow your imagination to work. Use its very smallness to expand the visage of your imagination. Oof!" it puffed. "Think of her, constrained yet dreaming big, and be inspired. Think vast. Think, deeply, yourself."

Couplet sat.

I watched it as sunlight filtered in, draping us in calming light that suggested a timeless serenity.

"You've recently awoken. So I'll give you time."

A ray of light tore through me. Maybe in these constrained yet metaphorical spaces I could be both Aa-Aa and myself.

"Couplet, care to join me for a cup of Ethiopian coffee?"

"Don't!" Couplet shrieked. "That was part of my torture routine!"

"Sorry. I'll switch to synthetic Darjeeling tea."

"I prefer to wait outside," it said, bowing gravely.

I returned to see Couplet swinging in the lotus that was circling round and round in the circular pond.

"This ride makes one dizzy," Couplet said, jumping off, "but then which worthwhile experience doesn't?" It rubbed its hands. "Are you ready?"

"What is expected of me now, Couplet?" I felt unpleasantly hot, as if it were afternoon already.

"You will follow her routine. And," Couplet pressed its hands together, "the best part is she wandered around the City in disguise. You'll follow suit. I'll accompany you."

"And?"

"The bad part is you will have to keep recalling her unfinished speech *ad infinitum*. Till you come up with the ending." Couplet shrugged.

Light seemed to splinter in shards.

I closed my face with my hands. I asked, "What if Aa-Aa's secret was inane? What if her death was another silly mistake?"

"That's a risk we…"

"But… but even if she had a dangerous secret, hers was just one voice."

"Clone," Couplet beamed, "How can the Global Community tolerate this… this delightful aberration?" Couplet patted my hands. "Open your eyes. What if grief and memory and tenderness are again stirred up?" Its voice sparkled so that I opened my eyes. Its antennae sparked; tiny starlights scattered. Its antennae seemed shorter but it did not seem to notice.

"Promise, Clone, that you will do your best!"

"I promise."

Couplet pirouetted towards the door.

"Wait! I have something to tell you."

"Nothing more now, dear Clone, or I shall collapse from a surfeit of hope! You realize, don't you, that the sensitized are especially susceptible to its winged weight?"

I felt that days, years, centuries had collapsed into me; yet this gravity was acting as a springboard. I felt I were simultaneously buried and flying. It was an altogether curious emotion.

~ 54 ~

I thought of him. But thinking of him, I did not know what to think. Was he in pain? Buried in memory? Was he safe in the midst of subterfuge? Was he thinking of me?

I felt as if I was in a swirl of dry neem leaves spun by a hot current, their serrated edges on my skin.

I decided to re-live Aa-Aa's life as closely as possible.

Waiting for Leader to reappear, I ordered the food she liked; I wore cherry-coloured slippers awaiting her secret to reveal itself to me.

By mimicking her gestures could I become her?

How does one become another?

For this to happen, needn't one first know who one is?

Who am I?

I sat by the water's edge watching the crescent moon's enlarged reflection dapple the surface.

What lay beneath? Water? Darkness? Or not even this?

Who has the answer?

The moon followed its ancient trajectory in the sky, and passed below the earth's curve.

I fell asleep by the dark water, darkness swirling me into even darker stillness.

<h2 style="text-align:center">❦ 55 ❧</h2>

"We commence re-tracing your Original's secret routine," the Superior Zombie (Hawk-Eye Resolution) said, handing me a replica of his costume. "She travelled in disguise. Wear it."

I wore the thigh-high clanking boots of granitodine leather, the breastplate and back-guard, the shoulder-high gloves, its fingers encased in fishscale miristeel.

"The weapons are phoney," he said, handing me the arsenal, "She was never armed."

The weapons magnetized on my armour, on ankle, thigh, hip, back, palm.

"Walk."

I followed him through glowing cochineal corridors, into a surveillance pod.

"Hello, Clone," said Couplet from the rear. "I'm accompanying you, and am, myself, being accompanied as you see."

Next to it sat a Superior Zombie (Type K6) the only ones capable of neutralizing Firehearts when they threaten to explode with outrage. "This gambit is foolproof," Couplet said. "Of course Aa-Aa did not tour in quite these circumstances, but then what's to be done?"

I thought it best not to reply.

"The ritual you will undergo is called Testing The Lama Spirit, so named after an archaic rite of Tibetan origin wherein priests presented contenders to the Spiritual Throne with a series of choices," Couplet said. "Only the contender possessed by the spirit of a late High Lama responded correctly, and was chosen. We shall monitor how close your responses are to your Original's to ascertain how far you have evolved." It paused, and added, "By the way, you understand the meaning of the word *spiritual*, don't you, Clone?"

"No."

"I see we have a long way to go," murmured Couplet.

"We have arrived at the Plasma Transfusion Centre," said my Superior Zombie. "Disembark."

The pod hovered at the upper reaches of the Centre, near a small tunnel-like opening.

"She used the catwalks to observe unseen," the Zombie said. "Wear this."

I wore the helmet. My vision was blinkered, only the path straight ahead was visible.

"Did she wear a helmet?" I asked.

"Yes, but hers permitted all-round vision. Yours is like ours. It is sufficient for you."

"I demand a hovering chair," said Couplet, "to keep up."

"Request foreseen," said its Zombie, pulling out just this from the pod.

From below, the sound of engines grew louder as did the noise of thumping, compression, and a quirky swishing sound.

We walked on with Couplet keeping up in the hovering chair. The noise grew louder and louder. And hotter.

"Armour, induce air-conditioning and reduce noise pollution for team," said my Zombie.

The air cooled, the noise faded. We proceeded down the tunnel.

"I need my special frequency to communicate with the Clone," said Couplet, hovering beside me.

"Request foreseen," said its Zombie.

"Observe the preparation of the Originals' Sanitation Dip composed of tiger saliva and Komodo dragon blood extracts. Highly antiseptic. Mixed with the herb Prunella vulgaris or Self-Heal," said Couplet. "Extracts of all species that existed before our Trans-Species Epoch are stored and replicated."

"Fireheart, complete the sentence: 'For the betterment of The Global Community'," said my Zombie.

"Well, you have." Its antennae twirled and dipped. "Of course they are all extinct."

"Move." I was prodded down the catwalk. "Stop."

"The Plasma Transfusion plants extract high-energy plasma for the Originals' weekly dip," whispered Couplet, "otherwise they'd be doddering." It stuck out its long tongue, then giggled.

Was Leader similarly susceptible without immersions? How little I knew of him who had been in me.

The tunnel opened to an atrium filled with blinding saffron light.

"Up darkening visors," said my Zombie.

Our vision cooled and darkened. Far below I spotted small shadowy figures, Clones working in the noise, heat and light. With periodic regularity some fell at the base of the machines. These were carried away on stretchers; others replaced them,

I remembered 14/53/G had worked here. Nausea overcame me; I clutched the guardrails.

"Steady," said my Zombie. "Or we shall retreat and this mission will be deemed a failure."

"I have recovered."

"We shall stand by the forklift to permit you to have a good look."

"I am prepared." I watched, holding tight to the rails.

From below more of the same followed.

"I have a question for the Fireheart," I said.

"Permission granted."

Couplet's chair rose to hover near my shoulder.

"Why aren't those Clones provided with visors like ours?" I asked. I saw the terror and vulnerability of my actuality and that of the others. "Couplet, is cruelty embedded in us at the Birthing Place, or is it instilled in us in Behaviour School?"

"Ah-ha!" It rubbed its hands. "You're on Aa-Aa's track, Clone, though simplistic in your formulation. But then you're a Clone. However, there are no easy answers because nothing is easy. Aa-Aa, according to the archival access I've been temporarily granted, raised similar issues at the High Council. For a start, she suggested the Global Community 'wipe its eyes with dewdrops,' that is, refresh its vision. She faced derision and ordered to wear ancient spectacles to correct her 'long-sight'—which she wore as a symbol of protest. Further, she was informed she could miss her weekly plasma dip as a Conscientious Objector. This option, according to my research, she didn't take."

I did not know what to say, so I said, "I see." I felt as if a moth was fluttering in my throat.

"Hey Zombie! Yes, you, dragontail," said Couplet turning to its Zombie. "Notify your superiors that the Clone responded in a manner similar to her Original. I consider this part of the mission a success. Get it? Now move the Clone out of here!"

"Recording this part of mission successful," its Zombie repeated.

We turned. As we retraced our steps a vision appeared: I was standing, holding the rails, and looking at 14/53/G being carried away. Everything went black.

"Awaken, Clone, awaken."

"This dear Clone is reviving. Just as soon as she awakens all that she saw will pass like a fading dream. She will only remember the real—the Dream in which we live," sang a

Nurse Clone. "We don't want the Dream to break, do we? So we must revive!"

I squeezed open my eyes.

"Get up, dear Clone! You have been fortified," she beamed, patting my hands. "You are ready for your next mission. Do sit up!"

I was in an unaccustomed place. Everything was white, even the light. Couplet's eyes were white and round. Its mouth was a round white hole. Whiteness swam around me.

"I am well," I said, struggling up. "Initiate next mission." My armour had been removed.

"You still need a helping hand, dear Clone,' said the Nurse Clone, inoculating me. "Count till ten, then heave yourself up. We're on standby. Ready? One, two, three, wheeeeee!"

I stood.

"Another helping hand," she said, inoculating me again. My head cleared.

"Please take this for me, dear Clone," she said, forcing four pink gems into my mouth. "Swallow!"

I felt close to normal though the light was still white.

"Proceed to next destination," I said. "Couplet, remove me from here."

"Tadpole feet! You, I mean you, Zombie!" Couplet cried. "Proceed!"

I was marched into the pod. Exhaustion overcame me.

Sweet scented breezes blew, birds chirped above the sound of running water, I could hear tree shadows dipping and swaying. I sighed, and snuggled deeper in my seat.

"We are here."

A pristine light jewelled the grass, the dew on the grass, and flower buds and flowers; the light ran over gentle hills that shone with butterflies afloat; the light spread glimmering up to the vast trees and sky then again fell on the earth like a kiss. I knew where I was: paradise.

I was up, and running. A rain of laughter led me on. Then I saw them: children. The children wore crowns and skirts and shorts in the colours of rainbows, they danced in the soft valley, clapping and shouting.

I followed.

They gathered in a circle, holding hands and singing something faint and sweet, something soft as honey.

"We are in School," said Couplet, puffing to keep up. "Observe from a distance. Aa-Aa sought forbidden glimpses of her children."

"She was lucky," I murmured.

"If you insist," shrugged Couplet. "Crawl towards them, the way she did."

"Yes, of course, yes," I said, falling on my knees. My child might be here.

I crawled in the fragrant dew-smirched grass till I could see every detail: their chubby feet and dimpled hands, their wind-tossed curls, their neat tiny teeth. They looked so delightful that I gasped. I heard their silvery chanting. As I crawled nearer, I heard better.

> *"We are Originals, we're the Best.*
> *We're kind, we rule at others' behest.*
> *Firehearts are liars we suppress*
> *Or The Truth they will repress.*
> *Strong Zombies we keep in check*
> *Or our Order they will wreck.*
> *Clones are those we guide and shield,*
> *they must work or to death yield.*
> *The mutants too we put away*
> *For they are ill and shouldn't stray.*

This we do for the Common Good
And not from hatred, it's understood!"

The children stomped their feet and fell laughing to the ground.

My body seemed to be filled with a thousand fluttering moths, beating wings against each other.

"It's their School Song," said Couplet.

"Do they know what they are saying?" I asked. Then threw up.

An Original, wearing sequinned wings, traipsed around them.

"Their Teacher," Couplet said unnecessarily.

Fireworks burst overhead like promises. Balloons and chocolates rained upon them. A few children grabbed at the raining sweetmeats. Most tussled with each other, baring teeth, tumbling and mock-fighting.

The Teacher clapped. "Children, disperse to your Guardian Units. Tomorrow we shall begin a new fun topic. It's called History."

Flowers showered from the pristine light above, falling in an arch on the grass to spell "History."

"What are we learning tomorrow?" the Teacher asked. Her wings beat furiously.

"His-treeeeeeee!" the children screamed, tearing in different directions.

I wished to sink beneath the grass.

"Clone, do you now understand why Aa-Aa tried to commit suicide after her first visit here?"

"What is 'suicide'?"

"Oooo," it sighed. "You've reverted to Clone-Mode mindframe as a protective device. Enough for today. Pull yourself together and we'll leave."

I felt embedded in swampy chill; like my DNA had drained out. "It is difficult to speak," I managed.

"You are experiencing depression because you've sensed the pervading horror that lies beneath normalcy. I shall report that this part of the experiment too was a success. Now rise."

"I cannot."

"Zombies!" Couplet called. "Toad-horns! Rat-legs! Haul the Clone into the pod. Depression has incapacitated her."

I felt like a log in a bog.

I was to feel like this for days.

⊸⊱ 56 ⊰⊶

I would see, yet not register movement.

I would hear, yet not respond to sound.

I would sit still for hours.

I was overcome by "Depression."

I was staring at the artificial water and did not hear the flourish of trumpets. I did not hear Duke bark, but he stood close by. Wagging his tail, he licked my face.

"Duke." Now I heard the dog whine as he circled me. I stretched out a hand to touch his passing body. He padded back and settled at my feet. I stroked him. "This means the Leader is here," I said, turning my head.

Maybe my vision had not as yet recovered, for I did not see him.

"Duke, where is the Leader?"

Duke yawned, licked his maw and sank his head between his paws.

I slowly rose and wandered through the rooms looking for him. When I returned I heard Leader's voice: "...am detained. Duke should be fed in an hour's time. Ask the Unit for Duke's menu." A thumb-size image of Leader's face issued from Duke's vision-collar.

I did not know what to do with Duke. I decided to take him for a sail. "Follow me," I said.

Duke stood, stretched and followed.

At the pond I called, "Lotus." It came towards us. I stepped in saying, "Follow."

Duke remained on the shore.

I disembarked and repeated the action. Duke still stood on the shore. "Come."

I caught Duke's collar and dragged him in. "You will like this," I said, still holding him. "Lotus, proceed."

With a jerk we were on our way, circling the pond. Duke began to bark. I let go. He jumped into the water and swam ashore. By the time I reached the shore, he was shaking himself, scattering droplets. He ran up and down the pond edge barking, then retreated to the veranda. I followed him.

He seemed content to sit at my feet. I too found it companionable. Occasionally he would get into a frenzy of trying to catch his tail, or he'd squirm on his back, four paws dangling in the air. Hours slipped away.

The Food Dispensing Unit served Duke a large bowl of meat and rice, and a bone. He took a long time gnawing the bone, holding it between his forepaws. The sight was calming. Both of us were absorbed.

Leader's face again appeared on Duke's collar and said, "I have been further detained. Please escort Duke to the Zombie stationed outside your back door. I shall see you soon."

"Come, Duke," I said, tickling the underside of his throat. Duke's pink tongue hung over black gums; I stroked his forehead, his eyes rolled back, he panted. "Enough. You must go," I said.

He padded behind me to the back door that was camouflaged to look like the wall.

"Open the door. Return the dog to The Leader," I called

to the Zombie. The wall-door parted. The Zombie saluted, Duke slid into the garden.

From behind the window, I watched Duke bound down the pebbled path towards a long silver glider. It took off.

ᴈ 57 ᴄ

He arrived. Immediately without a word we mated. I pulled him to me, my back to the wall, his body against mine, his desires my want, his hands my need, my body seeking to pass into his, further and further around him till we went blind with joy and our eyes reopened at last and we parted.

Then he spoke.

"I didn't realize it would be so hard for you to do Aa-Aa's rounds," he said, lying in my arms.

This made me stand. "14/53/G used to work at the Plasma Centre." I walked towards the windows. With his words I realized how far we had parted, and how quickly, though I still smelt of him all over.

"I forgot you used to be one of them." He ran a hand through his hair. "Come now, sit beside me."

"I still am 'one of them', am I not? I too was meant to work till my actuality ran out. I too was supposed to live under the rules the children sang about," I said, circling back towards him. "Their song was 'depressing'."

"I see Couplet has been teaching you emotiwords," he said, reaching to pull me on the bed, "which you understand." He pulled me to his side, his arm lay across my breasts and shoulder, his legs tangled with mine. "Lie still, will you now?"

"I haven't told Couplet that Aa-Aa was your mother," I said, pulling myself away and looking into his face.

"Tell it so that it will trust me. I need all the support I can muster. My plans are falling into place." He rose and paced.

"That's what detained me. I'm fine-tuning operational details with select mutants and Firehearts. We are on track for The Celebrations."

"Will you tell me your plans?"

He stood still. "The less you know, the safer you will be."

"If you are worried that I'll speak under torture, don't be. I haven't had any further visitations. Once I was scared of what I'd next become—maybe a leech in the twentieth century or a politician in the twenty-first—any lowly life-form. But the condition I'm reduced to seems worse. The ability to write or create voice-tombs has deserted me." I slid on the floor with my head in my hands. "I'm just a Clone."

"A mutant. A mutant Clone."

My hands rose to pull my hair, to pull my head back. "I miss it. I miss the writing so."

"Aa-Aa 14/54/G," he said cupping my face in his hands, "what do you miss about the writing?"

"I miss—being away from myself, yet being myself." I shook myself free and paced. "Am I making sense?"

"Not really."

I felt like a pebble rolling down a mountain slope on a long journey.

We sat side by side in silence.

"I think you should go for a spin," he said. "Get up. Let's go."

"You mean I may leave the Comfort Capsule?"

"You will have to be implanted with a temporary tracking device even if you accompany me. But that's a small price to pay," he said, pulling me up.

He called our clothes towards us. We dressed.

At the back door he said, "Zombie, the Clone is accompanying me. Track her."

The Zombie kowtowed. Leader strode ahead while I was inoculated.

When I recovered, I noticed a fleet of gliders parked in the thoroughfare.

Some had whirring red lights on their domes, others were thorny with arsenal and the last was sprayed with a Red Cross. Leader was standing near a long glider that looked like a smooth golden fish.

"Come!"

I entered what seemed like golden mist. When my eyes adjusted to the fragrant light, I saw divans draped in gold damask, golden tables and a gold fountain shedding golden water. The bouncy carpet gleamed with embedded pearls.

"Sit," he said to me, then, "Glider, take off."

"Proceeding on target, Gracious Leader." The glider had a soothing voice.

"We are journeying far into the suburbs of Old Bombay and will take almost five minutes to reach. It's in ruins."

"Security tracking our movements, Gracious Leader," the glider said.

"Acknowledged," he replied and turned to me. "There have been rare reports of scavenger-raiders ambushing lone gliders at the ruins." He laughed. "Even the Global Community's hold occasionally slips."

I remained silent. The gold was suppressing my voice.

"This," he said, waving his hands, "is normal for Originals. It's far less ostentatious than my colleagues. One of them travels with a circus on board."

I looked out of the rose-tinted window. The city was a blur below.

"Have a soma-nectar," he said, pushing a glass of golden liquid towards me. "There will be nothing where we are going."

"Where is that?"

"One of Aa-Aa's secret places. She visited it twice. It's called Gandhi Bhavan."

We landed as I was gulping down the drink. I felt strong, as if I had just been released from the Birthing Place.

Used tesson parts, seebege, tangled robot limbs and discarded prototype heads lay strewn around. We picked our way through the garbage of body parts. I sensed the heat of a force field.

"We are here," he said and mouthed a code that made visible a ruin beyond the force field. "Come." He held out a badge and we passed through the force field. It seared only slightly.

Within lay a room of old brick, plaster peeling off the two standing walls. Faded red floor tiles lay scattered. A length of wooden banister hung preserved in cobalt forsickaline. A wooden wheel, or possibly a spindle of some sort, was similarly hung between sheets of clear acryfoam.

"Make yourself comfortable," he said leaning against the acryfoam.

I did likewise.

The silence was immense.

"Activate hologram," he said to the ruin.

Within the faded hologram, I discerned what seemed to be a spindly tortoise or a shrunken old man. It was a man; his arms were moving, turning a spindle.

"He was called the Mahatma," the Leader said, "who apparently was an apostle of peace and instilled courage in the weak. My mother, as usual, didn't concur with him—or anyone else—completely. But she noted she largely agreed with his views."

I waited.

"All trace of the Mahatma is obliterated from the Archives. There is only this ruin—that stands due to typical bureaucratic oversight—and her comments spirited away in the margins of a voice-tomb I am researching."

"What did he do?" I asked.

"I don't know. I believe he lived in the twentieth century. He possibly led an uprising."

I knew this was a special place, and special for Aa-Aa and him. But the Mahatma did not evoke any response in me. I felt no poetry, or curiosity. Even the sense of time past was missing, for what lay beyond were heaps of recent garbage. This was a lone derelict, long elided from memory.

For me this place was special because we had passed through a force field.

"Thank you," I said, "for the trip."

"Think about this place. Maybe it will inspire you."

I nodded.

We stayed so long that the silence and ruin seemed to become part of me. All of it entered, and settled into me.

I became the discarded body parts, the crumbling walls, the faded holograph, the forgotten memory of the Mahatma, the distorted force field light. I felt the implacability of time. As if its mouth had opened and I and he, the convoy of gliders, the entire Global Community, the cities, all that moved and did not, all of memory, history and misinformation was being sucked down time's endless throat. My hair stood on edge. I was not even discernible in this grand onrush. Everything passed, and continued to pass.

What sense could I make of it?

What use, then, my struggles and despair? Or was it because all things passed in such quick succession that my struggles took on—significance? Does The Great Fading That Awaits Us All impose on each one an astounding accountability?

Was this the secret Aa-Aa had been moving towards?

Before we passed through the force field again Leader slipped a small diamond medallion into my hand. "Keep this memento. It's merely second-grade protection against force fields," he said, closing my fingers over it.

I looked at him.

"Stash it away in your favourite hiding place. The sole of your right shoe. No one will think of searching there again. Be quick."

I did.

On the return journey we held hands.

Alone in the Comfort Capsule, I felt strangely still. As if I had already passed, unwritten, into history.

Yet, my breath hammered against my chest. I wondered: What is the weight of one's actuality? Doesn't this emerge from accountability, from grasping the moment?

I felt a vastness within me, a vastness without meaning, yet deeply beautiful. Yet, who was I? To what species did I belong?

❧ 58 ❧

I laid an array of lipsticks on the floor. These were my tools.

The walls spread white around me, like the endless empty pages within the Computer I'd seen at the Museum.

I tried to write but felt my limbs were hacked off.

I tried to compose voice-tombs but felt pressed between thick airless sheets. I tried to think but felt trapped within a hollow crystal cube that was morphing. The air within was petrifying into tar. I too was petrifying. I was tearing at my veins but no blood flowed.

This sensation was ceaseless as the blank white sheets.

I became accustomed to this state.

I lay within the whiteness trying to think of something comforting. I could think only of mating, this lone desire had not left me. Rather it quickened my blood and grew to fill the spaces of my mind. I thought of the long sleek hunger that pushes one onwards, onwards to becoming part of another's body, I thought of the blinding moment after which I'd fall back into my own body, knowing again my body's limits; I thought of the body's silence when it rests, satisfied and calm after this voyage.

Had Aa-Aa also been trapped by this desire that grew in me like an endless cavern? But Aa-Aa had mated with many different Originals so it must have been different with her. What does constantly being mated do?

I thought of Leader, the nape of his neck against which I rested, breathing in its scent of salt and lime, the throb of his pulse. I pretended he was asleep and ran my hands all over him, revisiting the places I knew. The mole between his shoulder blades, that small dark bump that my palms would slide over, that my fingers would try to smoothen out, the nick below his ribcage to which I would fasten my lips, trying to suck the hurt skin out and make it even, the softness between his legs that I would hold and watch as it grew, the slight hair curling on his thighs that I liked to straighten which would spring back as soon as I let go, the skin of his heels that was softer than mine. He would let me run my fingers, run my breath, my lips, all over him as we rested; he would let me put my ear to his body and hear the sounds it made inside.

I dressed him in the various costumes I had seen in my visitations: in rough hide and fine muslin and brocade and yellow silk. I changed his jewels, his garlands, the length of his hair, his footwear. I dressed him and undressed him, skipping through centuries. I liked him best as a monk, head tonsured, draped in a single loose cloth. When I could quickly undress him and he would be ready within.

My body was in pain by the time I finished my voyaging.

I paced.

My body continued to cry.

❧ 59 ❧

"Visitor!" called a songbird. I tried to press my way out of the numbing whiteness that surrounded me when I try to work; my hands were splayed against solid air.

"What are you doing, Clone?" asked Couplet.

"I can't do anything."

"Pardon. I'll rephrase my question. What are you trying to do?"

"I was trying to write. But I'm stuck. I can't breathe."

"Oh, you're in that hell, are you?" said Couplet. "Don't worry. It will pass."

"What is the name of this hell?"

"The Writer's Block." Couplet chuckled. "This is good news."

"I don't think so," I said, still trying to push my way out.

"It's metaphoric, Clone." Couplet called for a hovering chair, and slouched with legs crossed. "You are so disturbed that you are petrified. But eventually, the unfolding, whenever it happens, should be creative. Keep faith."

"Couplet…"

"Clone, soon words will roll off your tongue like an elixir. You will be revitalized, as will your listeners."

This was oddly comforting, though I was by now convinced that there was no usefulness to literature except its momentary fragrance. Nothing changed because of it, yet it survived as visitations.

"I see you disagree, Clone."

The air began to circulate. "Aa-Aa died," I began, "while the Global Community—"

"Clone, I am sorry to state that this is not the time for a discussion on the merits or demerits, such as there may be, of literature. There's much to be done," Couplet said, its antennae twirling. "Though, come to think of it, maybe you could use the lessons I have to teach you as a displacement technique, in order to get back to creativity."

The light seemed brighter, blood oozed into my limbs at the thought of work.

"Hey, you are also scheduled to do a rushed tour of Aa-Aa's ambit before you focus on her last voice-impulses for The Celebrations," Couplet said. "Remember, Clone, you will have to deliver her exact words. The secret they want silenced, the secret that's kept you alive."

I remembered what I had to say. "Couplet, I have to tell you certain things."

When I finished, Couplet's antennae stood upright, its eyes and mouth were round. "Are you sure The Leader is Aa-Aa's last child?" it asked.

I nodded.

"Well then. Well indeed."

"Couplet, you are lost for words!"

"Of course not. I'm merely stunned." Couplet turned a shade red. "Well, this explains his extraordinary attachment to you. It also 'rationally' explains why a non-literary Original leads the Cause. I don't believe in pure altruism, Clone. Outside poets, I mean."

"You are wrong, aren't you Couplet? You are being narrow."

"Of course not. Poets are never narrow. It's only by being deeply yourself that you can become others, you ninny."

A sea seemed to ebb within me, exposing exhausted sediment.

"I didn't mean *ninny* literally," Couplet said. "Come on, Clone, up!"

I sat where I was.

"Poets don't apologize; they transform. This is the best I can do." It shrugged its shoulders. "If you think you have literature running through your cloned DNA—act! Literature is never selfish. Keep faith."

In the silence, the air shifted its colours of light.

"Oh," said Couplet, "I almost forgot! I bring you good tidings of great joy. Because of the voice-tombs you have relayed—capped with sure-fire proof of the Writer's Block you currently exhibit—you have been admitted into the Firehearts' Council."

"What does that mean?"

"No greater honour can be conferred on you. Understand this, Clone." Couplet raised its right hand and said, "You can take the oath. Repeat after me."

Raising my right hand, I repeated: "*I promise to secure for all: justice, social, economic and political; liberty of thought, expression, belief, faith and worship; equality of status and opportunity, and to promote among them all fraternity assuring the dignity of the individual...*"

"Congratulations," said Couplet. "Clone, you are now an honorary member. Though some among us demur about the oath—they think it is out of date and requires refashioning. It is, in fact, very old."

"I do not fully comprehend the oath," I said. "Somehow, the significance seem to overflow the words. Though all I've repeated seems... like a river of stars, yet close as the lines on my palm."

"That's grand," Couplet conceded. "You can't fully understand because you are still a Clone. But don't let it bother you. Overly, I mean."

It seemed to me that significance was like the light of a great star that had exploded eons ago in the universe. Now its dead light reached us still; and we still sought its light, believing it was still true and alive. Yet, because we still see its light in the distant sky the star *is* alive.

In other words, one has to trust one's self in order to understand significance.

"It's the best you can do," said Couplet.

The path to the star seemed to have hit the hard cementerrene of the thoroughfare.

"What is the work I have to do?" I asked.

"Well, with Leader leading us things look brighter," it began. "However, begin to memorize…"

We set to work, Couplet and I, pretending to work for the Global Community while working for The Cause.

Even as I was discovering words, I was learning of their betrayal.

Even as I was discovering myself, I was learning how to wear masks.

Was this the way of the world?

Was this all my actuality amounted to?

∽ 60 ∾

Supervised by a Superior Zombie, two JE Clones with gecko DNA walked up the wall to install an air-sheet within my cramped quarters. The sheet curled at the ceiling and floor.

"When He appears on screen, do not attempt to see His visage," the Zombie said. "Or else…"

I kowtowed. All thought fled.

Ethereal music filled the capsule. I kowtowed and lay in front of the sheet.

"Clone, are you prepared for what you are about to receive?" a voice sang.

I murmured into the floor, "This Clone is unworthy and begs pardon in advance for any untoward mistake." The old words returned like close companions; like trees standing together in a forest.

"We accept you acknowledge your failings."

A blast of trumpets followed. I shook.

"Clone, your responses to stimuli are as predicted," a new voice said. "Now you must strive to do better."

"Gracious Sovereign, this Clone's only enterprise is to fulfil your command." I knocked my head ten times against the floor.

"However, you have not recently had any visitations nor produced any voice-tombs. This does not bode well."

A chill drained my blood. "Forgive me Great Lord. This Clone begs permission to say that, in spite of her best efforts, nothing has manifested itself."

"Clone, focus on your Original's last voice-tomb to prove your worth to the Global Community."

"Long live the Global Community."

"Clone, deliver. So that you too may be delivered to Paradise Island."

Paradise Island! I jerked. Squinting I glimpsed the face of the Supreme Commander on the air sheet. His chin and forehead were curled on its margins.

"Most Honourable One and Highest Lord, this Clone begs forgiveness. But nothing comes to me. This Clone is helpless." I shuddered at the blatant words that spilled out of me like milk. From what source do the weak gain courage?

"Make it happen. Or you shall be withdrawn very slowly."

The face on the air sheet faded. Trumpets blasted.

I thought the trumpets were blasting from within me. My Writer's Block had protected me. There was nothing I could reveal.

∼ 61 ∼

The sensation of trumpeting was short-lived. I had to remember, and could not. Or I had to concoct, and could not. I lay in blankness. And blankness lay ahead of me in the form of my reward, Paradise Island. Tremors shot through my body. I huddled. Twitched.

This is how he found me.

"I heard what transpired between the Supreme Commander and you," he said. "Calm down Aa-Aa 14/54/G. You've resisted enough for the moment." He stroked my head.

I jerked away. "Nothing manifests," I managed.

"Visitor!" the songbird chimed.

Couplet entered. It saluted. "Leader!" it beamed. Its body sparked.

He saluted Couplet. "She's become a blank. This can have serious repercussions for us and them. And," he added, "her."

Couplet was still beaming. "That Which Should Not Be Mentioned has descended on her. I vouchsafe it's a genuine state." Couplet saluted again, beaming. "The Writer's Block is a savage and savaging silence."

"What then do we do?"

"We wait for it to pass." Couplet beamed. "It will, I assure you, Leader."

"But the game plan hinges on her focusing everyone's attention on Aa-Aa's secret during The Celebrations. On cue!"

"Sir! Maybe the Clone will, maybe she won't," Couplet saluted, "but I've heard resistance is growing. The FBI/1 unit has reported abnormal behaviour as has the ISIL-RAW, the KGB/0/CIA and the 007/…"

"Curtail your enthusiasm, Fireheart."

"Sir."

"What is the average timespan required for this Block to lift?"

"Leader, we are speaking about artistic creation. There are no averages."

"I just have to take your word for it, do I?"

"As the pre-eminent poet of the realm I suggest you do, Leader." It bowed.

He ran a hand through his hair. "We'll hope for the best. Couplet, do not use her to reach me. Go through your old contact. I want her safe." He turned to me. "You'll recover." He kissed me and left.

Couplet was blushing. "Well, Clone I'll see you soon. In the meantime, be prepared for tedium, Exalted One." It bowed extravagantly.

They had spoken of me as if I was not present.

Was this part of The Block? Does not writing equate to not being?

❧ 62 ❧

They refurbished my Comfort Capsule. The supervising Superior Zombie (Type D Onion Head) said, "Most of the floor has become a treadmill to simulate your Original's pacing. Recorders that culled her voice-thoughts from the surfaces of her palace have been initiated." They left.

The floor began to move. I had to keep walking to stay on the spot.

The Capsule said, "Children play games called Riot-Riot. The weak are disposed. Dissidents are bled in public squares. The strong flee into the freedom of blindness while commerce continues, rulers rule, slaves slave and accords on border walls and sanitized zones are signed."

I paced on a tile.

"What kind of beast am I?" the walls repeated. "How am I immured?"

With effort I made my way to the veranda. Two tiles were stationary. I sat on these. The step said, "I have no tears. I have no sanctuary. To what moral community do I belong?"

I leaned against a pillar that said, "Not for the first time or the last is atrocity blanketed by even more atrocities. But do we learn or do we forget? Are we lost?" My body shrank from the pillar's cool contact. I ran towards another post that said, "I fear we are lost."

Standing on a stepping-stone at the pond's edge, I looked into the quiet green water. "I cannot turn the other cheek, nor say forgive them for they know not what they do. What, then, do I demand of myself?" The waters of the pond repeated lapping against zeebed water lilies. Buds sprang open. Fake fragrance spread. It was a no-moon night.

I turned. Running on the spot and leaping, I reached the Food Dispensing Unit. It said, "Give me water, hope." It served a scarlet froth.

I covered my ears. I hopped to Level Two over sliding tiles. As I lay in bed it said, "I have a dream."

"Do not forsake me," said the pillow.

I shivered. I reached for the coverlet. It said, "I pray to myself, my only God. May my talons grow towards tenderness. May I redeem myself in my eyes. May I be what I am meant to be."

I passed out.

∾ 63 ∾

Day after day, the rooms and I repeated Aa-Aa's thoughts.

What kind of a beast am I?

There was no respite, and no answer.

To what community did I belong?

I did not know what I was meant to be.

Then how could I redeem myself?

Light tore like petals.

The voice lapped my mind, clinging like barnacles. These thoughts were not mine, yet refused to fall away.

It seemed as if I was wearing my insides out, on the floor

and walls. This exposure made my very skin alien to me. I did not seem to know where I began or ended.

My breath swayed like elephant ears in a storm, strong yet helpless.

I lost all sense of meaning.

There was one place I had not visited recently that might help me remember: Aa-Aa's lotus workstation. Permission was granted.

I sat on the swing within its petals. We sailed. It began to speak.

"*Hail! Members of the Global Community. Let us give thought and thanks to…*"

The swing began to rock. "Delete the word 'thought.' This is alien. Find another. *Let us ***** and give thanks. Let us be and give thanks.* Better. 'Be' is ambiguous, suggestive of both 'being' and 'freedom.' How sad I feel."

The swing rocked faster. "*I stand before you on this day of The Celebrations to proclaim…*" The swing stopped. "I can't go on."

We stopped sailing. "This won't do. Let me remember."

Water recomposed itself around the base of the lotus, quivering with reflections.

We sailed. The lotus began again: "*All that I have written repeats the same theme. Whether dog or tree, fish or bird, woman, man, child, whatever beast we are—we are, intrinsically, the same.*" The swing rocked furiously. I held its edges. "Control yourself. Delete three last sentences." The swing slowed. "*I stand before you on this day of The Celebrations to proclaim…* This stinks. Delete last sentence. *On this day of The Celebrations, I am honoured to stand before you.* Better, for I feel honoured to address you today." The rocking began; the lotus spoke faster. "Cut the slack. Remember you have two minutes to make your stand. Be yourself. Build to the secret."

The lotus slowed. "Second draft. *Hail! Members gathered for*

The Celebrations. I remind you," the lotus spoke in a rush, "*of the power and the potential of this Global Community of which each one of you—whether Zombie or Fireheart, Original or Clone—is a part, not apart...* No! Think quiet, think true. Be yourself." The swing rocked furiously.

"Courage. Words come to me. "

The swinging was so fierce that I clung to it, upside-down. "*Hear me well. This is my last testament.*" The swing buckled and leapt. "*I stand before you to share with you a secret that is small yet immense. This is the secret of my life, and yours. Realize it!*"

The swing shot through the lotus. I hit the water gasping. I doggy-paddled.

When I reached the shore the lotus had capsized. It was drowning.

It went down, glug, glug.

Glug.

ஓ 64 ‰

"What transpired? The lotus was thought to be unsinkable."

Leader was wrapping me in a towel that did not speak.

"It spoke too much."

"Indeed?" He shook his head. "You are hallucinating, Aa-Aa 14/54/G. The lotus was mute. No voice-thoughts could be culled from the workstation. Those died with her."

"It was leading me to Aa-Aa's secret. Rather, her drafts."

He stopped drying my hair.

I nodded.

"The secret?"

"Not revealed."

His body sagged. "When will you speak to me?" he asked softly, holding my face in his hands. I knew it was not me he was speaking to. "When will you be only mine?"

"Leader." Maybe there was something in my look that quickly made him turn his face away, something like an arrow going into my eyes. He focussed on drying my hair. I felt I had shrunk.

"Still, this is wonderful news." He was already standing. "I will immediately inform them that you will take the stand." He walked away. At the door he turned. "I'll order a Nurse Clone for you."

I lay where I was left.

Nothing moved.

Nothing spoke.

I slept.

"How long have I been sleeping?"

"Long enough," he said. He was sitting on the veranda steps that were covered by the long shadows of evening. "I have Aa-Aa's parrot, stuffed. I have holographs of her striding through the meadow, reading, even sleeping. My favourite is of her feeding her parrot slivers of guava. She called it Sweety."

He placed my head on his lap. "She took her time feeding the parrot; she was singing a song that's erased. She was smiling." He stroked my hair, smiling. "And she refused to colour her hair. Her long hair was greying."

I looked up at him.

"Would you like the parrot?"

"No."

"Just as I thought. The impressions culled from Sweety will be mine, not hers. I've had it for seventy years."

I nodded.

"You are tired. I've ordered her favourite dish."

We stood.

At the door he turned. "One more thing, Aa-Aa 14/54/G.

I have entered her holo-fantasy. It's of the sea." He paused. "But you don't know the sea, do you?"

"No."

"It is water without end. Salty water."

I ate the food. Sprout salad with yogurt dressing. It was crunchy and not particularly tasty. Then I returned indoors.

The rooms seemed larger and more empty. I wished he was here, or his holograph. I made my way to Level Two and sat on the bed.

"Turn down lights," I said.

The room was in darkness, and quiet. The darkness extended.

I cupped my eyes. Colours flickered beneath my lids. Flakes of sunlight drifted to settle over shades of blue. Scales of sunlight, like clipped nails, covered the blues. The light smoothened and stretched. Its glow grew more luminescent, and thickened. A blanket of light shone like a metallic paste over a vast stretch of water.

Sheets of moonlight rested on water. These moonlit sheets heaved and breathed like dreams remembered.

The water turned, grew dark, lifted and rolled like balls over each other. The water rose, lost its curves to angles and quick-rising cliffs that quickly fell. A random geometry of triangles and lines it became.

It became the sky at sunset, yet more fiery.

It was water without end, with rhythms unforeseen, through which shoals of whales blew and dived. Mountains of ice drifted on it, and coconuts.

I knew the sea was a creature unique.

◦◦ 65 ◦◦

"We suggest you put yourself on double time to imprint impressions," said the Tourist Guide Clone. "The City is preparing itself for The Celebrations."

"This is your only tour," said the accompanying Superior Zombie (Type P-Dragonfly-Viper), "unlike your Original who visited two thousand and eighty-four times."

"Acknowledged." I turned up my bioclock. My systems functioned at the same pace. I turned it up to Grade Four. My systems still functioned at the same rate.

"Bioclock not responding," I said.

"Are you reporting a malfunction?" said the Zombie.

"No. I shall compensate with attention. Proceed."

A temporary tracking device was implanted. I was hauled into a Tourist pod. The floor and sides were made of transparent sifteen polymestics.

"We are approaching the Originals' palaces. The metreonic domes insulating their inhabitation offer gamma, ultraviolet, sonic and X-ray protection. Further, their palaces are earthquake, atomic bomb, gene warfare and tsunami proof. The security systems offer…" the Tourist Guide Clone continued.

I looked.

The sky was ashen. But within the domes it was twilight. Sunset streamed green, purple and peach. Brilliant honey-coloured lights dripped off trees, spires, minarets, tall towers and temples. Lakes shone like sheets of reflecting diamonds. Leader lived within this magnificence—like a parrot in a gold cage.

"…of the Superior Zombies. Look farther right. These peresitic domes are made of jigmadolite which enhances aggression. Their inhabitation is difficult to perceive as they are quartered underground. However…"

Lightning, smoke, thunder and fire swirled within the domes.

"Request closer look," I said.

"Requesting exaggeroscope," she said.

"Visibility computations do not deem request necessary," said the Zombie.

"Begging pardon. We shall now proceed to the dwellings of the Firehearts."

I strained my eyes in the fading light. Domes of moonshine approached. Hamlets floated within, sparking, shimmering or wrapped in intense darkness.

"Firehearts requested that absolute clarity rain through their 'inner and outer spaces,'" the Guide Clone said. "However, this notional scheme was vetoed. They then demanded that their habitations reflect their moods. Therefore you will detect changing hues. That one for instance," she said pointing to a dazzling spot, "reflects a Fireheart having an inspiration."

Maybe Couplet was composing.

Night was drawing into our pod, and the surroundings. A sticky greyness smudged the windows.

"Below, try to observe the Clones' cell-towers that do not manifest protective domes. Rather—"

"I know Clone cells."

"We shall skip this part of the tour," the Guide Clone said when lighting sprang open, far beneath. The thoroughfares were lit; the towers remained cloaked.

"Why is this?"

"Power is drained from Clone cells to enhance the illuminations," she said. "Preparations for The Celebrations have begun. Look."

I perceived faint figures. "What are they doing?"

"Request exaggeroscope," said the Guide Clone.

"Permitted," the Zombie said.

My vision cleared. Clones in costume were dancing and playing instruments. They thronged the thoroughfares as a glued mass.

"Request greater clarity of vision," I said.

"Enhance exaggeroscope capabilities," said the Zombie.

Some Clones wore tinsel hats, others played paper accordions, some beat cellophane drums, others hooted kikodees, some others sprinkled starwinks in the air; all kicked up their legs. Not a single Clone smiled. But then I remembered: Clones do not know how to smile.

"Note the final rehearsal for the Grand Parade," said the Guide Clone.

"Acknowledged," I said.

"Clone, you will have two minutes Free-Time after you purchase a memento against labour on your Free-Day," said the Guide Clone. "What will you buy?" She showed me miniatures of the four types of habitations.

"The Clone cell-towers."

"All tourists buy Originals' palaces," she said.

"Cell-towers, if it is permissible," I said.

"Permission granted," said the Zombie.

My fingers curled around the cell-towers. This is from where I came.

"Clone, what do you want to do with your two minutes Free-Time?"

"Visit The Neitherlands," I said, "if it is permissible."

"Checking," said the Zombie. "Permissible."

The land was dark. The sky was dark.

The Neitherlands held nothing.

Suddenly far ahead, firelight glowed.

"Go there," I said.

The enhanced exaggeroscope capabilities were still in force.

Figures were running, figures were chasing. Flame-throwers were in use. But the running figures were not immediately extinguished. They ran in flames, fell in flames.

"The flame-throwers employed do not use extemporine," said the Guide Clone, "but ancient napalm or kerosene that take considerable time to consume the victim. This follows the logic of the runners who follow an outmoded way of thought, a.k.a. 'rebellion against intolerance'. Those aflame disturb the harmony of the Global Community."

Some figures were tumbling, trying to extinguish the flames.

I saw flaming hands reach for the skies.

I saw faces aflame.

"Return to base," said the Superior Zombie. "Extinguish last vision."

"Acknowledged," said the Tourist Guide Clone.

My mouth seemed extinguished; my vision was aflame.

৵ 66 ৵

"Fireheart! Couplet! What has become of you?"

It shivered. Its antennae had wilted; its body was a mauve-grey with black splotches.

"Alas. I could not predict when your Writer's Block would lift. Therefore…"

"No one could, Couplet. Refresh yourself with soma-nectar. I have a few drops. "

"I need elephant memory infusions," it whimpered. "Clone, get used to my state. It should not be long."

A stone seemed to have plummeted from my chest into my feet. "What are you saying?"

"To our release, thou ninny." It grinned weakly. "The Celebrations are on. Thou shalt take the stand. Everything will change; the earth will glow again."

I pressed the capsule of soma-nectar to its lips.

"Fie! Thou shame thyself and me. We do not partake of such mortal juices. We are the sigh of the breeze, the fragrance of thought, the passion of..." It coughed and crumpled.

I rubbed soma-nectar on its forehead; tore open the cherry heel of my right slipper to pass the diamond medallion over its face, ripped the left heel to extract Bullet's eye and rubbed it over its limbs.

Couplet revived. "'Tis thy love, naught else." It flopped.

"Couplet, rest. I shall soon be back."

"Zombie, inform the Supreme Commander and the Leader that I remember."

I was summoned to the Cloaking Room.

In darkness I spoke to darkness. "Hail! Members of the Global Community! We are gathered together on this day of The Celebrations. Hear me well. This is my last testament. I stand before you to share with you a secret that is small yet immense. This is the secret of my life, and yours. Realize it!" I paused, and continued wildly, "Aa-Aa's Lotus told me this. But I am distraught. I cannot remember further because Couplet is unwell."

"You are addressing a simulation of the Grand Presences. Your ploy has not succeeded."

"I am beggared." I slipped to my knees. "Help Couplet. Please!" I wept.

"Your distress is convincing. The Fireheart shall be revived. You shall henceforth co-operate in a proactive manner and yield your secrets to us."

"Your Gracious Lordships, I shall do better than my best. I swear on My Elder's remains."

I felt like a dry riverbed remembering rain.

When I returned, Couplet was sitting on the floor, its legs splayed. "Clone, what Faustian pact did you strike with the devil?"

∽ 67 ∾

Kneeling on the shore of the siffrine pond in rippling morning light, I tried to make Aa-Aa's secret glide though me.

Water lilies turned their buds upwards. With a faint popping sound, each flower opened, one after the other, inexorably, till my vision filled with separating petals. Over and again I mouthed her words in the spaces between their colours. "Hail! Members of the Global Community! Hear me well. This is my last testament. I share with you a secret small yet immense. This is the secret of my life, and yours. Realize it!"

The words rose and sank like a fever. Sweating, I rose and paced.

I touched each wall in the Comfort Capsule; each dwarf bamboo, each artificial shrub with its twinkling flowers. Aa-Aa must have done the same. I plucked flowers. The grifferline blossoms left sparkling dust on my hands from which words emerged on my palms. "I wish to make known that each one of us is imbued with a sacred power. Apprehend this power."

The words did not make sense. Had I lost Aa-aa? Part of a mystery revealed only makes the mystery more awesome.

I remembered the vision of Aa-Aa leaning against a pillar, twirling marigolds, looking at the distance that hung within her eyes.

I found a gelex marigold plant growing behind the pond. I crushed the stem; a mild fragrance of sap and sinexx spread. With the torn fragrance more words appeared. "I speak but am I too late? Am I complicit by being complacent so long?"

I sickened and sank.

I remembered Aa-Aa turning her face away from the man who stood near her bed.

I shed my clothes and rolled in its silk, rubbing my face in its folds. The bed rocked as it floated. With the rustling of sateeniquin, I heard a murmuring: "If we have forgotten the bed of tenderness that supports us, what are we?"

I rubbed my face harder into its depths, rubbing till my face flamed. There was only silk, softness; the gentle rocking.

I fell asleep in silk.

This was the routine I repeated day after day.

Night after night I fell asleep with the same desire: may Aa-Aa's words flow through me.

I never thought: may I find the words.

One night I dreamt my first dream.

People stared from behind barbed wire while holding out lollipops. Children bled and sang. Men were beheaded, their arms ran after their rolling heads to screw them back on their necks. Women had their bodies torn, they revived and began sewing themselves up. It was crowded. "I need to rest," I said to the Leader, who was picking his way through the mutilations. "Rest on this mound," he said, pointing to a heap draped with a flag. I clambered, the heap crumbled. I lifted the flag. Bones lay beneath; also my head, my eyes staring back. I screamed. Then the dream began again.

I resolved not to sleep.

I sat by the pond that had fallen silent.

Silence ate me like tendrils of hair whipping my body.

Late in the afternoon I crouched by the toolbox near the floating bed. I wrenched it open. It was empty and dark.

The lid fell on my knuckles, blood appeared. As I licked

it, my blood said, "I am the cowering darkness in which we live."

The bleeding would not stop. I licked it again. "Once I was quiet, am I therefore this terror that refuses to stop?"

The words stopped.

I sat licking my wound till darkness enveloped me.

Like a flood, darkness filled the house, the waters, the sky, the air I breathed out.

The Celebrations drew near.

⋘ 68 ⋙

"A platoon of my bodyguards will escort you to the High Stand. I shall be there. My trusted force will man the wave-amplifiers. You will make Aa-Aa's speech which will be heard by all. Simultaneously, my mutants will take over key centres. The Uprising will be complete in a matter of minutes." He swept a glistening shawl over his shoulders. "Then we shall be free to speak."

"How is this possible?" I said.

"The Superior Zombies' command code will be reprogrammed in their Control Unit. They will henceforth obey me. Do not fear," he said. "I am not alone."

My hand rose to my chest, he looked like a true Leader. My heart glowed, yet I trembled.

"Focus on Aa-Aa's words. This is all that is required of you."

"What if I cannot recall? I've tried—"

"Don't worry. Aa-Aa believed in pushing things to the edge. Her spirit will not betray you."

"Even if I manage, do you expect words to change the course of history?"

"Of course not. Originals are obsessed with knowing the powerful secret for which she died. This is their flaw. I merely require their auras to be focussed on your speech to affect the shift in the Power Lobes."

Aa-Aa's words. I was to provide the distraction while the heroes worked. We were to hold centre-stage, yet not.

The Cause was noble. Yet had Aa-Aa meant her words to be used as spectacle?

I felt I was standing on hedgehogs.

"What if—"

"The Fireheart has memorized the escape route. It will lead you to safety."

My ribs squeezed my breath. "And you?"

"Don't worry about me. I am protected by a secret mantra force shield."

Like a mountain, a wave of tremulousness rose within me.

"This is the only way," he said. He was on his knees before me, whispering into my sex. "Trust me."

Kneeling before me was the child who had crawled on Aa-Aa's knees, the child I longed for, beseeched that he be left with me; my lover knelt before me. She had wept for him and herself, and abandoned both in her quest for something other.

"Trust me."

I cupped his face in my hands. Never should he leave me again!

He rose, his hands like a thousand comets heading home to me. Our hands and lips reached across time; our bodies traversed infinite spaces to mould into one. Darkness brightened.

Faced with parting, was this hunger uniquely ours? Surely it has been the fate of all lovers, each time.

My tongue tasted tears. Whose were they?

Stars opened their petals into my flesh. With the descending calm we felt our dark bodies separate.

He left.

I imprinted his retreating figure in my memory: the shoulders, the shawl, his stride, his curly hair.

I had forgotten to tell him I was pregnant.

∞ 69 ∞

I hadn't slept. My eyes looked like a Superior Zombie's at the end of its term.

I trickled sweat. It smelt different.

My skin broke out in rash.

I felt I was carrying the City on my head. With each step I took the City moved.

I had not as yet fathomed Aa-Aa's last words.

"Your Honour looks ghastly!" said a Clotheshorse Clone Type Cleo, "If you will kindly pardon this lowly observation."

Two were in attendance.

"There is much work to be done," said the other. "Tut, tut, Your Honour has been skipping her beauty sleep. Your Honour has aged beyond expectation!"

"She has grey hair!" chimed the first.

"And wrinkles on her brow, oh woe!"

They stood on either side of me, wringing their hands.

"I was attempting to write. This ages one."

"That's a paltry excuse for neglecting Your Honour's beauty routine," they chimed, "if we may be permitted to say so. And," they shook their heads in unison, "Your Honoured Self is somewhat overweight. Tut, tut."

They busied themselves with my body. My skin glowed a smooth gold. My robe was scarlet and gold, on my hair a snood of dripping golden dewdrops. They had even stopped the sweating.

"Honoured One," they said, clutching my feet. "Wear these Cinderella shoes."

"I shall continue to wear my cherry slippers," I said. "Leave. Or I shall tear off my golden snood."

"Our task is incomplete, Honoured One," they said. Their nails grew into talons.

I ripped off the snood and cast it down.

"Ooooh!" They flung themselves after it.

They refastened it, shaking each golden dewdrop. "There," they beamed.

"Leave."

"You must carry the Staff of Certitude," they chimed, thrusting a golden caduceus into my hand.

With each step I took gold dust spilled from the staff's snake head. My path was carpeted with gold.

"Leave."

Alone, I was immobilized.

My mind was a blank yet felt like a circlet tightening.

I do not know how long I stood thus.

"Awaken from your spell. May your spell begin."

Couplet!

"You look regal; right for the game," it chuckled.

A sparkling net surrounded Couplet like shards of glass. I opened my arms.

"Do not touch me. I am within a force field," Couplet said. "This is supposedly for my protection but it's my entrapment, etc." It airily waved its hands.

"Couplet, I still cannot recollect Aa-Aa's last speech."

"So?"

"So what am I to say when I take the High Stand?" I began to sweat again.

"She'll deliver." It chuckled, its antennae swung.

"But what if she doesn't? Couplet, what am I to do

facing the crowd? What if I betray the Cause?" I stood on my hands.

It marched around me while I was still in handstand. "What pity of mediocre writer are you if you cannot deliver under intense pressure?" it huffed. "How dare you go by the name!"

I righted.

"You will deliver. Delve into yourself and the words will come forth. Enough tarrying! Now is the time for action. You are graced to speak. So speak!"

Within the sparkling net it had turned deep red. "Do not betray us," Couplet said. "Do not forget the massacred. Or they will be uselessly dead. We might as well be dead."

Maroon droplets broke from its body. "Do not betray yourself. Or there is no forgiveness ever." It spat. The spit sizzled as it hit the force field. "Now march, Clone, towards The Celebrations."

Beyond the door, two squadrons of armed guards waited. Behind them another five platoons in full battle regalia waited. I stepped out. They surrounded me.

We marched towards the transport gliders.

✎ 70 ✎

It was a bumpy flight.

We flew through clouds.

Through drizzle I saw the Artificial Glade. The arena, the river, the stands full, the outer ring of trees standing silver in the rain.

We disembarked and marched into an underground vestibule near the High Stand. There was barely standing room. A slit of light entered through a high window.

"I wish to observe," I said.

"Sir," replied the Guard Clones. They passed me on their shoulders towards the slit.

"The Fireheart too."

A path was made for Couplet. Within its force field it sparked near the legs of the guard on whose shoulders I sat.

Through the slit I saw scuffling feet in the distance.

"The War Games salute," said Couplet. "It's used as a dull refrain after each event. I'd say we've missed the first six hours—most of the speeches and the allosaur routine. Thanks be to the Global Community for small mercies."

My palms were slippery with sweat. The golden snood was tight, my temples throbbed.

"Though you are her DNA replica your brain scan patterns are dissimilar, for these are formed by each one's experiences. That's why you are anxious. Relax. You'll have your last visitation on the stand."

"Or else? Couplet, what will happen to me?"

"For the last time I say: become her, and deliver. She's the character who made you!"

I closed my eyes and chanted, "Aa-Aa, Aa-Aa, appear. Appear!" I don't know how long I repeated the chant. Another chant of grunts and snorts filled my consciousness. "What is this?"

"'Songs without Music'. Music is banned during The Celebrations. It is considered impure."

The Songs without Music sounded like half-eaten things were crawling out of mouths to a deafening beat. I shut my eyes and ears. Another sound, more familiar and rending, wormed its way in. Wails, shrieks, screams—as if the arena had grown a voice that bled.

"What is that?" I shouted to Couplet.

"'The Exemplary Massacre of The Others.'"

"Who are The Others?"

"Anyone—or any group—designated as 'The Kafir

Others.' There are no markers to identify The Others. It's arbitrary, and keeps changing with each victory and each Celebration." Couplet shrugged.

"What have The Kafir Others done?"

"Nothing in particular, Clone." Couplet was turning scarlet within its sparkling net. "But The Kafir Others live, don't they?" It whimpered and crumpled into a purple ball. "They are never saved."

I stuffed my fingers into my ears. Even listening to Songs without Music and the wailing arena seemed better than knowing about this. All that was within me seemed to want to spill out in a fleshy red mess.

Suddenly I almost slipped. The guard beneath me was saluting. A Superior Zombie had entered.

"Guard Clones, remove helmets. We proceed to The Stand."

As the guards whipped off their helmets, I slid and fell. Each one looked like Leader. The same eyelashes, the same hair, the same mole near his lips. Hundreds like him.

Had I held them all in my arms?

"Where is the Aa-Aa Clone?" said the Superior Zombie.

"Here." I made my way to the front.

We marched, five platoons of Leader's Clones behind Couplet and me.

Sunlight dazzled.

In the far distance, the Supreme Commander hovered in a chair of crystal, holding aloft a small ruby bouquet. Above him hovered a baldachin of dew and pearls. Surrounding him were children in jewelled robes. Row upon row of Originals sat behind, waving to the crowds. They dazzled more than the sunlight. Their magnified faces shone from holograph screens suspended between crowded stands. A few screens showed crowd reactions—Clones cheering without smiles. The clapping was deafening.

An Original in a feathered crown took the High Stand that flapped purple and gold beneath his feet. "We have for you a spectacle that was presented only once in the grand history of the Global Community. This involves breaking through the force field that is erected before Us and…"

"Are you ready?" he asked. He didn't look like his Clones. He looked pale. His mouth was tight. His hands were cold as they clasped mine.

I saw his eyes and went mute.

"Good. Your voice will be heard. My personal guards are manning the transmission systems. They will not fail. Now distract the Originals. Give me forty seconds."

I bowed to him, my robes sweeping the floor, my heart at his feet.

I banged the snakehead Staff of Certitude and rose. Gold dust spilled before me. Each step seemed a mile long. Originals slowly turned their glances towards me, children waved in slow motion as I approached the Supreme Commander. I walked and walked, and prostrated myself at his feet.

"Arise, Clone," his voice showered from the sky.

A voice that was not mine began from within me. "*Hail! Members of the Global Community! Hear me well. This is my last testament. I stand before you to share with you a secret that is small yet immense. This is the secret of my life, and yours. Realize it!*" I lay at his feet. The gold dust spilling from the caduceus was so profuse it filled my nostrils. I coughed and spat. His hovering chair rose higher.

"Rise, Clone, and address the gathering. You are here to speak your Original's last words." The Supreme Commander's lips smiled at me. "Obey."

I rose. I seemed to keep rising until I realized his Guard Clones had lifted me to the High Stand. They set me down. I heard a muffled bang as the Staff of Certitude hit the flapping carpet. The Supreme Commander's replicas withdrew.

I saw my face surrounding me, or was it Aa-Aa's, reflecting in gigantic proportions in the holographs around the arena. My mouth open and voiceless, eyes pale and wide, hand clutching a staff that endlessly spewed gold dust.

I cast my eyes down. The ground of the vast arena was splotched with blood. Some of it was still pooling, curdling red; other parts glistened silver and black with clotted gleam. I shut my eyes.

I opened my eyes. The blood was still there, dyeing the earth.

This spilt blood gathered itself into a tongue that spoke through me: "The secret is that I am human. Each one of us is human. We still have the capacity to live as humans."

This voice that was mine yet not mine alone ricocheted from every part of the arena. "Remember with me: I claim my birthright to be human."

I lifted the Staff of Certitude and shouted, "None can stop us, for we are human!"

Blood writhed on the ground.

❧ 71 ❧

"Repeat: I am human and I am not alone!"

The stands rose, the chorus rose from every section.

"I claim my birthright to be human."

"I claim my birthright to be human!" The arena echoed and echoed with voices.

The crowd holographs filled with Clones standing, arms raised and shouting.

The Staff of Certitude was spinning, thumping the carpet, spewing clouds of gold dust. It was an automat. Ice slid through me: could the Clones merely be mouthing my words on command, no more?

"Retreat," he said, pulling my arm. "You—"

"You have betrayed us, Leader," said the Supreme Commander.

Protecting me with his body, Leader asked, "What will you do?"

"I am human," I shouted. No echo followed. My voice had been silenced. Had theirs been too? I saw scuffles break out in the crowd holograms. Guard Zombies were pushing Clones down.

Leader was dragging me towards his Guard Clones. The Supreme Commander shot after us in his hovering chair. Everyone else was transfixed, as if blocked in a dream.

"How far will you go for power? Would you revoke the sacred mantra with which you shod me at birth, Father?" he called, still pulling me towards his Clone Guards. "For only you can cause my premature death."

"I revoke the mantra with which I protected you since your birth, my son," said the Supreme Commander. He mouthed words in silence.

The Leader leapt and writhed at my feet. His skin peeled. He screamed. I dragged him towards his bodyguards.

"Reveal your chain of command and you shall be saved."

"The G7 South…" he writhed.

"Have been vanquished," said the Supreme Commander. "Your transmissions are silenced. Don't you hear?"

There was nothing to hear.

"What else, my son?"

"The F/12 A Sub-Species…"

"Shall be attended to. For your co-operation you deserve a reprieve."

Leader's skin stopped peeling. He moaned. Red froth flecked his mouth.

"Revive my son," said the Supreme Commander.

Nurse Clones tore him from my arms. When they parted from him he lay gasping. But his skin was sealed, though some pink patches still bled. His eyes had stopped rolling. He stopped moving.

"What else, my son? Tell your father."

Leader vomited.

I huddled near Couplet.

"This is the end," it whispered, "for all of us."

"No. He'll survive. We will win."

"The two are not synonymous," it said.

"Is this all you can say?" I spat. I pointed to the disorder in the arena. "Look."

"It's too soon to be certain. They are Clones, after all." Couplet whispered, "I must break out of this force field or I'm no good to man or beast, or in-betweens like myself!"

I tore the heel of my right slipper. The diamond medallion lay in my palm.

Duke whined near the Leader, circling round and around. I rushed to Leader, lifted him, holding him up against me.

"What else?" said the Supreme Commander. "Renege, son. We take no pleasure in seeing you in pain. Confess and you can survive…"

"Father, kill me."

"…on Paradise Island." He smiled. "Or would you rather she is destroyed?" He swivelled his hovering chair in my direction.

Leader heaved and swayed. "I never will live on Paradise Island."

The Supreme Commander pointed the ruby bouquet at my head.

"Father, look for rebel mutants among your core 13/A Clones."

"This is a lie."

I tossed the diamond medallion towards Couplet. The sparkling net bursts into flames. Couplet screamed. The spray of ruby flowers was aimed at me.

"You will not get her again!" Leader shouted and lurched in front of me, "You won't get Mother again," as red beams hit him. He yelped like Duke, leapt from my arms, somersaulted bleeding into the air.

He is falling, I'm rushing to hold him, rushing, but not rushing fast enough. He falls, shoulders first, legs in the air and I'm shouting, "The Leader is killed! Attack! Attack! The Leader—"

His Guard Clones open fire. Superior Zombies and Originals open fire. Running feet, screaming, noise all around. Time plunges ahead, dizzyingly.

"Hoist him up and run," Couplet said. "This is what he said I must do. Move!"

Leader's face was a mask with eyes sockets bleeding. I slung him over my shoulders and ran after Couplet. Duke ran after me.

Voices, firing, ran after us, and faded. Faded, like histories forgotten. Like truths made into lies. Into darkness we ran.

Towards what were we hurtling?

"Duke," Couplet panted, "stop. Sit." It hoisted itself onto Duke's back, clutching his collar for support. "Now charge!"

We raced down a narrow tunnel that closed like weeping flesh around us.

Silence reigned; then noises grew again.

"Couplet, where are you taking us?" The sound of gongs, drums and cymbals tore into my ears.

"Think I'm betraying you?" Couplet's laugh was a whinny. "This is our best ruse. Into the ring!" it shouted as sunlight tore into my eyes.

✒ 72 ✑

To be lost in the crowd is a cliché," said Couplet. "Now test its truth."

We stared into the mouth of the arena. Beyond the outer ring of trees, the arena was teeming with sounds, movement.

"The show must go on, Clone. We'll mingle with the entertainers and live to tell our tale."

A stream of purple and black rustled before us, rising and undulating.

"The Cobra Dancers form the outer ring. If you must know, they symbolize the poison that should be kept out. To escape, we must charge between the hoods as they rise," Couplet whispered. "Dodge, and follow me."

Lugging Leader, I darted between the dancers' scaly legs, then stopped. We faced a milky wave that sighed and swished like a soft sea washing on white sands. Deeper in, it rippled in blues and greys ablaze with lasereene spots; dancers dazzled as they bobbed, like sunlit swell in rhythms graceful and hypnotizing. "Beware, the Siren Sea," Couplet called. "It returns your past to you."

Beyond, on waves of midnight blue, rode sheets of moondew haze. I held my breath for I saw Leader in perfect health walking towards me on the waves, I saw Aa-Aa opening her arms, I saw my child toddling in my direction, I saw 14/53/G dancing towards me. Leader smiled and beckoned.

"Don't be lost," Couplet hissed. "We have to cross its seductive heart and get to the other side. Shut your eyes and follow the lub-dub throb of the dance till it fades to a stop."

It darted across the white froth, across the blazing blue-greys; at the central spot of serene midnight blue waves, it turned. Couplet rushed back, lashed my dress to Duke's collar and dragged me on. The heartbeat rhythm told me what I wished to hear.

"Couplet," I murmured, "I must stay. Leader is calling."
I stalled.

A sizzling shot cracks at our feet. Leader's arm that is
trailing behind me, hanging over my shoulder and dragging
the air, this arm is singed. My love's arm; my child's.

"They've tracked us! Run!"

I looked up. Fighter-gliders swarmed like mustard seeds
above the dome. They were shooting into the sea around us
that writhed when hit, and stilled in spots.

"They can't be accurate because the dome's curvature
deflects aim, they won't annihilate The Celebrations for lack
of face," Couplet shouted. "Clone, are you now awake?"

Leader's weight on my shoulder sang its own song. I ran
between darting feet, between the rhythms of defeat.

We dodged through the ring of naked nymphs curled within
pearly globes that bounced and rose. Their hands broke out
of the bubbles to scatter fragrances that caused delirium.
I saw myself carried on a ruby litter, I saw masses bow to
me; a halo glimmered on my head. I did not need Couplet
to tell me what this was: Risen Pearls of Future Fantasy.
Leader's blood dampening my shoulders brought me back;
the dank metallic smell of lost blood swarmed through the
other fragrances. Laser fire made me dodge. I glanced up at
the suspended holograms. The Superior Zombies seemed to
have regained control of the stands though turmoil reigned
in a few spots.

"Prepare for the Joy of Liberation that lets dreams come
true," Couplet yelled. "Don't let go now!"

The arena darkened. A smog of drones let out smoking
dark.

Suddenly fireworks spewed from high that spilled,
spiralled, twirled though the dome. It was so splendorous that
I gaped.

"Clone, move your butt before it's too late," Couplet shouted. "The Bloodbath precedes the Joy of Liberation. Move!"

The earth began to heave. From beneath our feet, grunting armoured soldiers appeared like bloodthirsty teeth sown in a forgotten mythical disharmony. The creatures that emerged were neither beast nor human nor in-betweens, but something else, imagined by the dark within us and the innocent dark of technology. These were alive, and not. The armoured soldiers grew full-size. They fell on each other and slaughtered. Their scentless blood spattered us till we were drenched.

"Are both of you bathed in blood?" Couplet swivelled to ask.

I nodded.

"Right. We are temporarily disguised from global surveillance, however, dodge the warriors' blows! And follow." Couplet shouted. "Or there's no hope!"

For the first time, Couplet was redundant, for if this was the Joy of Liberation, it dispelled all spells. All that the fireworks left were etched negatives in the sky; the fireworks left starkness. And starkness opens one's eyes to slaughter, most of all.

I recognized a trapdoor that led to an underground chamber above which once a fake river flowed. It was the same one where I had spotted the dismembered lavender hand.

"Couplet! Here?"

Body parts of armoured soldiers were falling around us like sparks.

"Dig!"

I fumbled and heaved open the trapdoor. Below lay a chamber that revealed another tiny door that opened into a widening tunnel. Couplet and Duke eased through. I struggled through, scraping myself. Then I pulled Leader's heavy silence through. He stuck and bumped, but I pulled him through. I smoothened his clothes and wiped his eye sockets. "We are safe, I think," I whispered to him.

"Clone, get going down this tunnel! I can't see a thing," Couplet shouted.

"Nor can I."

Terrible sounds rushed upon us as if the soldiers had found new prey.

"It's us they have found through their blood scent," said Couplet. "Hurry up or be dismembered!"

I looked at Leader looking back at me with empty eye sockets. I smoothened his hair.

"Get going!"

I tore open the left heel of my shoe. Bullet's eye glowed. Holding it aloft as a torch I dragged Leader through, kissing him, heaving him down the tunnel's long length, asking, "Are you in pain?"

He doesn't reply.

Has time frozen?

∾ 73 ∾

"There." Couplet pointed to an ancient pod resting at the tunnel's lit opening. "It's so old that it has been declassified. Once we are on it, we can't be traced."

Couplet clambered off Duke's back. I collapsed with Leader in my arms. I bent against his chest, my arms running down his torso like the streams of blood. His pulpy body is a whirlpool into which I'm sinking, in which I want to be.

"Identify yourself to the pilots. Your voice-print alone will make the doors open. Your voice has been fed to it, come on!" Couplet's voice said from some other time. It kicked me somewhere. "Move! Or you are putting us at risk."

I was in the maelstrom of his blood leaking endlessly. Nauseous.

"He may yet have a spark of life that could be re-kindled if we can get him help."

Duke was whining over Leader. I knew Couplet was lying.

Couplet pounded me. "Act! If we are caught, before we are deliciously tortured you'll be forced to see the Leader's body fed—not to fijzt crocodiles that chomp—but to squishlisk maggots. They crawl from inside out and gnaw the skeleton last. His body will be devoured ever so slowly. Clone, are you up to seeing it? Are you?"

Couplet kept repeating this, kept pounding me somewhere.

Finally the idea of Leader exposed thus coagulated into an unbearable image. I saw robotic maggots crawling out of his body; his body becoming a fester of worms. I said, "No I won't let him be taken away again."

"Think later about pain," said Couplet, pulling me up. "Help us. Up!"

I stood. I reached to pull off the gold snood. My hair came off in my hand like a wig. I stared at my hairy hand. I guessed I was bald.

Couplet stared. "It's the shock, Clone. But now perform! Be human!"

I left my hair lying near his body.

"Requesting permission to come aboard. Passenger identification: the dead Original Leader, his dog Duke, the Fireheart Couplet and Clone Aa-Aa 14/54/G."

"Climb aboard," the pilot's voice said. The door opened.

I carried Leader in and cradled him, his head to my breast. Duke followed, then Couplet. The door closed.

We took off.

I wiped blood clots away from the hollows of Leader's eye sockets. I shut my eyes.

Is this what it means to be human? This cradling pain?

❧ 74 ☙

When I opened my eyes I saw Couplet sniffling. It was singed all over and bleeding.

"When did this happen?"

"Breaking out of the force field."

"Are you in pain?"

"Who isn't?"

Leader was turning cold in my arms. "Leader," I whispered into his mouth, "Leader, Leader." I kept whispering till I became his name. I am sure I saw him exhale. He was alive yet.

I am sure I saw him breathe. I put my ear to the cloth over his chest. It was lumpy and soft, unlike the taut flesh on which I had so often rested my head. I ran my hands over his body. It was pulpy, oozy. That's when I understood how his father had killed him: he commanded Leader's organs to burst outwards. Everything that once was inside him was out.

Then what remains inside the inside?

What are we made of? Are we only what is seen, and known? What of the spaces of thought and emotion, and that something else that makes us human, that something else that makes us grieve with others? What makes us feel thankful precisely because we are, in the end, not different, but governed by the same vast laws of life?

What is this sanctifying space within us?

I lay with my love's body in my lap, my head bent over his chest, waiting…

I saw stars edge like city lights outside the portholes, and pass.

Where were we heading?

⤳ 75 ⤳

"Where are we heading?"

"Ask the pilots," said Couplet. "They should know."

I crawled through the passageway to the cabin. A single pilot was manning the craft. In the windows wrapping his seat, stars shone like lights in deep wells. I spoke to the back of the pilot's head. "What is our current destination?"

"The dark side of the moon."

"Why are we heading there?"

"Oh!" said Couplet, crawling towards us, "We're heading towards the 'abandoned' colony on the moon, are we? The Resistance…"

"…is marshalling a counterattack from there, as The Leader had planned in his Die-Hard strategy," said the pilot. "We are exposed; the game plan has gone awry though some Clones are on the streets shouting, 'We are human! We claim our birthright to be human!' It's probably too late but this is a now-or-never battle."

"Well…" said Couplet. "All's well that ends well."

"Not necessarily so, Fireheart," said the pilot. "We've passed the classical framework of knowledge with the old, marker, Dwarf Star X83 fading to your left. We are now looping in open space. Anything and everything is possible here." The pilot turned around. The gladiator.

We looked at each other.

"You know each other, do you?" asked Couplet. Its eyes sparkled.

"We've met," I said.

"Your scalp is bleeding," said the gladiator. "Were you tortured?"

No words issued from me.

"I suspect she's numb with pain," said Couplet. "But now is not the time to pause, dear Clone, nor yet to mourn. For

there is a time to mourn and a time to reap the mourning.
There is a time for outrage and a time for action. And there
always is the time for tenderness and human dignity. It is in
this time that you have to plunge yourself, Clone, and you will
have to struggle hard. For you are human."

I understood what Couplet was saying. I tried to call up
the sanctifying space that I am sure is within each one. This,
that lies inside the inside.

It seemed a long distance away. It seemed alien.

When I heard them again Couplet was saying, "Give her
time."

The gladiator nodded.

They kept talking to each other like actors in a silent
movie I had seen in that other lifetime when I had worked
at the Museum. I saw their lips move but heard no sound. I
remembered the soundlessness of grief through which the
Dumb Madwoman spoke as she wandered in the killing
fields of the second century BCE. She had asked: what is the
wellspring of compassion? Can it spurt from a source other
than sorrow, born in blood, flowing?

Is this what it means to be human—that we need bloody
hands to touch compassion? Is this all I exhorted my fellow
Clones to aspire to when I demanded that they be human?

Yet, why do we crave tenderness so deeply that we risk our
actuality for it, time and again?

A truth must lie here, even if I do not gain it.

Where are we heading?

What does it mean to be human?

The foetus kicks in me. I place a hand on my belly, trying to
stroke my unborn child, this child of mine and Leader's and
Aa-Aa's.

Stars keep travelling in space like specks of ice embedded

in dark sliding glass, with a light so pure that it seems unreal and unreachable. I watch the vastness. The vastness expands into yet more vastness.

The vastness makes me conscious of my smallness, and my body. My body feels as if uncontainable things are bursting into strange new life, for resistance to horror throws out new lifelines, each more desperate and subtle. Gradually I hear again the lure of words though I wish to draw into myself and turn into silence.

I hear again; I hear myself again. Suddenly I know what I should do: love tremendously beyond myself. This is the only way.

"What's your name?" Couplet was saying as the voices coalesced.

"What is yours?" the gladiator was asking. "We are beginning a new adventure and it's known Firehearts change their names with each new episode."

"I could be Renga," said Couplet blowing on its singed fingers, "a form of medieval Japanese linked verse. Or Madrigal. Maybe Ghazal. Oh, I don't know. Maybe I'll name myself Palimpsest. Not terribly poetic, but appropriate, what say?" It blew on its blackened antennae that lifted slightly. "Quit stalling, gladiator! Answer."

"Gladiators were given ironic names. I'm named after a poet," he said. "My name begins with the letter 'S.'"

"Unfair! This encompasses the entire universe, in a manner of speaking." Palimpsest protested. "Why, you could be Saigyo, Shelley, Sappho, Suresh, Soyinka, Simic." Palimpsest huffed and turned to me. "And you, Clone?"

"Whaaat?"

"What will you name yourself?"

Duke barked; he was guarding Leader's body lying in the hold. Leader without eyes, movement, thought. Leader: I shall hold you in me and affirm your life till my last breath; till the end of time.

But, after a person dies shouldn't we change their name too? For the loved one transforms into a memory of memories, a cocoon, a deeper part of oneself, as deep as air in lungs that is never stirred by breathing, still and sustaining.

I have many such cocoons of memories, and so much love, and yet a feeling of incompleteness that makes my body ache. I am surely not the first to feel this way, nor the last. But what do I do with this bursting tenderness? What did Aa-Aa do, I wonder. By creating voice-tombs did she put this to rest and escape, or did her love live more fully?

Yet Aa-Aa did not complete all her stories. As I see Duke guarding Leader's body I think of Trichaisma, fur raised, guarding Vrikama on a battlefield as an axe descended towards him. Maybe I will have another visitation. Or maybe I will tell it my way some day…

Death is taking Vrikama on a slow path, dragging him along with a slack noose, this hero who with one lightning lasso could jerk a foe to the ground, then pull, so that, before he is reined in, the man is dead, lips blue, biting his tongue. Vrikama moans and gurgles; gurgles blood softly from himself as a newborn does the first milk.

And death comes to him. He opens his mouth to call and his spirit emerges. Yes, I see it. I, Trichaisma, the Three-Eyed, have become true to my name. Third eye open, hair bristling, I, Trichaisma, see.

Open-mouthed, his spirit rises, coloured by his life; it streams like a river, like a storm wind, a swift cry, running loud with his fears, his loneliness, joy, his great tiredness, his courage and questing. Open-mouthed and many coloured, his spirit trembles out of him like a lake skin touched by wind; open-mouthed I gaze upon the face of my master Vrikama, the half-breed, the hero Vayuvega, and get ready to do that for which I am trained.

I see his spirit sheet rip and curl, fall about his body like snakes, whip around his corpse trying to enter his ears, his nostrils, his fine mouth; I am bewildered by the fury spurting from his limp body. Like beeswax torched, my bones melt, yet I move into this conflagration and stand amidst its flaming shreds. I suck into my third eye his envy, his sorrow, his bloodlust; I am in a maelstrom. I accept him in order to free him.

May he wander free in the heaven of the shining sky. Tomorrow my death awaits me. Vrikama's spirit quivers in the air, quivers and fades like a mirage, like a tear in a child's eye. I stand over him and howl, lifting my head to the skies. I am not just a dog. I am a wolf. I stand over my master's corpse, his head beneath my four paws; I bay. I see the skies part. I bay and bay.

Heaven, Earth, Breeze of the mountains and of the plains, may the killings stop.
Shining sky and splendid waters, may we not live in a dream.
Pollen, all that moves and does not, may we be at peace.
Hear this call of Trichaisma, the Three-Eyed.
Hear me, you Gods.

Acknowledgements

I unreel a skein of gratitude to:

The memory of my parents
My mother Saroja Kamakshi for morphing into as many
roles as I required: assiduous co-researcher, first reader,
confidence booster, seeker

My father Vasu Gopalan Sarukkai, teller of magical tales
during my childhood, for teaching me the art of suspense—
such as I possess—through our episodic nightly listening
and his then singular taste in reading sci-fi and
spec-fic in our family

My grandmother Meenakshi Pattabhiraman for
recounting the *Ramayana*—particularly the sections
with animals—over lunch when my mother was
carrying my sister Malavika, the gifted dancer

To my publisher Urvashi Butalia
for taking on this book when it was a risky proposition,
for her courage, moral compass, enthusiasm and
unsparing effort, *Salut!*

Writer Anita Roy who was an inspired editor,
working with her was an unalloyed joy;
writer Sucharita Asana-Dutta for the delicacy of
her mind and sharpness
of fresh editorial suggestions

The book's designer Jojy Philip and its cover designer,
Sukruti Anah Staneley for entering the *Clone*'s world with
aplomb and acute sensitivity

To my husband Suresh Chabria with love and admiration